You're About to Become a

Privileged Woman.

INTRODUCING
PAGES & PRIVILEGES.

It's our way of thanking you for buying
our books at your favorite retail store.

— *GET ALL THIS FREE* —

WITH JUST ONE PROOF OF PURCHASE:

◆ Hotel Discounts up to 60% at home and abroad

◆ Travel Service - Guaranteed lowest published airfares plus 5% cash back on tickets

◆ $25 Travel Voucher

◆ Sensuous Petite Parfumerie collection ($50 value)

◆ Insider Tips Letter with sneak previews of upcoming books

◆ Mystery Gift (if you enroll before 6/15/95)

*You'll get a FREE personal card, too.
It's your passport to all these benefits— and to
even more great gifts & benefits to come!*

There's no club to join. No purchase commitment. No obligation.

As a Privileged Woman, you'll be entitled to all these Free Benefits. And Free Gifts, too.

To thank you for buying our books, we've designed an exclusive FREE program called *PAGES & PRIVILEGES™*. You can enroll with just one Proof of Purchase, and get the kind of luxuries that, until now, you could only read about.

BIG HOTEL DISCOUNTS

A privileged woman stays in the finest hotels. And so can you—at up to 60% off! Imagine standing in a hotel check-in line and watching as the guest in front of you pays $150 for the same room that's only costing you $60. Your *Pages & Privileges* discounts are good at Sheraton, Marriott, Best Western, Hyatt and thousands of other fine hotels all over the U.S., Canada and Europe.

FREE DISCOUNT TRAVEL SERVICE

A privileged woman is always jetting to romantic places. When <u>you</u> fly, just make one phone call for the lowest published airfare at time of booking—<u>or double the difference back</u>! PLUS—

you'll get a $25 voucher to use the first time you book a flight AND <u>5% cash back on every ticket you buy thereafter through the travel service</u>!

$\mathcal{F}$REE GIFTS!

A privileged woman is always getting wonderful gifts.
Luxuriate in rich fragrances that
will stir your senses (and his).
This gift-boxed assortment of
fine perfumes includes three
popular scents, each in a beautiful
designer bottle. <u>Truly Lace</u>...This luxurious
fragrance unveils your sensuous side.
<u>L'Effleur</u>...discover the romance of the
Victorian era with this soft floral. <u>Muguet des bois</u>...a single note
floral of singular beauty. This $50 value is yours—FREE when
you enroll in *Pages & Privileges*! And it's just the beginning of
the gifts and benefits that will be coming your way!

$\mathcal{F}$REE INSIDER TIPS LETTER

A privileged woman is always informed. And you'll be, too,
with our free letter full of fascinating information and sneak
previews of upcoming books.

$\mathcal{M}$ORE GREAT GIFTS & BENEFITS TO COME

A privileged woman always has a lot to look forward to.
And so will you. You get all these wonderful FREE gifts and
benefits now with only one purchase...and there are no additional
purchases required. However, each additional retail purchase of
Harlequin and Silhouette books brings you a step closer to
even more great FREE benefits like half-price
movie tickets...and even more FREE gifts like
these beautiful fragrance gift baskets:

L'Effleur ...This basketful of
romance lets you
discover L'Effleur
from head to toe,
heart to home.

Truly Lace ...A basket
spun with the sensuous luxuries of
Truly Lace, including Dusting Powder in
a reusable satin and lace covered box.

$\mathcal{E}$NROLL $\mathcal{N}$OW!
***Complete the Enrollment Form on the back of this card
and become a Privileged Woman today!***

Enroll Today in *PAGES & PRIVILEGES*™, the program that gives you Great Gifts and Benefits with just one purchase!

Enrollment Form

☐ *Yes!* I WANT TO BE A *P*RIVILEGED *W*OMAN.

Enclosed is one *PAGES & PRIVILEGES*™ Proof of Purchase from any Harlequin or Silhouette book currently for sale in stores (Proofs of Purchase are found on the back pages of books) and the store cash register receipt. Please enroll me in *PAGES & PRIVILEGES*™. Send my Welcome Kit and FREE Gifts -- and activate my FREE benefits -- immediately.

NAME (please print)

ADDRESS   APT. NO

CITY   STATE   ZIP/POSTAL CODE

PROOF OF PURCHASE   SAMPLE ONLY

Please allow 6-8 weeks for delivery. Quantities are limited. We reserve the right to substitute items. Enroll before October 31, 1995 and receive one full year of benefits.

NO CLUB! NO COMMITMENT!
Just one purchase brings you great **Free Gifts and Benefits!**
(See inside for details.)

Name of store where this book was purchased_____

Date of purchase_____

Type of store:

    ☐ Bookstore   ☐ Supermarket   ☐ Drugstore

    ☐ Dept. or discount store (e.g. K-Mart or Walmart)

    ☐ Other (specify)_____

Which Harlequin or Silhouette series do you usually read?

_____

Complete and mail with one Proof of Purchase and store receipt to:
U.S.: *PAGES & PRIVILEGES*™, P.O. Box 1960, Danbury, CT 06813-1960
Canada: *PAGES & PRIVILEGES*™, 49-6A The Donway West, P.O. 813, North York, ON M3C 2E8   PRINTED IN U.S.A

"There is a simple remedy for the situation," Hale said bluntly. "Marriage.

"If you accept, you will become my wife, the mother of my second family and a woman with a secure position in the community. If you refuse, I have no choice but to ask you to seek other employment."

Maya swayed as emotions burst within her. The turmoil was followed by the eerie calm that had always overtaken her in the past when life had forced her to choose among disasters in order to survive. Yet this time was also different. This time she might also be choosing for an unborn child....

Which meant that there was no choice at all. She would never permit a babe to pay for her sin with a life of misery and want.

"I...I accept."

And then, for the first and last time in her life, Maya fainted.

Dear Reader,

This month, Harlequin Historicals is very proud
to include *Redwood Empire* from the acclaimed
writing team of A. E. Maxwell in our list of titles.
This sweeping saga was first issued in 1987, and we
are delighted to have the chance to bring it to you
again. Thanks to the combined talents of Ann and
Evan Maxwell, this tale of a woman who braves the
lawless wilderness in search of her destiny sizzles
with excitement and passion.

Also this month, Margaret Moore returns with
The Saxon, the sequel to her award-winning book,
The Viking. Adelar, the brooding Saxon youngster in
The Viking, comes face-to-face with a young woman
who has haunted him since their encounter years before,
but now she is married to the man to whom he owes
allegiance. And keep a look out for *The Welshman*,
in December, the sequel to *A Warrrior's Way*, which
earned the author a 5* rating from *Affaire de Coeur*.

Our other titles this month include *Highland Heaven*
by Ruth Langan, another story in the series that includes
The Highlander and *Highland Barbarian*, and from
contemporary author Susan Mallery, her first historical
for Harlequin, *Justin's Bride*. We hope you'll keep
an eye out for all four titles, wherever Harlequin
Historicals are sold.

Sincerely,

Tracy Farrell
Senior Editor

Please address questions and book requests to:
Harlequin Reader Service
U.S.: 3010 Walden Ave., P.O. Box 1325, Buffalo, NY 14269
Canadian: P.O. Box 609, Fort Erie, Ont. L2A 5X3

A.E. MAXWELL

REDWOOD EMPIRE

Harlequin Books

TORONTO • NEW YORK • LONDON
AMSTERDAM • PARIS • SYDNEY • HAMBURG
STOCKHOLM • ATHENS • TOKYO • MILAN
MADRID • WARSAW • BUDAPEST • AUCKLAND

To *Kate Duffy*,
gone but not forgotten

ISBN 0-373-28867-0

REDWOOD EMPIRE

Copyright © 1987 by Two Of A Kind, Inc.

Book One

1869

Chapter One

As the schooner *Brother Samuel* slowly emerged from gray fog into sunlight, Maya Charters stood at the rail, letting the brilliant warmth pour over her. Many times she had doubted the wisdom of her flight from the past, but not now. She had never seen anything more beautiful than Cape Mendocino, California, where sunlight infused the water with liquid diamonds. Today the Pacific Ocean was living up to its name. The surface of the water was so calm that it had the appearance of satin. The sunlight was warm and clear, the air crystalline in its perfection.

Suddenly the smooth surface of the sea was pulled apart by five sleek, gray shapes as dolphins surged upward to play in the schooner's bow wave. The dolphins were so close to the ship that Maya could hear the hollow rhythms of their breathing. She stood motionless, straining forward, electrified by the lithe, powerful creatures. Never had she seen anything so free, so perfectly made for the world they inhabited. She both admired and envied the dolphins' ease. She had traveled thousands of miles in the hope that she, too, would find a world where there was more to life than war and starvation, misery and death.

The dolphins vanished as suddenly as they had appeared. Maya scanned the water almost urgently, trying to catch sight of the animals once more. They weren't part of the vast blue brilliance that was the open sea. Nor were they stitching their way through the dense shadow cast by the bank of fog that clung to the margin of ocean and land, an impenetrable gray mist that rested moist and thick upon the water and rose several hundred feet into the air.

Above the reach of the fog, a ragged line of dark green marked the presence of land a mile away. Trees were out there, trees lifting their evergreen branches to the sunlit sky, trees thousands of years old.

Taller than God they were, a green so dark it was near black and so thick the sun never touched the ground.

The words of her dead father haunted Maya as she leaned forward over the rail, peering above the glittering mist as she tried to see more of the miraculous trees her father had told her about as he lay dying. Farther inland, beyond the towering redwood crowns, the fog gave way to green upland forests that luxuriated in the sunshine. Like the sea the land was tranquil, untouched, endless, enduring, shades of green stretching to infinity.

There were no people about on the deck to disturb Maya's absorption in the land and sea. In the cool early morning she had the flat deck of the lumber schooner to herself. Even the helmsman at the big wheel amidships no longer stared at her with barely veiled sexual calculation in his eyes. He was nearing the end of his four-hour wheel watch and was too intent on his warm bunk below to pay much attention to the beautiful young woman who stood at the stern rail and half vowed, half prayed that she would somehow find a secure home for herself among the magnificent redwood forests.

Maya moved from the shadow of the yellowed canvas mainsail and turned her face to the sunlight, letting warmth fall on her in a silent benediction. The schooner had sailed in and out of fog since San Francisco. She had suffered for the lightness of her clothing, but there had been no choice. She owned no more than the clothes she stood in, and those had been worn for so many years that the dress was ragged and too small to conceal the curves of the woman she had become.

There had been times when she thought that she would be cold for the rest of her life. But now there was sun, a cataract of warmth, and she was standing in the hot center of it.

Her relief was so great that Maya for once lifted the iron control she had learned to keep on her impulsive, sensual nature. She reached up and pulled the cloth bonnet from her head, leaving the shapeless fabric to dangle casually by its strings down her back. Laughing softly, she shook out her thick mahogany hair, which shimmered in heavy waves down her back as she ran both hands through it, lifting its weight from her neck, letting the sunlight caress her smooth skin.

For the first time in her life she felt alive, free, hopeful—and very grateful that fate and the Civil War had prevented her from marrying at seventeen. If she had married she would have had two children by now and would have been pregnant with a third. She would have been like her mother, trapped by her impulsive nature into a lifetime of poverty and bitterness.

*Never marry a man of your own generation, Maya.
They mean well, and they're handsome and winning
in their ways, and they can make a silly girl's head
spin, but they can't support the children they get on
your body one after another. Marry a widow man who
wore out his first wife getting set in the world. He
won't be at you all the time, and he'll have the means
to see that your babes grow straight and strong, instead of hungry and crooked and crying. You're a
beauty, girl. Don't throw it away on a charming boy.
Use it to make sure that your babes don't die so wasted
that their tiny bones rattle in the wind.*

It had been Maya's fifteenth birthday when her
mother had said those words while she hacked a babe-
sized grave from the cold Ohio soil. Although that had
been almost four years ago, Maya remembered each
word. It had been the first time that she had truly understood her mother's bitterness toward the charming, handsome man she had married. There were six
crosses on the small farm, marking the graves of six of
her brothers and sisters. Seven others had survived.

Within a few months Maya had helped to dig another grave. Her father's. Her mother had died two
years later, an old woman at thirty-three. The younger
children had found homes with relatives and neigh-
bors. Maya had been too old. Nor had she wanted to
be taken into another hard-scrabble farm family. She
knew that there was more to the world and life than a
miserable piece of dirt that could barely feed the people who worked it. Her father had been a forty-niner.
He had returned broken in health, poorer than ever,
but with a mind full of wondrous sights. He had
poured out his experiences to Maya, for his wife had

been too tired to listen. But Maya had listened, and as she listened she had yearned for a larger world.

Maya had known that she wouldn't have an easy time working her way West alone. Her mother had been very blunt about the ways of the world when she spoke with her beautiful, oldest child. Maya had been shocked at first. Now she was grateful. It was that hard, clear-eyed view of male lust and female foolishness that had saved her from repeating her mother's errors when Maya started out to find her own way West....

On the first day after Maya left the farm, Joe Dockerty saw her walking along the dusty road. When he found out that she was alone and that her baggage consisted of nothing at all, the wagoneer politely invited her to join him and his wife. In return for receiving bed and board, Maya would take care of the wan, consumptive Mrs. Dockerty. It was a duty with which Maya was familiar; her father had died of consumption. In addition to nursing tasks, Maya was to cook for the three of them and to be available to Dockerty in emergencies that required a second pair of hands.

The arrangement worked well for several days before Dockerty began to brush up against Maya at every opportunity. Though sexually inexperienced herself, Maya knew precisely what Dockerty had in mind; the thin walls of the farmhouse where she had been raised had provided Maya with a thorough education in how babies were conceived. When Dockerty's advances went from "accidental" encounters to an attempt to demonstrate the fullest meaning of the term "bed and board," Maya was prepared. She had hidden a kitchen

knife beneath her pillow the first time she had seen
Dockerty's eyes lingering on her hips as she worked
over the cooking fire. Seeing the knife in her hand had
cooled Dockerty's ardor considerably. As soon as he
retreated, she grabbed a blanket and ran into the concealing undergrowth to wait out the night.

The next morning Maya had awakened to find
Dockerty and the wagon gone. She fought back tears
of anger and fear, telling herself that she was no worse
off than she had been in Ohio. In fact she was better
off, for she was seventy-five miles closer to her desti-
nation.

And better off, too, in that her possessions had increased by one knife and one blanket.

Maya walked alone that day, refusing several offers
of rides with westering wagons, for the offers came
from men who were traveling alone, men whose
glances had kept falling to the place where the worn
fabric of Maya's dress strained over her full breasts.
Finally, toward sundown, the smell of frying meat
drew her irresistibly. When she saw a small, plainly
dressed family gathered around a fire, she walked
forward and offered to pay some of her precious cash
for food.

The Buckner family were Quakers. They accepted
the hungry girl without hesitation. The wife, Judith,
was barely older than Maya in years. In looks, a decade might have separated the two women, for Judith
had had four children in four years. Only two of the
children had survived. She was pregnant with her
fifth. Royal, her husband, was a kind, restrained,
worn man who was two years older than his wife. They
had sold their small Pennsylvania farm to seek an

easier climate in the West, in a place called Los Angeles, California.

The Buckners wouldn't hear of Maya paying for a meal. They drew her into their tranquil family unit with the same quiet grace that they thanked God for their food. Maya was attracted and put off at the same time and for the same reason: she knew that there was no place in the Buckner family for the hot currents of life that she felt running in herself so strongly, the same currents of sensuality that her mother had warned her repeatedly against. Although Maya knew that she would be safe with the Buckners, she sensed also that she would be stifled.

Judith took Maya aside after dinner and offered her the protection of the household as far as Omaha, where the Buckners would dispose of their wagon and board the new railroad train for the West Coast. Then Judith added, "Omaha is a new city, a bustling city. A girl with your pleasing looks should have no trouble finding a decent, God-fearing man to marry."

Maya accepted the offer of a ride west, although she had no intention of settling in some "proper position" in Omaha. She could curb the restless yearnings of her body, but not those of her mind. She would have nothing less than the towering magnificence of the redwood trees that her father had talked of as he lay dying.

With outward calm Maya settled into the Buckner family routine so completely that by the end of the second week she was all but indispensable. Judith was in the throes of a difficult pregnancy, a condition with which Maya was all too familiar after caring for her own mother. Maya was able to make herbal teas that eased Judith's nausea and cramps. Maya knew clever, quiet games to keep the children absorbed so that Judith could get the rest her body so desperately needed. Maya knew how to handle the team so that Royal could slip back into the wagon with his wife and hold her while she wept silently. And best of all, Royal never watched Maya with barely veiled sexual hunger in his eyes.

When Royal Buckner sold his wagon and horses and paid forty dollars each for emigrant-class railroad tickets on the Union Pacific, he bought a ticket for Maya as well. She accepted, knowing that Judith would need her desperately on the last leg of the westward trip. The transcontinental route was just over a year old and still crude. The forty dollar tickets were a bargain compared to express passage, but the emigrant boxcars were rough and inhospitable. The cars were mixed with freight boxes in trains that made their way west at a pace barely superior to that of a man walking. The accommodations consisted of rough wooden benches. The cars were crowded with all manner of people, clouded with tobacco smoke, stinking of spittoons and ''honey'' buckets, unhealthy in the extreme.

Judith and the two children came down with a raging fever. Maya nursed all three for the ten days it took to reach the western terminus of the railroad in Sacramento. The children survived. The babe within Judith did not. She miscarried on the ninth day. Despite that, she was on her feet and caring for her family on the tenth.

Maya watched Judith with a combination of admiration for her determination and rage at the kind, sad-eyed man who so obviously loved Judith, yet put her through the endless hell of childbearing when the family barely had enough money to survive, much less to provide the kind of care that an overworked, oft-pregnant woman needed. Every time Maya looked at the other woman, her own mother's words echoed again.

Never marry a man of your own generation, Maya. They mean well, and they're handsome and winning in their ways, and they can make a silly girl's head spin, but they can't support the children they get on your body one after another.

At the end of the road Royal Buckner tried to talk Maya into staying with the family. Gently, firmly, Maya refused. She had promised herself that she would see the trees taller than God that her father had talked about so often.

And she knew that the Buckner family was too like her own for her to bear. Decent, God-fearing...and doomed. Judith would be dead before Royal had gathered enough wealth to ensure his family's health and security. If he ever did. Her father never had.

When Royal realized that he couldn't sway Maya, he pressed two ten-dollar gold pieces into her hand.

"It's little enough," he said. "Judith would have died without you. You were God's answer to my prayers."

Maya stared at the lustrous coins in disbelief. "I can't—"

"You must," he interrupted firmly. "My conscience would not rest if I cast you without money into the world. It can be a cruel, wicked place for a woman without a man's protection."

In the end Maya had tucked one of the pieces of gold into the hidden pocket in her petticoat. The second coin Maya held in her hand until she kissed Judith goodbye. Then Maya pressed the money into the other woman's fragile hand and whispered the same advice that Maya's grandmother had given her mother years before.

"You'll soon be pregnant again. Take this and buy a young cow fresh with milk. It will go easier on you and your next babe and the next one after that if all your strength doesn't go to milk."

Tears came and Judith clung to Maya suddenly. "Stay. You are like a sister to me."

Maya hugged her in return, but did not stay. She loved Judith too much to watch her die of poverty and childbearing.

With twelve dollars and twenty-one cents in her petticoat and tears burning her eyelids, Maya left the Buckner family and headed north. Two days later she found herself in front of the stage depot on Montgomery Street in San Francisco, trying hard not to stare at the four- and five-story buildings, for she knew that such gawking would mark her as a stranger, and a naive one at that.

San Francisco was an outrage of a city only a decade removed from the wild days of the Gold Rush. The city was making motions toward respectability; there were sidewalks and some of the buildings were brick or stone. But there was still an active, aggressive seething of humanity in the streets, a hoarse, barely controlled rumble of ambition that fascinated Maya.

She stood on the sidewalk trying to look inconspicuous while she watched the traffic flow past her—men, mostly, but a few women, too. Many were dressed in city finery, but some, like herself, were rudely dressed in clothes of the country. Two men walked by in buckskin shirts and fur caps. Maya caught their scent—campfire smoke and sweat and dead animals—at almost the same moment that she realized they carried pistols and knives in their belts.

Next a short, slender man walked by, dressed in dark, loose-fitting shirt and trousers. Maya was surprised by the odd color of his skin and by his startling face. His eyes were almond shaped and his features flat, blunt and broad, almost like an Indian's but with no sign of an Indian's arching nose. He wore a small, round cap and his hair, black as a crow's wing, hung down his back in a tight pigtail.

He was the most exotic person Maya had ever seen. She guessed that he must be one of the Chinese she had heard tales of, the industrious, wiry men and women from across the Pacific. She had been told that there were many Chinamen in San Francisco, so many that they were beginning to make some of the Occidentals uneasy. But this one looked mild and self-effacing, not at all threatening. He walked in the manner of a serving maid, with his eyes cast downward so as not to stare at those better than he.

Although the Chinese man didn't meet Maya's glance, other men noticed her ill-concealed, wide-eyed stare. She turned and caught a tall man leaning casually against a streetlight studying her. He was in his late twenties, a loose-limbed, handsome kind of rounder. He wore a bowler hat, a white shirt with a bow tie, and trousers hung from colorful suspenders. When she glanced in his direction, he grinned, revealing tobacco-stained teeth.

Instantly Maya turned and began walking away, only to find that the man's indolence had been just a pose. He intercepted her quickly. He stood over her, watching her in a way that reminded her of Dockerty.

"Take your hand off my arm," she said coolly, despite the fear racing through her blood.

As she spoke her hand went into the slit pocket she had sewn in her skirt. The knife lay inside, its handle ready to her fingers. Never had anything felt quite so comforting to her as the cool curve of the haft in her palm.

"Now, there's no need to look so ruffled. We know just what's what, don't we?" he said.

"I don't know you at all."

"Sure and you do, ducks. I'm your new master."

Maya drew the knife. Only the man's quickness saved him from being cut as he snatched back his hand. He feinted toward her, saw that her inexperience was as great as her determination to be free of him, and grinned.

"All right, Reggie. You've had your fun," boomed a big voice from the corner. "Now leave the little dove alone."

"I saw her first. She's mine."

"She don't want a hair off your dirty arse."

The language made Maya flush, despite the fact that she had heard far worse on the train coming West.

Suddenly a big, barrel-chested man moved between Reggie and his prey. The barrel chest was covered in a blue coat that was decorated with brass buttons and a huge, five-pointed brass star.

"Shove off, copper," Reggie said. "You know that I get first call on the girls off the train."

"Not this one, Reggie. Even a soiled dove has rights. She don't want you, so be gone with you." The policeman turned and saw Maya's face for the first time. Abruptly he decided that she wasn't a whore after all. "Well, well, what have we here? First time in the big city?"

"Yes, sir," Maya said.

The policeman's face gentled. "Get separated from your family?"

"My parents are dead."

The barrel chest heaved with a sigh. He turned back to Reggie. "This isn't one of yours, whoremaster. Now quit leering at the poor girl, or I'll take my stick to you."

Reggie left, streaming a banner of foul language behind.

"Sorry, my girl. There aren't many decent women traveling alone in the city. It will be much safer if you get off the streets. Have you a place to stay?"

As Maya listened to the policeman's hoarse, booming advice, she realized that her legs were shaking. She also realized that scarcely anyone on the street had noticed the encounter. It was as though the spectacle of a woman fending off an attacker with a knife in her hand were commonplace on the streets of San Francisco.

"You can put the sticker away now," the policeman said calmly, but he watched her as though he weren't sure what she would do next.

Maya lowered the knife a bit. "Who was he?" she asked. "What did he want? Why did he think he had a right to call himself my master?"

For a moment the policeman thoughtfully scratched his muttonchop whiskers. "If you don't know, I don't want to be the one to soil your ears with it, darling," he said finally. "Where would you be going, then? I ought to see you there, else another of Reggie's ilk will grab you, and you'll find out more about life than any young girl should know."

"I don't know exactly where I am going. I just know that I don't want to go anywhere with the likes of him."

The policeman shook his head sadly. "Slam in the middle of the Barbary Coast and you don't know where you're going, darling? Do you have any money?"

Maya hesitated. "A little. I can pay my way."

"Pay it, but not find it," he said ruefully. "Tell me, can you read and write?"

"I taught my brothers and sisters when there was time. But there was never enough time. They loved the stories so much...." Maya turned aside suddenly, trying to conceal the unexpected tears as she thought of her siblings' young, eager faces gathered around the fire to hear about elves and kings, fairies and wicked witches. That time was gone forever. Crying for it wouldn't help, and she knew it, but sometimes the tears came anyway.

"Come along then, darling," the policeman said gruffly. "I know some ladies who might take you under their wing."

After a moment's hesitation Maya followed him down Montgomery Street. She had to walk quickly to keep up with his long strides. When he led her up Sacramento Street, she found herself slowing out of curiosity. There were more and more of the small Chinese people on the sidewalks. Some of the men were dressed in the odd, loosely fitted clothes that resembled black and gray pajamas. Other men wore western clothing and had the look of miners or seamen. There were even a few women, mostly plain

women with broad, blunt features who were dressed
like the men in dark, often quilted pajamas.

Maya couldn't help stopping and staring when she
saw a pretty Chinese girl, years younger than herself,
dressed in a shining purple tunic and black trousers
and wearing an intricate, dazzling headdress of gold
and silver and glinting mirrors. After a few steps
alone, the policeman realized that he had lost his
charge. He stopped and followed the direction of
Maya's gaze, watching the Chinese child who proudly
marched down the middle of the sidewalk, her steps
small and mincing because the thick platform shoes
she wore had a convex curve on the sole just below the
arch, forcing their wearer to perform an intricate balancing act with each step. The girl's head was high and
proud. She was fully aware of the attention she attracted.

"The shoe merchant's concubine," the policeman
said, his voice a mixture of appreciation and derision.

Maya knew of concubines from the Bible, but she
had never before seen one. The girl looked beautiful,
carefully kept, exotic and . . . innocent.

"You'll see more of them where I'm taking you,"
he said cryptically as he proceeded on up the hill. In a
few moments he stopped in front of a large, woodframe Victorian house that had the aura of a mansion
in steep decline. A sign on the front door said Meth-
odist Mission to the Chinese. The policeman mounted
the steps and rang the bell.

"These women take in Chinese slave girls and make
Christians of them," he said while he waited for the
door to be answered.

"But I'm not Chinese, and I'm already Christian. Though my faith has been shaken," Maya added honestly.

"San Francisco would shake anyone's faith. The mission always needs tutors to work with the Chinese girls. You'll have a proper place to stay while they find you a good workingman for a husband."

An attractive middle-aged woman answered the door. "Sergeant Marley, how wonderful to see you! Come in, come in. We have coffee and fresh cakes."

"Good morning, Mrs. Wyatt. I've brought an odd sort of waif to you." He paused long enough to introduce the two women, adding for Maya's benefit, "Mrs. Wyatt is the wife of one of San Francisco's most prominent bankers." Then he launched into an abbreviated description of what had happened to Maya.

Mrs. Wyatt gave Maya a quick, assessing glance, taking in everything from her threadbare clothes to her startling beauty, and nodded. "Quite right, Sergeant," she said briskly. "We can't have her wandering the streets. She'd fetch quite a price at some slaver's auction."

Maya's eyes widened. She had thought that her mother had covered everything bad that could happen to a beautiful young girl on her own in the world, but apparently the barbarism of San Francisco's waterfront had been beyond her mother's experience.

"Come, child," Mrs. Wyatt said, holding out a warm, dry hand and taking Maya's confidently. "At least we won't have to steal you, and then spend months teaching you English."

In the next eight weeks Maya learned about a world that would have been beyond her mother's comprehension. The mansion at the edge of the Chinatown ghetto was home to thirty young Chinese girls, all of whom had been "freed from terrible slavery" in the delicate description of Mrs. Wyatt and the other women involved in the mission. Some of the girls were barely ten years old. The uses to which they had been put by their masters were appalling.

Maya discovered quickly that the "slaves" were Chinese prostitutes imported to service the men of the Chinese enclaves along the Pacific Coast. The young girls lived and worked in squalid conditions, often dying before they were twenty, their bodies wasted by abortions, disease and opium. The whoremasters didn't care about sick girls, for younger, healthier prostitutes were always coming onto the market. China was overflowing with unwanted girl children. Their price rarely exceeded that of a bowl of rice.

Maya learned that despite their tender age, most of the girls accepted the facts of slavery and prostitution without question. Those girls who fled to the mission of their own volition did so only because their masters had been egregiously cruel, violating the implicit terms of the slave-master relationship.

Yet hearing the girls' soft, childish voices murmuring of unspeakable sexual practices was not as terrible to Maya as the realization that each of these girls had been sold into slavery by a family unable to feed its own children. When Maya discovered that, she understood why none of the girls had a higher ambition than to become the concubine of a wealthy old man, a man who was powerful and generous enough to support the children he would get from his concubines' young, willing bodies. Instinctively those girls knew what Maya's mother had learned only at great cost.

Never marry a man of your own generation, Maya. They can't feed the children they get upon your body one after the other.

Through the days and weeks, Mrs. Wyatt watched Maya's increasing silence with compassion and a motherly worry. She suspected that Maya had seen too much of violence and perversion that ungodly men visited upon unprotected girls. It was giving Maya a morbid view of what was a divinely sanctified act whose purpose was the creation of children who would be raised to worship the all-benevolent God.

When Mrs. Wyatt discovered through the Church that a small northern California logging town called Eureka had taken up a collection and was looking for a young woman of high morals and decent education, she immediately thought of the restless young girl with haunted green eyes and a womanly body that drew men's glances. With Mrs. Wyatt's intercession Maya was hired sight unseen to teach the first six grades of Liberty School in a place called Trinidad on the coastline north of Eureka. She would be paid twenty dollars a month plus board.

Within hours of accepting the offer, Maya was walking onto the sturdy little lumber schooner *Brother Samuel* in San Francisco Bay. She left the mission without regret. The soft, high, childish voices of the prostitutes had become confused in her nightmares with those of her own little sisters, her dead mother and Judith.

The first mate of the ship, a buck-toothed Swede named Swanson, showed Maya the tiny cabin in the bow that would be hers and called her attention to the heavy latch with which she could secure the door to her cabin.

"The captain likes his Mexican brandy," Swanson said matter-of-factly, "and he knows you have no man's protection. Consider yourself warned. If your door is open when the captain comes calling, no man will raise a hand to stop him."

Maya absorbed the words without comment or blush. After what she had seen and heard in the past few months, the only surprise to her was that the door had a latch at all, and that the first mate had bothered to issue a warning.

"Am I the only passenger?" she asked.

"No. The Hawthornes will be boarding soon."

"The Hawthornes?" Maya asked, for the respect in the man's voice made it clear that she should feel herself privileged to be sharing the boat with them.

"Willy and Beth, the children of Hale Hawthorne, owner of Tres Santos Lumber Company and of this ship. You'll know them when you see them. Little Beth is blind, and Willy is a strapping lad bigger than most men."

An hour after Maya came aboard, a small steam launch carrying the Hawthornes pulled alongside the *Brother Samuel*. The crew rigged a chair-swing on a cargo block and lowered the seat into the launch. The girl allowed herself to be strapped in without complaint, until the chair moved. Then she called out in fear.

"Will! Oh, Will, where are you!"

"It's all right, Mouse. I'm right here."

Only then did Maya realize that the tall, muscular man who hovered near the chair was Will Hawthorne, the young son of Hale. Though Will's voice was deep, it had the subtly changing timbre of immaturity rather than the steady timbre of a fully grown man. That, and the careless exuberance of his body, proclaimed Will to be younger than his size and brawn suggested. Yet he was anything but careless as he tucked in Beth's skirts and soothed her with words spoken too softly to be overheard.

He raised his hand, signaling for the lift to resume.

"Will, it's scary," the girl called out after a minute.

"It's just like the swing in the madrona tree at Tres Santos," Will called back. "You're always telling me to swing you higher and faster, remember? Well, now I'm doing it. Isn't it wonderful, Mouse? Doesn't the breeze feel grand?"

Maya saw the girl's clenched hands relax on the lines of the swing, as Beth turned toward the sound of her brother's voice and smiled tremulously.

"Yes, Will. It feels grand..."

The chair rose to the level of the *Brother Samuel*'s deck, and then suddenly stopped as the wooden cargo block gave a shuddering creak and froze. At that moment the wake of an incoming ship rocked the *Brother Samuel*, swinging the chair in an arc that quickly widened from two feet to five.

Beth sensed the sudden movement with the acute sensitivity of the blind. She shrieked and clutched at the ropes of the swing. Her actions intensified the dangerous sideway arc. The chair swung slowly toward the wooden rail of the schooner and then away, out over the cold gray water. It was clear that on its next inward arc, the swing would smash against the railing, injuring the helpless girl.

Will realized the danger instantly. He grabbed a line that hung down from the schooner and tested the rope with a savage jerk. When it held, he leapt onto the rail of the launch and pulled himself hand over hand up the side of the schooner's hull, climbing with the speed and grace of a cat. Before the chair started back toward the ship, he had scaled the hull and was level with the deck. He hooked his arm over the wooden rail and placed his body between the rough, scarred planks and the swinging chair. Holding himself by one arm, he waited, then reached out and grabbed the chair as it swung toward him.

He cushioned the blow with his own body and at the same time tried to catch the chair, ending its wild motion. The force of the impact knocked him backward against the hull. Somehow he held on to the rail and the chair. As he struggled for balance, it became obvious that the rocking motion of the schooner would jerk the chair and the girl out of his grasp and over the water again.

"Hold onto me, Mouse. Quickly!"

Beth obeyed with a trust that wrenched Maya's heart. The girl's thin arms wrapped around her brother's neck and clung with surprising strength. Will let go of the chair, grabbed the rail with both hands and held on until the crew members shook off their surprise and leaped forward to help. Two of them reached over the rail and lifted Beth and the chair-swing aboard. Another crewman started forward to help Will. Before the sailor took two steps Will had levered himself up and over the rail with a fluid power that made Maya stare.

The entire crisis was over in less than fifteen seconds, yet Maya thought of it many times during the voyage, especially when she saw the powerful, lithe dolphins at play. When she thought of Will's easy strength, a curious fluttering warmth uncurled along her nerves, leaving her heart pounding and her knees weak.

And in her mind, her mother's warning rang again and again:

You're a beauty, girl. Don't throw it away on a charming boy. Use it to make sure that your babes don't die so wasted that their tiny bones rattle in the wind.

Chapter Two

Will Hawthorne lay alone on the bunk in his cabin listening to the water slide by the thick-planked hull of the *Brother Samuel* and thinking about the beautiful girl with worn clothes and eyes as green as a lowland forest. He had heard her light footsteps on the deck above him and knew that she was standing by the rail. He wondered what she was thinking about, where she was going and what lucky man had the right to kiss those high breasts and lie between those long legs.

She wore no ring. That he had discovered for himself. She was called Maya Charters and comported herself modestly enough, if one overlooked the fact that she was without a man's protection in a world where no decent young woman traveled alone—especially one so attractive. She was going to Eureka to teach children, she said.

Privately, Will doubted that she was half so modest as she appeared. No woman of her beauty could have been left untouched by men. She had to be at least his own age, perhaps even older. He was almost seventeen and had learned years ago what it was that made men hard and women soft. Most girls of eighteen had at least one babe in their arms and one growing inside as well, and a husband twice as old as they were en-slaved for life by God and law in order to keep the young wife in silks and fancies.

That life wasn't for Will. Despite his father's wealth Will couldn't afford a wife or a fancy woman. He and his father hadn't been on comfortable terms since they had stumbled over each other in a whorehouse ante-room three years ago. After that incident Will had worked at the mill to earn his board and keep, and Hale Hawthorne wasn't known as a generous em-ployer.

Will didn't mind the work. He had always been big for his age, strong, and imbued with a headstrong masculine arrogance that was equal to his father's. The education that Hale had paid to have tutored into his stubborn son had been thrown over by Will with-out a thought. He knew that he had been born for the wind and the sun, the fog and the tall trees. He hadn't been born to bow to four walls, a tutor with a squeaky voice and a father who couldn't accept the fact that his son was a man in all but years—a son with a man's needs.

It was manly need that had awakened Will, a hard yet pleasant ache in his groin. He kept thinking of the worn print fabric straining across Maya's breasts. Maybe she was as hungry as he was. Maybe she longed to have her soft belly kissed and her legs pressed open by a man.

With a stifled groan Will rolled onto his back. His mouth twisted into a wry smile as he thought what his friend Henry Ising would think if he knew Will's di-lemma. It had been Ising who had understood Will's woman hunger at a time when most other boys were still turning scarlet if a girl walked by. Ising had been the one who had shown Will the simple delights of moderate drink and immoderate whores. Nothing in Ising's words or actions—or the life of Will's father—had suggested to Will that there was any reason to prefer one woman over another when his blood ran hot.

Since that first time years before Will had had his share of women in the rough logging camps and in the scented bordellos of San Francisco, but the sight of Maya watching him with wide green eyes as he boarded the *Brother Samuel* had shaken him to the soles of his feet. He had wanted her then with a violence that he barely had been able to control. He still wanted her. Not just any willing woman would do. He needed one particular woman. Maya.

All he had to do was figure out a way to have her. They had been introduced at dinner last night, but she had made no attempt to encourage him with fluttering eyelashes and sidelong looks from her magnificent green eyes. In fact, she had said barely three words to him. It had been different with Beth. Maya had talked to her and had looked after her needs with the unconscious skill of someone accustomed to caring for others.

Perhaps Maya had been a rich man's governess. That would explain her obvious education. Perhaps the man had remarried and the new wife had been jealous. Or perhaps he had lost his wealth, for it was plain that whoever had been keeping Maya had been even more niggardly with money than Hale Hawthorne. Maybe that was why she had run away. If that were true she would be desperate. At the very least she wouldn't be too expensive in her tastes for a logger to afford. She couldn't even afford a coat to keep the chill north-coast fogs at bay.

Perhaps she would rather wear him.

With a curse Will shot from his bunk and dashed cold water over his face. He might have been sexually experienced, but he had no experience at all in dealing with his response to the aloof, shabbily dressed girl-woman whose body haunted him even when he slept. Sexual hunger wasn't new to him; he had wanted sexual relief in the past and he had learned how to get it. He hadn't learned how to control a lust for one particular female. For the first time in his life Will was beginning to understand why a man paid one woman a king's ransom—or even enslaved himself in marriage—rather than simply going on to find another woman willing to slake his hot male desires at far less cost.

"Ising would be doubled over with laughter if he could hear me," muttered Will. The big half-Yurok had always been amused by white men and their peculiar notions of life. But then, Ising was also amused by Indians and their equally odd perceptions of what was good and what was not.

Impatiently Will combed his thick chestnut hair into a semblance of civility that would be destroyed at the first touch of the sea wind. He pulled on his beautifully made gray slacks, white shirt and suit coat. Hale had paid for the wardrobe, but only because it galled his pride to have his son go to San Francisco looking like a woods ruffian. The Hawthorne name meant something among the city bankers. Hale meant to see that it remained that way.

A quick glance at a heavy gold watch told Will that he had some time before Beth would need him. She usually slept later than he did, particularly after a trip to San Francisco that had been as disappointing as it had been exhausting; the new, highly touted society doctor had had no more idea how to cure Beth's mysterious blindness than he had known how to fly. The fall that she had taken several years before would continue to hold back the light from her limpid, pale blue eyes.

Will climbed the ship's stairs two at a time, as though trying to flee from the bleak reality of things that could not be changed by a strong back and quick hands. As soon as his head came above deck, he forgot about Beth. Maya was standing by the stern rail, her back arched and her breasts thrust forward as her fingers combed through the rippling glory of her hair. She stretched languidly, smiling as though it were a lover rather than sunlight that warmed her flesh.

Desire clawed Will, a feeling more of pain than pleasure, an urgent need that made him shake. He stood motionless as he fought for self-control, appalled by the wildness of his emotions. He had felt nothing so intense before in his life. All that kept him from going to Maya and dragging her down on the deck was his own pride. He had never been ruled by anything in his life, even his hard, stubborn father.

Deliberately Will turned away from Maya, toward the bow of the boat. He walked the deck with measured steps, feeling his self-control return with each moment. Gradually the rigid evidence of his lust subsided.

When he reached the bow he saw the wall of fog shrouding the land. Frowning, he studied the sea with eyes that knew each shade and color of weather as intimately as any sailor's. With every passing minute it became clearer that Captain Trowbridge was going to sail them right into the soup.

"Damn Trowbridge," Will muttered. "He should heave to and wait. The fog will burn off soon and there will still be enough tide to carry us over the bar."

The ship continued to sail on.

Abruptly Will turned his back and completed his circuit of the ship's deck. In doing so he inevitably came to Maya.

"Good morning, Miss Charters," he said, coming up to stand close to her along the rail. "I see that you enjoy sunlight as much as I do."

In the shimmering light of morning Will was even more handsome than he had been by lantern light at the captain's rude table. Will wore no hat; wind combed restlessly through his lustrous chestnut hair, making it spill in a thick wave over his forehead. The temptation to discover if his hair felt as smooth and warm and thick as it looked was so great that Maya unconsciously clenched her hands to keep them at her side. Her glance moved from his hair to the strong, intriguingly curved lines of his mouth. Temptation lay there, too, an invitation to touch, to taste.

With an increasing feeling of confusion Maya looked at Will's eyes. Gray with expanding black centers. A gray so pure it was like crystal. He was watching her with a barely leashed intensity that was at odds with his unlined, unformed, almost boyish face. Almost, but not quite. There was something in his eyes as old as time.

Maya forced herself to look away from the eyes that were the same brilliant gray as the sun-shot mist. "Good morning, Master Hawthorne. Yes, I prefer sun to fog."

She sensed Will bridling at being called "Master" Hawthorne rather than Mister. She knew that she had scraped his pride, but she had learned that he was not yet seventeen despite his size. He was a boy, not a man full grown. He should not make her feel breathless, light-headed, weak-kneed. She resented it almost as much as she feared it. Just by standing there looking at her, he could reach past her control to the impulsive sensuality that she had spent a lifetime trying to extinguish.

"I'm afraid old Trowbridge will take us back into the soup when we cross the Humboldt Bar," Will said, glancing toward the fog-shrouded shore. "He thinks of this coast as an enemy to be bested rather than a woman to be cajoled."

"You talk as though you know the way better than the captain, who is a man of considerable years and experience."

Will no longer doubted that her reference to his youth was intentional. Desire turned to anger, and with it came a need to shake the aloof Miss Charters.

"I was raised on this coast. Trowbridge was not. The Humboldt Bar can be dangerous. One miscalculation and the surf will throw a ship like this on the sandbar and snap her back in an instant. The fog makes the passage all the more dangerous because a pilot has no landmarks to guide him to the safe channel. There's a light on the north jetty but it's no good in the fog. My father has been trying to convince the Lighthouse Service to install a bell, but the federal government believes that the lives of the people sailing the Redwood Coast aren't worth the cost of a few hundred pounds of bronze."

"If you think the passage is so risky, why don't you order the captain to wait until the fog clears? This is your father's ship, isn't it?"

"No captain is going to listen to a sixteen-year-old," Will said bluntly, "any more than he would have listened to you if you hadn't latched your door last night. A girl your age shouldn't travel alone unless she is looking for...company."

Maya felt a flush climbing her cheeks. "I'm nineteen today. Hardly a girl any longer."

"And I'm seventeen tomorrow. Hardly a boy."

"You don't look it."

"Neither do you. Sixteen maybe. Fifteen probably. Why are you traveling alone?"

Maya's flush deepened as Will's gray eyes took a slow inventory of her shabby clothes and adult curves. "You are impertinent."

"I'm honest. What about you, Miss Charters?" he asked, catching her chin in his hand, forcing her to look up at him. "Are you honest?"

Will's hand was warm, hard, surprisingly callused for a son of wealth and privilege. His touch sent sensations shivering over Maya, frightening her.

"Since I left Ohio, I have twice taken a knife to men who touched me," she said distinctly.

At first Will smiled, believing that Maya was joking. Then he looked more closely at her and saw the lines of tension drawing her face. Beneath his fingers he felt the fine trembling of her body. Slowly he released her. For a long time he simply looked at her, trying to understand her. The women he knew were either decent and under a man's protection or they were available. There were a few exceptions—one of the cooks at the logging camp was a woman. At least, she was rumored to be. A man would never be sure until he had undressed her, and it would have taken a very desperate or very brave man to do that. Miss Perkins was another exception. No one would have accused the erect, gray-haired spinster of harboring so much as a loose thought, much less of committing a loose act.

But Maya was neither mannish nor too old to bear children. That made her incomprehensible to Will, who was too young to have encountered the women from whom the Civil War had taken all men who would normally have protected them.

"If you don't want company, why are you traveling alone?"

"I have no choice. I am forced to depend upon the decency and chivalry of strange men until I reach Trinidad, wherever that might be. Perhaps there I will be safe from attentions that I have never sought and don't want."

Pride and anger were clear in Maya's voice, but it was the underlying tremor of fear that made Will step backward in an instinctive effort to soothe her.

"I'm sorry if I've upset you. I meant no harm." He looked at her curiously as he struggled to rearrange his view of the type of woman who traveled without the shelter of a man's presence. Almost absently he added, "Trinidad is north of Eureka about twenty miles. That's where the big stands are."

Maya knew that she should turn on her heel and leave Will standing alone on the deck. But it was dank and gloomy in her cabin. On deck there was sun and fresh air and open space and...gray eyes as deep as the sea itself. Besides, she had no reason to fear Will. Despite his size he was a boy two years younger than she.

And despite his brash forwardness he had been raised well. Once he had realized his mistake he had apologized and ceased his unwanted attentions. That was more than any of the other men she had met had had the decency to do.

"Stands? What are they?" she asked softly, implicitly accepting Will's apology.

"Stands of timber. Trees. God's own trees, so big twenty people can't reach around them."

Will's voice deepened when he talked of the big redwood trees. His eyes became focused on some distant magnificence that only he could see. The change both aged him and paradoxically made him appear even younger, untouched, as though he were an altar boy dedicated to something that was both far older and more powerful than he.

"You call them stands?" Maya asked.

"I can see you're going to have to do some learning as well as some teaching," he said, smiling. "We're timber beasts up here. We have our own language. It's mostly English but there are a few foreign words."

"If I learned some Chinese, I imagine I can learn some words in 'timber beast' as well."

"Where did you learn Chinese?"

For an instant Maya closed her eyes, regretting that she had mentioned knowing some of that language. She didn't want to think about young girls and men's unspeakable lusts.

"I stayed at a mission in San Francisco for two months. I taught English to Chinese girls who had no families."

Will looked at the young woman who suddenly appeared far older than her nineteen years. He had been to San Francisco often enough to know the probable occupation of Chinese girls who ended up in a Christian mission.

"Is Chinese very hard to learn?" he asked quickly, afraid that he had inadvertently offended Maya again. "I know Yurok pretty well, but I've never found anyone who could teach me Chinese."

"It's very different. Most of it involves the tone of your voice, rather like singing. You can say the same word with five or six different inflections and each time it means something different."

"So that's the trick. I've listened and listened to the Chinamen on Fourth Street in Eureka, but I could never make out what they were saying."

"You frequent Chinatown?"

"In Eureka it's hard not to. It's right in the middle of downtown, not far from the Tres Santos Mill. The one my father owns."

"I have nightmares about Chinatown," she said simply.

"The Chinese aren't evil. They're just different."

"Different?" Maya's full mouth turned down at one corner in a parody of a smile as she looked at Will's handsome, earnest, youthful face. "No, Master Hawthorne. They aren't different at all. They're just more honest about men and women and lust. Chinese men sell their girl children into slavery and concubinage. Western men force women to sell themselves into marriage by making it impossible for a decent woman to live alone without the protection of a man."

"Is that what they taught you at the mission?" Will asked, unable to hide his shock at Maya's plain speaking.

Maya thought of her exhausted mother, of Judith, of the high, childish voices of the prostitutes discuss-

ing the foolish, grunting men who rutted upon them.
Slowly she shook her head.

"It's something every woman learns for herself, if
she has the wit to look beyond a young man's charming smile to the babes she will inevitably bear. It's them
I feel sorry for. They don't ask to die too weak even to
cry out against their fate, but die they must, because
their mother married a man too young to care for the
babes he got upon her."

A chill swept through Will as he looked into Maya's
bleak green eyes, eyes so much older than her unlined
oval face. He didn't know what she was seeing in her
memories, what voices were speaking in the silences of
her mind; but he sensed that in this she was older than
he was, older than Ising, older even than his father.

Suddenly the sails snapped, and the masts creaked
as the wind freshened, bearing on its back a wall of
tumultuous clouds. The *Brother Samuel* shuddered
and heeled over beneath the force of waves that had
steepened and deepened as Will stood talking to Maya.
He had adjusted to the new motions of the deck without noticing. She was not so accustomed to the demands of the sea. When a particularly large set of
waves came, she staggered and caught herself against
the rail. Automatically Will braced her with his hands,
then let go when the heat of her body threatened to
burn through his careful self-control.

Will turned and stared toward the shore. He caught
just a glimpse of the high point called Table Bluff before the wind shifted, backing around to the northwest, blowing hard. On the seaward side a storm raced
toward them, and on the landward side fog and the
Humboldt Bar waited.

The schooner rose up the ten-foot swells and then slid down the other side into the troughs. Where there had been sunlight there was now only a ghostly gray illumination. Powered solely by aging canvas sails, the *Brother Samuel* was hostage to the weather. The hard, steady wind gave the schooner the maneuvering power it would need to cross the bar, but the same wind was also speeding the ship along too quickly. At this rate they would be crossing the bar against a falling tide. And at the Humboldt the tide was fierce, especially now, after a long, dry summer, when the river itself was low.

"What's wrong?" Maya asked, caught by the sudden stillness of Will as he stood listening to wind and wave.

"If I were captain we would be heading out to sea."

She followed Will's glance and saw only dark clouds and heaving swells whose tops unraveled in the fierce wind. "Why?"

"We're going to be caught between the storm and the bar if we head in now. Better to go out, where there's room to run. The *Brother Samuel* is a good ship. The storm would be nothing, so long as there were clean fathoms beneath the keel."

There was a shout. Sailors leaped to the masts. More canvas unfurled. Captain Trowbridge had made his choice. He was going to race the storm to the point where he believed the fog-shrouded channel to be, then turn inland and run past the bar for the shelter of the bay. The captain had made that run up the narrow channel past the river bar dozens of times. He was trusting his skill and instinct to find the hidden slot despite the fog and the storm waves pushing him against a falling tide.

"He's going to run for the bar," Will said.

A cold wind bore down on the deck. Maya shivered. With fumbling fingers she retied her bonnet and turned to go below.

"No," he said, grabbing her arm.

Maya's automatic protest at being touched died on her lips. There was urgency in Will's expression but no desire. He had the same intensity about him as he had shown when he had pulled himself up a rope hand over hand in order to prevent his blind sister from slamming into the railing.

"I'll be back," he said, yanking off his coat and putting it over Maya's shoulders. "I've got to get Beth."

"But—"

"Stay here," he interrupted curtly. "If we hit the bar you'll have no chance at all below decks."

Maya shot Will a look that was both fearful and disbelieving, but he was gone before she could protest that he was making too much of a matter that the captain had decided to his own satisfaction.

The wind was running at fifteen knots from the port quarter and the fog had cut visibility to twenty yards by the time Will reappeared leading Beth. He stationed her in the shelter of the wheelhouse, then went to get Maya.

"Do you really believe we'll go under?" Maya asked, searching his gray eyes, which were now intent on scanning the water off the bow.

"Captain Trowbridge will do his best. If that isn't good enough, we damned well better be ready to swim for it." Will stopped suddenly, as though he had just had a disturbing thought. "You can swim, can't you?"

Maya flushed as she remembered the delicious, forbidden pleasure of sliding through warm water, feeling it flowing over her nude body. Her mother had given her a thorough strapping for her brazenness; and then, knowing her daughter, she had taught Maya how to swim so that she would survive her next inevitable foray into the warm, silky waters of the farm's small lake.

"Yes, I can swim," she whispered.

A light, misty rain began to fall, chilling everything it touched and reducing visibility even further.

"I'm going to the railing to watch," Will said. "Beth, do you remember what I told you?"

The twelve-year-old's blind, earnest face turned toward her brother. "If we're separated, I'm to swim away from the sound of the ship. If I bump into a piece of wood in the water, I'm to hang on until you come for me."

"That's my girl," he said, giving her a quick hug. "Don't worry. The railing isn't far. I'll be able to hear you if you call."

"Will?" Beth asked as she clung to his broad shoulders. "This is just a game, isn't it?"

"Sure," he said. He kissed her cheek. "Just a game. But you can't cheat, Mouse. You have to pretend it's real."

Gently Will lifted Beth's hands, squeezed them and went quickly to the railing a few feet away. Maya forgot her own uneasiness as she realized what it must be like for the blind girl, alone in a darkness that knew no end, waiting for a sudden blow that would send her spinning into the cold sea.

Damn Will for frightening her like this, Maya thought fiercely. *It isn't necessary... is it?*

"Would you mind if I held your hand?" Maya asked. "It would be a comfort. Games like this frighten me."

Beth turned toward Maya's voice with a tremulous smile. "Oh, would you? It would comfort me, too."

Will, wearing a wool lumberman's coat he had grabbed from his room below decks, stood by the rail, watching the heavy mercury ocean that both bore them forward and at the same time carried traces of the land ahead in the countercurrents and bits of debris that swirled past the schooner's curving bow.

Trowbridge himself was at the helm of the schooner, though his pilot was standing at his elbow. The captain called out a string of orders. The ship turned sharply toward the unseen land. The sail that had been let out was taken in, and more besides, until the schooner had just enough canvas up to make way. The captain stood with one hand bracing the varnished oak wheel, scanning the fog ahead and the ocean to the landward side of the boat. Three of the dozen crewmen were at the bow, trying to take depth soundings in the heaving ocean with a lead line. The rest of the crew stood ready at the masts, awaiting further orders.

No one remained below decks.

The *Brother Samuel* sailed forward blindly for six or eight minutes. Will watched the water as closely as the sailors. The color had changed subtly, tending more toward brown than gray and varying in shade as well, as though the bottom were irregular. Bits of debris were present, material that might have come from the outwash of the harbor.

"Thirty feet and holding!" called the sailor with the lead line. Then he added under his breath, "And may God have mercy on our miserable souls."

Suddenly Will turned and shouted at the wheelhouse. "Deadhead! Port side! It must be the harbor. The current would have carried it south. We should bear to port!"

Maya looked over the side. Just at the edge of visibility she saw a huge log floating, mostly submerged. Even with the sails trimmed, the ship seemed to be moving at tremendous speed, for the log was quickly lost in the mist.

Trowbridge shot Will an impatient, dismissive look, but said nothing. Nor did he move to steer a course to port.

Beth started to say something, only to have Will shush her sharply.

"Quiet. Everyone quiet."

From somewhere ahead came a distant noise, as though a giant animal lay in ambush ahead, concealed in mists but for the rhythmic sounds of breathing.

"Surf!" Will shouted suddenly. "Surf dead ahead, Captain! It's breaking over the bar! Bear to port! The channel is to port!"

No one ever knew if the captain heard Will's warning, or if he believed it. A towering wave hit the *Brother Samuel*'s stern, shoving it forward in a massive surge of gray water. As the wave crested and the schooner started to slide into the trough, the partly submerged bar of the Humboldt River loomed up before them in the rain. The sailors at the bow saw the white explosion of the breaking waves ahead. One of them had time to scream a warning, his voice shrill above the grinding of wave over sand.

Trowbridge put the wheel hard over, trying to come to port and slide across the end of the bar in a desperate thrust toward safety. For a moment Will thought that they would make it. Then the water simply vanished and the schooner crashed onto the sandbar with staggering force just as a wave broke over the stern.

Tons of cold water swept the decks clean of all but a few feet of the masts. Not even the wheelhouse remained. The shock of collision was so great that it took a few seconds for Will to realize that he was buried in cold water, fighting for his life. When he broke the surface and drew his first choking breaths, he found himself in a porridge that was half earth, half sea, filled with struggling men and the jagged wreckage of masts and sails and lines. The ship lay between him and the shore, for the wild swirl of water over the ship had caught him in an eddy.

As the boiling rush of the wave subsided, Will fought to free himself of the deadweight of the lumber jacket. Another wave broke, dragging him down, but he was a strong swimmer. Once free of the jacket he surged to the surface again. Now he was beyond the reach of the bar, but not of the breakers relentlessly pushing him toward the broken ship.

Thirty feet away a man floated facedown within the tangled wreckage of the wheelhouse. The back of his head was covered with blood. No one else was within sight.

"Beth!" Will screamed. *"Beth!"*

Another ten-foot wave broke over Will, hammering him beneath the surface of the water once more. When he fought his way to air again he knew he had to swim away from the bar or die beneath the tons of pouring water. Yet he had to find Beth, who had been near the wheelhouse where the dead sailor floated. Grimly Will fought his way free of the wave, looking for his sister and for the girl who had stood next to her, holding her hand.

In one way Beth and Maya had been more fortunate than Will. Trowbridge's last desperate maneuver had deprived them of the shelter of the wheelhouse. The force of the breaking wave had swept them over the bar and into the calmer water beyond. The next wave brought with it a few scraps of wreckage, including a spar. Maya seized the floating beam and clung to it, dragging Beth along.

"Hold on," Maya said urgently. "Quickly, Beth. Hold on!"

Choking, crying, Beth clung to the spar.

When Maya was certain that Beth wouldn't let go, she looked around in the water. They were utterly alone, nothing but a cold mercury sea below and a lid of misty rain above. The spar was small, slippery, floating low in the water, unable to bear their combined weight. Another wave rolled over them, threatening to pull them apart.

Maya struggled against her long dress and petticoats as she tried to keep her head above water without putting too much weight on the spar. In the end she was forced to let go of the spar, or drag the blind girl under. The next wave washed over Maya, choking her as she frantically tried to stay afloat. She knew that it would be the same with the next wave and the next, until she could float no longer. She tried to call out for help but choked on seawater.

"Call—out," she said hoarsely to Beth. "Keep calling."

Beth's thin voice lifted above the sound of the breakers as she called for her brother.

Will was trapped in the maelstrom just behind the bar when he heard the wavering sounds of Beth's cry. He looked around, trying to orient himself. The *Brother Samuel* lay hull to the waves, half buried on the bar. The ship's landward side had been smashed by the weight of the waves. The hull showed great rents. Even as he watched, pieces spun away on the boiling crest of a wave, and other chunks shot into the air under the pressure of the wave's backwash. To stay there was death, yet he thought he heard Beth calling to him from the wreckage.

With a dozen strokes Will swam the length of the hull, dodging the planks that it had already begun to sluff under the pounding of the waves. He saw the bodies of two crewmen tangled in the lines and the torn canvas of the mainsail. Beth's voice came again, terror making it shrill.

Will realized that he was on the wrong side of the bar. Somehow he had to cross it without getting hammered into the wreck, tangled in the debris or ground into the sand. He spotted a piece of wreckage floating nearby. It was a section of starboard rail to which the barrel used to catch rainwater was still attached. The nearly empty barrel gave unusual buoyancy to the wooden rail.

Treading water, Will dug out his pocketknife and slashed away at the tangled lines that held the railing to the disintegrating hull. Once free the buoyant barrel floated high, easily carrying Will and the rail over the bar, toward the invisible shore. He had only to steer it in the direction of Beth's voice.

But Beth's voice no longer came to guide Will. The achingly cold water of the Pacific had already sapped her frail strength.

Maya kicked out of the last of her petticoats and tore at her dress. The worn fabric finally gave way, freeing her. Wearing only a thin chemise and pantaloons, she swam the few feet to the spar and grabbed Beth, who had almost slipped away. The girl's mouth was a purple gash in her bloodless face. A bruise swelled along one cheek.

"Hang—on!" Maya said, coughing up the seawater that she had swallowed. "Beth—hang on!"

Slowly the girl's grip on the spar tightened. Maya floated beside her, supporting her. Maya tried to call out, to let any possible rescuer know where they were, but she was unable to do more than to cough rackingly. Swift currents tugged at the spar and the girls clinging to it, carrying them farther and farther from the wreck.

Eventually the coughing passed. When Maya wiped the tears from her eyes, she saw only Beth and the spar, mist and the cold sea. Beth's grip on the spar had slackened. Maya called out for help.

No one answered.

"Beth," she said urgently. "Beth! Can you hear me?"

Beth's eyes opened, glazed with the cold that was sapping her life.

"You have to hang on!"

Beth's eyes closed wearily. Her hands slipped from the spar. Maya grabbed the thin girl and drew her head above water.

"Oh God," Maya said, "Will! Will, where are you! Help us! Oh God, she's dying! Help us!"

Maya drew in a ragged, choking breath, then froze. From out of the fog behind came a sound that could have been Will's voice calling her name.

The tide was running against...

Chapter Three

The tide was running against Henry Ising as he pushed his heavy redwood canoe into the rough water at the mouth of Humboldt Bay. The wind had risen, driving the cold rain ahead of it like sleet. He ignored the discomfort because he was determined to locate the heavy redwood logs a fishing-boat captain had seen in the mouth of the bay. The weather was ugly and becoming more so every minute, but Ising had enormous faith in his own ability, his own strength and his luck.

In addition he was broke, which was a condition of considerable discomfort for a Yurok of any age, much less a half-breed of twenty. When bastardy was combined with penury, there was more than enough incentive to send Ising into the teeth of a storm to scavenge logs. He had been raised among Yuroks, which was to say that he had been thoroughly inculcated with what white men called avarice and the Yuroks called an appreciation for the standard measure of anything's worth. Money. If Ising hesitated to take on the storm, he would remain poor, for the storm would scatter the logs beyond one man's ability to gather them.

The risk Ising was taking was real but not foolhardy. He knew the rough waters of the river bore very well. He knew that as long as he stayed behind the shelter of the river bar he would be reasonably safe. If he were lucky, he could round up the loose logs with the long pike pole he carried, hitch them together with the heavy iron dogs and chains that were lying in the bottom of the canoe and tow the valuable logs back on the turning tide before the storm made such work impossible.

With a steady rhythm Ising dug his paddle deep into the roiling water, pushing the canoe forward as he scanned the edges of his misty world for a sign of the deadheads that would bring cash to his empty pockets. Suddenly something grabbed the paddle as he tried to draw it back. At first Ising thought the problem was a tangle of kelp, but as he wrestled the paddle aboard, he discovered that it had become tangled in a snarl of sodden manila rope. He pulled the paddle free and was untangling and coiling the rope to keep when he saw other debris floating, almost concealed by the mist and currents and wind-whipped froth.

Instantly Ising realized that there must have been a recent shipwreck. Nothing else could explain the concentration of debris in an area of such strong, divergent currents. The only nearby obstacle capable of wrecking a big ship was the bar at the river's mouth. The bar was somewhere in front of him, lost in the mist and rain.

Even as Ising reached that conclusion, he put his back into paddling, sending the heavy canoe gliding forward into the storm with redoubled speed. Although mist and rain obscured all landmarks, he could tell by the action of the currents that he was at least three hundred yards short of the bar. The waves in this section of the bore were several feet high. They broke over the bow of the canoe until it began to ship substantial amounts of cold water. He didn't turn aside. He simply kept the bow to the waves and stroked toward the bar with every bit of his considerable strength. He knew that any survivors would probably be clinging to the wreck or swimming nearby. He also knew that men didn't live long in the bone-chilling sea.

When Ising's short canoe finally reached the shelter of the sandbar, he turned north again, paralleling the shore. The atmosphere was so thick with moisture that he had to judge his distance from the bar by the rhythmic thunder of waves breaking over the waterlogged tongue of sand. He saw no ship's masts looming out of the mist to guide him. He didn't need to see the ship to know that it must be there; the plumes of debris streaming by would lead him to the shipwreck as surely as his eyes could.

After a few minutes the sound of the crashing waves altered subtly, as though they were breaking over a hollow rock instead of a solid bar of sand and mud. Ising stroked even closer to the hidden obstacle. Suddenly through curtains of rain, he saw the hull of a lumber schooner lying like a beached whale on the seaward side of the bar. He fought closer, shooting the canoe through the waves and wild water, dodging the most dangerous pieces of debris.

A body turned over and over on a wave, then vanished. It was the only sign Ising could find that the ship had been sailed by men rather than ghosts.

Ising hailed the wreck repeatedly, his deep voice carrying over the thunder of breaking waves. Nothing came in response to his call but the rhythmic roar of waves tearing themselves apart on the bar. The force of the rushing water was so great that it wrenched off planks and launched them like javelins into the relative calm on the landward side of the bar.

For several minutes Ising called out in the lull between waves. No shouts came in return.

There was no way for him to get closer to the shipwreck without destroying his canoe and probably himself. Nor was there any reason to go closer. Anyone clinging to the hull would have answered him by now. There was nothing on the bar but the ocean and the wind and the ship brought to an early, shallow grave.

Ising turned the canoe's stern to the wreck and dug hard for shore. He paddled several hundred yards before he felt that it was safe to stop and bail out the gallons of cold water that sloshed about his feet. The biscuit tin he used for bailing made a dull, ringing noise against the solid redwood of the canoe. In the damp air it sounded as though he were beating on a wooden drum.

"Help . . . here . . ."

Head up, eyes narrowed, Ising froze, feeling a chill hand from his Yurok past scraping down his spine. A *woge* was calling to him, luring him to his death.

"Help . . ."

Ising shook off the superstitious dread. He was no longer a Yurok to avoid the dark places of the forest and call the names of gods long dead. He wasn't much on calling upon the Christian God, either. He believed in what he could see or touch or hear.

And what he heard sounded like a drowning man.

The call came from Ising's right, where the mist and rain were thickest. It was a man's voice, hoarse but still able to carry across the water.

"Over . . . here."

The paddle dug in. The canoe shot forward.

"Where?" Ising shouted. "Call out so I can find you!"

"Here . . . over here."

A few moments later an odd shape condensed out of the rain. Ising stared at it and slowly realized that the shape was a piece of ship's railing and a big barrel. Two survivors were draped limply over the barrel. A third survivor lay partly in the water, only his head and shoulders free, as though he had been propelling the awkward, makeshift raft with no more than the power of his legs.

As the canoe drew abreast, Ising saw that two of the survivors were women. One was dressed only in underclothing that was all but transparent in the rain. Though obviously weak she was alive, conscious and able to hold onto her precarious position. The second female was a girl who lay unconscious with her face partially in the cold water. Her skin was pale and discolored.

Ising dismissed the second woman as dead and therefore beyond his help. He looked back toward the man. There was something familiar about the shape of his skull and the thick, water-slicked hair.

"Will? Great God, is that you?" Ising called.

As the canoe bumped against the railing, Will swam forward with surprisingly powerful strokes and seized the side of the canoe. Instantly the raft became more buoyant, lifting Beth's face above the water.

"Henry? Damned glad you found us," Will said hoarsely. "Beth couldn't have lasted much longer."

At that moment Ising realized that the slender, motionless form was Will's blind sister. The Yurok started to speak, to say that it was too late, that Beth was dead; but Will had already turned away.

"Maya, climb up onto the rail and then into the canoe. Easy, sweetheart, easy. That's it," he encouraged, the words gentle despite the raw sound of his voice.

Ising steadied the canoe with one hand and used the other to pull the woman onto the rail and then lift her into the canoe. She was cold to the touch. Her skin was tinged with purple and roughened all over with gooseflesh. The scant clothing she wore wasn't enough to serve the needs of modesty, much less to turn the cold wind from her body. She collapsed in the bottom of the canoe and stayed there, breathing raggedly, barely conscious.

Ising eased Maya into a half-reclining position and quickly covered her with his jacket. Her eyes were glazed with exhaustion and chill, yet she tried to thank him. Her lips were too stiff to form the words.

"It's all right," Ising said quickly. "Save your strength. And don't move around. Understand?"

She nodded slightly even as her eyes closed once more. She leaned against the bow seat, too spent to do more than breathe.

Ising stepped over Maya and went to help Will aboard. But Will wasn't there. He had gone back to the raft, scrambled onto it and pulled his sister into a sitting position. There was no sign of blood in the girl's face, no warmth, nothing but the waxy stillness of death as she lay doubled over his arm.

"It's too late, Will," Ising said. "Come aboard. If we don't get the other one to shore right away, she'll die too."

Will shot Ising a look of anger that was frightening in its fierceness. The Yurok said nothing. He knew that white men felt differently about death than he did, and he knew how much Will loved his gentle, helpless sister.

"Get aboard," Ising said gently.

"I'm not leaving her."

"All right. I'll put a line on her and—"

"God damn you!" Will screamed hoarsely. "She's not dead!"

"Listen to me." Ising's deep voice was calm and his black eyes were compassionate as he looked at the still form folded motionlessly over Will's arm. "There's not enough room in the canoe for three people and a—and Beth."

It was true and Will knew it. He and Ising had often used the canoe together. It settled well into the water when it held just the two of them. With Maya aboard the canoe would ride even lower. If even Beth's slight weight were added, the craft would be dangerously overburdened.

"Put a line on me," Will said.

"If I tow you through the water, you'll drown or freeze before we're halfway there. Beth won't."

Suddenly Beth stirred and began vomiting and coughing violently, clearing her body of seawater. Ising stared in disbelief but made no more protest. He knew that there was no choice now but to risk all their lives in a crowded, too heavily loaded canoe.

As Ising moved to help Will, the Yurok's boot rang against one of the pieces of log-scavenging equipment that he had carried in the canoe so long that he thought of heavy iron tools as part of the canoe itself. They were the means of his livelihood. Without them he would be just one more shiftless Indian to be stared at disdainfully and then ignored by Yuroks and whites alike.

Saying nothing Ising began picking up the heavy iron dogs and chains and dropping them over the side into the sea. When Will heard the rattle and splash he realized what Ising was doing. And he realized what it would cost his friend in self-respect.

"I'll buy more for you," Will said, his voice raw.

Ising simply shook his head. He knew that Will and his father had barely spoken to each other for several years. Despite his wealthy heritage and expensive city clothes, Will was essentially as penniless as Ising himself.

The last of the expensive, handmade tools sank into the dark water. The pike pole floated away into the rain on the back of a swirling current. The canoe was one hundred pounds lighter when Ising reached over and took the violently shivering girl from Will's arms.

"I'll replace everything," Will said. "I swear it."

"Why bother? It wasn't much of a living anyway." Ising grinned suddenly, showing a wide slash of white in a tanned, handsome face.

While Ising cared for Beth, Will slipped off the raft and into the water. It didn't even feel cold. When it came time to pull himself into the canoe, he was surprised to discover that his body wouldn't obey his commands. He could rise partway out of the water, but not enough to lever himself aboard the canoe.

Strong hands wrapped around Will's biceps. Within seconds he was aboard. Ising laid the three of them out like fish in a tin, grabbed his paddle and bent to his work. He knew if any of the three were to survive, they had to be gotten warm and dry. Even that might not be enough for Beth, who had not moved but for tiny, shallow breaths while he wrapped his wool flannel shirt around her and pulled his knit cap onto her head.

Will lay on his back, feeling the frail weight of Beth resting along his right side and the more substantial weight of Maya on his left. He looked to his right and recognized the colorful red and black of Ising's flannel shirt. To his left Maya lay wrapped in a heavy wool logger's jacket that was also black and red. Her eyes were closed, her face wan and Ising's jacket so big and thick that Will couldn't tell if she were breathing. Nor could he see a pulse, for her hair had come undone and lay in wet, heavy ribbons that concealed her throat.

Suddenly fear shot through Will. He freed his hand and slid it into the jacket's opening. The thin cotton chemise was wet, cold, as was her full breast with its nipple drawn into a hard point; but her heart beat strongly beneath his palm. Slowly her eyes opened in response to the intimate touch. They focused on him.

"Will . . . ?"

"It's all right, Maya. Everything is all right."

She stirred toward him, instinctively seeking greater contact, shared warmth against the chill pervading her body. With a shuddering sigh her head fell onto Will's shoulder. Beneath the jacket her hand found his and pressed it even closer to her breast as though she were afraid of losing him. He brushed his cold lips over her forehead and brought her weight more fully onto his body. Her fingers tightened beneath the jacket, holding him against her. Eyes closed, he held her in return, feeling a tenderness more fierce than any emotion he had ever known before in his life.

After a few minutes Will eased his hand from Maya's and pulled the jacket closely about her once more. When she stirred, he kissed her very gently, murmured reassurances and saw the suggestion of a smile curve her full lips. He kissed her again, tasting salt and something more, an indefinable suggestion of Maya herself.

When he looked up, Ising was watching him.

"Known her long?"

"That doesn't matter," Will said simply. "Maya is mine."

Ising's eyes widened at the certainty in Will's voice, at the matter-of-fact possessiveness with which his friend looked at the woman lying beside him in the bottom of the canoe and at the gentleness with which he touched her pale flesh.

After a moment Will turned and checked on Beth. When he was reassured that she was still breathing and as comfortable as possible under the circumstances, he slowly eased himself out from between the two semiconscious women. He lifted Beth, pulled the second paddle from beneath her, and then arranged her carefully alongside Maya so that the two girls could share whatever warmth they had between them.

The first few strokes Will took were uneven, clumsy and agonizing for his icy hands. Then old habits reasserted themselves. Within a few minutes the canoe was parting the cold waters quickly, leaving a wake that currents turned and twisted until the disturbance vanished beneath curtains of mist. Silently the two men drove through the rough water toward the mouth of Humboldt Bay.

Small boats appeared suddenly around them. News of the shipwreck had already reached the town. Ising shouted across the water, telling what he had seen, but he never hesitated in his strokes with the deep, broad paddle.

Very quickly the two men brought the canoe to shore. The Hawthorne house was empty when they finally arrived, for everyone had hurried down to the docks to learn what they could of the fate of the *Brother Samuel*.

"In here," Will said, kicking open the door to Beth's room.

Ising looked around the room with its pale yellow wool blankets and yellow-flowered wallpaper. It was like nothing he had ever seen, as though summer had been captured and put into the service of a blind girl.

"Quickly," Will said, ruthlessly stripping away Beth's cold, wet clothes.

They wrapped the two girls in down comforters and settled them before the bedroom hearth. By then Will was shivering uncontrollably, utterly unable to remove his own clothes. Ising undressed him, covered him with the last down comforter and immediately went to work on the fire. Within minutes flames leaped high against the soot-blackened stone of the inner hearth.

"Not too close," Ising said, easing Beth farther away. "If they warm too quickly the heart stops."

Will accepted the warning without protest. The Yuroks had dealt with the cold sea much longer than he had. It was the same when Ising held a cup of hot water to Will's mouth and told him to drink. He drank without argument and was rewarded by a delicious feeling of heat unfolding through his body.

"Beth?" he asked, gesturing toward the water.

"Not yet. She would choke. The other one might drink." Ising hesitated. "In the village we hold the people against our naked bodies, and then wrap blankets around."

Although the suggestion outraged every idea of proper conduct between unmarried men and women, much less between white women and Indian men, Will said only, "Yes. Quickly."

When Will reached for Beth, Ising brushed his hand aside.

"You haven't enough warmth to do her any good."

Ising threw aside the clothes that he hadn't already given to the two girls. At the last moment he decided to keep on his long underwear. The cloth was neither wet nor thick enough to interfere with the task of warming Beth, and the idea of shocking the gently bred young girl with his nakedness was unsettling to Ising. The thought of how Hale Hawthorne would react if he found out wasn't comforting either. Ising wanted to save Beth's life, but was in no hurry to lose his own in the process.

As he pulled Beth's cold, frail body against his own abundant heat, Ising wondered at the fact that she still lived at all. There was no warmth in her, no color, nothing but a tiny, fluttering heartbeat as though a moth were trapped against his chest. With a silent prayer to whatever benevolent gods or God might be listening, Ising wrapped the down comforter around and settled in to find out if the girl would live or die.

Will watched Beth vanish beneath the enfolding blanket and the embrace of his friend and knew that there was nothing else he could do for his sister. When his own shivering abated enough that he could pour water without spilling it, he refilled his cup and went over to Maya.

"Maya? Are you awake?"

Gently Will's hand eased beneath the comforter to stroke Maya's cheek. She was cool but not cold to his touch. A faint flush of color showed beneath the flawless skin. Her body was shaken by erratic, violent shivering. Without hesitation he set aside the cup, opened the quilt and pulled her into the greater warmth of his body. He wrapped both of them in the quilt, and then lay down facing the fire as Ising had done.

Maya made a small, whimpering sound that was almost lost in the random chattering of her teeth. In an effort both to warm and to reassure her, Will stroked Maya's body with his hands, silently telling her that she was safe. Held between the warmth of his body and the fire, wrapped in soft down, Maya slowly stopped shivering and lay quietly in his arms, her back pressed along his chest, her hips and legs nestled against his, the two bodies fitting together as though they were two spoons lying in a drawer.

Beneath Will's hand Maya's heart beat steadily, strongly. Her breast was warm, silky, and her nipple had the texture of velvet. Long after her skin was no longer cold, he caressed her tenderly, shaping the flesh that had become more precious to him than his own. There was both reverence and desire in his touch, although he was conscious of neither. He was only conscious of the unutterable rightness of lying with Maya curled against his body, skin against skin, warmth against warmth, her breast a sweet weight in his hand, her hardening nipple nuzzling the sensitive skin between his fingers.

Neither awake nor asleep, Maya was aware only of warmth stretched along the length of her back and hips and legs, a living, resilient heat that was the most beautiful thing she had ever known. Relaxed, defenseless, stripped of etiquette and fear, she luxuriated in the sensations radiating from her breast. Because she had never been touched by a man, she had no defenses against the sensuous responses bathing her body. She didn't know that the taut aching of her nipple begged to be assuaged by the hands and mouth of the youth who even now was smoothing her belly and thighs with his broad, hard palm. She didn't know that she made a soft sound deep in her throat, a near-silent plea for more of the pleasure he was giving to her.

With a tenderness that was as new to Will as it was to Maya, he brought her even closer to his own body until she flowed along his length, fitting perfectly, and his warm breath bathed her cheek. She sighed and shifted until both breasts were nestled in his hands and then she cupped her own hands over his, pressing him closer. Her long hair was no longer cold; its damp warmth trapped between their bodies gave a sea- and woman-scented intimacy to the very air Will breathed.

Suddenly he trembled with emotions that were far removed from cold or fear. He had taken women before, had known the swift release from sexual urgency; but he had never known sexual intimacy, never known the clawing of violent desire held in check by an equal reverence for the fragile life that lay so trustingly against him. Dimly he was grateful that Ising was only a few feet away. His presence was all that kept Will's hands from sliding down Maya's body to the tangled nest of hair between her legs and the feminine warmth that he longed to stroke. But if he did that he wouldn't be able to hold himself back. He would smooth apart her thighs and thrust into her. And it would be good, so good.

Will stifled a groan and tried to think of other things. Half of his mind urged him to go ahead and take Maya; he was alive, she was alive and warm and there was no better way to celebrate their survival than in the explosive release of sexuality. Modesty wasn't even a consideration. He and Ising had taken whores in one-room shanties before, where privacy was a word without meaning.

But that was just the problem. Maya wasn't a whore.

Nor did he have any intention of sharing her, not even to the extent of letting another man overhear the tiny, soft sounds she made when he touched her. Those sounds, her softness, the heat of her body, the scent of her—they belonged to him, not to anyone else. Not even to Ising, his best friend, the man who had saved his life, saved Beth's life, saved Maya's.

No matter who or what Maya had been before Will had seen her on the deck of the *Brother Samuel*, whether she had known men or was as pure as a rainwashed dawn, she was Will's now. He had taken her from the sea and held her, fighting off the deathly cold. She was his in a way that no other woman had ever been or ever would be. He couldn't explain it and felt no need to try; he simply accepted it, and her.

Gently he kissed her bare, warm shoulder. With equal care he eased his body from the warm tangle of flesh and down. She whimpered softly when his hands left her breasts. The sound threatened to undo all his resolve. Then he realized that she was asleep; her responses to him were instinctive rather than the planned seductions of a coquette. A feeling of tenderness suffused Will for Maya's vulnerability. He wrapped her securely in the comforter, stole a kiss from her sleeping lips and reluctantly pulled a blanket around his own nakedness.

"How is she?" Ising asked.

"Warm. Asleep. Beautiful."

Ising's black eyes narrowed. He had known Will for several years, but never had heard that particular emotion in his voice, nor had Ising seen such emotion in Will's face as when he looked down at Maya.

"How is Beth?" Will asked.

"Alive."

Will knelt and reached inside the blanket that wrapped the girl to Ising's warmth. Her skin was chilly but not cold. Her lips no longer looked purple. The faintest suggestion of pink showed beneath her blue-white skin.

"Should we hold her between us? I'm warm enough now."

"I noticed," Ising said dryly.

Will realized that his own blanket had parted, revealing the state of his sexual arousal. He flushed as though he were ten rather than seventeen and hastily rearranged the blanket. Ising's black eyebrows raised in surprise. He and Will had been through too many whorehouses together for either one of them to blush over anything as common as an erection.

"I'll be back in a minute," Will muttered.

Though Will spent most of his time away from the house, his room was still kept ready for him at all times. The fact both irritated and reassured him; it was his father's way of saying that, despite their differences, his son was always welcome in the Hawthorne home.

And that was the irritation. Hale's *son*. Not Will Hawthorne, a young man in his own right, but Willy Hawthorne, a strapping boy whom no one took seriously.

When Will returned he was dressed in dry clothes, though his shirt was unbuttoned to reveal the pattern of dark brown hair on his chest. He checked Maya, reassuring himself that she was still asleep, still warm. He tucked the comforter he no longer needed around her before he went over to where Ising held Beth between himself and the warm hearth.

"I'm not as warm as the fire," Will said. "Will that matter?"

"The heat of our flesh will be better for her than flames."

"Why?"

"A shaman would say that our spirits mingle, calling hers back from the shores of death," Ising said, but his tone made it clear that he didn't share that belief.

Will thought of the complex emotions he had felt while lying with Maya. He could still feel them, an invisible yet powerful web binding them together for all time.

"Maybe the shamans are right," Will said, lying alongside his sister's frail, cool body and pulling the comforter closed once more. "Ah, poor little Mouse. You're such a tiny thing to have known such pain."

Beth didn't stir as she lay between the two big youths, absorbing their muscular warmth with the innocence of a flower absorbing sunlight. She was utterly motionless, so still that Will became alarmed.

"Can you feel her heartbeat?"

"It is like a moth's wings, only stronger. She is as tough as any Yurok child."

"She doesn't look it."

Ising smiled. "White man, you have to stop looking at only the outside of people. I have seen loggers half your size fight men bigger than you and come out on top. Spirit, not muscle. Despite her size your 'little Mouse' is as determined to bend the world to her needs as you or your father."

"Beth? She's such a gentle little thing."

Ising laughed. "For all your brawn you are still young. You don't understand that life pours through some women in ways foreign to all men. Those women live half with us and half with the future, for they carry the future in their wombs." Ising nodded at Will's startled look. "Yes, even little Beth. She isn't aware of it yet but it's there deep inside her. A hunger. It made her live when a boy her size would have died. If she were Yurok, she would be marked now as a shaman. But she is white, so she will bend the world to her womb's needs in white ways. It is the same for the other one. Maya. The other men on the ship died. She should have died as well. She lived. She is set apart now."

"Yes. She is mine."

Ising looked into the gray eyes of his friend. "It is for the shaman to choose her own life. It is for her to decide whose children will grow from her body into the future. And she might not see the same necessities as we men do, for we live only in the present."

"That doesn't matter. She is mine."

Ising sighed and said no more. His friend was young and white. Some kinds of wisdom only came with time and at great cost. For whites an understanding of women seemed to be one of those painful things. They made no room in their culture for those women who understood life differently from men. White men saw only that all women bled monthly, all were soft; and therefore men assumed that all women were the same, born only to serve men and to bear their children.

It was not so. Some women could be passed from hand to hand as chattel, or owned by one man for life. And some would not consent to be owned by any man not of their choosing. Ising didn't know if Maya were a shaman who wanted to lie with men, much less if she wanted to lie with only one man.

But Ising did know that it would be the shaman's choice, not the man's.

Chapter Four

~~~~~~ ∞∞∞∞∞ ~~~~~~

Maya awoke slowly, reluctant to leave the delicious warmth of her dreams. In the first few instants of waking she was surprised to find that she was alone. Then she wondered why that should seem unusual to her. She had become accustomed to sleeping without her sisters in the months since she had left the farm. She certainly hadn't returned somehow to the farm again to share a bed with her sisters. The view through the window wasn't of tiny fields and fences, but of a forest so beautiful that she could scarcely believe it was real.

Perhaps she was still asleep after all, still dreaming. She had never seen such magnificent trees before, towering evergreens with graceful branches and trunks the color of rusted iron. A breeze moved through the dark green boughs, making them shiver and sigh as though they were women being caressed by their lovers.

Maya's heart beat faster at the thought of being caressed like that. She blushed as she remembered her dream, the sensuous warmth of a man's hands holding her naked breasts, the heat of a man's body pressed along hers. A shimmering feeling condensed deep inside her, a bud of desire whose soft petals were wrapped closely around a secret warmth. She felt boneless, deliciously pliant and…restless. Her breasts were full, the nipples achingly peaked as though straining toward a man's warm hands.

Maya moved fitfully. The sheet caressed her sensitive breasts and thighs. With a feeling of shock she realized that she was naked. In the next instant she remembered the *Brother Samuel*, Will Hawthorne, blind Beth and an ocean of icy water pouring over everything. Maya wondered where she was, how she had come to this warm bed when her last clear thought had been the certainty that she would never be warm again. She remembered calling out to God that Beth was dying and hearing Will's voice coming back to her through the mist. Somehow God must have heard and saved her.

Or had it been Will who heard? He certainly had been big and strong enough to survive the cold sea.

Hadn't he?

Still more asleep than awake, Maya called Will's name urgently. Her voice was shockingly hoarse, hardly more than a whisper. Yet the door opened instantly. Her eyes widened. Will looked so much younger than she had remembered, his face unmarked, unlined, a youth despite the dark beardshadow lying beneath his skin.

"You survived," she said.

He smiled at her hoarse voice and wide, startled eyes. "Yes. So did you."

"Beth?"

"She's still sleeping, but the doctor said that she should be fine. With luck, she won't even remember what happened. He said it's often that way with peo-

ple exposed to cold. They forget." His gray eyes
searched her face, wondering if she remembered being caressed by him, being naked with him, being tied
to him in the ways that had no words. "How do you
feel?"

"I . . ." Maya swallowed painfully.

Will was beside her in an instant. He poured a glass
of water from a carafe on the bedside table and slipped
his arm around her shoulders to support her while she
drank. The smooth warmth of her skin was a delicious shock. She turned toward him so quickly that
her hair tumbled and slid over her bare shoulders in
deep auburn waves. He remembered how it had felt to
have the long strands pressed against his skin, warmed
by the heat of their bodies.

"Oh, you mustn't! It isn't proper. . . ."

Maya's voice faded into nothingness. She wanted to
tell Will that his touch disturbed her, made her feel
flushed and weak and that she was as afraid of that
weakness as she was oddly hungry for it. She wanted
to say all that and more but her voice was too bruised
from crying out for help to do more than make soft
rasping sounds now.

"Drink this," Will said, ignoring Maya's protests as
he propped her up and put the glass to her lips.

The sheet slid down and caught the swell of her full
breasts. The sight shortened his breath, yet as soon as
she finished drinking, he pulled the bed covers back up
around her chin. He saw the realization of her nakedness sweep up her skin in scarlet waves. He knew then
that despite her blunt speech on the ship, she wasn't
accustomed to being naked with strange men.

"Don't," Will said softly when Maya turned away,
too embarrassed to face him any longer. "There's no

need for you to be ashamed. There can't be anything improper between us.''

She faced him again, her eyes wide and very green. ''Why?''

Before Will could explain that Maya belonged to him, therefore it was impossible for anything improper to occur between them, the door opened. He knew without turning around that it would be his father standing in the doorway.

Hale Hawthorne wasn't as tall as his son, who stood well over six feet, but where Will's physique showed the long bones of a youth still growing into his full power, Hale had the heavily muscled body of a mature man. His hair had been black, but was now liberally mixed with silver. Despite his age his hair was still thick and neatly trimmed, as was the nearly pure silver beard he wore. He was handsome in the way that proud, self-confident men often are, a matter more of bearing than of any regularity of feature.

''I will have a word with you, Willy. Immediately.''

Hale's voice had the depth and resonance that Will's had not yet fully attained and a commanding edge that never failed to rasp on his son's masculine pride. It had been that way since the morning four years ago when Will had stood next to his father and discovered that he was the taller of the two. As Mrs. Hawthorne had died when Will was eleven, there had been no woman to stand between the two men, no mother to encourage the boy's natural hurry to be a man and no wife to soothe the older man's equally natural resistance to being outgrown by his son. Nor had there been anyone else to take Mrs. Hawthorne's role in helping the arrogant Hawthorne males to a better understanding of themselves and each other.

"Excuse me for a moment," Will said, looking down at Maya, who was watching Hale with measuring green eyes.

Slowly Maya looked away from Hale to his son, seeing the father in the son's face, a youthful echo of the man to come. She said nothing to Will, simply nodded, for she felt as though she was suspended between generations, dangling over a void of uncontrollable time.

The door shut behind the two men. Maya slumped heavily against the pillows and looked around the room, seeing its details for the first time. The bed she lay in was long and narrow, as though it had started as a child's bed and then had grown with the child. The child had been a boy, not a girl. There was nothing feminine in the rich, rust-red wood that framed the bed and comprised the dresser with its military ranks of drawers. It was the same for the wardrobe whose open door revealed a man's shirts in neat array. Yet the hand-crafted model ships and random iron tools tacked to the wall suggested a boy rather than a man. Or a boy becoming a man.

At that moment Maya realized that she was in Will Hawthorne's room, lying in his bed, naked. She knew with an instinct too deep to question that it had been his hands rather than his father's that had undressed her. As the realization came, Maya flushed to the soles of her feet. She would rather have been undressed by Hale Hawthorne; his touch might embarrass her, but it wouldn't disturb the hidden depths of her sensuality. She didn't know how she could be so certain of that fact, but she was; just as she was certain that Will's touch would make her as weak-kneed and mush-brained as the women her mother had had such scorn for, women who lay with the wrong men because they couldn't hear the pathetic cries of their future children. All those women had heard was the wild roar of passion in their own blood.

With a muffled sound Maya turned her attention from her restless body to the shafts of sunlight pouring through the multipaned bedroom window, light that made the jeweled colors of the bed quilt come alive. Slowly she pulled her hand out from under the covers and placed it in the radiant center of a shaft of light. The autumn sun still had enough strength to warm her skin. It felt delicious and reassuring, a soothing balm for her troubled thoughts.

For a few moments Maya lay motionless, content simply to be alive. Then she studied the stained-glass transom above the window, watching the sunlight set fire to the colors. It was the same for the sunlight outside, bringing vivid life to everything it touched, especially the red-barked evergreens stirring gracefully in the wind. The sunlight was so dense, so real, that she felt as though she could float away on it. Only gradually did she become aware of the raised, angry voices slicing through the bedroom wall and closed door.

"...told you to stay out of her room. It's bad enough that you undressed her and put her in your own bed, but to visit her in her helpless nakedness passes all bounds of decency!"

"You are overstating, Father. She was wearing bed covers to her ears. She is still weak, barely able to talk and had awakened in a strange place. When I heard her call my name, what was I supposed to do? Yell to her through the door that my father is so consumed by his own lustful thoughts that he won't allow me to enter a girl's room without an armed escort?''

"She is a woman, not a girl, and you are being impertinent!''

"She is but two years older than I, and you are constantly harping on my youth. If she is a woman then I am a man!''

"When I was your age—''

"Yes, I know," Will interrupted impatiently. "You were the sole support of your starving family overseas and simultaneously began a family here. In addition you apparently supported whores from Eureka to—''

The sharp crack of a hand against flesh stopped the flow of Will's words.

"You are not too old to be thrashed," Hale said icily. "You have been too big for your britches ever since you discovered that you woke up with a stiff member every morning. That is the least part of being a man, but I don't expect a boy like you to understand that.''

There was a long silence followed by Will's low voice, vibrant with anger.

"Don't ever strike me again.''

"You will keep a civil tongue in your head, Willy, or you will leave my house until the hard facts of earning your own living teach you manners.''

"I have been earning my own living.''

"In *my* mill.''

There was nothing Will could say to that, because it was the truth.

It was also true that Hale had made it clear around town that anyone who hired Will would have Hale to deal with. Hale was determined that his son would succeed him as head of Tres Santos Lumber Company—after a suitable apprenticeship, of course.

As always the temptation to simply walk away from his father swept through Will. And as always the idea of leaving Beth in Hale's unemotional, puritanical hands made leaving impossible. Hale simply didn't understand the fears that sometimes brought Beth awake and screaming in the night. He hadn't understood how to deal with Beth's menarche. It had been Will who had reassured his sister that the onset of the monthly bleeding was a sign of health rather than illness in a woman. Nor did Hale understand that Beth needed gentleness and laughter every bit as much as she needed Bible studies and food. But Hale had neither tenderness nor laughter, so he gave what he did have: money and an unbending sense of God's will.

Hale had ruled Will with an iron hand and a stern sense of moral rectitude. Will had believed in his father's rigid morality until, at fourteen, Will came across his father leaving one of the cribs at the Stock Exchange. Hale had still been in the act of tucking himself into his pants, fly unbuttoned, his eyes and mouth heavy with satiation. Will thought he had escaped his father's notice, but he hadn't. Nor had Will been big enough to avoid the lash of the belt when he came sneaking in through his bedroom window late that night. It wasn't the first time he had been strapped by Hale. It was the first time Will had fought back, however, and he had fought with all the fury of a boy betrayed in his beliefs.

It had been the last whipping Hale had delivered to Will. It had also been the end of Hale's ability to control the half-grown stranger who had once been his son. After that night Will had rarely spoken to Hale, and only then as employee to employer. For his part Hale spoke only to Will as father to child.

"I will move Maya out as soon as she is well," Will said finally.

"You will do no such thing. Have you no decency at all? Will you take a helpless girl and make a harlot of her in the eyes of society? Is that your idea of how to be a man?"

Will had no quick words of refutation. He hadn't thought about anything beyond the irretrievable fact that Maya belonged to him. In truth he hadn't thought of the future at all. The contempt in Hale's gray eyes told Will that his father knew it.

"Go see to your sister. She was calling for you, but her voice was too weak to carry to your bedroom."

Guilt struck through Will's anger, making him feel even more immature and irresponsible. His feelings about Maya were so new and so intense that they had overshadowed even his concern for Beth. Without a word he turned on his heel and walked down the hall to Beth's room.

Hale looked after him broodingly, then faced the closed bedroom door. When he had walked in a few moments ago and seen Maya's wide green eyes and her magnificent unbound hair, her beauty had struck him like a blow. It had been all he could do not to drag his son from the room by the scruff of his young neck. He didn't blame Will for being drawn to Maya, but he was going to make damned sure that it went no further. She was much too beautiful to be wasted on a randy boy.

The sound of knuckles rapping on the door with leashed impatience startled Maya from her thoughts.

"Yes?" she said. Her voice was husky but no longer raw. The water that Will had given her had washed away much of the raspiness.

The door opened. Hale walked in, the sound of his heels ringing clearly even through the padding of the rug.

"How are you feeling, lass?"

Maya smiled at the echo of a long-lost Scots brogue softening the brusque voice. "Fine, sir. Thank you."

The smile heightened Maya's already vivid beauty. Hale didn't smile in return. It was not like him to soften, even in such small things.

"As usual Willy was too scatterbrained to remember his manners. In the absence of proper introductions, you'll have to forgive my informality. I'm Hale Hawthorne, Willy's father. And you are . . . ?"

"Maya Charters, sir."

His glance fell to her left hand, which was curled like a sleeping kitten in a shaft of sunlight. "Miss?"

"Yes."

"Was your family aboard the *Brother Samuel*?"

"No."

"You were traveling with family friends, then?"

"No."

"Forgive me for prying," Hale said. "Perhaps it would help you to understand if I say that you, Beth and Willy were the only survivors of the wreck of the *Brother Samuel*. I was afraid it would be my unhappy duty to inform you that you had lost family or friends."

"I was traveling quite alone, sir. My parents are dead. The only respectable work I could find was in Trinidad. I am to be their new teacher."

Unlike Will, Hale had no trouble imagining circumstances that could force a young woman to go alone into the world. His own mother had traveled across an ocean and half a continent alone, and she had arrived at her future husband's doorstep as virginal as the day she had been born.

"Well, Miss Charters, there will be no traveling for you for several weeks. The doctor wants to make certain that your experience hasn't upset the notoriously delicate female constitution."

"I'm all right. I just needed a few hours of sleep."

Hale smiled grimly. "You've slept near a day, Miss Charters."

Maya's eyes widened, giving him a glimpse of startled green depths. He nodded in response to her unasked question.

"What of Will's—Master Hawthorne's—sister, Beth? Is she well?"

"She is awake. She is very weak, but then, she has always been frail."

"She is very brave. She faced the sea and the storm with nothing more than her brother's voice to guide her."

"A slender reed," Hale agreed grimly.

"That's not what I meant. Will—Master Hawthorne—saved our lives. Had it not been for his insistence, I would have remained belowdecks and drowned. Had it not been for his foresight, Beth and I wouldn't have been at all prepared for the worst. And had it not been for his courage and strength, we would have died despite our best efforts. You have a son to be proud of, Mr. Hawthorne."

"Perhaps. He's a headstrong young devil."

Maya smiled, remembering her own brothers. "Boys, even good boys, are like that."

Hale nodded slowly, watching Maya's smile with curious intensity. "Some boys grow up much later than girls, it seems. You are young, yet you aren't foolish. Life hasn't always been kind to you, has it?"

"Is life kind to anyone?"

"Some believe it will be to them."

"I do not."

Maya's soft, husky words struck a chord of curiosity within Hale. She was unlike any woman he had known. She had neither a harlot's calculating eyes nor the blushing modesty of a sheltered girl. She was forthright without being actually improper. It was the kind of honesty that frontier life often bred in women, but she displayed none of the coarseness of feature or language that women roughly raised often had.

"Do you grieve for your parents, lass?"

Unexpectedly Maya felt her eyes sting with tears. "Sometimes, but not for their deaths. For their lives. . . ." Her lips curved into something much sadder and more adult than a smile. "Father had so many plans. Mother had so many children. And in the end they died."

"Death is part of life. It's up to the living to bury the dead and go on."

She looked at the sunlight pouring over her hand. "That's what mother told us when father died. That's what I told my sisters and brothers when mother died. Now I tell it to myself."

"It is but the simple truth. Life is all that we are given. The rest we make for ourselves. That is God's way. To ask for or to expect more borders upon blasphemy."

Maya looked up. The gray eyes watching her with barely veiled masculine approval were the same color as Will's, but all resemblance ended there. Hale's glance held strength but no warmth, goals but no dreams, assurance but no empathy, pride but no laughter. The same lack of emotion was repeated in his somber clothes, grave expression and unyielding mouth. He was a man who would never go haring off after rainbows and rumors of gold. He was a man who understood that security didn't come from wishing or dreaming; only hard work and a clear-eyed view of life's possibilities brought security for a man and for those who depended upon him for the very necessities of life itself.

There was great strength in Hale, even if it had been built at the cost of gentler, more beguiling human qualities.

And did that matter, really matter, next to the relentless demands of survival itself? There may have been little laughter or warmth in Hale, but what good had her father's laughter and warmth done her mother when it was winter and there was neither food nor adequate clothing for her children? What good had empathy and dreams done the woman who had died far too soon, worn out from miscarriages and from seeing her children shiver with cold and misery? What good had dreams done when life came down to burying babies who weighed no more than a breath?

"My father lacked your wisdom," Maya said. Then she added softly, "A child who can't learn from her parents' mistakes is doomed to repeat them."

"I wish Willy had half your common sense."

"He is young and has always had enough to eat. If he had lived my life, he would have learned the same lessons I have learned."

Hale grunted. "He's young, I'll grant you that. If he keeps on hanging around with that half-breed Ising, he'll never learn anything useful."

Vaguely Maya remembered a canoe and a black-haired, half-naked man paddling with great strength. "Ising...did he help us?"

"Willy said he picked up the three of you in his canoe."

"I should thank him for saving my life. And Master Hawthorne, as well."

"I gave Ising twenty dollars for his trouble. As for thanking Willy, there's no need. He only did what common decency required."

Maya looked Hale Hawthorne straight in the eye. "That selfsame decency requires that I acknowledge my debt."

For a moment Hale was taken aback. He couldn't think of a time when any woman had ever spoken to him quite so forthrightly. Nor could he disagree with her conclusion: even a stubborn boy and a footloose half-breed deserved recognition for their deeds. It irritated him that Maya was beholden to Will in any way, but that didn't soften the necessity of facing one's Christian duty.

"You are quite right," Hale said abruptly. "The fact that you have to instruct me simply means that it has been too long since a woman's gentler spirit lived in this house. Willy acquitted himself well for a boy. So did the half-breed."

"I'm sure Henry will be overcome by your generous words," said a sardonic voice from the hall.

Will was leaning against the door frame, his glance going angrily from his father to Maya, who had been talking to Hale as though she had no awareness at all that her naked shoulder and arm were continually drawing Hale's eyes. Without a word Will stalked to the armoire and yanked out one of his dress shirts. He bent over the bed with the shirt in his hand.

"Cover yourself," Will said, his tone angry but too soft for Hale to overhear.

Maya flushed deeply. She hadn't felt naked in Hale's presence, but it took only a single look from Will to remind her that she was wearing nothing but her own skin beneath the bed sheets. Ignoring the shirt, she hastily put her arm beneath the covers and pulled them right up around her chin.

"I'm glad you agree that we should be generous," Will said, turning to confront his father. "I've sent word that Mrs. Granger should send over a complete wardrobe for Maya. It's the least we can do for the girl who saved Beth's life."

"Since when do you address a woman in such a familiar way, Willy? The least you can do is show some respect to Miss Charters by not usurping her Christian name."

"I saved Maya's life. She has no objections if I call her Maya, any more than I object to her calling me Will. As for Henry, I knew that you would see your Christian duty and replace the equipment he jettisoned in order to make room for us in his canoe. I took care of that as well."

Maya looked from son to father and back to son again. They very much resembled one another at that moment—stubborn, proud, angry and not willing to back up one inch. But Hale had the advantage of maturity and success, the very things that Will was striving to claim as his own.

"You are very quick to spend money that you haven't earned," Hale said.

"Take it out of my pay."

"You may depend upon it, Willy. If nothing else it might keep you out of dens of iniquity for a brief time."

"Dens? Do tell me their names, Father. I stand ready to receive instruction from your far greater experience with such places."

Maya saw the color staining Hale's cheeks above his beard and knew that Will had gone too far.

"You are disturbing Miss Charters's rest. Go see to Beth."

"After you, Father. I know you wouldn't want to permit any breath of scandal to touch Maya's name by staying alone in a bedroom with her. Would you?"

For an instant Maya thought Hale would strike Will again. So did Will. His stance shifted subtly, proclaiming his intention of fighting back. In fact he seemed eager for it. Hale turned to Maya.

"I apologize for Willy's loose tongue and coarse manners. But as you pointed out to me, he is very young for his age. If you will excuse us?"

Will shot Maya an angry, disbelieving look. She was too startled by Hale's words to do anything more than nod her head, acknowledging Hale's manners in asking her permission to leave. The door closed firmly behind Hale. A few minutes later she heard raised voices once again, but they were filtered through too many walls for her to understand the words. Nor did she want to know what was being said. She had learned all that was important; Will and Hale were strangers united by an accident of birth. There was neither love nor indulgence in Hale's glance when he looked at his son. It was the same when the son looked at the father.

After a time another knock came on Maya's door. It was opened by a Chinese woman of plain appearance and indeterminate years. She set a tray of food on the bedside table, bowed and withdrew. Maya pulled on the shirt that Will had ordered her to wear. The fabric was soft, thin and very white. She had never worn anything half so fine against her skin. With a murmur of appreciation she ran her fingertips over the cloth before her gnawing hunger demanded that she turn her attention to the tray the woman had left. She went to work on the food with an appetite that increased with each bite. Soon there was nothing left on the tray but plates and silverware.

Another knock came at the door. Thinking that it was the cook returning to pick up the tray, Maya called for her to come in.

Will opened the door, arms full of packages. As he looked at Maya propped up in his bed, wearing one of his dress shirts, her lips parted in surprise, he wanted to lock the door behind him and lick the tiny crumbs of cake from the corner of her mouth. All that prevented him was the knowledge that his father would throw him out of the house if he ever discovered anything improper happening. Will didn't want that. He needed time to find and rent a suitable place for Maya. Until then he would tolerate his father's overbearing manner and hypocrisy on the subject of women.

"You look very beautiful in my shirt."

Maya looked down at herself. Until then she hadn't realized that the fabric was almost sheer in the intense sunlight. The darkness of her nipples made twin circles beneath the cloth—and as she watched, they changed, rising and tightening until they showed clearly against the soft shirt. Maya flushed, feeling embarrassed and lighthearted at the same time.

"In fact," he murmured, watching her, "I'm tempted to send all this right back to Mrs. Granger and keep you just as you are." Despite the words Will deposited his paper-wrapped burdens on the bed. He removed the tray and put a package into Maya's hands. "Go on, open it."

With fingers that trembled, Maya took off the string and paper. A lace-trimmed chemise spilled out, followed by pantalettes. When she saw the intimate apparel, her flush deepened.

"Lord, what a lovely color," Will said, laughing softly.

"It isn't proper that you see these," she said, trying and failing to conceal the delicate underwear beneath the wrapping again.

"It's not as though you were wearing them, sweetheart."

Maya's head snapped up at the endearment. She realized that Will was bending over her, watching her with dizzying intensity. She felt surrounded by him and caressed by gray eyes that blazed like sun-shot mist. Heat spread through her, an awareness of his presence that was almost painful.

"Don't," she said huskily, looking away. "When you look at me like that, I feel . . ." Her voice died.

"How do you feel?"

"Naked," she whispered.

"Why should that matter? After all, I'm so 'young for my age.'"

She winced at the bitterness in his voice. "That's not what I meant. It's simply that I am too old for mine."

Will didn't know how to answer the bleak appraisal in Maya's tone. In hungry silence he watched her open the packages, envying the cloth that she stroked, the petticoats that spilled caressingly over her lap and the sunlight that warmed her face. When all the packages were undone she sat amid rich colors and textures as though surrounded by gorgeous spring flowers. Yet she was more beautiful to him, more perfect, than any flower that had ever unfolded into the golden sun.

"It is too much," Maya said finally, stroking a satin bodice with unconscious longing. "I could never repay you."

"You lost everything you had when the *Brother Samuel* went down. It was my father's ship. The least the Hawthorne family can do is to indemnify you."

"I never had anything a tenth so fine as this."

Will looked at the slender fingers sliding over smooth fabric and had to clench his hands to keep from pulling Maya into his arms. "You should have had fine things surrounding you. And you will, Maya. I swear it."

She shook her head without meeting his eyes. "Take them back."

"They're yours. I picked out each one. They match your hair, your eyes, your skin."

She closed her eyes. The intimacy of wearing clothes chosen by Will frightened her, making her feel hot and cold and unable to breath. "No!"

"For the love of God, be sensible. You haven't a stitch to your name. You saved Beth from drowning. Father is too much of a cold fish to say so, but if there's anything on earth that he cares about, it's Beth.

He'll hardly begrudge the cost of a few dresses to her savior.''

Maya's eyes opened. "But your father didn't buy these. You did."

"He has an account at Mrs. Granger's."

"Did you have his permission to use it?"

"I'm not a child! I don't need his permission to—"

"It's his money," Maya interrupted. "His to spend or withhold as he pleases."

"But he wouldn't have thought of it. He wouldn't have known what you wanted, what colors would suit you, what fabrics would pleasure you. I did!"

Will was right and Maya knew it. And that, too, frightened her. He knew her too well, and he was too young, and she was a fool to feel dizzy every time he came so close that she could sense the heat of his body.

"You're too young," she whispered. "Please, Will. You're too young!"

Chapter Five

It was one of the rare, crisply sunny autumn days that were scattered like diamonds amidst the Redwood Empire's rain-washed seasons. It was also the first day that Maya had been out of the house since the wreck of the *Brother Samuel*. She was wearing one of the dresses that Will had selected. Hale had ultimately insisted that she keep them—and then had brought home twice as many more for her in the bargain. The green of the thin French wool intensified the color of her dark green eyes and made her skin glow as though a lamp had been lit within.

Hale watched Maya as much as he watched the horses he was driving through the forest, as he took a roundabout way into the small, raw town of Eureka. Normally he would have been at the mill or at the bank in which he had a significant interest or on the waterfront discussing repairs with the captain of one of his lumber schooners. In the last few days, however, his work schedule had been changed. He had taken to coming home for lunch. Only at that time could he be sure of having Maya to himself; Will had his work at the Hawthorne mill, a job that required dawn to darkness management. Hale had much work as well, but he had the option of shirking it from time to time. Will did not. Nor was Beth along for the buggy ride. She still ran a fever in the afternoons and was thus consigned to Mrs. Chou's care.

"How long have you been in the redwood country?" Maya asked, looking sideways into Hale's admiring glance. He was a good-looking man, with an aura of strength and capability that she found subtly reassuring. She couldn't imagine him unable to cope with the demands of feeding and sheltering a family.

"I've been here most of my life. I suppose I was about the fifth or sixth white man to settle here. I cut bolts, split shingles and rails and finally saved enough capital to buy a mill." Hale made a sound of disgust. "Then some careless ship's lad dumped my consignment of mill equipment on the bottom of the bay."

"Did you get it back?"

"No. Too deep, too muddy. So I bought a steamboat, a side-wheeler that was hull-rotted and cost but a pittance. I took her out into the middle of the bay at high tide. There I built up a good head of steam and ran her up onto the flats as hard as I could without destroying her. Then I removed the side wheel and used the steam engine to power my saws. That same engine is still running the edger at Tres Santos mill, and the steamboat itself is still being used as a dormitory for mill hands."

"That was very clever of you," Maya said, smiling. "It takes an unusual man to turn disaster into good fortune."

"In this country a man has to make use of what's at hand. Careless accidents and trees are always in full supply around here. It's the will to shape their own destiny that most men lack."

Again Maya couldn't help thinking of the difference between her father and Hale. Her gentle, wistful father hadn't been able to make a secure living, much less to shape his own destiny. Yet he had had magic in his speech and dreams, if not in his hands and deeds. He had loved the tall evergreen trees with their thick bark the color of rusted iron. He had yearned to live and die among them.

In that, too, he had been unsuccessful. He had died among the frozen cornstalks of another failed crop.

"My father came through the redwood country years ago," Maya said. "Perhaps you knew him. Asa Charters, from Ohio?"

"I remember one party of Ohians in particular. They had been chasing fool's gold in California. They came here for a time. Most went back. One of them stayed. Good worker, if a bit rough on the men beneath him. He works for me now. Runs the green chain at the mill. Name of Sambito."

"Al Sambito?" said Maya.

"You know him?"

"I must be mistaken. I thought that Father told me Mr. Sambito had been killed out here in a logging accident. It must have been some other man."

Maya did not add that Sambito's wife and three children had thought him dead. Mrs. Sambito had mourned her husband for the requisite year, and then had remarried.

"Sambito was broken up in a felling accident a long time ago, but he survived. In fact, he's done well for a man with no education and less religion. He has one or two timber claims that I've considered buying from him. That would give him a nice piece of change. In truth, it would make Sambito quite well-to-do."

Hale looked at Maya for a moment, and then back at the horses' brown backs and the rutted road ahead. The storm that had brought the *Brother Samuel* to its grave had remained for several days, turning the roads into a greasy mire.

"Your father should have stayed here. A man with an eye for timber can do as Sambito has. If Sambito's eldest son is careful and smart, they could found a family fortune. But good blood is no guarantee," Hale said, frowning. "Look at Willy. Half the time he shows no more sense than a chicken in a hailstorm, running about and pecking at whatever bounces highest. With him as an heir the Hawthorne money will be gone before my grandsons even get a chance to find out what they're made of."

"He is young yet," Maya said softly.

"Is he? At his age I was saving for my first mill, sending money back to Scotland and supporting a wife as well. It wasn't an easy time, but I hadn't grown up expecting one. This country can make a timberman rich; it can also kill him the first time the wind blows the wrong way on a falling tree. The forest is only for the quick, the strong and the clever. It's our destiny, if we're willing to claim it. The good Lord saved us the best forests in His creation. Now it's up to us to exploit those trees, to turn them into the lumber to build the greatest cities and industries in the world. It's not a job for the common run of man, and certainly not one for a boy."

Hale looked sideways and nodded at Maya, who was watching him with eyes as deep and shadowed as the forest around them.

"You'll see what I mean soon enough. The trees here are good, clean lumber, and they look impressive against the sky. But these are only the edge of the forest. There are trees out there so big we don't know how to cut them down, and even if we did cut them, there would be no way in creation to saw them into lumber."

" 'Trees taller than God and older than Christ,' " Maya murmured, drawing a startled look from Hale. "That's what my father used to say."

"He must have seen the big ones, then." Hale looked up as they came to a clearing. Sawed-off stumps big enough for two to have dinner on stood above the returning undergrowth. In the distance, hills and mountains rolled to infinity, an endless evergreen sea. "This country has enough timber to last us a thousand years. We've barely begun to scratch the potential of the forest. We may never be able to, but by God I will do my part before I die. I will leave the Hawthorne mark upon this land."

Maya thought about the worn old man her father had become, working the little farm in Ohio, trying to keep all those mouths fed despite the wasting lung disease he had brought back from the cold rivers of the California goldfields. Her father had left his mark upon nothing. He had lived and died in penury, taking a good woman and five babes down into darkness with him, and leaving the others to charity and chance.

Hale was nothing like her father had been. Hale exuded an enormous confidence, a determination that could accomplish great things, a raw strength of body and will that would never simply give up and vanish into a shallow grave as though the man called Hale Hawthorne had never been born at all. He was one of the men who had opened up the country for lesser men, men who wouldn't have been able to survive the rigors of a wilderness. Hale had not only survived, he had thrived in the savage land. He had built and would continue to build a secure future for himself and his children.

"Your wife was wise in her choice of husband," Maya said quietly. "And your children are very fortunate to have you as their father. They will never know want."

"My wife was like Beth, more frail than a wilderness woman should be. She died not too long after Beth was born. As for my children being fortunate... Willy wouldn't agree."

"He hasn't yet found out how cruel life can be to those without money. I have. You provided well for the babes born to your wife. No woman can ask more of a man than that."

Beneath the brim of his hat Hale gave Maya a considering glance, wondering at the intensity of her low, vibrant voice. She was not talking for the sake of flattering him; she had meant every word. He looked at her high, proud head and the green eyes far too old to be found in such a youthful face.

"You will not go on to Trinidad. You will stay with us."

"I can't impose—" she began, only to have him override her words.

"You will stay. I will arrange it with the school. You will be both companion and tutor to Beth, who has reached an age when she requires a woman's softer touch. You will receive bed and board and an amount equal to what you would have earned at Trinidad's schoolhouse. You will learn to run my house as a wife would; you will buy that which is needed and see that everything is in readiness when I return at night. You

will instruct Willy, as well. That young savage needs
more schooling.''

"Mr. Hawthorne, I can't—"

"It is settled," he said, interrupting her. "Hi-up
there you lazy beasts," he called, snapping the reins
across the horses' broad rumps. "We have a town to
show off to its newest resident."

The horses picked up the pace, shifting into a crisp
trot. Dazed by the sudden turn of events, Maya said
nothing, but deep inside her an icy knot of fear began
to loosen slowly. She would not have to go off to a
strange new town and make her way with her wits and
a knife concealed in her pocket. She knew with great
certainty that no man would dare to harass a decent
woman in Hale Hawthorne's house. Nor did she have
to fear Hale himself. He was a hard man, but a decent one. If he decided that he wanted her in his bed,
he wouldn't break down her door and take her. He
would ask her to marry him.

And she would accept.

"Thank you, Mr. Hawthorne," Maya said, her
voice husky with the force of her emotion. "Thank
you from the bottom of my heart."

Hale looked at her for a long moment, then nodded as he turned away.

"Hi-up!" he said.

The horses snorted and bore the buggy closer to
town. Where logging had taken place the forest
thinned, letting through more sun. All the remaining
tall trees were lightning-struck, twin-trunked or old,
old snags whose dead boles had been polished by the
seasons until their wood shone nearly white. Piles of
branches trimmed from felled trees dotted the land. In
most cases the slash piles were charred by past fire and

overgrown with vines. Surviving trees showed burns high up on their trunks where slash fires had gotten away and swept through the uncut forest, or where fires had burned long before men with steel axes had come to cut down the tall trees.

The closer Hale and Maya came to town, the more ragged and raw-looking the land became. The hills resembled a cow with mange, for the cover of forest had been gnawed away unevenly. Much of the logging had been so recent that no undergrowth or regrowth had occurred. Every scar that man had put upon the land was still there.

Yet for all that the green of the forest still predominated, for only those trees that would yield the most lumber for the least work had been felled. The smaller trees remained, as did the larger trees that were too big for man's mills to process. The result was an uncurried, half-tamed forest where deer and small game thrived among weeds and vines, wildflowers and evergreen seedlings.

Only along the tidal flats and at the very outskirts of town did the forest disappear. Here the trees had been transformed by mills into the lumber that built wharves and pilings, bakeries and homes, churches and bars. New homes and small businesses grew like mushrooms from the mud. Eureka was a town less than two decades old and, like a teenager, its exuberance was rarely accompanied by a well-reasoned consideration for what the future might bring. Men built where there was bare land without consideration for high tides, violent storms or floods. As a result the town's three thousand people were crowded on the narrow margin between an ocean thousands of miles wide and an evergreen sea that was scarcely smaller.

Hale guided the high-wheeled buggy straight down First Street. The road was even more churned in town than it had been in the empty forest. The constant traffic of lumber wagons had made the streets into narrow ribbons of muck and mire. A teamster was hard at work spreading fresh sawdust from the mills to dry up the mess. The pungent perfume of turpentine and pine resin swirled up from the sawdust wagon with the breeze. It was a sharp, clean, exciting smell, as fresh and vivid as the sunlight itself.

"What a wonderful smell," Maya said, watching a fragrant, golden mound vanish into the mire. "Although I'm afraid that man's work is futile. There is far more muck than sawdust."

"Then we shall simply have to cut more trees," said Hale, controlling the horses with casual skill on the busy street. As they slowed to a walk, he pointed out landmarks. "That's the biggest of the three banks in town. It was capitalized to the extent of fifteen thousand dollars in 1860 and has never had an unprofitable year since then."

Maya saw the bank's name painted in subdued gilt on the building. "Tres Santos Bank. And your lumber company is also called Tres Santos."

He nodded. "I was a founder of the bank. The bank's profits are largely a result of the loans it has made to Tres Santos Lumber. The loans were always paid back on time and at current rates of interest, of course. The management of Tres Santos Bank observes all proprieties. That," he continued, pointing the buggy whip toward a handsome three-story building, "is the finest hotel between San Francisco and Portland."

Maya looked at the hotel's graceful bay windows and the ornate detailing of the wood trim. She had no doubt that Hale was correct in his estimation of the accommodations; the exterior of the building was certainly finer than anything she had seen while she worked in the Christian mission.

"And next door is the best gentleman's saloon in the entire state. The bar itself is over a hundred feet long and made of cherry wood from England."

"Why did they use imported wood with all the beautiful trees that were already here for the cutting?"

"We have the wood, but we don't yet have the craftsmen—the millwrights and cabinetmakers. Nor do we have hardwoods, not like those of Europe and our own country east of the plains. What we have on the West Coast are magnificent pines and a red cedar every bit as perfumed as the incense cedars of Biblical fame. But better than even our pines and cedars is the redwood. It's a marvelous wood to work, as clear and straight grained as any lumber you can buy. It resists insects, rot and is even proof against fire."

"A wood that won't burn?"

"Redwood is hard to ignite and easy to extinguish. A city built of redwood would be almost indestructible."

"It sounds too good to be true."

Hale's mouth shifted beneath his beard into a hard smile. "You're a skeptic, lass. It's a good thing to be. Redwood isn't perfect. It tends to split easily unless handled carefully. But in the hands of a wise man rather than a fool, redwood is workable, durable and as beautiful as any wood God ever made. What's more, we have the only trees like it on earth."

Maya remembered the massive grace of the trees just beyond the Hawthorne house. "Truly?" she asked. "They are found nowhere else?"

"I'm told a similar tree grows in the Sierra Nevada Mountains of central California. At least the wood is similar in that it doesn't burn easily and rots not at all. The trees are called sequoias. They are huge beyond my ability to describe and certainly beyond man's ability to utilize. The wood is very brittle, much more so than our redwood. In sum, we in Eureka have the only accessible supply of the best building material in the world. Some day the world will understand this, and the demand for redwood will far outstrip that for the many pines that grow alongside redwood in the forest. All we have to do to make our fortunes is to figure out how to cut down and saw up redwood trees that are twenty feet through at the butt."

Hale frowned suddenly, thinking of the problem that bedeviled every mill owner—how to saw the huge trees with saws invented by men to whom a log six feet in diameter was a monster worthy of an article in the local paper. Right now the Tres Santos mill was working with a jury-rigged double saw that got the job done most of the time, and the rest of the time came spectacularly, dangerously undone.

"We'll stop at the mill. I'll show you what I mean. Hi-up, Brownie."

The voice and a whistling snap of the buggy whip set the team off at a smart trot. A sideways glance told Maya that Hale's mind was suddenly elsewhere. She felt no particular resentment at the fact. Common sense told her that a man as successful as Hale Hawthorne had little time and less reason to answer frivolous questions. It had been very good of him to bother to take her for a ride.

The horses trotted through the heart of the prosperous downtown area, past hardware and general stores, hatmakers and restaurants. Hale turned right onto A Street, making good time to the waterfront through the tangled traffic of lumber wagons and delivery drays.

The wharf area was a forest of schooner and cutter masts where ropes hung like Spanish moss. Longshoremen and sailors milled and swore on the heavy plank wharves while eight-horse teams hauled five-ton loads through the deep, clinging mud of the streets.

"This is a rough area," Hale said, nodding to the row of waterfront bars and seedy hotels along Front Street. "The people who live here are no better than they have to be. It's not a place where decent young women walk alone."

Maya looked at the roughly dressed men on the plank sidewalks and at the women who lounged in the doorways of the buildings that advertised ground-floor bars and "temporary lodging rooms above." Though less crowded it was very much like the tawdry quarters from which the Chinese slave girls had come. There was little doubt about the nature of the work engaged in by the unkempt women who displayed themselves with complete disinterest to passing men. As always, the meeting ground of sailors and landsmen called forth the worst elements of both.

"It's not a safe place for young men, either," Hale said. "It goes beyond the danger to their immortal souls from the attentions of loose women. Young men who drink in waterfront bars have been crimped and sent to heathen lands."

"Crimped?"

"Impressed. Drugged and taken aboard a ship and then forced to work as sailors."

"That's terrible!"

"Boys who don't listen to their betters have to learn about life the hard way. No one is taken from the respectable establishments, only from the dregs of the waterfront bars."

Hale kept the team at a smart pace while they crossed the waterfront toward some buildings sprawled on a small rise. As the buggy drew closer, Maya could see that the buildings were really open-sided A-frame shelters surrounded by stacks of bright, newly cut lumber and rough-barked logs. A short, squat smokestack thrust up from the center of the tallest A-frame, belching smoke that was thick, black, pungent—the result of burning green wood. Next to the chimney were several shorter, thinner pipes that bled white streamers of steam into the blue sky.

Above the rumble and shout of the waterfront came an immense pounding, as though a heart made of iron were racing in fear or exertion. Maya listened to it, her head cocked, her eyes wide.

"Steam engines," Hale said, catching Maya's startled glance.

Then came a hair-raising sound, a metallic scream that rose quickly to painful heights and keened at an unwavering pitch for thirty seconds.

"That's the head saw," Hale said, pride clear in his voice as he pulled up in front of the mill. "Reverend Cleary often uses it in his sermon to warn sinners what a condemned soul will sound like on Judgment Day."

Maya shuddered and said nothing.

As though he had been waiting just for them, a Chinese liveryman trotted out from behind a stack of drying lumber. He held the horses while Hale helped Maya down from the buggy onto a handsome herringbone sidewalk made of fresh lumber.

Hale led Maya into the mill, waving or nodding in acknowledgment of the respectful greetings of mill workers along the way. Oddly, even in his dark coat and vest, starched white shirt and knotted necktie, he seemed very much at home in the mill. Indeed he seemed to relish the relentless clamor of machinery and the brawny, sweating men with sawdust clinging to their uncombed hair and beards.

It was several minutes before Maya could sort out the noises and activities of the big room. The pounding of the great steel heart of the mill was easy to understand. It took her longer to realize that the slithering, metallic clanking noise came from a chain snaking on or off a spool, and that the rumbling thunder was the sound of a saw carriage moving tons of log to their rendezvous with the whirling teeth of the saw.

And then there came a faint, metallic hum, an urgent mechanical sound unlike anything Maya had ever before heard. From somewhere overhead there was a sudden heavy thump, as though a huge weight had been thoughtlessly dropped. She made a startled sound, but realized that nothing was amiss when Hale made no move to investigate the odd noise.

"There's your former neighbor," Hale said, pitching his voice to carry to Maya despite the cacophony of the mill. "Yo, Sambito!"

A short, thin man who stood at the bottom of a chute with a metal crook in one hand and a crayon in the other looked up.

"Sambito is one of the best graders we have," Hale continued. "He has a real eye for timber that will yield good lumber."

"Sambito, say hello to Maya Charters from Ohio," Hale said, drawing Maya after him toward the lumber grader. "She tells me you knew her father."

The grader stepped away from the freshly sawed planks of rich dark redwood. He had a narrow look about him and sharp teeth that showed when he smiled uncertainly. He watched Maya carefully, as though he were trying to guess in what context the connection with her father had been mentioned.

"Charters," he repeated. "Ohio. Are you sure you're not mistaken, Miss?"

"It's been many years, Mr. Sambito," she said carefully. "I'm probably mistaken."

Silence hung between them for a moment. Then Sambito realized that Maya intended to say nothing more.

"Charters ... Would that be Asa Charters?" Sambito asked.

"Yes."

"Sure. I remember now. Good enough man, I suppose, but real unlucky. Nothing ever came right for him." Sambito smiled slightly as he looked at Maya standing next to Hale. "He has a right pretty daughter, though. Must be a real comfort to him."

"You're very kind," Maya said stiffly, disliking everything about Sambito from his sly smile to his calculating eyes. He reminded her very much of Reggie, the San Francisco man whom she had belatedly understood was a pimp. Unconsciously she drew closer to Hale.

"How is Asa, anyway?" asked Sambito. "He get any luckier?"

"My father is dead."

"Oh. Sorry to hear that. I told him he should stay here in California. Only a fool would go back and wear himself out on Ohio's winters."

"He had responsibilities at home."

Sambito's eyes narrowed, but whatever he might have said was lost in a loud rumbling noise.

"Look over there," Hale said, touching Maya's arm and then pointing toward the center of the building. "They've got a big log on the carriage. Come this way. I'll show you what I meant about the problems of cutting redwoods."

Hale looked at Sambito, nodded in dismissal and drew Maya toward a place where no machinery inhibited their view of the saw pit. Men called out to each other or used hand signals to communicate through the staggering noise of the saw.

"The sawyer is the man at the front of the log," Hale explained. "He determines how the log is placed in front of the saw, which never moves. He's the most skilled and highest paid man in the mill. He can make or break a log with the first cut. See his hand? He's signaling to his dogger how to set the log. The dogger is the second man on the carriage. He has the hardest physical work in lumbering. Levering those big logs around takes a lot of muscle."

Maya's breath came in suddenly as she recognized the dogger who worked on the carriage. "Will."

Hale didn't hear. For all of his response the dogger might have been a complete stranger.

"See the circular saws, the upper and the lower? They act like a single large blade cutting through the big logs. We need two blades because no single blade can cut a log thicker than the blade's own radius. That's not nearly deep enough for these trees, so we use one blade on top and another on the bottom. But cutting that deep puts a terrible strain on the saw blade and the log itself. When a knot is hit, there can be real trouble. Most of the time the blade chews on through the knot or the log shatters. Sometimes the blade just explodes and pieces of metal and splinters fly everywhere."

"That sounds . . . dangerous."

"It is. No part of logging is safe. It's men's work and nothing comes free. That's why I put Willy down there. To make a man out of him."

Silently Maya watched as Will carried out the sawyer's instructions, levering the big log a few inches this way or that in the cradle, visibly straining every muscle in his big body. She realized then how he had become so powerful despite his youth.

"How long has he been working in the mill?"

"Since he was as tall as I am. When he's half as smart, he'll be promoted."

Maya glanced quickly at Hale's hard profile. The pale clarity of his glance was emphasized by the silver radiating from his temples into the darker backdrop of his hair. He looked as obdurate as the spinning blades awaiting the equally unyielding log. Whether the blade or log would be ruined or whether they would work together to create something useful to man was a thing that only time would tell. It also was a thing which did not seem to interest Hale in any personal way. His strength and his position in the world had come at a cost to whatever more gentle qualities he might have been born with.

But as Hale had said and Maya had learned to her sorrow, nothing was free in this world.

A deep-throated, demonic howl gripped the room. It was the same banshee cry that Maya had heard as they drove up in front of the mill; but here, inside the mill, the howl was not simply noise. It was a living force, a thing as tangible as sawdust or wood or the steel blade itself, spinning blindly through the log.

Instinctively Maya clapped her hands over her ears to protect them as the howl continued. Hale tried to point something out to her but his words were lost. Finally he took her arm and led her up some stairs, steadying her among the drifts of fragrant sawdust. Each step brought them closer to the numbing, overwhelming sound. The howling grew so intense that it vibrated in her very bones.

From the top of the stairs Maya looked down to where Will and the sawyer rode on the carriage, which was a long, narrow, sawdust-covered platform. The carriage held a redwood log that had been peeled of its thick bark. The platform was like a small, steam-driven railcar that moved back and forth on a ten-foot track, carrying the log past the point where two large circular saws whirled in midair like flaming swords set to guard the gates of Eden. The saws were being spun continuously by an intricate system of overhead belts and pulleys. The blades were free of the log at the moment, singing their high, unwavering note of metallic expectancy.

Hale waved at the man who sat at the close end of the steam carriage, a set of control levers in front of him. When Maya realized that Hale was trying to speak to her, she removed one hand from her ear. He bent down and spoke loudly.

"That's Albert Fowler, the best head sawyer in Eureka. Not a log gets cut in this mill except by him."

Fowler flashed a hand signal to Will, who adjusted the machinery that held the log in place. Then Will took a heavy metal bar and used it to lever the massive log over until it rested flush against the plank gauge. Despite the coolness of the day Will wore only a light cotton shirt whose sleeves had been ripped away to give his arms greater freedom. Sweat made the shirt cling to him like a second skin. The muscles of his upper body bunched like steel cables as he shunted the log around on the carriage. Both he and the sawyer were liberally sprinkled with the bright red sawdust that was redwood's signature.

At a signal from Will, Fowler shoved the control lever forward and the steam carriage slid down its track, moving the huge log into the spinning saws. As steel teeth bit into the butt of the log, the metallic scream of the blades went through Maya's head like a knife. A great gout of blood-red dust leaped into the air behind the top saw. She clamped her hands over her ears to diminish the unearthly shriek.

The twin spinning saws were perfectly aligned, one above the other. Together they cut a single, four-inch slab of redwood lumber the length of the log. The slab fell onto a heavy conveyor and rattled off into the bowels of the mill as Fowler shot Will another hand signal and brought the carriage back to its starting place.

Once more Will levered the log into position while sweat washed dark trails through the red dust coating his body and the saws sang their inhuman song of anticipation. Once more the steam piston shoved log and carriage through the saw. Once more a gout of blood-colored dust leaped high as blades whirled a third of the log's length, two-fifths, halfway—

And then it all came apart in a shattering report that brought Maya to her knees.

Instantly Fowler ducked behind the sheltering bulk of the uncut log. Will leaped for safety too, but he had farther to go. Maya saw neither man move, for Hale had known what the sound meant as surely as the sawyer and Will had. Hale grabbed Maya and fell to the floor, covering her body with his, protecting her from flying bits of metal.

There was a rending screech as machinery ground to a halt. Suddenly the entire mill was filled with a silence that was as eerily expectant as the sound of a freely spinning blade.

Maya heard a man's deep voice cursing steadily, viciously, the kind of language associated with teamsters or sailors or timber beasts. With a feeling of unreality she realized that it was Hale swearing. He came to his feet and began calling out orders.

"Find out the damage! Quickly, now! We have three schooners to fill!"

Hale's voice galvanized the mill workers, who swarmed to look over the machinery.

"What happened?" Maya asked as Hale lifted her to her feet with careless strength.

"The saw hit a branching point or a knot. Broke some teeth from the sound of it and froze the entire assembly. They'll be hours getting it operating again. If we're lucky."

Maya leaned over to look at the carriage. The first thing she saw was Will sprawled across the frozen controls. Blood welled from his scalp and arm.

"*Will.*"

Hale spun around and stared toward the carriage. Fowler had just come out of his shelter and was bending over Will.

"Get the doctor!" Hale shouted at a knot of mill workers. "Move, damn you! Move!"

One of the men turned and began running toward the door. Maya hit the bottom of the stairs, picked up her skirts and ran across the sawdust-drifted floor to the carriage. Fowler heard and turned toward her. His hands were covered with blood.

"Stay back, Miss. There's a lot of blood. It's not a fit sight for a woman."

"Do tell. Have you ever attended a birth?" she asked crisply, bending over Will. "I've attended eight. Will? Will, can you hear me?"

He groaned and tried to sit up.

"Be still," she said, holding her hand against his shoulder. Her fingers were almost steady despite the fear racing through her. She had faced accidents on the farm, and injuries, and births. Blood was no stranger to her.

Will's eyes opened, cloudy with pain. They focused on her with disbelief. "Maya?"

"Hush now," she said. "I'm going to look at your head."

There was too much blood welling for her to determine the seriousness of the injury. Without hesitation she bent over and ripped off a length of new petticoat, folded it and pressed it to the wound.

"You'll ruin it," Will said.

"Better to be used for this than for a winding sheet."

Will's eyes widened at Maya's matter-of-fact tone.

"Here. Hold this," Maya said, putting his hand over the wad of petticoat.

Will made no complaint when Maya probed lightly at his upper arm. There was a ragged cut where a flying chunk of wood had scored the flesh. The wound bled freely, contributing to his rather horrifying appearance, but was not deep enough to maim him. With a silent prayer she lifted the bloody cloth from his scalp wound and probed very gently. After a moment she bowed her head.

"Thank you, Lord," she whispered. Then, more steadily, "It's messy but not serious."

"I could have told you that," Hale said, kneeling by Maya's side.

"Then your eyesight is far superior to mine. From the stairs I thought Will was dead."

Will's hand closed over Maya's and squeezed reassuringly. "I'm all right. I just caught a few splinters on the way by."

"Splinters?"

"To a timber beast anything smaller than a stove log is a splinter." He started to sit up, swore and settled back until the dizziness passed.

"A doctor will be here in a minute," Maya said.

"He won't need it," Hale said. "On your feet, boy. There are empty ships waiting to be loaded."

Will came to his feet, stood very still for a moment, then took the bloody strip of cloth from Maya's fingers and wrapped it around his head to keep blood from running into his eyes while he worked. In stunned silence Maya watched as he went over to the log to assess what might be done to get the saw free. Gradually she realized that she was the only one who was horrified; the other mill workers simply assumed, as Hale had, that a man who could stand up could work.

"Come, Miss Charters," Hale said, lifting her to her feet. "We're in the way here."

Maya said nothing until they were in the buggy again, headed back for the house.

"Does that happen often?"

Hale looked at Maya's pale, tense face. "It's those big trees," he said simply. "We have to jury-rig our saws to handle timber that size. Things go wrong when you use equipment that way."

"Why don't you just cut smaller logs?"

"Economics. The bigger the tree, the better the yield of lumber per man-hour. The better the yield, the more competitive the price per board foot. The more competitive the price, the more board feet sold. If I don't cut the biggest tree I possibly can, somebody else will. Then I will be undersold in the marketplace. And then I will be bankrupt."

Maya looked at the blood on her hands, shuddered and said nothing at all.

Chapter Six

"Oh, Will, it's just not fair," Beth said, turning her blind, beautiful eyes toward her brother with the gesture of a girl who hadn't lost the habits of sight. "I've so looked forward to this picnic, and Maya has worked so hard with Mrs. Chou to make the food, and it's not raining and—"

The plea abruptly ended in the deep cough that had plagued Beth since the wreck of the *Brother Samuel* a few weeks before.

"Father would peel me like a log headed for the saw if I let you go out in this weather, and you know it," Will said. "And he'd have every right. You're not well yet."

"But he had to go to San Francisco. He'll never know if—"

"I'd know," Will interrupted firmly. "If you took a chill I'd never forgive myself."

Two tears shimmered in Beth's blue eyes. Will closed his own eyes and said quickly, "When you're better, Mouse, and not a minute before."

"But you'll be gone by then."

Maya turned toward Will. "Gone?"

"Henry wants me to go timber cruising with him, but I don't know if I'll go."

What Will didn't say was that he was reluctant to go on a trip that might last eight weeks. Before he did, he wanted to make Maya admit that she belonged to him. He had had great hopes upon seeing her anxious face hovering over him just after the accident in the mill, but since then she had systematically avoided every attempt he had made to talk to her alone.

"What about your work in the mill?" Maya asked.

Will shrugged. "If I go, I'll be docked a few weeks' pay."

"You might not be taken on again."

"Doubtful."

"Because you're the owner's son?"

The accusation implicit in Maya's words stung Will. "No. Because I'm the best damned dogger in a hundred miles and father pays me half what I'd make at another mill."

"He's just trying to teach you the value of money."

"By not paying me an honest wage?"

Looking down at her hands, Maya said nothing. She had tried very hard to keep her distance from Will since the accident at the sawmill. It had shocked her to know how much she had cared whether or not he was badly injured. She had tried to tell herself that she would have felt equally torn if it had been an utter stranger lying senseless and bleeding amid the sawdust, but she hadn't believed it. There was something about Will that simply went through her defenses with the terrible ease of a saw slicing through air, setting everything to humming with wild expectancy.

Perhaps it was simply that she owed her life to him. And perhaps it was something more complex and far more dangerous, a passion that would bring her to her knees as surely as had the shattering, triumphant cry of a steam-driven saw biting into wood.

Restlessly she turned away from Will. Like Beth, Maya had been shut up in the house for too many days. She hungered for the oddly intimate, endlessly wild expanse of the forest where ancient trees grew in a silence disturbed only by the wind. The thought of a picnic in the woods was all that had kept her from pacing the house during the long hours when Beth had slept and there hadn't been enough for Maya to do. Using skills learned at the mission, she had inventoried the kitchen and the linen closets, the larder and the liquor cabinet, until she knew what the Hawthorne household had and what it lacked. There was nothing left for her to do but embroider or tutor Will. She hadn't the patience for the former and dared not attempt the latter. The idea of bending over a book with Will was unnerving.

Maya looked out Beth's bedroom window and sighed with unconscious longing. The view from the second story of the big white house was lovely. The house itself stood on a gentle rise at the edge of Eureka. From the front gatepost the road went in two directions. Along the road that led toward town, Maya could see distant, orderly rows of little houses, all painted white with dark trim, and beyond them, the taller buildings at the center of town. Farther on the business area with its blocky, three- and four-story buildings gave way to a jumble of ships and mill stacks at the water's edge. From there, there was nothing but the choppy blue surface of Humboldt Bay. Off to the west beyond a thin peninsula, the cobalt surface of the Pacific shone through salt spray cast up by the surf.

Maya had the sudden heady sense of standing on the rim of a continent that had been scrubbed clean by storm and wind until unlimited possibilities glistened everywhere. She wondered if this elation was what her father had felt before he turned his face east and went back to Ohio. If so, it must have all but broken his spirit to return to a land that gave life grudgingly and then only at great cost, a land where farms rather than vast forests sprang from the ground. Had her father known that he would never return to the redwood country again? Was that why it had haunted him to the point that he returned to it in his mind as he lay dying?

"Trees taller than God and older than Christ."

She didn't realize that she had spoken aloud until Will answered her. He was standing very close to her back, so close that she could sense the heat of him through the cotton of her blouse.

"I'll take you there, where redwoods rule the sky from river benches. There's one grove..."

The warmth of Will's breath stirred the soft tendrils of hair against Maya's cheek.

"Yes," she whispered. "I want to see that."

They left Beth sleeping fretfully, disappointed by the loss of the picnic but too weak to argue the point any more. Mrs. Chou sat by the girl's bedside, embroidering silk handkerchiefs with exquisitely small stitches.

"Can you sit a horse?" Will asked Maya, pausing outside his bedroom door.

"If it's gentle."

"Put on that riding outfit I brought you, the one that's the color of your hair in the sunlight."

Maya's breath caught at the look in Will's eyes. She started to object, but he was speaking again, giving her no chance to cast up obstacles.

"Hurry. The grove is several miles away. I'll meet you by the kitchen door in fifteen minutes."

He was gone into his room before she could say yea or nay. Torn between refusal and currents of excitement that tickled her nerves, she stood outside his door. Then with flushed cheeks and a faster heartbeat she hurried to the room that had become her own, the room that had once belonged to Hale Hawthorne's wife.

Though Maya changed quickly, Will was ready before she was. He stood at the back step holding the reins of two horses. His gray eyes kindled when she walked into the luminous mist that so often swathed the redwood coast. Before she could say anything, he lifted her into the saddle. His fingers tightened convulsively around her waist when he felt her body shiver at his touch.

"Will, you're hurting me."

He loosened the steel grip of his hands. "Sorry. I had forgotten how soft you are, how fragrant your hair is, how..." But he couldn't tell her how velvety the tips of her breasts were and how hard they had become when he lay next to her in front of the fire. "I've worked in the mill too long. I'm not used to handling anything more fragile than steel levers and logs ten feet thick."

Will's hand went out to the saddle horn, and he swung up onto the horse's back with a single easy motion that underlined his strength and coordination. Maya watched him with an intensity of which she was totally unaware. At moments like this he reminded her almost painfully of the dream she had had many times since the wreck. In the dream she was caught between sleeping and waking, sensual longing and rationality... and Will's power and warmth were calling to her, flushing her body with anticipation.

Maya closed her eyes against the shimmering, fluttering feelings that came to the pit of her stomach whenever she remembered her wanton dream of lying caught between the hearth and his naked body, two fires melting her until she became as soft as honey left out in the sun.

"Maybe we should stay here with Beth," Maya said, swallowing suddenly.

Will's only answer was to urge his horse away from the house. Maya's horse followed immediately, giving her other things to think about than the unnerving response of her body to Will's presence.

The woods began fifty yards beyond the house. A solid rank of wild blackberry bushes came first, their last fruit withering darkly on the spiked canes. Then came the head-high alder brush, still green but showing the first signs of impending winter in leaves that were spotted randomly with dark brown. The berry bushes and the quick-growing alder were a buffer between man's presence and the untouched forest beyond.

Soon fir and spruce and shaggy-barked redwoods rose on either side of the crude wagon road, but Maya's eyes went more often to Will than to the forest. He was wearing a plaid mackinaw, a felt hat and cloth trousers, which were tucked into a pair of heavy leather boots such as loggers wore. There were no calks in the bottom of the soles, however, simply a deep tread that would grip well even on rain-slicked bark.

His wide shoulders, narrow hips and long, powerful legs made Maya forget that Will was only a boy wearing a man's appearance. Though he was unquestionably courageous and unreasonably strong, he was not yet mature. He thought nothing of blithely leaving his job for a jaunt through the woods. He hadn't the steadiness of purpose or character that came with maturity—or for some men, like Sambito, never came at all.

Nor for men like her father, who had left his wife once to chase a dream of gold and again to pursue a nightmare of war, and in between he had made babies in his wife's body and spun words in her mind; and the babes had died or grown sickly and the glistening might-have-beens had never come true.

Yet even knowing this, Maya couldn't stop the catch of her breath and heartbeat when Will watched her with hunger blazing in his gray eyes.

Desperately she concentrated on the forest that surrounded her, forcing her mind away from the boy she wanted but would not sacrifice the lives of her future children to have.

"Such a grim face. Are you uncomfortable?"

The touch of Will's callused fingertips down her cheek startled Maya. She realized that he had reined in to walk beside her on the narrow road.

"You mustn't touch me like that," she said tightly.

"If you don't want me to, why did you come with me?"

"My father saw the big trees once. He talked about them until the day he died. I have to see them. I want to know if they are worth what he sacrificed for them."

"What was that?"

"His wife's health, his own health, his children's future. All to scratch an unreachable itch on his soul...."

"Men are like that," Will said finally.

"Men, or overgrown boys?" Suddenly Maya turned to face Will. "Women are not like that, living only for the moment. They can't be. They carry the future within their bodies. The women who don't understand that have to watch their babes die for mistakes their mother made."

As he stared at her intense, unflinching green eyes, uneasiness shivered through him. Ising had been right when he spoke of shaman-women who chose their men not for the present, but for the future that would be born of their bodies.

Will tried to speak. No words came, for he could think of nothing that would remove the bleak acceptance of destiny from Maya's eyes except his touch, and she had forbidden that.

They rode side by side in silence until the road dwindled to a trail. After a time even that vanished, leaving only two people and two horses walking through the vast primeval forest. The trees were bigger here, so much bigger that an awareness of their size only sank in when Maya realized that the horses seemed to shrink in comparison to the roadside trees. Pines and cedars grew to wondrous height, only to be dwarfed by the towering elegance of the redwood monarchs. Each redwood trunk seemed bigger than the last, darker, taller, more furrowed by time and scarred by fire, trunks reaching to the sky until branches unfurled above the tops of the tallest fir or cedar, and still the redwoods reached upward, until at last the tallest wore crowns of diamond mist.

Will led the way deeper into the forest without hesitation, looking back only long enough to be sure that Maya still followed. He pressed forward until they crossed a meadow and the horses drank from a crystal stream. At the far edge of the meadow they dismounted. He led her across a springy loam of needles and moss, then stopped.

"Close your eyes," he said.

She looked up, startled. "But I can't walk that way."

"You won't have to. Close your eyes."

Slowly Maya closed her eyes. The next thing she knew she was being lifted into Will's arms.

"Will!"

"Hush. I won't drop you. You can trust me. It's not far. I just want to keep it a surprise for a bit longer. Hide your eyes, sweetheart."

Maya opened her mouth but no words came. He was so near, so vivid and suddenly so perfect to her that she couldn't bear seeing him. Her eyes closed as she turned her face against his shoulder. For a few minutes she knew nothing but his strength, the warmth of his body and his clean male scent mingling with that of the evergreen forest.

"Still awake?"

"Yes," she whispered, although in truth it felt more like a fragment of her sensual dream.

The sight of Maya's long eyelashes lying darkly against her flawless skin and the sweet warmth of her body in his arms went through Will in a ripple of dark fire, searing him with conflicting desires. He wanted to strip off Maya's clothes and take her right here, and simultaneously he wanted to cherish her as gently as the mist cherished the redwoods. He wanted to bury himself instantly in her satin heat and at the same time to seduce her so slowly, so gently that fear or denial would never darken her eyes.

But most of all he wanted to stay forever within this moment, sensing the slow unfolding of her sensuality deep inside her and knowing always the piercing sweetness of her body lying trustingly in his arms.

"Don't open your eyes until I tell you," Will murmured, admiring the flush that stained Maya's cheekbones. "I'm going to put you down now."

The reluctance in his voice was reinforced by the way his arms barely loosened as she slid down his body. The ground gave slightly beneath Maya's leather shoes. The forest loam was a resilient compound of moss and herbs and evergreen needles that hadn't been disturbed for thousands upon thousands of years. She trembled as she tried to find her balance. Instantly Will's hands returned, steadying her by nestling her slender back against his chest.

"All right now?"

She nodded.

"Open your eyes."

There was a parklike openness to the climax forest that surrounded them. Giant redwoods rose in massive elegance from the loam, their deeply furrowed bark darkened by the mist that had swathed their bases during the night and still ran in diamond streamers through their crowns during the day. The trunks were straight and clean, dark columns supporting the sky itself. The sun was overhead, but it was more sensed than seen, its incandescence muted to a gloaming presence by the silver mist and the cloud-embracing reach of the tall trees.

And in the center of it, dwarfing all attempts at comprehension, was a redwood titan that carried the sky in its arms.

Mist veiled the tree's true height, but each movement of the breeze revealed another aspect of the redwood's magnificence. The trunk rose uninterrupted by branches for more than a hundred and fifty feet. Long after lesser forest species had given up and spread their branches to the sunlight, the gigantic redwood still climbed toward the sun.

"If the world were a ship, that would be its mast."

Will's deep voice swirled through Maya like mist through the forest. Her vision blurred and ran as she wept at the beauty of the moment, the man who shared it with her and the tree that had lived long before she was born and would live long after she had died, rising above man's hopes and dreams with an indifference that was both humbling and sublime. Pain and exaltation swept through her, shaking her.

It was worth it, all of it, all the hunger and privation and fear, to stand just once in the presence of the great tree.

As though Will understood the turmoil of Maya's feelings, he said nothing more, simply stood behind her, giving her a solid warmth to lean against in the vortex of time and emotions spinning around her. She didn't know how long it was before she could see the tree again; she only knew that in some enormous and unspeakable way she had touched eternity.

"The Guardian has been alive since before Christ," Will said quietly, "and it will be alive long after I'm dust. Can't you hear it laughing at tiny man, who lives only three score and ten years?''

"Laughing? I'd think any tree in this country would keep still to avoid attracting the woodsman's ax.''

"This tree doesn't need to worry. It would take two skilled fellers nearly two weeks to bring down the Guardian. And there would be no point. We don't have a sawmill big enough to turn this trunk into lumber.''

Maya reached out tentatively and stroked the bark. It was rough, cool, damp, but she knew beyond argument that the tree was alive. She sensed the redwood's life just beyond her touch, hidden in mist and mystery and time. She looked up, trying to follow the straight thrust of the tree to its conclusion. Her head tilted so far back that it gave her a sudden feeling of dizziness. Will, who had had the same problem the first time he had tried to see the top of the Guardian, was prepared. He caught Maya's shoulders, steadying her.

"Now you can look," he said.

The mist still concealed the tree's height, but Maya didn't care. It was extraordinary to feel Will's warm living strength supporting her as she touched the cool manifestation of eternity that man called redwood.

"Thank you for bringing me here," she whispered, brushing her lips against the strong hands holding her shoulders. "I have never known anything half so beautiful.''

Will's fingers tightened briefly before he forced himself to release Maya. "I have to tend the horses. Stay here. It's safe to look if you keep your hands on the tree itself.''

She was unable to turn away from the huge redwood, so she simply nodded.

When Will came back with blankets and a saddlebag full of food, Maya was still standing where he had left her, looking up into the mist with a rapt expression. As he shook out a blanket to serve as a table, she turned toward him and gave him a smile that made his heart turn over.

"How did you find this place?"

"After my mother died, I wandered the forest a lot," Will said. "That's how I met Henry Ising. Like me, he was restless. But I was alone when I found the Guardian."

"The Guardian?"

"That grand redwood. It seemed to me that it guarded the forest against harm." Will smiled crookedly as he unpacked the saddlebags. "I was pretty young when I named that tree."

"And lonely."

He looked up suddenly. "How did you know?"

"I think everyone is lonely."

"Not my father."

"He must miss your mother greatly."

"Must he? Why? The waterfront is full of women."

"Love is more than that."

"Who said anything about love? He married my mother because it was convenient for him. She ran his house according to his requirements, gave him a son to inherit his empire and never complained when he spent more nights in bordellos than in his own bed."

Maya thought of the Chinese girls and the unkempt, empty-eyed women lounging in waterfront doorways, waiting for men whose needs had overcome their pride or self-control.

"Perhaps he wanted to spare her more childbearing," she whispered.

"My father never spared anyone his or her duty. Or what *he* saw as their duty."

"Does he spare himself?"

Will gave Maya an angry, glittering look that reminded her of Hale.

"No. But there is a great difference between doing your duty as you see it, and doing your duty as someone else sees it. I am quite tired of doing his idea of my duty!"

Maya remembered Hale's words in the mill to the effect that when he was half as smart as Hale, Will would be promoted from dogger. Hale, of course, would be the one who determined Will's progress, and Hale was a hard man to please. In fact, he was a hard man in every way.

That was why he had gone from penniless immigrant to timber baron. That was why his wife had never lacked for food or shelter, and his children had grown up without ever knowing want. The world was a brutal place for those who had no money. It took a hard man to win security for himself and his family using nothing more than his hands, his sweat and his determination.

Maya looked at Will and tried to imagine him without wealth, thrown on the mercy of a world that cared nothing at all for his hopes or dreams or his empty belly. She knew that if physical strength was all that was required, he would make his way. But the woods were teeming with strong men who made barely enough to feed their families in good times. It took more than a strong back to survive, much less to thrive in the harsh realities of the world. It took the kind of experience that only came with maturity.

With a sorrow that Maya neither understood nor wanted to admit, she looked from Will to the stately forest rising around them. As they ate their picnic in a silence that was neither uncomfortable nor wholly serene, her glance kept returning to the magnificent tree. In the time since she had opened her eyes and seen the Guardian, the mist had thinned until it was little more than a thin silver sheen across the face of the cerulean sky. In the presence of sunlight the trees changed magically, ghostly grays and blacks giving way to the living textures of rich brown bark and needles that came in shades of green both too vivid and too delicate to name.

Will followed the direction of Maya's glance and smiled at her obvious love of his favorite place. Quietly he cleaned up the last of the picnic and set it aside. With the supple ease that characterized all his motions, he removed his mackinaw, flinching only slightly when the heavy wool scraped over his arm. The wound left by the flying "splinter" had almost healed, but the skin was still tender.

"There's only one way to enjoy the forest without getting a crick in your neck," Will said.

Maya looked from his smile to the impromptu pillow he had made for her by folding his jacket. "Won't you be cold?"

"This isn't Ohio. Even in late autumn the sun is still strong here. Don't worry."

"But I do worry. Ever since the mill accident . . ."

Maya's voice died away. She had barely admitted to herself how much it bothered her that Will went off to his job as dogger each day, risking his life for half wages. She understood why Hale was being so hard on his son, yet she still was haunted by the memory of Will lying motionless on the log carriage.

"I healed," he said matter-of-factly.

"Did you? I saw you wince when you took off your jacket."

"I thought you were looking at the trees."

She had been, but she was intensely aware of him as well. And that, too, was a fact that she didn't want to talk about. Especially with him. Especially when he was lying on the blanket, his hands clasped behind his head, looking up at her with eyes more clear and brilliant than any silver mist.

"Come on," he said, holding out his hand. "Let's look at the trees together."

"Will . . ."

"What are you afraid of?"

"It's not that."

"Then what is it?"

"It's not . . . proper."

"Oh, bother 'proper.' If you end up walking around for a week bumping into things because your neck is stiff, don't come to me for sympathy."

Maya looked at Will. He ignored her, apparently too lost in the vista overhead to be worried about whether she was going to join him. She tilted back her head and looked up at the Guardian's spectacular height. After a few moments of that she felt distinctly dizzy. She put her legs in front of her, her hands behind and braced her weight that way. It was an improvement, but not a solution. Within a few minutes her neck and shoulders were feeling distinctly stiff.

Beside her Will stretched and smiled up into the sun. He looked so young, so innocent, as he lay there relaxed in the pouring sunlight, that Maya chided herself for being so wary of him. No matter his size, he was simply a boy. With a smile at her own foolishness in being afraid of him, Maya lay down and pillowed her head on Will's jacket. Immediately the mixed scents of wool and pine resin and Will himself swirled over her. Each time she inhaled, it was as though she took a part of him into herself.

That thought was as dizzying as trying to see the top of the Guardian while standing.

"Are you all right?" Will asked, suddenly rolling over onto his side and looking at her.

"Of course. Why?"

"You made a little sound."

Maya looked up into his clear, silver-gray eyes and felt as though the world had dropped away beneath her. "I'm . . . fine."

"You're pale. You haven't got Beth's fever, have you?"

As Will spoke, he put his hand on Maya's cheek. She closed her eyes and shivered, feeling his touch all the way to the soles of her feet. When he felt the telltale tremor, his breath shortened. He knew how much he wanted her, but it had never occurred to him that she might want him in the same way.

"You don't feel feverish, but there's only one way to be sure," he murmured, coming closer, inhaling the delicate, subtly spicy fragrance that he had come to associate with Maya.

The first touch of Will's lips against Maya's cheek brought an inchoate sound of protest and pleasure from her throat.

"Shh. There's nothing wrong. This is how my mother used to check me for fever."

The voice was so close, so deep, that Maya felt as much as heard the words.

"You aren't . . . my mother."

"Thank God," Will said, turning Maya's face toward him with a gentle pressure of his palm.

His mouth brushed over hers, stilling her inarticulate objections. The smooth heat of his lips surprised her, as did their softness. His hand stroked her cheek slowly, gentling her, reassuring her. There was no demand in the kiss, nothing to frighten her. There was simply warmth and sweetness and a feeling of being cherished that was unlike anything she had ever before experienced.

After the first instant of surprise and hesitation Maya's mouth softened, and she returned the kiss with a tenderness matching Will's. Will murmured a sound that had no meaning beyond the pleasure of the moment. He kissed her again and then again, each brush of his mouth more lingering, until her breath sighed out. With infinite gentleness he took her parted lips, rocking his head slowly against her mouth, opening her for a more intimate kiss.

She made a startled sound as the tip of his tongue touched hers. She looked at him with wide green eyes. He knew then that despite her unusual forthrightness in action and thought, she wasn't an experienced lover. The realization sent a fierce shaft of pleasure through him. He would have wanted her if she had had a thousand men, but he was glad that she hadn't. Eyes open, watching her, he slowly touched her tongue again and again, stroking its sensitive surfaces until she made a tiny sound deep in her throat. After a long, aching moment he lifted his mouth a fraction.

"You taste like sunlight to me," he whispered. "What do I taste like to you?"

"I don't . . . we shouldn't. . . ."

"Taste me."

Before she could object, he lowered his head and joined their mouths once more. This time, when his tongue stroked hers, she trembled and returned the caress, learning the textures of his mouth even as he savored her. She couldn't decide which was more intriguing, the incredible softness underneath his tongue or the exciting roughness of its surface. She kept touching first one texture and then the other, not realizing how much the kiss had deepened until the slow, rhythmic stroking of tongue against tongue finally ended in a complete mating of their mouths.

Will groaned almost soundlessly and threaded his fingers through Maya's thick, soft hair, removing combs and riding hat until waist-length mahogany tresses tumbled over his hands and fell in a gleaming fan across the blanket. He pulled back long enough to admire the picture she made with her lips rosy from his kisses and her cheeks flushed and her bodice straining over her quick breaths.

She opened her mouth to say something, but whatever it might have been was lost in the gliding sweetness of his sudden kiss. Trembling, arching her back in an instinctive attempt to ease the aching of her breasts by pressing them against his hard body, she gave herself to the kiss. His hands slid beneath her back, arching her even more deeply, rubbing her slowly against the clenched muscles of his chest. He claimed her mouth with slow, penetrating movements of his tongue, which she met and matched.

When the kiss finally ended Maya was breathing almost as raggedly as Will. She didn't realize that her riding jacket and blouse had been unbuttoned until she felt the sudden coolness of the air over her chemise. With fumbling hands she tried to rebutton her blouse. He brushed her hands aside and in the same skimming motion caressed her breasts. She couldn't control the husky sound of surprise and pleasure that came as her nipples tightened.

"Ah, you are so beautiful," he murmured, bending low, kissing the soft curves that were barely concealed beneath the thin chemise.

"Oh no, you mustn't," she said as he began pulling the chemise up her ribs.

"Why?" he murmured, never looking away from the flawless skin being revealed to his eyes, his hands, his mouth. "I've held you naked against my own naked body, your back to my chest and your beautiful breasts filling my hands. Like this, sweetheart. Remember? Like this."

Maya made a tiny, broken sound as Will's hands caressed her naked breasts. A sunburst of pleasure radiated through her when he caught her nipples between his fingers and rolled them gently. It was her dream all over again, sweetness claiming her while her body turned to honey and her breasts filled, rising to his touch. Then he bent down and licked a tight ruby crown. Maya stiffened as pleasure speared through her.

"Will, ah God, Will . . . !"

"Hush, sweetheart, it's all right," he murmured, catching her hands in his and pulling them up above her head. "I won't hurt you. You know that. I've been waiting to do this since I pulled you from the sea. And you've wanted it, too. That's why your breasts are pouting so prettily at me right now. I've kept my mouth from them much too long. They know how gently I'll love them. And I will.''

Helplessly Maya watched as Will's head bent down to her. The sight of his tongue teasing her sensitive flesh sent wild shivers through her body. When his teeth very lightly scored the tight tip of her breast, her back arched and she cried out in surprise and pleasure. He fitted his mouth to her breast and then began fitting her breast to his tongue, stroking her with its rough satin surface, tugging on her rhythmically, pulling her deeply into his mouth until pleasure shattered within her, and she gave a broken cry with each breath she took.

Slowly he released her hands, knowing that she wouldn't think of pushing him away now. And she didn't. Even as he slipped one arm around her, her fingers spread into his chestnut hair and held him against her breast as though she would die if he lifted his head. He groaned and smoothed his hand down her body from her shoulders to her thighs, stroking her continually, finding and freeing the fastenings of her riding skirt and pantalettes, easing his fingers closer to the intimate heat and softness of her that he hungered to caress.

At the first touch of his hand between her legs, Maya gasped.

"What are you doing? Will, what—"

The question was cut off in the instant that he took her mouth. He retreated momentarily from the tantalizing heat he had uncovered and contented himself with teasing and caressing her nipples until she forgot that she lay with blouse unbuttoned and chemise rid-

ing on the upper curve of her breasts and her riding
skirt and soft pantalettes pooled around her knees.
She forgot everything but the waves of sensuality
sweeping through her body as his mouth and hands
stroked her. She had no defenses against him or herself because she had never known that her body held
such incandescent pleasures concealed within its
depths.

Maya didn't feel the slow withdrawal of clothing
from her legs. She only knew that after a time she was
free to respond to the tender urgings of Will's hand.
With a sigh she parted her legs enough to allow his
fingers to glide along the sensitive surface of her inner
thighs. Shivering with pleasure, she stroked his thick
hair and gave herself to the wildness of his mouth on
her breasts and his hand caressing her.

The second time Will's fingertips drifted over
Maya's hidden warmth, she shivered and gave in to
the gentle pressure urging her legs apart. He cupped
his hand around her and caressed her with the heel of
his palm until she moaned and melted into his touch.
A fine mist of sweat bathed him as the heady scent of
her swept over his senses.

Will would have taken any other woman long before that moment; but this was Maya, whose life and
body were his to cherish; Maya, whom he had pulled
from the sea. He would never forgive himself if he
hurt or frightened her with the fierceness of his own
need. He didn't want to come to her for the first time
with his boots on and his pants around his knees as
though she were no more than a whore bought for a
few drinks. So instead of unfastening his fly and
pushing his rigid, aching flesh into her as he desperately needed to do, he held her hard, close, caressing

her until she twisted slowly against him, and he smiled down at her through the pain of his own abstinence.

"Will?" she said raggedly as pleasure spread through her body, a wildness called by his touch. "Will!"

"Yes, love," he whispered, rubbing against the hard nub of her passion. "Soon."

Reluctantly he eased his hand from her moist, soft flesh and began removing the rest of her clothes. She didn't fully realize what was happening until she wore nothing but the riding boots that were even then being gently pulled from her feet. Suddenly she looked the length of her naked body to Will kneeling between her legs. She flushed wildly, feeling both shame and a curious white-hot pleasure when she saw that he was looking at the dark hair that concealed her feminine softness. With a hand that trembled finely, he reached out to her and eased through the warm nest of hair until his fingers could caress her. She moaned, and her body rippled with sensual pleasure.

Will clenched his teeth against a cry of need as Maya's warmth bathed him. He had never known a woman to respond as she did, helplessly, her body begging for him even as shame stained her cheeks. He closed his eyes, fighting for control while he stripped away his own clothes. When he opened his eyes he saw Maya staring at the heavy, rigid proof of his need. There was more fear than passion in her face as she watched him.

Shaking with the violence of his own desire, Will lay down next to Maya and turned her onto her side with her back to him, sensing that she would feel less threatened if she didn't have to face him until she was passionately aroused once more. He pulled half the picnic blanket over their bodies, further concealing his nakedness and adding to her feeling of shelter. His arms slid around her, pulling her against his body.

"Will, I'm afraid. I can't. What if..."

The words ended in a throaty sound as his hands found her breasts, and he held her as he had when he warmed her in front of his bedroom hearth.

"There's no need to be afraid," he said softly. "I'll never hurt you. I'll just give you pleasure. Like this."

Maya tried to answer, but his fingers had found her nipples once more. Sensations seared through her, radiating from his touch. Both anxiety and fear vanished in a burst of melting pleasure. He tugged at her breasts again, felt again the currents of ecstasy ripple through her, melting her. Her hands came up and wrapped over his as though she were afraid that he would leave her again, and she couldn't bear that thought.

"This is the way it should have been weeks ago," he said, biting her nape with care, hearing her breath break. "I held your breasts, and you put your hands over mine, and I made your nipples as hard as I was. Oh, love, I wanted you then. I wanted to slide my hand down your body."

For a moment Maya's right hand lifted as though to free him for whatever caress he wanted to give her. His breath wedged as he remembered how innocent and wanton she had looked lying with nothing but her riding boots on, how she had let him touch her so intimately. The image sent such a burst of heat through him that he thought he had lost control.

Almost desperately Will's hand stroked down Maya's torso, then detoured up and over her hip until he could trace her spine with his thumb. But no matter how he tried to prolong the moment, the temptation of her hidden heat was too much. His thumb traced the crease in her buttocks down and down until his hand was deep between her thighs, opening her for his caress. She made a muffled sound as his fingertips dipped into her again and then again, deeper each time, until she shuddered and moaned at the knowledge of him within her body.

He withdrew his touch from her, pausing only to tease the knot of ultrasensitive flesh that had risen from her softness. When she was twisting and turning against him, crying brokenly with each breath, he eased her over on her back once more. Her eyes opened, glazed with sensuality and need. When he pressed her thighs apart she gave him all that he asked for without hesitation, wanting only to know more of the shivering, shattering pleasure his touch brought.

"Touch me again," she said huskily. "Oh, Will, I'll die if you don't touch me like that again."

"So will I," he said roughly.

He covered her with a smooth, powerful movement, parting her thighs even more, pushing slowly into her, fighting not to lose control of his own body. But she was so hot, so close, so perfectly made for him that he could restrain himself no more. After a single thrust of his hips he began pouring himself into her, his body shuddering and driving against her in paroxysms of completion that left him spent.

"I'm sorry, sweetheart, I'm sorry," Will said hoarsely when control returned. He kissed Maya's face swiftly, repeatedly. "I didn't give you what you deserve. Love, I'm sorry."

Maya was too dazed to do more than respond to the unhappiness in Will's voice. She stroked his hair and

naked back soothingly, her mind and body in utter
turmoil, a wild restlessness consuming her. Will turned
his head and tasted the tears on her cheek and remembered the instant of resistance before he had taken
her completely. With a feeling of disbelief he realized
that despite the wild, helpless responses to him, she
had been a virgin.

"I hurt you," he said, his voice raw.

He started to withdraw from her body, only to stop
as she moaned.

"It's all right, Maya. I won't hurt you any longer."

Her hips moved instinctively, taking him fully into
her body once more. He realized that her moan had
come not from pain but from pleasure, the pleasure of
having him inside her. Desire swept through him in a
surge more powerful than anything he had yet felt.

"Is this what you want?" he asked, moving his hips
slowly, deeply.

The words meant nothing to Maya. All that mattered to her were the expanding rings of sensation
welling up from the hard, hot, gliding pressure of Will
moving within her. Blindly she reached for him,
wanting his mouth, needing it, needing to be surrounded and permeated by him, for she sensed that the
tension coiled within her could only be released by
him. She called out to him, her words incoherent,
tumbled, frantic, the world spinning away until nothing was left but the shivering tension of her body. Her
nails raked down to his hips in unconscious demand
for release from the sensual vise he had created, and
he laughed and thrust again and again until her tension burst into shimmering waves of ecstasy, pleasure
sleeting through her with a sweet violence that almost
sent her into unconsciousness.

Slowly Maya returned to a sense of herself and the reality of the forest and the sky overhead. She heard Will's voice, felt his weight along her body, his warmth inside her and knew that she was joined to him in an intimacy that was stunningly beautiful . . . and terrifyingly dangerous, a betrayal of everything that she had ever believed about herself.

"My God, what have I done?" she whispered.

"You've enjoyed me as much as I enjoyed you," Will said, tenderness and triumph clear in his tone. "You're so beautiful, sweetheart. Perfect. No woman has ever come close to giving me the pleasure you just gave me. You were made for me, and now you are mine."

For a long moment Maya was silent as the truth of her situation reverberated through her. She had believed herself immune to the passion and stupidity that led women to risk the future of their babes for the pleasures of the instant. She had been wrong. Even now her body rippled with the aftermath of ecstasy each time Will moved. Even now his words were a sweetness that made her want to whisper love words to him with each breath. Even now the touch of his lips against her neck, her shoulder, her breast made her want to moan. Even now, understanding what the outcome inevitably would be, she would come to him again and again, joining her body to his because there was nothing in her life that had ever felt more right, more beautiful.

You didn't tell me about this part of it, Mother, Maya thought bitterly. *You never told me that you don't have to die to go to heaven . . . and having once been there, how can I not go again, and in going, doom my babes to hunger and misery because I chose the wrong man?*

Maya shuddered convulsively in the grip of a despair that was as great as her ecstasy had been.

"You're cold," Will said, kissing her gently one last time before moving aside.

She said nothing. Even when he dressed her, she lay as passively as a doll, her eyes closed. He pulled on his own clothes, watching her with increasing uneasiness.

"Maya, love, are you all right?" he asked as he buttoned her jacket.

Her eyes opened. He felt a chill at the bleakness he saw within those green depths.

"Maya? What's wrong?"

"Can't you guess?"

He simply looked bewildered. "I pleased you. I know that."

"You ruined me."

Maya heard the echo of her own words and knew that they were wrong. "No. That isn't true. I ruined myself...and my babes. May God and Jesus forgive me, for I know that I will never forgive myself."

"What babes? That's impossible. You don't have any children. You were a virgin!"

"I was, yes. And I could be a mother within nine months." Maya smiled bitterly as she watched understanding sweep through Will. "You didn't think about that, did you?"

"We'll be married as soon as it can be arranged."

"No."

"Don't be silly, love," he said, smiling down at her as he traced her trembling lower lip. "I'll take care of you, and, if you're pregnant, of our baby as well."

"How? By charging it to your father's accounts?"

Anger flushed Will's face. "I have a job."

"Ah, yes. Your job. Tell me, does your father pay you so generously at the mill that you can keep yourself and a family as well?"

Again Maya watched understanding sweep over Will. Too late. But she couldn't blame him for his youth and his lack of foresight. He hadn't seen babes die and children grow up pale and sickly for lack of food. She had. She had known better, and yet she had opened her legs and joyously welcomed the seed that never should have been planted within her body.

"I'll demand a raise."

For an instant Maya was torn between sad laughter and sadder tears. She knew what Will didn't suspect: Hale Hawthorne wanted her; he would do nothing to bring about her marriage to his son.

"If you try to marry me, your father will throw you out without a cent."

Will didn't deny Maya's flat statement. Deep inside himself he knew it to be the truth. Hale watched Maya with a possessiveness that had infuriated Will almost as much as it had made him deeply uneasy.

"I'll go north. I'll stake out my own timber claims, build my own mill. I'm not a boy, Maya. I can support you."

"Me, yes. When it's too wet for you to cut trees, I can always work at a lumber camp as a cook so that we can eat. But what about our babies?"

"For God's sake," he said impatiently. "You act as though you think we'll starve."

"No man sets out to see his children starve and his wife die young. But it happens, Will. *It happens.*"

"It won't happen to me."

Maya looked at Will, young and confident of his own strength, his control over his own destiny. She had felt the same way once. And then she had lain with a boy beneath a magnificent redwood and learned that she was no different from other girls.

"Maya, did you hear? It won't happen to me. It won't happen to us!"

"I heard."

But she didn't believe, and he was too young to understand why.

"You'll see, sweetheart. I'll go timber cruising with Henry Ising and pick out the best place for us."

Maya said nothing, not then, not on the long ride back to the house, not even at dinner. She said nothing until late that evening when Will appeared at the kitchen door leading a packhorse laden with supplies.

"I'll be gone three weeks, maybe more. Will you be all right? Will you? Oh God, sweetheart, say something."

She looked into his anxious gray eyes, touched his mouth with fingertips that trembled...and whispered goodbye.

Chapter Seven

Ising looked over at Will, who was staring into the breakfast campfire as though demons or his own future were writhing within the orange flames. Ising knew that something less tangible than fire was gnawing at Will's mind. The Indian also knew that Will would tell him in his own time. Until then it was enough to know that part of what was driving Will was money. Or, more precisely, the lack of it.

That was something that Ising understood all the way to the broad soles of his feet toasting by the campfire. An accident of geography and fate had blessed the Yurok people with ample food—particularly fish—and a climate that neither sapped a man with too much warmth nor froze his ambition with too much cold. As a result the Yuroks had been largely freed of the daily struggle for survival. That allowed them to concentrate on other, higher things.

Money, for instance.

For a Yurok money was strings of dentalia. The scarce seashells served the same purpose among the ocean-oriented tribes as gold or silver did among the white man. Everything in Yurok culture had a monetary value; commerce, love and war were all conducted with an eye toward cost. Every dispute could be settled with money. Compensation in dentalia could be computed for seduction or rape, marriage or divorce, accidental death or premeditated murder.

Because everything had an ascertainable value, Yuroks were among the most peaceable tribes on the frontier. They were also among the richest. But, as with most human tribes, the Yurok social structure was both hierarchical and tended toward rigidity. A bastard born of a poor mother was locked into the lowest social rank. Ising could bond himself over to a wealthy family as a servant, or he could struggle along at the level of bare subsistence, but he stood little chance of becoming respectable—that is, wealthy—within Yurok society because all the sources of wealth were already owned. All the good fishing spots, all the meadowlands where a man could hope to bring down an elk or a deer and all the coastal areas where dentalia could be found were already under the private ownership of the Yurok well-to-do. There was nothing left over for the likes of Henry Ising.

Ising had been saved from a life of bondage by the introduction of a new element—the white man—into the Yurok social equation. Small numbers of Caucasians had begun arriving on the redwood coastline almost a quarter century before. The trickle of whites quickly had become a flood. By the time Ising was ten years old, the cities of Eureka and Union City had been established in the territory of the Wiyots, the coastal tribe whose lands bordered the Yuroks' territory to the south. The Wiyots had fought against the American incursions, a tactic that ultimately had proved disastrous for the tribe. Wiyots had been massacred by white settlers who sometimes acted out of fear for their own lives and sometimes out of naked avarice.

The Yuroks had escaped similar extermination only because their land was more distant and rugged than that of the Wiyots. White settlers did spread north toward the Klamath River, but not in such great numbers. The land itself seemed to turn them back, for it was a place of huge trees, trees so gigantic that they were immune to the white man's ax, enormous trees creating groves so thick that sunlight rarely touched the ground. Only ferns and moss thrived in such groves, and man could neither eat, wear nor barter ferns and moss. As a result most white men did largely as the Indians had always done; they avoided the land of the big trees.

Unlike other Yuroks Ising didn't feel ill at ease among the towering trees, a fact that he attributed to the influence of his white blood. Ising enjoyed the sky-climbing firs and redwoods and the subdued light of the open spaces beneath the sun-absorbing green canopy. His ease with the big trees was one of the things that had drawn him to the white culture and away from the Yurok. Since he fit in neither culture, how much worse could it be to live as a half-breed among the whites than as a poor bastard among the Yuroks?

It was a question that Henry Ising asked himself a hundred times over the span of his life. There was no single, simple answer.

Not all Americans were as antagonistic to Indians as the rogues who massacred the Wiyots. Even in a frontier town such as Eureka, there were citizens who objected to the mistreatment of Indians of any tribe. Will Hawthorne was one of them. The wife of a lay preacher had been another. She had taken in Ising when he was eight, fed him, clothed him and taught him the white language and ways. By the time he had reached his full physical maturity at fifteen, he was at least as much white American in his outlook as he was Yurok.

Unfortunately Ising was not white. He knew without being told that some things were forbidden to him, foremost among them the presence of a white woman in his bed. That was what had sent him back to the Yurok villages of the north coast when he had turned seventeen. Women. There were Indian women who were more than happy to ease his body. The Indian men welcomed Ising's white knowledge for the simple reason that Yuroks were coming out second in competition for material wealth with the whites. The Yuroks, being pragmatists, were ready to acquire whatever knowledge would lead them to greater wealth. Though part of neither white nor Indian culture, Ising had made a place for himself in both.

A raven's raw voice called through the early morning fog. Ising looked up and realized that he had spent too long staring into the fire. Time was money to both Yurok and white. It was one of the few things that the two cultures agreed upon.

"Will. Will! Time to quit mooning into the fire. There's a thousand miles of forest out there just waiting to be turned into money."

Will started, called back from his dreams of Maya. Though he had been away from her only five days, hunger was an agony within him. It was more than the simple clamor of lust; it was a need to hear her voice, her laughter, the whispering rustle of her skirts as she walked toward him. But he could not go back to her until he had the means to begin their future. Never again would she question his ability to provide for her.

Coffee dregs hissed as they hit the flames. Methodically Ising and Will crushed the small fire with their heavy boots, ensuring that a wind would find no embers to fan into flame. Not that there was much chance of fire here in the damp, cold silences beneath the big trees. But Ising and Will had fought timber fires before and had no desire to do so again.

They left their horses hobbled in the small meadow next to the river, for where Ising and Will were going a horse would be worse than useless. The deadfalls and rotting logs of the primeval climax forest could be negotiated only by sweating, powerful, determined men on foot.

Will pulled out his leather-bound notebook and a pencil. He flipped to the last page he had written upon, which showed the area they had surveyed yesterday. It represented a pitifully small amount of land against the broad sweep of the countryside. In the untamed forest it could take a strong man a full day of arduous work to walk three miles. A wide, irregular line down the center of the page represented the river Will and Ising were camped by. The river had a Yurok name that was unpronounceable to Will. Though only a few hours by boat up the coast from Eureka, the land itself had never been claimed and catalogued by whites. There were easier trees to be cut closer to home; and men had already claimed and cut many of them. Now it was Will's turn to stake out a piece of the new world upon which to build his life.

He smiled crookedly at the thought of what his timber claim description would look like when he filed it: "Five miles on either side of the No Name river..."

In the past five days he and Ising had seen more board feet of standing trees than Will had dreamed possible. The potential of the forest was almost overwhelming. Despite the persistently falling rain and the sometimes dangerous scrambles across ravines and over slick river boulders, he couldn't get enough of the wild land. He had been wet for so long that his feet were pale and wrinkled inside his boots, but he didn't care. Each step revealed to him more of God's own timber country, the most magnificent forest ever to grow upon the face of the earth.

Will was not a man easily impressed by trees. He had walked great groves of redwoods since he could remember. He had sat in his father's house listening to tall tales from lumbermen who had come from all over the world. He had huddled around camp stoves in loggers' shanties, hearing timber legends told and retold. But never in the wildest of the tales and legends had Will heard of country to match the reality of the forests through which he and Ising walked.

For mile after mile they had gone through redwood groves that seemed to support the roof of the world, trees three hundred feet high and more, whole groves of Guardians towering over the land. On upland slopes that caught the Pacific mists he had seen dozens of single trees twenty feet thick at the butt, hundreds of trees too big for the Tres Santos mill and thousands upon thousands of trees that challenged the highest technology available anywhere on earth.

Will had thought he understood the potential of the redwood country before this trip, but after only five days of wandering the watersheds of nameless Yurok streams he realized that Tres Santos and other lumber companies had not yet even seen the evergreen wealth of the northern coast, much less begun to cut it. There were billions of board feet of lumber locked within the mammoth forests of the Redwood Empire.

"You still scribbling?"

Will smiled at Ising's question but kept on taking notes. "Just writing down the best places to begin my future."

Ising shook his head. "These trees are just too much of a good thing. We need to get farther inland, where it's drier. Good trees there. And not too damned big for an overhead saw." With a grunt Ising shifted his pack into place. He gestured toward the opposite side of the river where a large stream came in. "But if you like big trees, that's where the biggest trees around are. The clouds and fog drift in from the ocean and pile up against the mountains. The big trees need moisture all the time. Not that they'll do you any good. They're still too damned big to mill."

"Some of them always are, no matter where you cut."

"All of these are."

"Are they?" Will asked softly. "Show me."

"You deaf? I told you they're too big to cut."

"They won't always be."

"Trees aren't like people," Ising said dryly. "They don't shrink as they get older."

"The saws will get bigger. Mark my words. And when they do, I'll have section after section of timber claims just waiting to be cut."

"You'll be dead before that happens."

"I'm betting that I won't."

Ising smiled. "There's a lot of your daddy in you after all. Just took awhile for it to show."

Before Will could think of an answer, Ising set off toward the river with the long, easy stride of a man accustomed to walking. Will followed, letting Ising lead the way, knowing that the Indian had a keen eye for moss-covered deadfalls or moss-slicked rocks that could break an unwary man's leg. Because there had been no real rainfall yet this year, simply the endless drizzle of the coastal redwood forest, the river itself was low. They forded it easily and went on to the broad bench-valley that Ising had pointed out.

Ising hadn't exaggerated. For as far as Will could see redwood trunks stood straight and solid, an army of giants in random formation. Dampened by mist, the boles were black columns rising to a hidden sky. There were other kinds of evergreens scattered through the redwood ranks, but not many. In the dense shadows of the climax redwood forest nothing else had much chance to survive. The redwoods were so dense, so huge, that their massive presence darkened the world.

"Does this place have a name?" Will asked.

"Just 'the forest.'"

"Then I shall call it Black Basin. How big is it?"

"Two miles along the flatland beside the river. Then the land rises up toward the ridges and the trees begin to get smaller."

"Are there any Yurok villages in the valley?"

"Indians have no use for this land. The fishing is bad in the river, the game avoids the shadows of the forests because there's nothing to eat and the trees are too big to be made into canoes." Ising shrugged. "Indians don't live on useless land, especially Yurok Indians."

"You call these trees useless?" Will said in amazement. "You don't have to be a lumberman to get some pleasure from their size alone. I'm surprised your people don't worship the trees."

"Most Yuroks fear these woods. This is where the *woge* live, the little people."

"Don't you fear the *woge*?"

Ising shrugged again and said nothing.

Will didn't press. He knew that Ising's ways and beliefs were not always white. Will respected that, just as Ising gave respect to white ways and beliefs that he didn't share.

"Most white men would be awed by these trees, too," Will said after a moment. "But their reaction would probably be to take an ax to them, rather than to avoid them."

"That's because white men have steel axes and bull teams. Yuroks have only stone axes and the power of their own shoulders."

"That would be something, wouldn't it?" Will said softly.

"What?"

"To take on one of these trees with nothing but an ax and a good friend working alongside you."

Ising's black eyes met Will's. Both men smiled, for they were young and needed tangible ways to measure their own worth.

Wordlessly they turned and walked through the ancient silence of the forest, their footsteps cushioned by humus that had lain undisturbed since before the first man had been born. Will saw trees that were thicker at their base than the Guardian, trees that were taller, trees with bark even darker and more deeply furrowed. Yet none of those trees moved him as the memory of the Guardian did. For him, no tree would ever have the sheer magnificence of the redwood at whose feet he had first known the shattering, transcendent ecstasy to be found within the woman he loved.

Will and Ising walked for the rest of the day, exploring Black Basin and the edge of the upland slopes beyond. It was late before they returned to camp. Will was weary in every limb as he rolled into his blankets next to the fire. Even then he couldn't sleep. He kept seeing the vast green promise of the forest sweeping back from the river with no name. Gradually a certainty formed within him. It was here that he would stake his claims. It was here that he would begin to build a new world for Maya and himself.

Long after Ising slept, Will stared into the incandescent caverns glowing beneath the graceful flames, dreaming of the life to come.

"You seem unhappy, lass. Do you not like it here? Do you wish to go home?"

Maya looked into Hale's pale, shrewd eyes and wondered if he somehow knew what had happened ten days ago while he had been in San Francisco. Fear burst suddenly in her, bleaching her skin of color. If Hale knew, he would turn her out to fend for herself. And what if she were pregnant? What would she do then?

"I have no home, Mr. Hawthorne. Even if I did, I wouldn't wish to return to it. I have never been happier anywhere than in this house."

Hale sensed the fear beneath Maya's desperately calm, soft voice and saw fear in the pallor of her skin and in the tension of her mouth. "You're afraid that

I've been listening to the loose tongues around town, aren't you? You're afraid that I'll send you away."

If Maya had been pale before, she went absolutely white upon hearing Hale's words. She said nothing because she could not force her tongue to work within her suddenly dry mouth. Fear hammered through her, making her weak. For a moment she felt a dizziness that sent the world spinning. She struggled against her own weakness, knowing that she had never needed strength more than she did now, when she was on the edge of being set adrift once again with nothing more than her own wits to provide for her survival.

"Aye, I've heard the gossips," Hale continued, his Scots accent strengthening as it always did after several whiskies. "I've heard all the plain women who tittle and tattle and tell each other that a beautiful girl such as you can't live with a widower such as I without impropriety." He looked at the rest of the whiskey in his glass and then back at Maya's womanly curves concealed beneath the dress that he had purchased for her. "And they are right, lass. They are right."

Maya saw the frank desire in Hale's eyes and trembled. "You would never...you couldn't..." Her voice cracked into silence.

"Of course not. But God recognizes the sins of the mind as well as those of the body." Hale sipped the whiskey before setting it aside with the air of a man who has made a decision. "You are young but you have known enough privation that you have a proper gratitude for such simple things as food and warm clothing."

"Y-yes. I am very grateful for your k-kindness." Maya took a slow breath, trying to control the shivering of her body, trying to prepare herself for the moment when Hale would accuse her of seducing his son and throw her out.

"I know that, just as I know what kind of life you could expect if you had not found a haven in my house. At best you would have ended up a poor man's wife and drudge, or a wealthy man's mistress. At worst...well, you've seen the women waiting in the doorways for ships to come in."

Maya closed her eyes against a wave of nausea.

"Ach, I'm doing this badly," Hale said, standing up suddenly. "I never was a man for words and dealing with women's emotions. A thing either makes sense or it doesn't, and talking about it either way is a waste of time. But you are a young woman. You haven't had time to discover that romantic notions of love and marriage are so much twaddle." He let out an explosive breath and ran his hand through his thick, graying hair. "I am fifty-three, and I find myself with a son and heir who isn't worth the powder to blow him to hell and an impoverished housekeeper who is too attractive for my peace of mind and who, my laundress assures me, undergoes the normal monthly bleeding of a fertile female."

Flushing scarlet, Maya looked aside. Hale saw, frowned and forged on to the main point with the bluntness of a man who is accustomed to giving orders rather than explanations.

"There is a simple, God-sanctified remedy for the situation I find myself in. Marriage. If you accept, you will become my wife, the mother of my second family and a woman with a secure position in the community. If you refuse, I have no choice but to ask you to seek other employment."

Maya swayed as emotions burst within her. The instants of turmoil were followed by the eerie calm that had always overtaken her in the past when life had forced her to choose among disasters in order to survive. Yet this time was also different. This time she might also be choosing for an unborn child. It was not just her life, her sin, her turmoil, her poverty or wealth that was in question; it was also that of an utterly innocent life that might have been conceived within the Guardian's fragrant silence.

Which meant that there was no choice at all. She would never permit a babe to pay for her sin with a life of misery and want.

"I . . . I accept."

And then, for the first and last time in her life, Maya fainted.

"So soon?" asked Maya. "It was only last night that we became engaged."

"I'm fifty-three. I don't have any time to waste getting another son and raising him properly," Hale said without looking up from his plate of pot roast, potatoes and gravy. "The good Reverend Cleary will be out tomorrow morning at ten. That should give you adequate time to dress or to wash your hair or to do whatever it is that females do to fill the time between rising and taking up their household duties. Beth, pass the carrots, please. The bowl is two inches from your left hand."

"Won't the haste lead to more gossip?" Maya asked softly, trying frantically both to conceal and to control the feeling of panic that she had awakened with in the middle of the night. She had felt such panic before, when her father had died, when her mother had died and when she had realized that she would have to make her way west alone. She didn't understand why she was feeling that same panic now, when her future finally was secure.

"Bother the gossips," Hale said curtly. "Thank you, Beth. Now the salt, if you will. It's just above your right hand. A man can't let his life be run by women's loose tongues. In nine months I'll be fifty-four. Nothing would please me better than to hold a baby son in my hands on my birthday."

"But Father, what about Will?" Beth said, her voice and face equally distressed.

"I made my own way at fourteen. Willy is seventeen, and less of a man than I was at twelve. Maybe my marriage will teach him to work for what he wants instead of waiting for it to fall into his hands as would a ripe fruit. When it comes to marriage and childbearing, women want men, not overgrown boys. If you don't believe me, ask Miss Charters, who will soon be your stepmother. And Willy's as well, I suppose."

Maya flushed and then went quite pale. Her heart beat erratically, making her hands shake. Very carefully she placed the heavy silver fork on the china plate. Then she looked up and met Hale's eyes.

"That's the way of life, Beth," Hale said, looking at Maya all the time as he spoke. "Women want men and boys want what men have earned. Your brother will have to find his own girl now, his own family, his own life. Or he can go on living here and being a boy and working for half wages at my mill." Hale nodded curtly. "My marriage will be the making or the breaking of him."

"I don't want Will to go away!" Beth cried. "Who will I talk to? Who will take me for walks and on picnics? Who will care if I wake up crying?"

Impatiently Hale set down his fork. Though Beth could not see his mood, she flinched at the sharp ring of silver against china.

"Willy must make his own life. You're too young to understand that, but it is true just the same. Miss Charters will see to your schooling. She will teach you what is expected of a young woman of good—"

"But I—"

"Silence, child! I am speaking."

Beth bit her pale lips against the words and fears crowding her into incautious speech. Maya wanted to reassure her but knew that Hale would rebuke her just as sharply as he had his daughter. There would be time to reassure Beth later, when Hale was not present.

"I have spoiled you because of the circumstances that caused your blindness. That was an error. It was God's will that you be blind, and it was grave arrogance on my part to feel responsible. If you hadn't run from my argument with Will three years ago and fallen down the stairs, God would have found some other means of taking sight from you. So dry your tears, child. They will no longer make me feel that I must be punished for that which is God's will. You are as you are, and you are blind. When Miss Charters is my wife, she will find something that you can do around the house. You are not too feeble or too foolish to know the rewards of a job well done. Now eat your dinner. You will never recover from the shipwreck if you don't put on some flesh."

There was a long silence that was relieved only by the clink of silverware against china as Hale finished his dinner. Maya moved her food from one quadrant of the plate to another so that she wouldn't have to watch slow tears fall from Beth's blind eyes. No one said a word until Hale swallowed his last bite and pushed back from the table.

"You have a point, Miss Charters. A hasty wedding will cause gossip. I won't delay the wedding, but I will take other measures. Saturday after next you will give a dinner here. I will give you a list of people to invite. In this way you will be introduced to the women who are your peers, while I talk over business concerns with their husbands. When the women see that I hold you in respect, they will hold their tongues or I will break their husbands financially." Hale pulled a big gold watch from his pocket, looked at the time and frowned. "Bring my coffee to the library, if you will. I have accounts to examine."

After Hale left, Maya reached for Beth. At first the girl pulled away, then she broke down and sobbed against Maya's shoulder. Maya held Beth in her arms, rocking her, stroking her hair, trying to calm her.

"It will be all right," Maya whispered again and again. "I'll take care of you, Beth. If you cry out in the middle of the night, I'll come to your room."

"I w-want W-Will!"

Maya closed her eyes in pain. "He'll be back soon."

"But it won't be the s-same. You'll be our s-step-mother and everything w-will change. Don't you understand? I want it to be the s-same!"

"Time doesn't go backward. You may fight and cry and rail until you're exhausted, but time only goes one way, and we are carried forward with it whether we like it or not."

Something in Maya's voice penetrated Beth's own unhappiness. Her small, delicate hands reached up to Maya's face. "You're crying."

Maya noticed her own tears with a feeling close to surprise. She never cried. "Why, so I am."

"But why are you sad?"

"It doesn't matter. It will pass. That's the only thing that makes life bearable. It passes." Maya smoothed fine blond strands back from Beth's forehead with a hand that was almost steady. "Mrs. Chou says there are mice in the kitchen. Do you know what that means? It means that there is a need for a cat, a need that even your father will understand. I shall bring kittens to you, little Mouse. The one that feels best to you we shall keep."

Maya watched eagerness replace tears on Beth's young face and smiled sadly. It had been that way with her younger brothers and sisters. The moment's unexpected pleasure could make them forget all but the worst belly hunger. That was how she had known when her sister was dying; she hadn't responded when a fluffy baby chick was put into her hands.

"Really? A kitten for a Mouse?" Beth smiled and clapped her hands in excitement. "Oh, wait until Will hears. He'll laugh and laugh."

Maya said only, "Come. You'll help me choose my wedding dress."

"But I can't see!"

"You can feel textures, can't you? After we've picked out the dress, we'll go into the garden for a bouquet."

"But the flowers are gone."

"Then we'll just have to choose something that smells good, won't we?"

Beth's face lit with a smile. "Oh, I'll be the best help you could have for that. Will says I have a very keen sense of smell."

"I'm sure you do, Mouse," Maya said calmly, but her voice and graceful walk were at odds with the silent glide of tears down her face.

"... Pronounce you man and wife." Reverend Cleary closed the Bible with a distinct thump and looked over his reading glasses at the couple standing in front of him. "May I be the first to congratulate you on your lovely bride, Mr. Hawthorne?"

Hale smiled and shook the reverend's thin hand. Maya stood quietly, her skin pale and her eyes very dark. A band of gold gleamed on her left hand, a ring that Hale had bought when he had realized that Maya was not only homeless, but levelheaded and utterly alone in the world. He had known then that she would become his wife or his mistress. Either way, it was just a matter of time until she was his.

From the bouquet in Maya's hands rose the fragrance of tiny redwood boughs bound in a white satin ribbon. The scent called up memories of the Guardian and Will, scent drenching Maya, drowning her, destroying her. She could not escape it or the forest green of the dress that exactly matched her eyes, a dress Will had chosen for that very reason and that Beth had picked out because the fine wool had been like a warm caress across her skin.

With a feeling of unreality, Maya stood beneath the dripping eaves of the front porch next to the man who was her husband. At Hale's urging she waved to the reverend's buggy as it disappeared into the mist and

rain. She didn't realize that she was shivering until
Hale put his hand on her arm and drew her inside.

"Come, Mrs. Hawthorne. We can't have you getting a chill on your wedding day."

Hale drew her into the parlor where a fire blazed
upon the hearth. Beth followed, moving with the
fragile confidence of the blind walking amid familiar
furnishings. Mrs. Chou had set out a cold lunch and
a plate full of sweets. A teapot steamed gently between pots of cream and sugar, and a bottle of champagne had been set out. Hale opened the bottle and
poured two glasses of the fizzy liquid. He handed one
to her.

"To the son and heir you will bear me," Hale said,
clicking the rim of his glass against hers.

Maya took a sip and choked, spilling champagne in
all directions. Amused by her lack of sophistication,
Hale took the glass from her and poured her a cup of
tea instead.

"Here, lass. Clear your throat."

Gratefully Maya took the cup of tea and wrapped
her cold fingers around it. She could not stop the random tremors of her body. Hale drank two glasses of
champagne in rapid succession while Beth nibbled on
the sweets that had been laid out. Maya sipped tea,
hoping its warmth could thaw the chill that had settled into the marrow of her bones. Minutes passed in
a silence that seemed to grow heavier with each second.

The gold watch at Hale's waist chimed loudly, proclaiming the noon hour.

"All right, Beth," Hale said, pouring himself another glass of champagne. "It's off to bed with you.

The fever came back yesterday. We dinna want you to fall ill all over again."

Maya couldn't control a start at Hale's hearty words and mellow brogue after the long, taut silence. Beth pouted but said nothing. She had come to look forward to the early afternoon when she could go to her room and shut the door and not have to explain what she was doing or thinking to anyone. She smiled in the direction of Hale's voice, then in the direction of the evergreen fragrance that to her was like a beacon in the mustiness of the room.

"If you don't need your bouquet, may I have it?" Beth asked. "My room smells of Mrs. Chou's moth potion."

"Of course." Maya gave the bouquet to Beth with a feeling of relief.

"Thank you... Maya. If I may call you that?"

"Yes," she said quickly, sensing that Hale was going to insist that she be called Mother. She couldn't bear that. "Please do that, Beth. I'd like very much if you called me Maya. There's not so much difference in our ages, after all."

"Seven years," Hale said stiffly.

"But as you get older, the years matter less and less." Maya bent and kissed Beth's soft cheek. "Sleep well, little Mouse. Later, if the rain stops, we'll go back to the garden. You did very well with the plants yesterday. I think you'll make quite a gardener, and it would be so nice to have flowers for the house."

Beth left with a bright smile and a light step.

"A gardener?" Hale asked. "Hardly a suitable occupation for my daughter."

Maya forced a smile as she looked into her husband's pale eyes. "Raising flowers is a worthy pastime for a gentlewoman. At least that's what my mother told me. She was raised in the South, and her parents were very wealthy."

Hale grunted and poured another glass of champagne. He held it out to Maya. "Drink it, lass, and then another. It will help."

Her eyes widened when she realized what he was implying. He wasn't going to wait for night to consummate the marriage. She started to say that she didn't need wine because marital relations didn't frighten her, that, in fact, she had found her single experience with sex to be stunningly beautiful.

And then the thought of lying naked with her legs spread and Hale naked on top of her made Maya freeze. The glass slipped from her numb fingers and smashed on the floor.

With a stifled sigh Hale picked up the bottle and the remaining intact glass and took Maya's arm. He walked her up the stairs and into his bedroom, which lay at the opposite end of the house from Beth's and Mrs. Chou's. Firmly he shut the heavy door behind him. He shook the bottle several times, flattening the wine, before he poured another glass.

"Try again, lass." This time he held the glass to Maya's lips. She swallowed convulsively because it was that or choke. "Good girl. Now another. It's easier now, isn't it? Not so many bubbles to tickle."

"Mr. Hawthorne, I don't—"

"Drink," he said curtly, cutting across her words, his voice gruff, his eyes narrowed and not unkind. "The Lord in His infinite wisdom did not see fit to curse decent women with the baser instincts that He gave so fully to all men. I don't want to hurt you, but I will have children of you. While I don't expect you to enjoy the marriage bed, I do expect you to do your duty as my wife without weeping or cringing."

Maya closed her eyes and drank.

In a few minutes she began to feel light-headed. Hale looked at her and nodded. He went around the room and methodically closed the heavy drapes, shutting out even the pallid illumination of the rainy afternoon. Though the room was nearly dark, he lighted neither candle nor oil lamp.

"Your nightclothes are behind the screen," Hale said, gesturing toward a folding oriental panel that closed off a corner of the room. "I'll change after you do."

It took Maya an unreasonably long time to change into the simple flannel gown. Hale listened to the rustlings and stirrings from behind the screen with increasing impatience. When she slipped by him and hid beneath the covers, he changed into his own nightclothes with harsh, jerky motions. He was fully aroused, a condition that had become not at all unusual since Maya's arrival. If she had shown the least hint of passion toward him in the preceding weeks, he would have made her his mistress rather than his wife, but her lack of desire told him that she could be had by him through no other means than marriage. He approved her aloofness; it was the very thing that made her suitable to bear his future heir.

By the time Hale climbed beneath the covers Maya was so tightly strung that she was shuddering. Hale stretched out beside her. Awkwardly he pulled her into his arms, trying to calm her, but the feel of her soft breasts pressed against him made him groan with a surge of need. He found her breasts with his hands almost roughly. The feel of them beneath his fingertips made his breath quicken as though he had been running. He felt Maya start to pull away from him as his hands clenched in a helpless spasm of need. He forced himself to release her breasts, knowing that it was unfair of him to take anything from her but that which he required for children.

"Lie on your back," he said hoarsely. "Yes, like that."

Maya gasped as she felt the nightgown being bunched up to her waist beneath the blankets. When Hale's hands pushed at her thighs she cried out and tried to pull away.

"Lie still, lass. Don't tighten so. I'll be quick as I can to spare you, but fighting will only make it worse." Hale gave a grunt of satisfaction as he separated her thighs. "Now lie still, lass, lie still, still, still still . . . *now*."

Maya screamed at the sudden, tearing pain, but Hale had anticipated her. His hard hand kept the sound from going beyond the bedroom.

"It's all right, all right, all right . . ." he chanted as he thrust into her again and again.

The words were meaningless for Maya because all she felt was the agony of having Hale thrusting inside her unprepared body. Rigid, suspended in nightmare, she waited for the pain to end while his motions increased and then increased again until he was hammering into her in a blind frenzy of need. At last his whole body tightened and then shuddered repeatedly. For a minute he sprawled heavily on her, and then he rolled aside, breathing harshly.

"You did well, lass," he said finally, adjusting his pajamas. "Dinna worry. You did well."

Chapter Eight

"Oh, this is a lovely texture," Beth said. She ran first her fingertips and then her whole hand over the tablecloth. "Is it the right color?"

Maya closed her eyes as she smoothed her fingers over the fine linen. Beth was right. There was a cool perfection to the weave that was very soothing.

"It's the color of freshly sawn redwood," Maya said reluctantly. "I'm sure your father would prefer something more formal for his table."

"Bother formal," muttered the young girl. "It feels beautiful. I wish more people saw with their fingertips the way I do."

Unbidden, the memory came to Maya of the afternoon when Will had gently traced her lips, her neck, the tips of her breasts, the hollow of her navel and the warm, shadowed secrets beyond. His eyes had been closed in order to focus his attention completely on the sensations communicated by her skin to his fingertips.

With an effort that left Maya shaken, she wrenched her mind away from the sensual memories. The difference between that afternoon and the reality of the marriage bed was a brutal fact that she was still trying to absorb. Without realizing it, she had assumed before she married Hale that sex would be about the same with any man. She had been terribly wrong.

Yet, even had she known her error, she would have married Hale just the same. Five minutes of acute discomfort several times a week was a small price to pay for the lifetime well-being of her future children. Though she was still healing from the first time with Hale, sex no longer was agony for her. She had quickly discovered that mineral oil could be used to ease Hale's presence within her body. He had objected at first, saying that it was a device used by improper women to increase illicit pleasure, but Maya had said that she used it not to increase pleasure but to reduce pain. Hale had talked the matter over with the Reverend Cleary, who had found nothing against it in the Bible. Reassured, and relieved that there was an acceptable way to get children without hurting his young wife, Hale had bought a crystal flagon for Maya and filled it with the lubricating oil.

"Maya? Maya, are you still there?"

She felt Beth's light touch on her sleeve and realized that the girl had been trying to get her attention.

"I'm here."

"You've been so quiet since the wedding."

"I have many things to think about. Running a house that will please your father takes a great deal of planning. You've been a real help to me, Mouse. Without you I would have had to count all the linens and china and silverware by myself."

Beth's smile of pleasure eased some of the hurt within Maya. Under her patient teaching, Beth had overcome some of the fear and shyness that previously had marked her dealings with the world beyond her bedroom walls. Maya hoped to be able to do even more to bring Beth into a full life. At the mission Maya had heard talk of something called Braille, which was a way of teaching the blind to read. She was determined to investigate that. Beth had an active, inquiring mind. She lacked only the will and the incentive to use it.

"Good afternoon, Mrs. Hawthorne, Miss Hawthorne. That's a lovely tablecloth, isn't it?"

Maya turned to face the shopkeeper. "Good afternoon, Mr. Gilbertson. The texture is indeed lovely, but the color is a bit bold for Mr. Hawthorne's needs. Do you have the same cloth in eggshell white?"

Mr. Gilbertson excused himself and went to search his stock without a glance at the other customers who patiently were waiting to buy a packet of needles or a bit of candy. Maya watched the owner's efforts on her behalf with an uneasy combination of amusement and bitterness. She was no different than she had been two months before, yet the same shopkeepers who would have ignored her then couldn't wait upon her quickly enough now. All that had changed was money. She now had the means to put her mother's teachings to work.

What a pity that you're dead, Mama. You thought I would never use all those things you taught me about proper comportment for a lady. Would you be happy to see me now? Would it soothe you to know that I didn't repeat your passionate error?

"Here you are, Mrs. Hawthorne. 'Tis not exactly the same weave, but 'tis close as you'll come this side of San Francisco."

"Beth?"

The girl needed no more urging. She patted air until she found the cloth then ran her fingertip over it.

"It's . . . all right."

The lack of enthusiasm was apparent.

"The color is excellent," Maya said to the merchant. "We'll take this and the red one as well. It will look quite festive on the sideboard at Christmas."

And if Hale objected, Maya quietly vowed to make the cloth into a coverlet for Beth's bed. There was no reason that Beth shouldn't be surrounded in her own room by textures that pleased her rather than colors that pleased someone else.

As the merchant took the purchases and wrapped them, Maya drew a deep breath and relaxed. The tablecloth was the last in a seemingly endless stream of details that had to be taken care of for the coming party. Taking Beth along had tripled the time needed to do errands, but Maya hadn't had the heart to leave the girl alone in her bedroom, her blind eyes staring toward the window as she waited to hear footsteps approaching her door. Hale had alternately spoiled and ignored Beth so thoroughly that she had no idea of how to care for herself. Will had done what he could when he was at home, but it hadn't been enough. Beth needed a gentle, firm, consistent influence in her life.

And, in any case, Maya doubted that Will would ever live under his father's roof again. At least, she hoped that he wouldn't. Memories of that forbidden afternoon were hard enough to cope with. She didn't know how she would be able to face him again. What she had permitted him to do had been very wrong . . . and unspeakably beautiful.

"Is there anything else you would like to look at?" Mr. Gilbertson asked Maya as he handed over the neatly wrapped parcel.

"No, thank you. If you'll bring me the bill...?"

"Thank *you*, Mrs. Hawthorne, but you needn't bother your pretty head over such things. It's all taken care of. Your husband told me personally that I was to put whatever you wanted on his account."

You needn't bother. It's all taken care of.

The words went through Maya like wind through a forest, stirring everything. Just a week ago she had gone to Hale with real trepidation; the food for the party that he had requested had come to more than thirty dollars. In addition there had been the cost of new clothes for Beth and herself, hiring extra help, replacing worn linens.... The list had been endless, but Hale had simply glanced over it, told her to order boots and heavy coats as well and to give thought to new drapes in the dining room; then he had gone back to the mill accounts without a word for the money she would spend.

In the past few days Maya had seen more than a hundred dollars pass through her hands, and she still hadn't ordered drapes. One hundred dollars. That was more money than she had spent in her entire life, and Hale had dismissed it as unworthy of his attention.

When Maya stepped out onto the boardwalk, she discovered to her delight that the late afternoon drizzle had given way to sunshine that was as thin as gold leaf. The air shimmered with light and moisture.

"Oh, it feels so very beautiful," Beth said, turning her face in the direction of the sun with unerring certainty. "Is it?"

The girl's intense sensual pleasure reminded Maya painfully of herself and Will. Beth, at least, would be spared the Janus-faced knowledge of sex. Though her father was wealthy, her blindness made it unlikely that she would find a man willing to marry her.

"Yes," Maya said huskily, touching one of the long, cool locks of Beth's hair. It was precisely the color of pale sunlight. "It's very beautiful. Come now, Mouse, the buggy is near."

Maya guided Beth's feet and hands as she mounted the buggy. The vehicle had been the major barrier to taking her out of the house; in the past, Will or Hale had always carried Beth into, over or around such obstacles. Once she had realized that learning to get in and out of the buggy was all that was preventing her from accompanying Maya on trips, Beth had stopped pouting and mastered the buggy step very quickly.

Handling the gentle horse was no problem for Maya, who had driven a reluctant mule through wet fields. It was much nicer to ride through Eureka's streets, though they were equally muddy. The lumbermen's clothes and shop windows were colorful in the autumn sun, and the pungence of sawdust drifted on the air.

As they passed the Logger's Emporium, Maya saw in the window a waxed yellow linen slicker. She wondered whether Will had one like it, and if he had worn it for the last two weeks to turn aside the chilly rains of autumn. The thought of his powerful body burning up with consumption or fever brought on by an extended chill made Maya's hands clench helplessly on the reins. Disease was so insidious, so deadly. She had seen it waste her father's life by inches; she knew what sickness and malnutrition could do to even the strongest boy. Will didn't know, any more than he knew how horrible it was to watch children who depended upon you go cold and hungry.

But she knew. She knew so much more than he did about the cruel decisions life forced upon people.

As the horse trotted through town, a cold wind off Humboldt Bay swirled up suddenly, wrapping the sun in gray clouds. Rain spattered down, randomly at first, then with a chill steadiness that made Maya bow her head and silently thank God and Hale Hawthorne for the good wool coat that she wore and for the warm house that awaited her at the end of the muddy road.

The flickering light of a dozen lamps threw shadows on the paneled walls of the Hawthorne dining room. The civilized tones of a violin quivered sweetly above the discreet clatter of china and silver and the mingled conversations of a dozen of Eureka's leading citizens as they ate sliced beef, roast Canada goose and a tenderloin of Roosevelt elk. More than a week of concerted effort on Maya's part had transformed the lower floor of the house into a home where furniture gleamed with polish and dusty corners were no longer overlooked by indifferent hired help who knew that Hale Hawthorne was too busy to worry about the fine points of housecleaning. Rugs had been beaten, drapes aired, silverware and lamps polished, sachets tucked into drawers, fresh lace coverlets laid out; everything proclaimed that a new and very careful mistress was in charge of the Hawthorne house.

Beth had been coaxed and lured into every aspect of the housecleaning. She might not have been able to see dust, but she had a keen nose for mustiness and fingertips that were very sensitive to the presence of dirt or grease. Because she had worked so hard, Maya had quietly insisted that Beth be allowed to share the social hour before the dinner actually began. Hale had objected until Maya had pointed out that Beth would never have any confidence in herself if she were locked away in her room whenever visitors came. She was a lovely girl whom any father would be delighted to display. In fact, it was a requirement for girls of her age and station to make brief appearances in adult situations. In the end Hale had given in with more pleasure than irritation; he was more than happy to leave baffling domestic and social matters in Maya's capable hands.

Looking as fragile as a porcelain angel in the white wool dress Maya had chosen for her, Beth had stood with Maya and Hale as the guests were greeted. The young girl's cheeks had glowed with pride as everyone complimented her father on her loveliness. When it had come time to go to her own room, Beth had been as reluctant to leave as she initially had been to be a part of the gathering. She went with a smile instead of a pout because she knew that Maya had left the tactile beauty of the red cloth across her bed as a reward.

While Beth learned not to be frightened of people, Maya made a concerted effort to draw out the wives who were married to Hale's fellow businessmen. She knew instinctively that people would rather talk about their own interests than hear about someone else's, so talking to the women wasn't difficult. Before the dessert was finished and the men withdrew for brandy and cigars, many of the women had decided that Hale wasn't as foolish as he had appeared to be in so hastily marrying such a young woman. She was modest, attentive and of excellent manners.

Hale watched Maya charm the women and listen gravely to the men. The dress that she had chosen for herself was dark, almost severe, and she wore no jewelry but the gold wedding band. Despite her youth and the beauty that made men nod to Hale in silent congratulations, Maya looked every inch the decent Christian woman that Hale believed her to be.

"A lovely, lovely girl," said Arthur Kroeber, as Hale shut the door to the den behind the men.

"Yes, Beth is turning into quite a beauty," Hale agreed.

"I was referring to Mrs. Hawthorne."

"My wife is not a girl."

"A fine thing that you remarried," Mr. O'Hara said quickly, heading off a confrontation between Hale and Kroeber. "Beth is at that tender age when girls need a womanly influence about them."

"Exactly my thoughts," Hale said. "Beth's welfare and my need of a hostess were foremost in my mind when I married Mrs. Hawthorne.

Kroeber grunted, unimpressed by Hale's high-minded reasons for marrying a beautiful girl.

Hale hid a smile. As one of his biggest competitors in Eureka logging, Kroeber had been invited for the sole purpose of showing Maya off to him. Kroeber's wife was sour, dowdy and every bit as old as Kroeber's fifty years. Hale knew that pride was a sin, but he hoped that the Lord would forgive the pride that he took in his young wife's beauty.

"I hear that Willy is out timber cruising," O'Hara said, throwing out the one conversational lure that no one in the room could ignore: lumber.

Hale looked at the glowing end of his cigar and said quietly, "Damn fool waste of time, haring off into the woods when I've got more Hawthorne timber than I can cut right in my back yard."

Hale's voice was cold enough that looks went around the room and men nodded silently to one another. Will's absence at the wedding had been one of the two questions that everyone tonight had wanted to ask but hadn't dared. Obviously father and son weren't on speaking terms at the moment. No one was particularly surprised. They had watched Hale ride roughshod over his son for years, and they had also watched Will's resentment grow.

"Ach, don't be too hard on the lad," O'Hara said. "Young men and fathers are forever fighting. 'Tis as natural as the rising and the setting of the sun."

"Anyway, you needn't worry," Kroeber put in smoothly. "The boy will be no competition. He still hasn't learned the hard facts of milling. He's way off in Yurok country, where the trees are twenty feet through the butt. Pretty enough to look at, I suppose, but useless as teats on a boar hog when it comes to turning timber into lumber. And money."

A faint stain of color showed on Hale's cheekbones. It was one thing for him to criticize his own son. It was quite another for Kroeber to do so.

"Willy's a dogger in my mill," Hale said curtly. "He knows just how thick a log we can handle."

"Then why is he camped on a river bench where the trees are three hundred feet tall? Have you discovered a way to mill those giants?"

Hale heard the sudden silence in the room. Every man knew that logging would be revolutionized if there was some economical way of felling, hauling and milling the big trees. Timber land that was now worthless would suddenly be valued in the hundreds of thousands of dollars, perhaps even in the millions.

"Ask Willy," Hale said in a cold tone. "He's the one out there, not me."

"I'd rather ask you a different question," Kroeber said. "Why haven't you joined the California Redwood Miller's Association?"

There was an uneasy stirring in the assembled men. That was the second question that the other men had wanted to have answered tonight, but not one of them had had the nerve or power to ask it. Kroeber had plenty of both.

"I don't like anyone telling me where and when to sell my lumber." Hale's narrowed gray eyes glanced from man to man as though he were counting and memorizing each face. "If I want to fill six schooners with lumber and send them to San Francisco, then, by the Lord God, that's just what I'll do—and no Johnny-come-lately from Wisconsin is going to tell me different!"

"The Association doesn't want to prevent you from selling lumber. On the contrary. We want you to sell as many board feet as you can at the highest possible price." Kroeber swirled his brandy and looked Hale right in the eye. "If you would simply wait thirty days to send those schooners, the price of lumber at the docks in San Francisco, Honolulu and Sydney would double."

"Undoubtedly. That doesn't make it a proper thing to do."

"Proper." Kroeber looked at his brandy and repeated the word again. "Proper. Tell me, Mr. Hawthorne, just what is improper about a businessman maximizing his profits through a trade association?"

"There is a difference between shrewd business and highway robbery. It's a difference that you Lake State lumbermen don't seem to understand. I will attempt to explain what should be apparent to any God-fearing man. If there are no trees, then the price of lumber will be very dear indeed. If there are many trees, then the price of lumber will be set by the demand for lumber. That is God's way. Withholding lumber to artificially inflate the price is not only immoral, it is stupid. Your short-term gains would be great, I grant you. In the long term, however, you would have doomed our logging industry. What we refuse to cut in Eureka, others will cut elsewhere. Then where will we be?"

"Other lumbermen all over the state—all over the West itself—will be brought into the association. When all of them are in and you are not, where will *you* be?"

"Here, just as I am now, cutting timber for an honest living at an honest wage." Hale sipped his brandy and then looked around the room once more. "Each must follow his own conscience, gentlemen. That, too, is God's way."

"You seem quite familiar with God's way," Kroeber said sardonically.

"More so than you appear to be, certainly."

There was a moment of uncomfortable silence before the men began talking among themselves about less explosive topics. Hale watched and listened in apparent serenity, but beneath his calm expression his mind was working very quickly. Kroeber didn't have the power to create the association without Hale, but that wouldn't remain true forever. The small mills couldn't compete with Hale's board-foot prices unless they banded together into one large miller's association. The only reason that the small mills had survived at all was that Hale's mill simply couldn't process enough timber to meet the demand for lumber.

If the demand were to fall suddenly, the small mills would be out of business. Some men were farsighted enough to know that. It was those men who were most eager to join the association, because a share of whatever market existed would be guaranteed to them as association members. In time all mill owners would realize that either expansion or association was the key to long-term survival.

When Kroeber finally succeeded in organizing the local lumbermen, Hale would then be in the position that the small mills were in now; he wouldn't be able to survive unless he joined the association. His only choice was to expand now, while he still could, and to keep on expanding until he was simply too big for the association to swallow. For that he would need cash— a lot of it. Part of the money could be borrowed from the local bank. The rest would have to come from San Francisco, which meant that he must plan to spend a long period of time in the city itself, courting bankers and builders, assuring Tres Santos Lumber of both cash and new markets for the greater amount of product he would have to sell.

But first, before he expanded, he had to ensure that he left his wife pregnant with a son who would be worthy of inheriting his father's redwood empire.

That thought brought a stirring to Hale's loins. Having Maya's lush young body beneath him in bed had made him feel more a man than he had in years.

Unlike his first wife, Maya hadn't cried bitterly and cringed against her duty. Maya had accepted her role in his bed with a fortitude that made him both humble and proud of his choice in a wife. She was industrious and intelligent as well. He was very grateful that she had found an acceptable means of making an embarrassingly awkward act easier for her and for him as well, and he was doubly grateful that the oil did not offend propriety even though its gliding lubrication certainly increased his pleasure.

He glanced sideways at the gilt clock and sighed. It would be several hours before he would be free to force himself into Maya's tight, oiled sheath and leave his seed within.

Maya's eyes were tightly closed, her hands clenched at her sides as she lay motionless, fighting silently with her own body, knowing that if she could just relax she would spare herself much of the pain. Above her Hale chanted reassurances as his hips churned with greater speed and force until his words ran into one another and became meaningless. Maya knew it wouldn't be long now. The realization was such a relief that her body loosened somewhat, making Hale's final frantic thrusts less painful for her. Finally he collapsed on her, breathing heavily, his hands gripping her breasts. She endured it for a few moments longer before she shifted her weight, silently urging him to roll off her and retire to his own room.

The sound of the front door closing downstairs came as a shock.

"Maya, Father? I'm home!"

Suddenly Maya could bear Hale's touch no more. She pushed against him so hard that he grunted in surprise.

"I hear him, lass. I hear him."

Reluctantly, with far more than the necessary amount of sliding and pressing, Hale separated himself from Maya. As he left the bed, he heard her pull the covers up to her chin, though she of course hadn't removed her long nightgown when he had come to her bed. He approved her modesty even as he secretly wished that he could see her naked in full light, just once. But that would be an improper thing to ask of his wife and the future mother of his children.

Hale was halfway out the door before he realized that he hadn't rearranged his pajamas. He shut the door behind himself, tucked his still-turgid flesh out of sight and started down the hall. Only then did he see his son.

Will was staring at him with an expression of horror.

"What were you doing in Maya's bedroom?"

Will's voice was low, hoarse, shaking with emotion. He closed his eyes frantically, but he could not banish the image of his father's sex thrusting through the pajama fly.

Hale brushed past his son and started downstairs.

"What were you doing!"

"Lower your voice, Willy. Your stepmother is trying to sleep."

With a feeling of chilling unreality, Will watched his father's thick body vanish down the stairway. After a few moments Will turned and ran after him, his boots drumming hollowly on the stairway. Hale had gone into the den. He was lighting a cigar with slow satisfaction when Will flung the door fully open.

A single look at Hale's face made Will's stomach turn over with rage and sickness. He had seen that heavy-lidded, flushed look of satisfaction before, when he had stumbled over his father coming out of a whore's room above the Stock Exchange. When Will had returned home, the resulting argument between father and son had so frightened Beth that she had run from her bedroom into the darkened hallway and from there to the stairs. She had tripped, fallen headlong and awakened blind.

"My stepmother," Will said carefully, unable to believe the extent of his father's treachery. And Maya's. *It couldn't be what it seemed,* he assured himself wildly. *Maya couldn't shed her virgin's blood in my embrace one day and then marry my father the next!* "May I ask your new wife's name?"

"Maya Charters Hawthorne." Hale looked at the color leave his son's face and felt curiously triumphant. He realized in that moment just how much he had resented growing old while his son grew in physical prowess. "You look surprised, Willy. Did you think that she couldn't see past a comely face and a charming manner to the improvident boy within? She knows the value of a warm coat and a secure roof over her head."

"So does a whore."

Hale's openhanded slap rocked Will, but he made no attempt to retaliate for the simple reason that he felt no pain. He knew it was there, deep inside his gut, and with it a hot tongue of fury burning up through his icy disbelief.

And he also knew that if he gave into pain and rage he wouldn't be able to stop himself from killing his father.

"I've seen you look at her with a boy's sly lust," Hale continued, his gray eyes blazing. "If I see it again I will horsewhip you until your very bones bleed. Do you hear me, Willy? Do you? Answer me, boy!"

Will said nothing, knowing only that he must get out, get away from the sight and sound of his father, and he must do it *now*.

Moments later a raw cry of rage and betrayal was torn from Will's throat as he ran out of the house and into the night. Maya heard the cry and screamed as though a knife had been driven into her body. But no one heard the scream, for she had turned her head into the pillows; she would have suffocated rather than let a sound escape.

Will ran on foot into the cold Eureka night, but no matter how fast he went he couldn't outrun the demon growing inside him. Even when each breath sounded and felt as though it were sawing him in half, he still ran on, trying to understand what had happened. His father's betrayal came as no particular surprise; it seemed that everywhere Will had turned in the past few years, his father was already there, forbidding him to go any farther toward manhood. Some fathers rejoiced in their son's accomplishments. Hale did not. In fact, he seemed to resent anything that Will did.

Yet his father's jealousy didn't explain Maya's treachery, Maya's betrayal. She had given herself to Will with a hot, sweet sensuality that could inflame him even in memory. He hadn't believed that she would turn and sell herself to another man for money.

The fact of a wedding ring made it no less of a sale and Maya no less of a whore.

Yet even that wasn't the worst of it. The worst was that Maya had so lacked faith in Will's worth as a man that she wouldn't marry him, wouldn't trust him to be able to support her and their children. He had loved her, and she had turned her back on him because she believed him to be a child.

A hard rain was falling before Will stumbled into the clutter of Indian shacks and sweat houses that sprawled on the mud flats east of the mills. Ising and three other Yuroks sat beside a fire of bark scalings and mill scrap, drinking from a crockery pot of whiskey. The fire was so smoky that the air would have been unbreathable were it not for the lack of chinking between the badly cut boards in the shanty walls.

Ising's cheeks had begun to flush with drink, but he had no trouble reading the wildness in Will's eyes. The Yurok didn't know what was wrong. He did know that Will was on the edge of explosion. It was a feeling that Ising understood for the simple reason that he, too, sometimes felt as though life were an elaborate joke played on man by cruel gods. The only permanent cure for that knowledge was death. Men, however, were not entirely stupid; they had invented an interim measure, a palliative for the times when the joke became unbearable.

Ising dangled the whiskey crock from one blunt finger. "Your people invented this stuff. Looks like you just figured out why. Here, maybe whiskey will treat you better than it does Indians."

With an abrupt, savage gesture, Will yanked out the cork and took a slug of liquid fire. He had drunk whiskey before, but the rawness of this made him gasp. Without hesitating he took another drink and then one more. Shuddering with the impact of the crude alcohol, he hammered the cork back in and handed the crock over to Ising.

"If you don't like it, why do you drink it?" Will asked.

"Ask me when I'm sober. I drink to forget why I'm drinking."

Ising uncorked the crock, drank and passed the container around. When it got back to Will there was nothing left but eye-searing fumes.

"Bastard's empty. Let's go have a real drink."

"This is as real as anyone needs," Ising said.

A breeze swirled through the chinks and pulled a streamer of choking smoke around Will's head.

"Then let's at least find someplace to drink where we won't be smoked like gutted salmon!"

With a sigh Ising looked at his young friend. The alcohol had done nothing to dilute Will's fury. It was there in his eyes, burning like sun behind morning mist.

"Will, this is the only place in town where an Indian can drink."

"What about the Humboldt House?"

Ising closed his eyes and wondered if he had been praying to the wrong gods. When he looked again at Will, he decided that Will's gods hadn't done very well by him, either. Ising sighed again.

"The Humboldt House. Friend, you're really hurting for it, aren't you? You walk into the Humboldt feeling the way you do, and one of the timber beasts would eat you alive even if you were alone. With a half-breed at your side, you'll bring down the house. Besides, most of the men in the Humboldt work for your father. In case you haven't noticed, your father's not the most popular mill boss in Eureka lately. You're going to hear a lot of names being called."

Will's eyes narrowed. "That's no skin off my ass. If I could, I'd trade my father for a dog and shoot the dog. But I'd a hell of a lot rather shoot *him*."

With that, Will spun on his heel.

"Where are you going?" Ising asked.

There was no answer.

"Well, shit," Ising said in disgust. He heaved himself to his feet and caught up with Will before he got out the door.

"You don't have to come," Will said curtly.

"If you can't get crimped or killed with a friend, what's the use of having one?" Ising looked sideways at his young companion. Only Will didn't look young anymore. His eyes were bleak, and fury had etched deep lines in his face, drawing it like a death's mask. "Will? Can I ask you something?"

"As long as it doesn't have anything to do with what happened after I left you tonight, yes."

"If I get killed, promise me you'll bury me in Black Basin, okay?"

"You said that wasn't Yurok country."

"It isn't. I'd just like to think my death had some meaning, if only by inconveniencing you. Be hard as hell to haul a stiff all the way into Black Basin."

Will smiled grimly. "My pleasure."

"You want to be buried at home?"

"I don't have a home."

Ising was silent the rest of the way to the Humboldt House.

Two bouncers the size of professional prizefighters stood watch at the door of the saloon. They eyed the

young white man and the Indian who pushed through
the double swinging doors into the smoky, raucous
saloon. Ising saw one of the bouncers, a square-built
man with arms as thick as the lower branches of a
Douglas Fir, start toward them as though to block
their way.

The bouncer's partner, a head taller and just as sol-
idly built, stopped him. They glanced toward the center table, where the Humboldt's manager, a gambler
named Shanker, sat playing cards and overseeing the
nightly action. Shanker didn't recognize either of the
young men at the door. He measured their size, their
strength and their youth, nodded almost impercepti-
bly and went back to cheating at cards. The two
bouncers withdrew, opening the way for the newcom-
ers to walk to the bar.

Will was too caught within the coils of his own fury
to notice the exchange of looks. Ising was not.
Shanker's nod had made Ising more uneasy than if
they had been thrown out. He tried to steer Will to the
quiet end of the one-hundred-foot bar, but to no avail.
Will had picked out a place right in the center of the
action. There he would drink and nowhere else.

The Saturday crowd was little different in size or
drunkenness from that of any other day of the week.
The Humboldt House was like the sea and the forest;
the bar was open for business twenty-four hours a day,
seven days a week, three hundred and sixty-five days
a year. The saloon dispensed a continuous flow of
crude alcohol, crude women and crudely rigged card
games. The long bar was scarred from fights and
stained by spilled drinks that had eaten through var-
nish to the wood beneath. The floor by the bar consisted of eight-inch planks of solid fir which were so

chewed up by logger's calk boots that after six months even those tough, thick planks had to be replaced.

The air in the saloon was even worse than in the shack on the mud flats. The only attempts at decoration were long mirrors behind the bar and a half-dozen fading prints of languid, nude women in what were presumably enticing poses. Ising purposely steered his glance away from the nudes; he had already caught several hard looks from white men who were surprised to find an Indian drinking in their midst. Ising had no desire to enrage anyone's racial sensibilities by leering at portraits of white women, especially white women who were about as attractive as the ass end of a pig.

The bartender had a bald head and a flourishing waxed moustache. He glanced once at Shanker, who nodded without looking up from his cards. The bartender turned and looked at Will with absolute disinterest.

"What'll it be?"

"Whiskey, two glasses," Will said. He bounced a silver dollar across the bar.

The bartender fielded the dollar and reached beneath the bar for a plain glass bottle filled with brown fluid. He turned, pulled two shot glasses off the shelf beneath the mirror, set them on the bar next to the bottle and walked away to serve another customer. The only sign of any displeasure came in the fact that the bartender performed the whole series of actions without once looking at Henry Ising.

Will poured two shots from the bottle and gave Ising a look of triumph before shooting down the glass of whiskey. It was even worse than the stuff in the crock had been, but Will forced himself to swallow without coughing. No matter how raw and how hot, the crude drink was not a patch on the demon burning within him.

Ising looked down the bar. There were a few other Indians present, but they were at the far end of the bar where no one would notice. They were also Miwoks, a tribe that had learned its place and stayed there. With an inner sigh Ising looked at the cloudy brown whiskey awaiting him. He knew that he shouldn't have any more, because if it came to a fight—and he had little doubt that it would—he wanted to be able to give a good account of himself.

So he watched the shot glass in front of him as though it were about to explode, but did not touch it.

Will poured himself another shot and sipped at it, grimacing over the taste. "Drink up, Henry. It's not that much worse than what was in the crock."

Ising looked up and down the bar. No one seemed to have the least bit of interest in them. That made him feel even more uneasy than if there had been murmurs of anger about pushy half-breeds drinking with their betters. Having a feeling that he would regret it, Ising reached out, lifted the glass, and knocked back the whiskey in an open-throated gulp. There was a bitterness to the drink that made him grimace.

The glass had no sooner been set on the bar when Will filled it again. Ising looked at his friend's eyes. Nothing had changed. Raw red hell still stared out, waiting only for the excuse to be released. Ising shrugged and sipped at his whiskey again. The oily bitterness was still there, but Ising no longer cared. A heavy warmth was pervading his body.

Suddenly Will shook his head. He could still feel a clear flame of rage burning, but it was as though he were experiencing it through the wrong end of a spyglass. Distant. Remote.

"Hi there, sweetie. How about a drink for me?"

Will turned to look at the bar girl who had appeared out of nowhere to stand beside him. She was a big, sturdy female with a square, heavily rouged face and a body that was squirming farther out of her low-cut dress with every breath. Suddenly he remembered the whore he had seen his father with three years before, and then the moment three hours ago when he had seen his father coming out of Maya's room looking heavy and sated.

"Me, too," said a fat Mexican girl in a dirty calico wrapper. She carefully readjusted the wrapper in such a way as to momentarily reveal the huge brown disk of her left nipple. After that she smiled up at Ising, showing off her gold eyetooth. "Buy me a drink, han'some?"

Something began to rub against Will's leg. He looked down and saw the first bar girl sliding her hip up and down against him. He opened his mouth to tell her to go away, he didn't want her, but no sound came out. His tongue lay in his mouth as though it were so much meat cut from a haunch of venison. He tried to turn back toward Ising. The movement threw Will off balance. He sagged against the bar. After an effort he managed to turn his head enough to see Ising was being propped up by the surprisingly strong Mexican whore. Only then did Will realize that he was being propped up as well. The woman had hands as rough and strong as a logger's. He looked straight ahead into the bartender's eyes. The man looked back with as much emotion as a snake.

"Don' wan' her," Will said, trying to pull free of the whore's grasp.

Shanker appeared behind Will and stepped smoothly into the increasing gap that was forming between Will and the rest of the bar's patrons.

"We'll have no disturbances in here." Shanker glanced at the bartender and nodded very slightly. The man vanished for a moment, then reappeared with his right hand held behind his back. "You boys are pretty drunk," Shanker said matter-of-factly. "The girls will take you to a place where you can sleep it off. Ned! Jimbo! Help Fanny with these boys."

As the two bouncers came toward Will and Ising, the crowd at the bar melted back without ever actually looking at what was happening. Suddenly Ising threw off the Mexican woman's hands, grabbed Will and tried to propel him toward the front door. The bartender leaned forward and brought a pump handle down on the back of Ising's head. Will turned but it was too late. The cold iron caught him over the ear. He went down without a sound.

As one, the bar girls bent and went through Will's pockets. They started fighting over his money. Shanker hit one with his fist and kicked the other. They ran off to the back of the saloon, where they nursed their bruises and counted the small change they had stolen. Shanker looked at the bouncers.

"Take 'em. A few months at sea will teach these boys not to drink with men."

Book Two

1874

Chapter Nine

"I like to keep plenty of water between St. George
Reef and my keel," said the burly, red-faced captain
of the steam schooner *Farallon*. "This coastline looks
lovely and green but it can kill you quicker than a
knife. St. George's rocks stole one hundred and sixty-
six souls off the *Jonathan* ten years ago this month."

Captain Olmstead stood just forward of the huge,
polished wheel, his feet planted firmly on the deck and
his glance moving restlessly across the calm ocean; the
constant, searching eyes and wide-footed stance were
the result of a lifetime at sea rather than of any anxiety about the ship's fate at the moment. The captain
was quite relaxed. He had been talking around the
stem of his pipe for more than an hour, reeling off the
coastal landmarks and describing their dangers, but
his audience of one showed no signs of becoming
bored.

Indeed, although the captain had no way of knowing it, Will Hawthorne was comparing the coastline of
today with his memories of it as he had seen it on a day
five years before, when he had awakened with a head
that felt as though an ax had been buried in it and had

seen the land of his birth slipping away astern. The coastline hadn't changed markedly since that day.

Will Hawthorne had. No one looking at him today would guess that he was only twenty-two; nor would anyone attempt to slip him a drugged drink. In fact, any man who looked into Will's eyes today wouldn't attempt to antagonize Will in any way at all.

"Have they replaced the light at Crescent City yet?" Will asked idly. "The old one used to be more of a danger than the rocks themselves."

Olmstead paused and took the pipe from his mouth. "You sound as though you know the redwood coast. I thought you were a stranger or I wouldn't have been running off at the mouth about the people and the coastline for nigh onto an hour."

Cold gray eyes studied the captain for an instant before shifting back to the ragged line where sea met land.

"I've been away for a long time."

"Been at sea, have you?" Olmstead asked, lighting his pipe with a sulfur match and drawing hard.

"Do I have the look of a sailor?"

"Not in your clothes. From that very handsome wool suit, I'd say you were a businessman or a gambler. But you stand the deck like a sailor and keep watch around you like a first mate."

Will's faint smile was as cold as his eyes. He watched constantly, yes, but not because he had been trained as a first mate. In the places he had been, men who weren't alert weren't alive for long.

"I was a sailor once," Will said softly. "Never a very good one, nor a willing one. A friend and I were drinking whiskey one night and woke up in the hold of a four-masted bark headed south around the horn for England."

"Lots of plowboys, loggers and loafers had the same experience," Olmstead said, nodding. "Some of them turned into pretty good sailors, too."

"I held my own. I sure as hell earned the twenty dollars a month the captain paid us when we finally hove to in the estuary of the Thames. Sixty dollars for three months of our lives, eating moldy salt pork and hard bread with weevils in it."

Though the words were harsh, there was no real bitterness in Will's voice. He had been stupid, and he had paid for it. That was the way life was. Whining wouldn't change reality. Being stronger, quicker and meaner than the next man would change it, however. Will had learned that lesson in some of the most brutal places on earth. He had learned it very well. There was little of emotion or mercy left in him.

"At least you were paid," Olmstead said. "A lot of captains who crimp their crews just dump the boys ashore at the other end without a penny to their name."

"He tried. He had a change of heart."

"Heard the voice of God, did he?"

"In a manner of speaking."

Will looked at his hands. They were rough, hard, scarred—and some of those scars had come from catching the captain ashore and beating every last penny out of him and his scabrous first mate.

"Five years, eh? You spend them in England, if you don't mind me asking?"

"My friend and I signed onto another ship, but this time voluntarily. We spent another two years before the mast. We set anchor in every port in the world from China to South America. Then my partner came back here, and I went on by myself. I stayed in Seattle, working in Henry Yesler's mill and cruising timber."

Olmstead nodded. "I know that part of the Pacific Northwest pretty well. We've hauled lots of Yesler's lumber out of Puget Sound. That country's still a touch rougher than Eureka. The lowland timber's about gone, down here. I understand Hale Hawthorne's thinking about borrowing money to build a logging railroad to open up the inland country."

"Yes. That's why I'm here."

"You a railroad man?"

"I'm whatever I have to be."

A puff of smoke escaped as Olmstead removed the pipe, examined the stem as though for flaws and replaced the stem in his mouth. He had seen many a hard man shuttling up and down the coast, but the man watching the shore with eyes the color of ice was well beyond the common run. Olmstead hesitated, then gave a mental shrug. If the stranger didn't want to talk, he could just turn around and walk away.

"In fact, Hale Hawthorne just built a fancy new house and moved his family into it," the captain continued. "Quite a showplace, I'm told. Built with redwood. That's a shrewd man, the kind of man we need out here. If it wasn't for him, some of the mills would have banded together and driven the price of lumber right out of sight, and driven ships like this one right out of business as well. Yes, Mr. Hawthorne might be a hard man, but he's honest and farseeing."

Will thought of his father walking out of Maya's bedroom. Had Hale foreseen that that night ultimately would bring his ruin? Because it would. Will had looked forward to that ruin for every minute of the last five, hellish years.

"Do you know Mr. Hawthorne well?" Will asked softly.

"I've met him several times on the run from Eureka to San Francisco," Olmstead said. "Big man, odd color eyes, strong face. You look a lot like him."

"I'm his son."

There was a long silence broken only by the creak of rigging.

"Odd," Olmstead said finally. "He only talked about his daughters. Three of them. One is blind, I take it?"

"Beth. My sister. The others ... well, I suppose they're my sisters, too. Half sisters."

For an instant the icy control Will kept over himself slipped, revealing the demon living deep within his soul. Olmstead saw the darkness beneath the ice and looked away quickly while gooseflesh stood on his arms as though at a chill. For several minutes the captain examined the spray cloud from the rocks of St. George Reef as though he expected the reef to set sail on a collision course with the *Farallon* at any moment.

"I would consider it a personal favor if you didn't mention my presence to anyone," Will said, turning and looking at the captain. "And I am a man who remembers such favors."

Olmstead glanced at Will's eyes and then away quickly. "Of course. A man's business is his own, I always say."

"You're a wise man, Captain."

Will watched the sea and the land in silence, holding memories at bay by sheer determination, allowing only useful facts to surface. He had had a lot of practice at that, at suppressing emotions and letting only what was needed filter through; the best way to set ax to tree, the best way to bet a poor poker hand, the best way to kill or survive, the best way to ruin an enemy whom you could not kill. Those were the things that it was worth remembering. All else was worse than useless.

It had cost five years of his life and all of the softness in him, but he had learned. Now it was time to put everything he had learned to work in the service of the demon within.

Will pulled out his spyglass and scanned the shoreline carefully as he had done throughout the trip. Signs of logging had increased since the ship had passed Trinidad Head. Everywhere it had been the same story: the biggest trees had been left behind. A handful of towering old redwoods and Douglas firs stood like lonesome monarchs above the slash and stumps of recent logging. From time to time there would be the shattered hulk of a big tree, epitaph to a giant felled by loggers and then dynamited in an attempt to split the trunk into manageable pieces. It rarely worked. Usually the dynamite blast blew the trunk into a useless stack of kindling. In Northern California, as in Seattle, the lumber industry was still struggling within the size limits imposed by rotary head-saw rigs and the hauling power of oxen.

Once the sight of uselessly felled monarchs would have saddened Will. Now it merely gave him a foretaste of triumph. His years in Seattle had taught him the strengths and weak points of the lumber business as it existed there. The industry was the same here, and his father was the same. Nothing had changed but Will himself.

And that was the trap into which his father would blindly stumble. He would believe his son still to be the biddable boy who had done nothing more than run away from the scene of betrayal.

As the ship shot through the channel into the bay, Will realized how much Eureka had grown. Buildings swept up from the shoreline like a solid wave that broke only in the distance, where the forest still rose in ranks of green. Fishing boats were mixed among the lumber and cargo boats. New wharves had been built, and ships were tied up while cargo was loaded or unloaded with the controlled frenzy that bespoke money to be made if only enough ships could be wedged into the bay and then sent on again quickly, holds filled with new cargo.

Once ashore Will walked through the waterfront, ignoring the coarse women leaning in doorways, calling to him. He had learned to control his sexuality with the same ruthlessness that he had learned to control every other aspect of his personality. Loss of control had cost him five years of his life. He would never lose control again.

The hotel he chose was newly built, yet close enough to the waterfront that the desk clerk neither asked nor answered questions about the guests. Will took a room, changed into the rough logger's clothes he had carried in a leather grip and went back to the waterfront again with his suitcase still in hand. Anyone who had seen the well-dressed man enter the hotel would have been astonished at his transformation. Despite his clean-shaven face Will looked as rough as any man on the waterfront.

He quickly found a small waterfront tavern that served fishermen, sailors and loggers alike. Even at midday, there were a handful of drinkers at the short bar—a salmon fisherman, a cashiered timber beast catching up on his drinking and two bullwhackers killing time while their teams were being outfitted by the local blacksmith.

Will dumped his satchel in a corner where he could keep an eye on it and went to the bar. He disliked alcohol but had trained himself to drink it, because there were times and places where a man who didn't drink wouldn't be trusted. This was one of those times and definitely one of those places. He ordered a neat whiskey, tasted it for drugs, found none and tossed back the drink with a flick of his hand. He ordered another whiskey, turned to survey the bar's occupants and calmly announced that he'd buy for the house.

Within fifteen minutes he had become the drinkers' best friend. Within an hour he knew exactly which areas around Eureka were being logged and which were not, which companies were hiring and which were laying off, and how far into the mountains around Black Basin Hale Hawthorne's railroad would have to go in search of manageable timber.

"They'll be surveying Yurok country next," said the logger. "Lots of good timber on them upland slopes above Black Basin."

"Black Basin?" Will asked, startled.

"That's what they call it now. First man who claimed a chunk of it named it Black Basin, I guess. Anyways, there's lots of good timber up beyond the basin itself. All a body needs is a way to bring the logs out. River's no good most of the year, even with splash dams, and ox trains are too damn slow. Haw-thorne's got the right idea. Lay track and let a ma-chine do the hauling.''

Will's expression didn't change, but he cursed him-self for not coming back to Eureka sooner. His father had moved very discreetly in planning for the rail-road, because the instant men knew, there would be a rush to claim nearby timber land. If Will hadn't bought up claims himself along the redwood coast in the last three years, he wouldn't have seen the pattern developing. But he had seen it, and he had moved to stalemate his father by buying claims he knew would be vital for a logging railroad's right-of-way. He had also claimed the flats where big trees grew, for he knew that without a yarding area, logging was impossible. If the land he wanted had been unclaimed, Will had paid others to claim it and then resell it to him. Al-though the practice was illegal, it was also so wide-spread that attempts to enforce the homestead laws were futile.

''I've been up that river all the way to the headwa-ters,'' continued the timber beast, a rangy man with a face full of scars that were the loser's trophy in a calk-boot fight. ''Ain't nobody taking up claims above the remnants of that Yurok village that was burned in '67. That's a good ten miles of prime timber, once a man figures out how to get the logs to the mills.''

''Shame to let it all go to waste,'' Will said, pour-ing another round. ''I'd like to invite you gentlemen to join me in claiming land up there. I claimed a piece of Black Basin years ago. I can guarantee you that you'll be well paid for your trouble if you take up claims next to mine.''

One of the bullwhackers spat on the floor, thinking it over, but the other shook his head.

"Mister, we're logging men, not sodbusters. Like as not we'll pull the tit and roll out of here for parts unknown tomorrow or the day after. We sure ain't going to hang around this country long enough to prove up a worthless farming claim in the big trees."

The whacker's partner grinned and spat again. "That's the whole point, though, ain't it, mister? You're trying to pick up a section of timber by getting the four of us to file together. Then you'll buy out our claims."

"But that's spec-u-lation, and it's agin the law," said the first whacker.

Will sipped his whiskey before he said calmly, "It's not illegal for a man to sell his claim if he has a good reason. The law only makes it illegal to stake a claim for the purpose of reselling it."

In silence Will poured another round of drinks and wished to himself that Congress would get off its collective butt and end the claims farce by passing the Timber and Stone Act. Then anyone who wanted to would be permitted to buy timber rights to as much land as he could afford. But Will couldn't wait until Congress got tired of hearing itself talk. By then Hale would have succeeded with his railroad, and the railroad would make him so rich that Will wouldn't be able to touch him for years—if ever.

It had to be done now, while his father was up to his lips in debt, overextended on every front, betting on the outcome.

"A 'good reason,' huh?" The bullwhacker spat. "What's a good reason to sell?"

Will glanced up. "One hundred dollars. Each."

The men looked at each other, tossed back their drinks and hitched up their pants.

"Sounds good enough to me," said the bull-whacker. "Where's this land we're claiming?"

Will got out four pieces of paper and distributed one to each man. Each piece held a different set of claim boundaries. Then Will set out four hundred-dollar gold pieces in front of him on the bar.

"I'll be here when you're finished filing."

As the men left, Will checked his watch. If the men hurried, he would have time to find Henry Ising before dark.

"Get up, you worthless bulls," Henry Ising sang loudly. "Up, *omewimar*."

Ising spoke to the bulls in Yurok, calling them "old ones" and accusing them of being lazy. The brawny bulls responded about as well to Yurok as to any other language, which was to say that they responded well so long as words were followed up with a judicious application of the brass-tipped hickory goad. But Ising used Yurok because it added to what had become his mystique. Even the stiff-necked Swedish and Finnish timber beasts seemed to half believe that Ising was a shaman who had special abilities to communicate with animals.

Secretly that amused Ising. What amused him even more was that the Yuroks seemed to believe it as well. Ising believed that his bulls responded better than other bullwhackers' animals because he made sure that his bulls were fed well, worked hard, but not to exhaustion, and had a dry place to rest at the end of the day. He also had a shrewd eye for temperament. He knew when an animal was lazy and when it was truly lame, when it was shirking and when it was ill, when it was going to balk and when it was merely bluffing. Ising also had a reservoir of affection for the big, patient beasts. As a result he treated them well, and they responded in kind.

In that respect oxen were unlike men. As far as Ising was concerned, most men responded badly no matter how they were treated.

"Up, you worthless ones!"

The eight yoked pairs of oxen stirred themselves. Two of the pairs had flopped down in the warm sunlight of the little meadow beside the skid road and were chewing cud. Two other pairs of oxen stood switching flies for one another at the edge of the woods. None of the oxen had had more than a half-hour break from their arduous work. Despite that, they turned out and lined up in correct order without a beating, to the amazement of the loggers who regularly lined up to view the phenomenon of the oxen and the Yurok shaman. Each day added to Ising's reputation, for each and every day Ising and his team produced thirty percent more work than any other team.

Ising laid the goad across the dusty back of a roan ox named Segep—Coyote. "Move smartly or I'll let them turn your worthless hide into shoes," Ising hollered. "You'll get some of the same, Johnny, unless you get that bucket and start swabbing the skids."

Johnny Ising rolled out of the shadow of a redwood where he had been napping. "Nobody else is going back to work, yet. What's the hurry?"

"You wanted to work for me—so work!"

Johnny sighed. He had thought it would be easier working for his brother than for one of the white teamsters. He had been wrong. And he had been right, too; the ox goad had never touched Johnny's body, which was more than any other sugler in the forest could say. Each of them had felt the prod when he hadn't pleased his bullwhacker by greasing the skids fast enough.

"Fetch the grease, boy. Hurry."

Johnny didn't bother to point out that water rather than grease was most often used on the skids to make the logs easier to pull. Bullwhackers called whatever was put on the skids grease, and nobody with a brain argued with a bullwhacker.

With hidden pride Ising watched Johnny fetch the bucket. Johnny was his half brother, a penny-bright youth with strong shoulders and an ingratiating smile. Ising loved the boy because his laugh could light up the woods on the dreariest misty winter day. But Johnny was too easygoing. He didn't have any gut appreciation of how rough life could be. He believed that it rained dentalia and gold eagles, and all a man had to do was walk outside with his hat turned upside down. Johnny also had a taste for whiskey that worried Ising. He didn't think Johnny was tough enough to survive being crimped.

"Move it," Ising growled, feinting at Johnny's thigh with the hickory goad. "The woods boss says we're going to have company this afternoon—Mr. Hawthorne himself. If that old bull of the woods catches you napping, you're going to be digging pennies out of full spittoons for your living and I'm going to be called a lazy redskin and fired."

Johnny ducked the goad with the same quickness that made him a good sugler. He treated the danger-ous job as a game, darting into the middle of a moving log train to swab a sticky skid and then dancing away in the instant before he would have been crushed.

"Old man Hawthorne already thinks we're lazy redskins," Johnny pointed out. "You could drive those oxen straight to hell and back, and you'd never change that man's mind."

"I don't give a damn about impressing him. I just want to make sure he keeps paying me one hundred dollars a month. Now shake a leg!"

Laughing, Johnny picked up the wooden bucket and foot-long rag mop he used to slop water onto the notched skid road. Above Johnny's laughter came the ring of steel biting into wood as the logging crew went back to work after the midday break. All around the bull team, shaggy redwoods and firs covered the slopes of the Elk River watershed. The trees were less daunting there than in the coastal stands, for not as much rain and mist bathed the forest. Even so, the biggest trees still went up to ten feet through at the butt. Timber cruisers had estimated that the watershed above Weeber Basin would yield at least sixty thousand board feet of lumber per acre, a figure that had staggered Lake State lumbermen such as Arnold Kroeber, who had been raised among much smaller trees.

The problem was that Weeber Basin was more than five miles inland from the Tres Santos mill. Logging the basin was an experiment to see if cutting the timber that far from a mill was economically feasible. In the past only the coastal trees had been taken, but now they were either gone or claimed or too big to log. Building a mill inland, where the smaller trees were, wasn't a workable solution because the river itself was too unpredictable, going from exposed gravel beds to full flood with only a day's warning. Plus there was the added cost of freighting finished lumber to the port for shipment to world markets.

The alternative to moving the mill was a railroad or a skid road and bull team. The former was more efficient in the long run and far more expensive in the short. Hale would build the railroad when he could, but in the interim he was going to use bull teams to haul the logs to the river. He had built a splash dam upstream. As soon as the winter rains filled the pond behind the dam, he would blow the dam and force a rise in the river of several feet. That would be enough to float the logs all the way to the bay, where the Tres Santos Mill would process them.

At least that was the theory. In reality Ising had his doubts—a whole lot of them. The rains simply hadn't been enough last year to bring the river up, even with the added impetus of a splash dam. Last year's logs still lay stacked behind the splash dam. This year's logs lay in the dust beside last year's, for the rains still hadn't come. Betting two year's worth of cut logs on a storm big enough to fill the check dam, but not so big as to make the river too dangerous for men to herd logs on, struck Ising as quite a gamble. On the other hand it was one hell of a lot cheaper than hacking and grading a railroad bed through steep, rocky country, especially when a man didn't have much money in his pocket because he had two year's worth of logs lying in a bone-dry "pond" behind a useless splash dam.

It was no secret that it had been a bad year or two for lumber companies. Forest fires, droughts followed by floods, unreliable foreign markets and the fast-rising cost of shipping lumber had ruined the smaller lumbermen. Some of the big lumbermen were feeling the squeeze as well. Ising suspected that Hale Hawthorne was one of them.

For a moment longer Ising stood motionless, listening to his own thoughts and the rhythmic chopping of axes as tree fellers took up their positions on springboards ten feet above the ground. From that frail, resilient platform the men would work, swinging razor-edged, three-pound axheads fastened onto the end of handles nearly four feet long. The axes were outright trials of strength and skill, longer and heavier than any that had ever been used before in the lumbering industry. And still the axes were too small to cope with the monster trees.

At times like this when the late summer sky was bright and the breeze was cool and the axes sang throughout the forest, Ising wished that he hadn't given up working among the men perched on springboards ten feet above the forest floor. He knew that he could still do it. His hands were still strong, still hard, for he cut his own timber after hours and sold the logs to Tres Santos Mill. He loved the rhythm of chopping, the feeling of using his entire body, the smooth swing and the rich bite of steel into wood, the leap of huge fragrant chips into the clean air....

"But fellers don't make one hundred dollars a month," Ising reminded himself as he hitched the ox team and walked them to the flat yarding area to pick up their load.

Even knowing how much money he was saving toward his own timber claim, Ising felt a stirring of regret as he saw all stages of the felling process in progress around him. Men circled a tree, deciding which way they wanted the trunk to fall. Then they went to work opening up an undercut on the falling side of the tree. While they worked, another pair of woodsmen cut down smaller trees along the fall line to cushion the impact of the big tree and—hopefully—to prevent it from breaking into useless fragments.

Finally the choppers went to work on the side of the redwood away from the undercut. Working ten or eleven hours a day, they opened a wedge-shaped cut that ultimately would be deep enough to hold a grown man standing upright. Sometime during the fifth or sixth day, if the choppers worked hard, the tree would start to groan as though in terrible illness. They might work another day, driving the wedge-shaped cut deeper and deeper into the dark red wood before a breath of wind or the tree's own weight supplied the coup de grace. Then there was a prolonged roar as the last strands of heartwood gave way and the tree came rushing down.

At such times no one needed to shout "Timber!" The man who couldn't hear a falling redwood was deaf. The man who couldn't run fast enough was dead.

As Ising approached the yarding area, where logs were prepared for hauling, he saw sawyers and peelers working over a nearby fallen tree. They were sawing it into eight-, ten- or twelve-foot saw logs. As he waited, two men put a slight taper called a "snipe" on the front ends of each of the logs. Peeled of all bark, shaped at one end, cut down to size and dogged together into trains, the logs awaited removal by Henry Ising and his famous bull team.

But instead of picking up a new load, Ising was given the job of restarting a log train that had hung up halfway down the skid road earlier that day. A poorly sniped lead log had caught on a skid. Men had spent an hour digging the errant log out of the soft dirt in which it had mired. Now the log was hanging on the wedge, waiting to be jerked back into the skid road's groove and from there on down to the dry pond at the end of the road.

Ising studied the slope and the terrain carefully and knew why he had been given the job. The slope was steep and the skid road heavily worn by friction until the skids were nearly smooth where the log trains had ground them down. Once the oxen bucked the first log of the train back into the groove, the big logs would very quickly gain momentum. That would have been no problem, if it weren't for the slight bend in the skid road. It was going to take an agile, highly responsive span of oxen to keep out of trouble if the logs got going too fast.

"We've got to keep this bastard under control for that dogleg, but the skids still have to be greased between here and there, or we'll never get the damn thing moving in the first place," Ising said to Johnny. "So don't stand there gawking. Get moving, boy! You're slower than a three-legged bull."

"Those damn bulls are slow no matter how many legs they have," Johnny muttered under his breath.

He moved off down the road, slopping water from the bucket onto the skids ahead of the team. His was an exercise in applied physics; he had learned that gravity took over once the logs started to slide, and therefore less water was needed to maintain the same speed. But until the bull team got the logs moving, the skids had to be watered, or the bulls wouldn't be able to break the log train from its resting place.

Ising turned away to check the traces of the team. Johnny disappeared down the slope, slapping his rag mop on the groove that had been worn in the skid road logs. As he wet the logs, he kicked a bit of dirt over the wet spot and then added more water to create a thin, slippery mud. Halfway down the slope Johnny refilled his bucket from a nearby redwood barrel that was kept there just for that purpose.

"Come on, you lazy redskin!" Johnny called back up the hill to Ising. "You get any slower and the forest will grow back over the skids before you're halfway to the pond!"

Ising turned around and opened his mouth to reply to the taunt, but when he looked down the hill to the dry pond he saw a black buggy pulled by a pair of black horses.

Hale Hawthorne.

Without a word, Ising turned back to his team. Hawthorne was a dour man, not given to joking in the woods—or anywhere else, as near as anyone could tell. Ising finished checking the traces, walked up to his lead ox and swatted it on the flank with his hand. The animals farther back in the line knew the signal. One by one they began leaning against their smooth, heavy oak yokes, digging footholds in the soft dirt that separated each ten-inch width of skid log that had been laid crossways to the road.

Ising quickly walked back to the head of the train and used a dead limb to knock the wedge out from under the sniped end of the lead log.

"Go, bulls," he called out, reaching out to touch the chainer team on the neck with the goad, making sure that they didn't slack off when they felt the full weight of the log.

The log train was hitched together with manila rope. The biggest, heaviest log was put in front. Once it was moving, it became almost like an additional pair of oxen, adding its weight to that pulling the rest of the train forward. But the chainer pair had to lean very hard into their yokes before that happened.

"Go, Segep! Hup!"

The bulls leaned into their yokes and dug great clods of earth from between the skids. The lead log of the train teetered for a moment, jerked, then slid forward smoothly. The rest of the train's logs stirred to life as the slack was picked up. The bulls strained against their yokes, their heavy necks and shoulders bulging. After the first few jerks the log train moved forward with unexpected speed and ease. Ising fell into step beside the oxen, feeling pride at the power and skill of his team.

The first fifty yards were easy, allowing Ising to take his attention off the bulls for a moment to check the log train itself. The oxen hooves and sliding logs had already churned up a cloud of dust in the dry soil, but the logs themselves were moving smoothly in the wet skids. Almost too smoothly. The slope was steep and the pace was increasing subtly with every downward inch of grade.

Ising turned and quickened his pace to a trot, wanting to reach the head yoke before the bulls got to the spot where the road broke off to the left. Ising came up next to the lead ox and dropped back down to a walk. As he did, he crowded against the leader's shoulder to make sure that the animals snubbed the first log in the train around the turn properly.

At that instant Ising realized that the oxen were going a bit too fast. Johnny had done his work of helping the oxen launch the train too well. The skids were slippery with mud and water, giving little resistance to the peeled logs in the train. The turn would be manageable, but just barely.

Even as Ising was thanking God that the skids would be dry after the turn, he came around the curve and saw Johnny industriously slathering water and mud on the last few feet of skid road leading into the dry pond.

Damn that Johnny, Ising thought to himself. *He's greased these skids up to a fare-thee-well, just to get even with me for calling him lazy. He thinks it's a joke. Damn fool kid! He's never seen what happens when a log train breaks loose!*

Ising trotted alongside the team on the balls of his feet, leaping from one half-buried skid log to another and praying that he wouldn't stumble as he looked over his shoulder to check the chainers, the pair of oxen that were closest to the log train. The sure-footed oxen seemed to be having no difficulty, but the chainers had been forced to break into a trot to stay ahead of the massive log that was threatening to overrun them.

As Ising watched, the pair in front of the chainers broke into a trot. It wasn't enough. The chainers were still crowding forward into the haunches of the next pair of oxen.

And so was the log train. In a few instants the train had gone from controlled to uncontrolled, a huge mass of logs gaining speed and momentum with every instant until they would be fast and powerful enough to crush everything in their path.

Ising went cold. The oxen who had worked their big hearts out for him day after day had only one chance of survival. They had to outrun the snaking, sliding, hurtling tons of logs before the train shot through the grooves and turned the team into a bloody pulp.

With a bellow Ising brought his goad down across the back of the lead bull. Segep leaped forward, dragging his yokemate with him. The downhill trot of the oxen quickly turned into a lope and then a gallop.

Wearing a wicked grin, Johnny worked over the last few feet of skid logs. At Ising's bellow, the boy looked up and saw the oxen breaking into a gallop. For a moment Johnny's smile increased; then he heard the thunder and thump of the log train and realized what he had inadvertently done. Instantly he dropped the bucket and ran forward, trying to undo the disaster by throwing handfuls of dirt at the wetted skids, dirt that would soak up water, leaving the skids dry and rough.

Nearby logging activity came to a halt as pondmen and swampers, fellers and teamsters looked up and saw the span of oxen galloping down the hill with a log train racing and tumbling behind and a cloud of dirt boiling all the way up to the treetops.

The normally slow oxen were quickly outdistancing Ising, who was having an increasingly difficult time maintaining his footing on the uneven logs of the corduroy skid road. Yet even at a gallop, the chainers were being crowded by the log train. The lead pairs were running well, but the oxen in the middle were, as always, lazy. If they didn't run harder, they would doom the whole span to be crushed beneath the heavy logs.

Ising closed in on the ox team in the middle of the span. One handed, he caught the brass-capped horn of the near ox. With the quickness of a cat, he swung onto the beast's broad back. Steadying himself with one hand on the yoke, he flailed away at the oxen he could reach with his goad and yelled like a banshee.

The entire span was in a lumbering gallop now, driven by their bullwhacker and by the groaning, rumbling log train that was bearing down on them. Suddenly the mate of the ox Ising was riding lost its footing and staggered crazily. Instead of leaping off and leaving the span of oxen to their fate as any sane man would have done, Ising leaned far over and jabbed the stumbling ox in the neck with his goad in a desperate effort to right the beast.

"Up, you useless, penniless bastard or I'll leave you to the *woge!*" he screamed in Yurok.

The ox's eyes rolled wildly, but the familiar voice and the unfamiliar pain of the goad penetrated the animal's panic. With an effort that corded every muscle on the ox's huge body, the animal leaped forward, easing the choking drag of the yoke and regaining his balance. After a few choppy strides the ox matched speed with his mate again. The faltering span regrouped and settled into a thundering run.

Ising's shouts, the ringing sounds of the hooves on the skid road and the groaning rumble of the log train had lured everyone who could hear out of the woods. Grim faced, they came to witness the bloody, inevitable end of a runaway log train. In silence men gathered to retrieve what was possible from the coming carnage.

Hale Hawthorne sat transfixed, fighting to control his increasingly nervous buggy horses and, at the same time, watch the spectacle of sixty tons of redwood sawlogs snaking down the hill on the heels of sixteen galloping oxen, one of which was being ridden by a madman screaming in an unknown language.

As the downhill slope flattened out on the final approach to the dry pond's shore, Johnny's frantic efforts to undo his mischief finally began to make a difference. The momentum of the lead log was immense, but the level land, dry dirt and newer, less worn skids of the lower road began to scrub off the log train's speed. The smaller logs at the rear of the train were still sliding down the greased, grooved hillside, but the heavier front logs were having much slower going. The smaller logs bumped into the bigger logs, but the bigger logs held position in the groove by their sheer mass.

As suddenly as the log train had gone out of control, it became docile again. Ising could hear the difference and sense it in the less frantic pace of the oxen as the logs' weight began to be felt against the yokes once more. He called out the span's names in Yurok, praising and slowing them at the same time. The oxen's gallop shifted to a fast trot, then a slow trot and finally a walk as the last of the log train hit the dry, flat part of the skid road. The lead bulls came to the unloading area and stopped of their own accord, panting and blowing and stamping.

A cloud of dust rolled toward the dry pond, enveloping the team and the bullwhacker. Ising dismounted and emerged into the sunlight, exhilarated and furious at the same time. All that prevented him from grabbing Johnny and beating him within an inch of his careless young life was the knowledge that Hale Hawthorne sat watching from his buggy not forty feet away.

"Afternoon, Mr. Hawthorne," Ising said, lifting his broad-brimmed whacker's hat and nodding briefly. He glanced at the pair of black horses standing nervously between the buggy shafts. The animals were trembling and sweating. "Looks like you've got a lively team there. I should put them in front of my bulls. They're feeling a touch lazy today."

The timber beasts who had come from the forest and gathered around Hawthorne's buggy stood dumbfounded for a minute and then, to a man, broke into uproarious laughter. Even Hale joined in. When the noise died down, Hawthorne brushed some of the dust from his black coat and cleared his throat. He and every man around him knew that Ising's deft handling of the oxen had prevented a tragedy.

"I've heard that bullwhackers will work hard to prove their superiority over a railroad," Hale said, "but that performance was truly extraordinary. Steel rails or skid roads, Ising, you'll always have a job with Tres Santos."

"Thank you, Mr. Hawthorne."

Hale nodded even as he spoke soothingly to the champing, restless buggy horses. "Do you think you could train your beasts to do more than pull logs down a groove?"

"Yes."

"Good. Take the remainder of the day off and rest your team. Report to John Johnson tomorrow. You and those wild-eyed beasts of yours are going to help me build a railroad."

Chapter Ten

Maya sat in a redwood lawn chair nursing baby Justine and watching her older daughter Emily with an indulgent smile. Emily had discovered a butterfly and was chasing it with all the speed her chubby four-year-old legs could muster. Beth sat nearby, reading a book with nimble fingers and cocking her head from time to time in order to better locate the delighted cries of her stepsister.

Sighing with rare pleasure, Maya leaned her head back and let the gentle sunlight pour down over her. She loved the feel of the breeze blowing over her unbuttoned bodice, caressing her skin as though it were precious. The warmth of the sun was delicious, as was the hungry tugging of the baby at her breast. It was wonderful not to have to withdraw to her room to nurse Justine and thereby avoid offending Hale's sense of propriety. It was wonderful to feel milk come to her breast at Justine's hungry cry, to know that her baby would be fat and healthy and fall asleep with a full stomach. It was wonderful to hear Emily's energetic squeals and to look at her round red cheeks and laughing eyes and chubby body.

And it was pure bliss to switch Justine from one nipple to the other and, for a moment, just a moment, to feel sunlight on her bare breasts before she pulled the fine lace nursing shawl into place once more.

Hale would have been appalled at her hedonism. He didn't understand why she had insisted on nursing both babies for the first few months when wet nurses could be hired for a pittance. Nor did he approve of her sitting bareheaded in the sunlight with her unbound hair streaming down around her shoulders. There was much that Hale didn't approve of that Maya saw as simple, harmless pleasures. Rather than argue with the man who was both her husband and, in the eyes of God and society, her master, Maya simply waited until Hale was gone from the house. Then she loosened the stays of her undergarments, unbraided and brushed out her hair and sat barefoot in the sunny garden with her babies and Beth, whom she had come to look upon and love as her own child.

Smiling, Maya reached beneath the shawl and gently smoothed back the fine, dark wisps of hair that covered Justine's tiny head. The baby's eyes opened, their gray-green depths dreamy with pleasure. Long lashes fluttered down once more as Justine resumed nursing hungrily.

"Ah, you sweet little babe," Maya murmured, caressing Justine's cheek with the back of her finger. "You gave Mama a terrible fright, but it's fine now. You're greedy and chubby-fisted just like a babe should be. I love you, Justine."

That love was clear on her face as Maya looked down at her tiny daughter. For a time Maya had feared that Emily would be her only child. Despite the ease

of Emily's conception and birth, it had been more
than a year before Maya had been able to conceive
again, and two years before she succeeded in carrying
to full term another child. Two miscarriages in rapid
succession had left her spent, worn and in a depression that only Emily's clear laughter and Beth's need
for love had been able to penetrate. Finally, a month
premature, Justine had been born. Although Hale had
been bitterly disappointed to have another daughter
instead of a son, he had sat by Maya's side at the baby's crib and prayed for her during the long, long days
and nights while Justine fought for life.

"Maya?"

"Mmm?"

"Are you sure there aren't any knights left anywhere in the whole world?"

Beth's wistfulness reminded Maya of herself many
years ago, when she had first learned that the fairy tales her mother told at bedtime were just that—lovely
stories that had no relationship to real life. Sir Walter
Scott's *The Lady of the Lake* was like that, beautiful
and impossible. It was Beth's favorite story.

Knowing that, Maya couldn't bring herself to destroy Beth's romantic illusions. Nor was it necessary;
Beth would never have to face hunger or privation or
the duty of the marriage bed. She would never have
either the glory of giving birth to a baby or the chilling fear for that baby's life. God was both cruel and
kind. He had taken Beth's sight and with it her chance
of motherhood's bittersweet joys, but He had left
colors in her mind, colors of richness and brilliance
that Maya had known only once in her life, in the arms
of a lover now forbidden to her by the laws of God and
man.

*Where is he now? Is he well? Is he hungry or tired
or cold? Does he fall asleep cursing me?*

After the first few, devastating instants Maya controlled her tumbling thoughts, forcing herself not to
remember Will. It was scarcely easier now than it had
been five years ago. She had assumed once that the
passage of time would dull her memories of him, but
she had been wrong in that. Will was a hurt and a
yearning and a darkness in her that only the presence
of her children could ease.

"Maya?"

"Somewhere, Beth," Maya said huskily. "Somewhere on earth there might be a place where Lochinvar still rides."

The quality of Maya's voice made Beth's fingers
pause over the stiff pages of the Braille book. Unerr-
ingly she turned toward Maya, whose patient teaching had opened up the world to the blind girl.

"You're feeling sad again, aren't you?" Beth got up
in a rush and felt her way across the few feet that separated the two lawn chairs until she could kneel at
Maya's side, putting her head in her stepmother's lap
and her arm across her thighs in a hug that didn't disturb the nursing baby. "I love you, Maya. Don't be
sad. Can't you hear Emmy's laughter? She is so quick,
so alive. Baby Justine is healthy now and growing so
fast—oh, how she's growing! When I hold her in my
arms I can't believe she's only three months old. She
loves you, too; I know she does. We all love you,
Maya. Don't go away into sadness again. If you do,
who will teach Justine to laugh?"

Maya looked from the babe nursing at her breast to
the seventeen-year-old girl whose blond hair lay like a
golden pool across her lap. Just beyond the chair Em-

ily laughed with delight as the first bright butterfly was
joined by another, and they turned round and round
in a graceful spiral dance. Maya's hand came up to
stroke Beth's soft cheek and even softer hair.

"It's all right, Mouse. I love you, too. You know
that, don't you?"

"Oh, yes, but I was so afraid before Justine was
born. I was afraid you would die like my mother did
and I would be all alone again. It was so very dark
before you taught my fingers to see words...."

"Hush, Mouse. It's all right. I'm not going to leave
you."

Maya felt Beth's deep sigh as the girl leaned more
heavily across her lap. She stopped stroking Beth's
hair long enough to shift Justine's weight then resumed the slow, soothing caresses that reassured Beth
more than any words could. Justine, too, seemed to be
soothed. Her nursing slowed and finally stopped, but
she didn't release the nipple.

"Sweet, greedy little thing," murmured Maya, but
she made no motion to move her breast.

Justine stirred and began sucking again. Maya
smiled, then let her head tilt back against the chair.
Gradually a feeling of tranquility pervaded her, as
though somewhere deep inside her a long-unanswered
need was on the verge of being assuaged. Justine became still again, then slept with the suddenness of
youth and health. Slowly the baby's mouth released
the rosy nipple it had held captive. An evergreen-
scented breeze whispered over Maya, lifting aside the
fine lace of the nursing shawl, revealing the babe nuzzling even in sleep against its mother's breast.

Thirty feet away Will Hawthorne stood in the
shadow of the surrounding woods as though he had

been turned to stone. He had been that way since he had first seen Maya and Beth sitting so quietly in the garden of their new home. He had heard their words, and it had been like scalding water dripping onto naked flesh.

He had told himself for five years that Maya was simply a whore out to line her own pockets with golden coins. Yet she hadn't looked like a whore as she sat barefoot in the sun with a baby at her breast and her hair in unschooled profusion around her shoulders. She hadn't looked like a whore when she had smiled to see her daughter running pell-mell after a butterfly. She didn't look like a whore now, even with her breast bared to the sun in what should have been coarse immodesty, but instead made a picture of beauty that was like a knife turning in Will's soul.

And Beth...blind, gentle Beth whose love for Maya overflowed with the transparent warmth of sunlight itself.

A shaft of baffling, wounding hurt pierced Will, sliding through the demon rage that had both guarded and ruled his emotions for so many years. *How could she love them so well and me not at all?*

There was no answer but the demon's howl... and for an instant it sounded more like a cry of agony than rage.

Will withdrew as he had come, silently, creating no disturbance in ferns or piled needles. Even so, Maya stirred. Her eyes opened, and she looked suddenly toward the spot where Will had stood.

"What is it?" Beth asked, sensing Maya's sudden tension.

"I thought I heard someone call my name."

"I heard nothing."

"Then there was nothing to hear. Your ears are much better than mine, little Mouse."

Smiling, Beth nestled her cheek into Maya's lap again. Maya stroked the girl's hair and watched the woods until tears blurred the outline of redwoods. For a long time there was only silence and the scented breeze and memories too painful to bear.

When Maya was certain that her voice wouldn't give away her emotions, she sat up, closed her bodice and tugged gently on Beth's pale hair.

"Come, Mouse. Your father will be back from the woods soon. We'd better check on Mrs. Chou and Emily's cake."

"And Mrs. Ashton's cleaning. There was dust on the top of the sideboard yesterday, and the pantry smells of mice rather than cedar. How do they find their way in so quickly? We've only lived here a few months."

"They come in the carpenters' pockets."

Beth giggled as she stood up. With motions of her hands that were both graceful and tentative, she searched out her book and the light cane that Maya had bought for her after they had moved to the new house.

"Emily, we're going in now," called Maya.

"Stay!" the girl said instantly.

Maya looked at her quick, willful daughter and sighed. Emily was grass stained and dirt smudged, and dandelions drooped in her small fists. Her cinnamon colored braids were more undone than done and far more tangled than smooth.

"Your father will be home soon."

"Catch butterflies?" she asked, holding out the bright, frayed flowers.

"Not now, sugar. We have to get you washed and combed. Your father thinks little girls should be clean and smell of rose soap rather than weeds. We know that we're not always so perfect, but we don't want to disappoint him, do we? Especially since he's coming back early just for your party."

Emily's odd, silver-green eyes narrowed in rebellion, but she knew her father well. "Yes, Mama."

The little girl ran forward, dandelions still clutched in her fist. Even as she raced past everyone to be first at the back porch, she was careful not to get in Beth's way. Emily had quickly learned that she would make her mother truly angry if she teased Beth or took advantage of her half sister's blindness by playing tricks on her.

"It has been such a lovely, warm summer," Beth said, turning her face toward the sun as she walked slowly.

"For us. For the loggers it's becoming a nightmare. Last winter there wasn't much rain. The rivers are little more now than pools and gravel runs. Even in the lowlands it's impossible to float logs down to the mills. The higher reaches of forest are terribly dry. Everyone fears a fire."

While Maya spoke, she watched Beth's progress with a careful eye as the girl tapped her way along the wooden garden walk. She moved with more confidence each day, but it had been a harrowing few weeks for everyone while Beth became accustomed to the new house. Maya hadn't wanted to change houses at all, knowing how difficult it would be for Beth to adjust to new surroundings, but Hale hadn't taken Maya's objections seriously. He had wanted a house in keeping with his growing family and his position as the biggest lumberman in northern California. And that was just what he now had. The house was an ornate, three-story, white Victorian mansion trimmed with forest green. It had bay windows and sloping dormers, and its three levels were edged with yards of carefully turned frieze designs and parapet moldings. There was even a widow's walk with a wrought-iron railing atop the crested roof. Inset in the doors and above the normal windows, there were elegant stained-glass windows that transformed light into jeweled colors.

In the end Maya secretly had been relieved to leave the white, two-story frame house that had once been on the edge of Eureka's bustle but during the past few years had been engulfed by the city's expansion. Not only had the noise and movement of strangers disturbed her at the old house, but the rooms themselves had reminded her too often of Will.

Even so, Maya's heart had ached for each bruise and scrape Beth earned as she felt her way through the new house. She had learned with remarkable speed, though. She rarely stumbled anymore unless one of the cleaning women replaced a chair carelessly.

"Do I need to change my clothes?" Beth asked as they climbed the back stairs to the kitchen porch.

Maya looked at the pieces of grass clinging to Beth's skirt and smiled. In some ways being blind had kept Beth as uninhibited as a child when it came to showing affection. If she wanted to kneel in the grass and hug someone, she did so without a thought for appearance.

"Your pale blue silk dress would look lovely on you this afternoon. That's the one with tiny little pearls sewn into the lace at the collar and cuffs."

Beth's face lit with pleasure. "Oh, I'd like that. It whispers to me so sweetly when I walk."

"Angie will bring hot water to your room." Maya saw Beth's hesitation and said quickly, "I'll be in to help you with your bath as soon as I've checked on the kitchen."

"I don't want to be a bother."

"You're no bother, Mouse," Maya said, touching Beth's cheek lightly.

Maya knew that since Beth's body had changed from that of a child to that of a young woman, she was uneasy at being washed or dressed by anyone but Maya. Beth had tried doing both herself. The results had been unintentionally hilarious. Eventually Maya knew she would have to teach Beth how to care for herself, but there was no hurry. It was enough for the girl to become accustomed to a new house. The rest could wait for a less upsetting time.

The arrangements for Emily's belated birthday party had progressed well in Mrs. Chou's capable hands. Maya had only to taste the duck sauce, approve the creaminess of the boiled icing for the cake and send back two pieces of silverware to be polished again. Within moments of entering the kitchen Maya was free to go to the ground-floor wing of the house that had become Beth's. There were no unnecessary pieces of furniture in the rooms, nor were there any loose rugs to trip a blind girl's feet.

"Come in, Maya," Beth called in answer to the knock at her door.

"How do you always know who it is?"

"Your footsteps all sound quite different to me."

Maya walked in and found Beth standing naked in front of a steaming hip bath. Sun streamed through the gauzy curtains, giving the girl's body a pale golden glow. Her breasts were high and full, untouched by age or privation or pregnancy, and her hips were sleek and rounded. Suddenly Maya realized that Beth was quite beautiful. Were it not for her blindness, she would have been beset by suitors.

Quietly Maya hoped that perhaps Beth would be lucky. Perhaps a Lochinvar wealthy enough to keep servants and nannies would ride into Beth's life and give her children of her own to love. But there were few men around who were wealthy enough to offer such a high degree of security to Beth; and of those few men, none were young. That was what Maya wanted for Beth, a young man who loved sunlight and saw with his fingertips and laughed when the sweetness of life overflowed in his hand.

Maya closed her eyes for a moment and prayed that she would never have to see Beth sold into the pain and cold comforts of an old man's bed.

"Are you there, Maya?"

"Yes. I'm here."

"You sound odd," said the girl as she stepped into the tub.

"I just realized how very beautiful you are."

"Am I really?" Beth asked, pleasure clear in her voice. With a total absence of embarrassment she ran her hands over her breasts and hips, seeing herself in the only way possible to the blind. "I can remember how I looked years ago, but I can't imagine how I look now. Sometimes I feel as though I'm wearing a stranger's body."

Maya smiled sadly, understanding too well. There were times when she saw her reflection and wondered who she was and how she had come to stand in front of a gilt-framed mirror in a darkened room and look into a stranger's haunted green eyes. After Justine had survived, the question hadn't come but once or twice, as though the world were slowly coming back into focus for Maya. The baby reminded her that she had been put on earth to care for those less strong and able than she was; in a very real sense she had been born for her own unborn babes. She had come to this realization slowly, many years ago. There had been an intangible condensation of certainty in her that had strengthened each time she had seen how her own mother had been caught within the cruel vise of a marriage choice badly made.

Her mother had paid for marrying the wrong man, but not so dearly as had her children.

Maya had paid for her marriage as well and continued to pay for it in ways that she understood with fresh pain each day, but her children did not pay. They laughed and thrived and grew as only healthy children could, full of curiosity and exuberance and the certainty that each new day was a shining present just waiting to be unwrapped. Maya knew that ensuring the well-being of her children was her destiny as surely as her husband's destiny was to ensure that men could build a new world with the clean, straight lumber that came from Hale Hawthorne's timber claims and mills.

And if sometimes she felt as though she didn't exist, as though she should be able to walk past a mirror unreflected, it was only a silly fancy. She would not change her marriage to Hale even if she could. Given the same circumstances she would make the same choice, even knowing full well the hidden costs of that choice. What was the occasional beat of black wings within her soul compared to the silver laughter of her living, healthy children?

"Mrs. Hawthorne?"

Maya paused over the tub as the nanny's call registered. She tucked the bath sponge into Beth's hand. "Rinse until your skin is squeaky rather than slippery. I'll go see what Mrs. Johnson wants."

"Is Emily with you?" Mrs. Johnson asked through the door.

"No," Maya said. "I thought she was with you."

"I bathed her and dressed her in that green dress you laid out and did her hair. Then I turned my back to change Justine, and she was gone."

"I'll find her." Maya turned back to Beth. "The towel is behind you on the floor next to the tub. Your undergarments are at the foot of the bed. Once you get into them, would it be all right if Mrs. Johnson helped you with your dress?"

"Of course. Where do you think Emily is?"

"Chasing butterflies again."

"In her new dress?"

"I don't think the butterflies would care, do you?" Beth laughed.

Maya opened the bedroom door. A large, vaguely tiger-striped cat shot through into the room. The cat was the ugliest feline Maya had ever seen. It also had the softest fur of any animal she had ever touched. As the cat was for Beth's pleasure and companionship, its wilted ears, crooked nose and crossed eyes mattered not in the least.

"Tickle is back," warned Maya as she shut the door behind the cat. "Don't trip over her."

As Maya walked down the hall, she realized that her hair was still loose and her feet bare. Hale would be irritated if he saw her running about like a hoyden. Yet if she didn't find Emily right away, only the Lord Himself could imagine what mischief the girl would do to her party clothes.

"Oh, *bother*," Maya muttered.

She didn't turn and go back to her own rooms to groom herself, however. She would rather have Hale irritated at her than at Emily. When Maya opened the back door, she saw that the yard was empty and muttered beneath her breath again. Then she heard her daughter's silvery laughter float from the forest at the side of the house.

"The gazebo," Maya sighed. "I should have guessed. She'll have every balloon untied and all the streamers in shambles before her father even gets to see them."

From the back porch the gazebo was little more than a flash of white seen through a haze of green foliage. The airy structure had been built on a small rise overlooking the city and the sea beyond. It was one of Maya's favorite places, which was why she had decided to hold Emily's belated birthday party there. Maya picked up the long skirt of her dress and began to run up the winding wooden walkway.

The change from sunshine to forest shade and from there to the gazebo's sunny knoll momentarily dazzled Maya's eyes. When the tall figure turned away from Emily, Maya at first believed that Hale had come home. When the man stepped from the gazebo's shelter into the pouring brilliance of the afternoon sun, Maya felt as though she couldn't breathe and time vanished while she stared at the man who lived within all her silences, touched all her secret agonies.

The man was both Will and not Will. He had none of Will's gentleness, neither in his eyes nor in the line of his mouth. He had aged more than should have been possible in five years, and none of that aging had been the result of kindly experience. He was taller, broader, far more powerful than her memories. He moved with the grace of a wild animal and watched her with eyes the color and pitiless clarity of ice.

Maya had never seen a man half so handsome, a tenth so compelling, had never known with such anguished clarity the price of her children's well-being. Nor had she ever sensed a man's hatred so clearly. Finally she had the answer to one of the questions she asked herself in the long stretches of night that came before sunrise: Yes, Will cursed her before he slept at night.

She shivered suddenly, shrinking from the cruelty in his eyes.

"Hello, Maya," Will said, a hard smile etching his lips. "Or should I call you Mother?"

"No," she whispered, feeling the last of her blood drain from her face. "Never. *You are not my son.*"

"That's just as well, all things considered."

Will looked at Maya with cold eyes that remembered her naked and crying for the locking of his body with hers. Maya felt naked, humiliated. She flinched as though she had been slapped. For years she had tried to imagine what would happen if Will ever returned. Somehow she had failed even to suspect how much it would hurt to be hated by the man she loved.

"Why have you come back?" she asked hoarsely.

"Doesn't every boy want to be reunited with his loving family?"

Motionless, Maya watched Will as she would a stranger. Neither his face nor his voice held emotion. He could have meant exactly what he said, or he could have meant the opposite. There were no clues in his tone or body. He was as controlled as his father—no, he was even colder, even more controlled, a stone where Hale was merely wood. Whatever had happened in the last five years had burned all emotions out of Will Hawthorne.

Except hatred.

Unable to bear the icy reflection of herself in Will's gray eyes, Maya's eyelids closed protectively, bringing blessed darkness. She wanted to flee or lash out or die, yet she had no choice but to go on from this moment as she had from so many others. The future lay before her, filled with the needs of her children. The past lay waste behind her. If she had just discovered that too much of her lay waste in the past as well, so be it. She would mourn the loss of herself in the hours before dawn. Daylight was for the living, her children.

"I see that part of your family has already greeted you," Maya said, opening her eyes once more. "Did you introduce yourself to your half sister?"

For a moment Will didn't answer. He couldn't. When Maya's eyes opened, she looked like a death mask of herself. The transformation from the woman he had seen in the garden to the woman who now stood before him was chilling. Somehow she had sensed the demon caged within his soul; she knew that he had come back to destroy her.

"I wasn't sure what our relationship was until Emily mentioned that we're celebrating her birthday today. Unless you had an unusually lengthy pregnancy, that leaves only half brotherhood, doesn't it?"

Emily had followed the only part of the conversation that mattered to her, the discussion of her birthday. "Today isn't my birthday, but the baby was sick then, and Mama was ill, and no one but me wanted to have a party."

Will turned and focused his eyes on Emily with sudden intensity. "How old are you?"

"Four years and three months," she said proudly.

Maya rallied, forcing words past lips that were suddenly stiff with the same cold that was freezing the marrow of her bones. "Emily, go to the house and tell Beth that her brother is here. Stay in the house. I don't want you outside in your good clothes until it's time for the party."

Emily started to protest, measured her mother's formidable composure and realized that protest would do no good. She turned and began running down the long path back to the house.

"You have come to tell your father about us?" Maya asked, but there was no real question in her tone. She knew.

"Yes."

"Do you hate me so much that you will destroy an innocent child just to ruin me in the eyes of my husband?"

"Yes."

Will's answers were so matter-of-fact, so final, that Maya knew instinctively it was no use to plead. She tried anyway.

"Even if that child is yours?"

"Is she?"

"Yes."

"I don't believe you."

Maya nodded slowly, understanding. "It's easier that way, isn't it?"

"When I came back from timber cruising five years ago, I saw my father coming out of your room. His fly was undone and he was still wet from your body. There is not the slightest doubt in my mind that he had just fucked you. Under those circumstances you'll understand my lack of eagerness to claim the child as mine."

Nausea rose in Maya's throat with a searing violence that choked her. She clasped her hands together until her fingers showed bands of white. She could not speak.

But it didn't matter. Will was talking again.

"You needn't look so distraught. I gave up the idea of having my father throw you out of his house when I saw you with Beth in the garden earlier this afternoon. I won't see my sister hurt. She is as close to sainthood as our wretched kind ever gets, and it's obvious that she loves you. That, my dear stepmother, is all that is saving you from being branded a whore and turned out on the streets to starve with your mongrel offspring."

Maya tried to speak, but her tongue would shape no sounds. Wordless, motionless, she stood lost amid the balloons and colored streamers until she heard Beth's cane tapping madly up the walk.

"Oh—Beth—careful!" Maya called out, but the words were no more than hoarse, broken sounds forced past the constriction of her throat.

Will's eyelids flickered when he heard Maya's ruined voice. Deliberately he looked away, putting Maya's reality out of his mind with the ease of many years of practice.

"Hello, Mouse," he said, stepping forward to catch his sister in his arms and hold her as though he were shipwrecked and she were a life preserver floating amid the storm-tossed debris. He remembered Beth as a thin, shy child, but the girl whose arms were wrapped so tightly around his neck was neither thin nor a child. "My Lord, you've grown. You're a woman!"

Beth said nothing, simply clung and clung to Will while tears ran down her cheeks. Finally words began tumbling out as fast as her tears. "Maya was right. Oh, thank God, Maya was right! When no letters came to me after the first one from England I thought you were dead, but she said you weren't, you were alive, she was as certain of it as she was that her own heart beat. She said that she would know if you had died. And she was right. Oh, she was right! You're alive and you're home and I've missed you so!"

Narrow-eyed, Will looked at Maya. She looked back, but not at him. Her eyes were focused on some inner horizon that only she could see. Uneasiness moved in Will, a feeling that Maya wasn't present in any way that mattered. The insight made him furious. He held her life and future within his grasp, yet still she eluded him as she always had.

"Oh, why didn't you write? Didn't you care about us, Will? Didn't you want to know if we were alive or dead?"

"Of course I care about you," he said hoarsely, burying his face in Beth's neck. "You're the only person on earth I do care about. I've kept track of you, Mouse. I know that you shop for clothes by touch and drive the housekeeper mad finding dust and read with your fingertips and have the ugliest cat on seven continents."

"How do you know? Did Maya write and not tell me? Is that how she knew you were alive?"

Will threw a hard look at Maya, but she seemed totally unaware of the conversation.

"Hale Hawthorne's business and private life are known in every lumber port," Will explained. What he didn't explain was that he had paid men for information about the Hawthorne family so as to keep abreast of Hale's business plans. When the conversation had turned to personal matters, Will had listened with an intensity that had left more than one of his spies quite uneasy. "Every miscarriage and birth, every timber grant and board foot, the cost of everything in that elaborate redwood palace in which you live. Your father is rather famous, Mouse."

"He's your father, too."

Will put Beth down on the gazebo floor. "So where is your famous cat?"

"Oh, Will, you're still upset with Father, aren't you? Just because he didn't want you to claim trees that couldn't be cut...."

"Upset?" Will asked, carefully keeping the sarcasm from his voice if not from the shape of his smile. "Is that what he told you? That's not why I left, Mouse. I grew up, that's all. I do things my way now, rather than his."

"Are you back here to stay?"

Will was looking at Maya. He saw Beth's question spear through the death mask to the woman living within. Her eyes changed; he was their bleak focus now.

"I'm back to stay," he said.

"Oh, that's grand! Did you hear that, Maya?"

Will's smile twisted cruelly as he saw the words sink into Maya. For an instant her agony was plain; then the mask came into place, and she eluded him once more.

"Maya?" Beth asked uncertainly.

"She heard. She's speechless with delight." Again, Will's victory existed only in his smile, not in his tone or words. He had meant what he said; he would spare Beth whatever hurt he could, short of giving up vengeance entirely. That he would not, could not, do.

"Maya?" Beth asked, holding onto Will with one hand and groping for Maya with the other.

Automatically Maya took Beth's hand, silently telling the girl where she was.

"You're like ice," Beth said. "You aren't pregnant again, are you? It's too soon after Justine! I heard what the doctor said. Oh, Maya, you mustn't!"

"What?" Will demanded, his voice like a whip as he turned on Maya. "Are you pregnant?"

She said nothing.

"Answer me!"

"I'm not pregnant."

"Are you certain?"

"Yes."

Beth flinched at the sound of Maya's voice. "Maya?" she whispered, releasing Will in order to hold onto Maya with both hands. "Your voice... frightens me."

Will saw the shudder that went over Maya, as though somewhere deep within herself a battle were being waged for control of her body. Slowly the mask of her face changed as she looked at Beth.

"It's all right, little Mouse," Maya said hoarsely. "Everything is fine. I'm coming down with a summer cold. That's all. Just a cold. It will make my voice sound funny for a time."

The relief on Beth's face was so great that Will felt a shaft of fear. His sister worshipped Maya. If he destroyed Maya, Beth would be bereft. He didn't want to cause Beth pain. Yet he could no more turn aside from his revenge than he could forgive Maya and his father for betraying him.

Grimly Will looked away from the sight of his sister embracing the woman he hated. As he turned, he saw the man who had just rounded the last corner of the twisting path that led to the gazebo. Will froze, wondering what his father would say upon seeing the prodigal son's unwelcome return.

Hale had been wondering the same thing ever since Emily had told him that Will had shown up at the gazebo. Emotions had surged within Hale at the news. Foremost among them was anger. He knew that Will would disrupt the quiet household that Hale treasured and had finally managed to procure for himself after the turmoil of the move into the new house. It irritated him that just at the moment of his greatest personal and professional victory, he would have to put up with Will's relentless rebellion all over again.

That could not be allowed. Domestic peace had been too hard won to be given over to a bragging, strutting boy. Just in the last few weeks Maya's eyes had begun to show more than exhaustion and the dark shadows that had nearly overwhelmed her in the years between Emily's and Justine's births. The doctor who cared for Maya had been quite explicit in his instructions to Hale: Maya must have peace and tranquility

if she was ever to build up enough strength to risk another pregnancy.

Hale was determined that she would have whatever
she needed. Maya's presence had made his own life
much more productive, more comfortable, more en-
joyable. As a hostess she had no peer. She ran his
house and his business dinners with an elegance that
had people vying for invitations. She had taken Beth
and transformed her from a blind mouse of a girl into
a self-possessed and useful young woman. When he
came home at night or after a business trip, all was in
readiness for him—his favorite foods, his favorite cigars, his favorite chair with his favorite books on the
table, his favorite hassock ready to receive and rest his
weary feet.

All that his life lacked was a son to mold into a
suitable heir. Hale was impatient to have access to his
wife's bed and body once more, yet the doctor had
told him bluntly that if Maya became pregnant too
quickly, she would surely miscarry; and the doctor
feared that this time he would lose Maya as well as the
baby.

The thought of living without Maya distressed Hale
in ways that he didn't really understand. He had accepted the loss of his first wife with the strength, serenity and dignity that God and society required of
men. But he wasn't sure that he could be so accepting
of Maya's loss. Though he had married her for un-
christian reasons of jealousy and lust, he had come to
value her highly. No matter what circumstances she
found herself in, she did not complain. In fact, she
expressed her gratitude for being his wife in quiet ways
that pleased him immensely. Never did she flirt with
or encourage in any way the young men who were

drawn to her haunting beauty. She was utterly unaware of herself, far removed from the squalor of lust;
yet never, not once, had she refused the duties of the
marriage bed.

And she loved his children with a clear, burning
flame that humbled him.

Hale stood at the bottom of the gazebo steps and
looked at the three people standing beneath the airy
lattice of white wood. Beth and Maya were unaware of
his presence, one blind and the other with her eyes
tightly closed. Maya looked unwell, which made Hale
both uneasy and impatient. It had been six months
since he had opened her bedroom door and left his
seed within her body. The need to do so had become
very urgent.

"Hello, Father," Will said.

Neither man made any move to close the distance
between them.

"Hello, Willy."

Hale looked intently at Maya and Will, but saw
none of the barely veiled lust in his son's eyes that had
made Hale so violently angry five years ago. Will
looked at Maya with no emotion whatsoever. And she
did not look to Will at all.

Deep within Hale a knot of fear loosened. Will
might have lusted after Maya's perfect breasts and
smooth hips five years ago, but he did so no longer.
Maya might have teased and smiled and walked out
alone with Will once, but she was a married woman
now. Whatever she had been five years before, she was
a thoroughly decent woman today. She would not hu-
miliate or degrade her husband with indecent
thoughts, much less indecent actions.

"Beth has worried about you," Hale said. "You might have written more than one letter from London."

"That's all right," Beth said quickly. "I understand. I'm so glad to have Will back. Please don't quarrel with him, Father. You'll make him go away again."

"Don't worry, Mouse. I'm grown now. I don't run away for any man. I've come to the redwood country to stay. Through the years I've bought timber claims. I'm going to begin logging."

For the first time Maya was grateful that Beth was blind. The look Hale gave his son was a bleak bend of betrayal and anger. "You would become my enemy?"

"Competitor, Father. To have enemies requires emotion. Like you, I have none."

"You didn't have to go this far, Willy. I would have backed you if you had come to me."

"Really? The way you backed my other dreams?"

Hale flushed. "You were a boy, then."

"I'll always be a boy to you...until it's too late. But that's the nature of being human. We learn too little, too late. Won't it be comforting when you find out that you're as human as the rest of us?"

"I don't know what you're talking about."

Will smiled. "You will, Father. You will." He turned to include Maya in his cold smile. "I was remiss five years ago, but I'll make it up to both of you now. Your wedding present will take some time to deliver, Mrs. Hawthorne, but I'm sure you'll understand the extent of my apology when you see what the present is."

Maya looked into Will's gray eyes and saw a demon pulling at its chains, grinning.

"I've thought about it for a long time," Will continued. "The perfect wedding present. I had all but despaired when it came to me: timber for a timber baron. What could be more appropriate? So I am giving you a very special part of one of my timber claims."

"Oh?" Hale asked, curious despite the uneasiness that came every time he looked at his son and a stranger looked back at him with a cruel, predatory smile. "Where?"

"I have river bench land that supports some of the most magnificent trees in all the world. I want to make a present of one of those trees to the two of you. A very special tree. It will make perfect paneling for your bedroom suite. When I was a child, the Guardian was to me the most perfect tree on earth."

Maya couldn't prevent the hoarse sound she made. She covered it instantly by pretending to cough, but it was too late. Will had heard and understood. He smiled.

"The Guardian?" Hale said. "That monster tree you dragged me into the forest to see years ago?"

"The very one."

Hale sighed. "And the rest of your timber claims? Are they full of trees like that, trees that no man can cut or haul or mill?"

"Some of the claims, yes."

"You haven't learned a damned thing, have you?"

"On the contrary. I've learned much from you. For instance, I have nearly seven hundred acres of river bench land, flat land, land with magnificent trees—"

"Useless," interrupted Hale. "Useless!"

"Unless you want to build a railroad through Black Basin. Then my land becomes very, very valuable, for it controls river access to millions of board feet of the best redwoods on the coast. Without my river bench and flatland claims, all the money you've borrowed to buy up Black Basin watershed is wasted."

"It's you! You're Redwood Enterprises!"

Will smiled, but there was neither comfort nor mercy in the gesture.

"Yes, I'm the sole owner of Redwood Enterprises. We'll have to get together after Emily's party and talk about the railroad that you just borrowed many thousands of dollars to build into Black Basin. I'm sure we'll be able to reach some kind of an accommodation. Won't we?"

Hale looked into his son's eyes and suddenly felt very cold. Will had finally grown up, but he had become a stranger instead of the strong partner that Hale had always wanted.

No, not a stranger. Like Hale, he asked no quarter and gave none. Not a stranger at all.

An enemy.

Chapter Eleven

The Delmonico Hotel became Will Hawthorne's new home. It wasn't the finest hotel in Eureka, but it was more respectable than the crib-houses on First Street. There was a rugged masculinity to the Delmonico that appealed both to Victorian gentlemen and to frontiersmen alike. The Delmonico was also among the more tolerant establishments in Eureka. The dining room and lobby bar were open twenty-four hours a day, and the desk clerk cast a blind eye on the goings and comings of hotel guests—or their companions, for that matter. As a result, the Delmonico vibrated with activity no matter what the time of day or night. It became home to dozens of men like Will who were trying to turn a dollar, or a thousand, in the lumber business.

There were at least a dozen ways to get rich on the redwood coast. Most of the residents of the Delmonico had tried one or more variations on each of a dozen themes. To such men lumbering was an all day, every day, no-limit poker game. All the chips were green, and each one represented a six hundred and forty acre parcel of forestland that had a potential profit of ten thousand dollars an acre.

Some of the Delmonicans were timber cruisers who roamed the unexplored land, locating unclaimed timber stands on behalf of Eastern or European investor syndicates. Other residents were themselves speculators who bought, sold or traded timber claims, often sight unseen, on the basis of hunches or inside information about the continually changing needs of the lumber business. There were already ten mills operating in Eureka with a new mill being proposed each month. Every one of those mills chewed up logs and spat out finished lumber by the millions of board feet.

None of the existing mills was as big as Hale Hawthorne's Tres Santos, but several large Midwestern syndicates had sent agents to the redwoods to explore the prospects of the country. There were rumors of impending investment by a number of Lake State firms that had watched Kroeber's success with great interest. Each rumor fueled a speculation concerning the future price of logs in a volatile market which in turn directly affected the price of timber claims. As with unregulated claims-and-shares markets that sprang up in every mining city in the West, the purchase, sale and resale of logging claims were based on paper transactions rather than on a tangible exchange of goods. Most of the logging claims had been seen by only a handful of white men and were years away from being cut, but that just made the profits—and losses—in trading timber claims all the more extreme.

So many fortunes were made and lost in the Delmonico bar, with its pastel portraits of Rubenesque nudes, that it became known locally as the Stock Exchange. Action in the Stock Exchange might have been a bit more genteel than that in the Humboldt House, but it was every bit as cutthroat.

Will Hawthorne rented a small suite in the Delmonico Hotel on a full-time basis, despite the fact that he expected to spend no more than ten days a month in Eureka. The rest of the time he planned to be on the road, traveling to Crescent City or down to the doghole ports of the Mendocino Coast, prowling for timber claims and brokering cargoes of lumber, mostly for the South Seas and Australian trade.

But before Will's expectations for the future could be realized, it was necessary to consolidate his gains along the redwood coast. That, in turn, meant raising Hale to such a pitch of frustration and anxiety over his thwarted Black Basin railroad that he would be willing to settle the matter in any way that Will offered. Thus, for five weeks after Emily's belated birthday party, Will vanished into the woods, leaving Hale with an expensive railroad loan and no way to put it to work.

Part of those weeks Will spent on one of Henry Ising's small claims, felling trees with a heavy axe nearly four feet long. From time to time Ising would appear, and they would work as a team while Ising told of surveyors working in Black Basin along what would be the future railroad line; that is, as soon as Will's Redwood Enterprises ceded right-of-way for a railroad to Hale Hawthorne. Will listened and chopped, soothed by the strenuous exercise and the knowledge that each passing day meant that his father was gambling more money on eventually being able to obtain the right-of-way through his son's claims. Technically the surveyors were trespassing, but Will had expected it. His father would wait for no man, least of all Will. Hale had a railroad to build, and he was going to build it.

That was exactly what Will wanted. It was essential to his plans that his father be so deeply into Black Basin that he couldn't get out without going bankrupt. Only then would Will step in and offer a salvation too tempting for his father to refuse. Once Hale took the offer, he would be the same as a tree marked for felling, still outwardly strong, still upright—and inevitably doomed to go down in agony beneath the onslaught of steel axes.

Until that day, however, Will concentrated on the other aspects of building his own redwood empire. Unlike many of the speculators at the Stock Exchange, Will had no reluctance to muddy his boots or soil his hands in the timber-to-lumber business. His years as a timber beast and as a seaman had taught him the value of staying in touch with the men who were actually doing the physical work; it was there, where ax met timber, that fortunes were made or squandered.

So while his father stewed, Will toured prospective claims and talked to woods bosses and timber beasts. He also called at the machine shops and smith works along Second Street, keeping an eye on trends in forest tools and machinery. Steam power and electricity were new forces in the woods. Will looked to them for the solution to the problem of hundreds of millions of board feet of lumber locked up in trees too big to cut, transport or mill. The day would come when the big trees were unlocked for man, and Will intended to be right there with a pocket full of timber claims.

After five weeks Will decided that it was time to set the rest of his trap. Although unavailable by day he became a regular nighttime participant in the poker games that were the Stock Exchange's hallmark. He ate roast beef and drank good red wine from Napa Valley with syndicate agents. He bought drinks for timber cruisers, pumping them for inside information about the latest claims staking. He played cards until dawn with the other Delmonicans, exchanging gossip for hard information. Within a few days he became known as a formidable poker player, drinker and conversationalist. None of the men he met and laughed with saw past Will's easy camaraderie to the bleak calculation in his gray eyes.

That, too, was as Will had planned. He had learned in the past several years that the most accomplished predators left no sign of their presence but the cleanly gnawed bones of their prey.

The Associate Members of the Stock Exchange— the women who were as loose below the waist as they were stiffly corseted above—found Will to be endlessly fascinating. His appeal was more than his stunning good looks and rumored wealth; it was the fact that he laughed and joked with them but made no attempt to buy them for a week or a night or even an hour. There was never a question of his sexuality. The whores were quite adept at separating men into those who wanted women and those who wanted other men. But more than one pretty prostitute had draped herself across Will in the middle of a card game, teasing his earlobe with a lacquered fingernail or rubbing her breasts against him, only to discover to her chagrin that Will kept his sexual responses as tightly under wraps as his poker cards. He ignored everything up to and including a skillful hand exploring his crotch for a sign of interest. The sign was there, and unmistakable, but when Will had turned his head and let the prostitute look into his unshielded eyes, she had removed her hand and herself from his vicinity with remarkable speed.

That had marked the end of the whores' games, but
not of their interest in Will. When he was at the table,
it was very well attended by the prettiest Associate
Members of the Stock Exchange.

Hale Hawthorne knew that, as he knew everything
about Will that could be bought from spies. Nothing
that Hale had learned in the past five weeks had comforted him. Whatever Will had been five years before, he had changed so drastically as to become an
unknown quantity in the present. Too late Hale had
discovered that more than one of his business disappointments in the past three years had been the direct
result of Will's unseen presence. A key timber grant
here, a lumber schooner there, a dockside lumber price
undercut by a few tenths of a cent elsewhere; all of the
setbacks could be traced back to Henry Yesler and,
from there, to Redwood Enterprises.

If Hale hadn't found himself locked in combat with
Will, he would have admired him in many ways; when
all was said and done, Will had become a shrewd,
honest and utterly ruthless businessman. Hale felt a
real regret for having missed the signs of the man-to-
come in the boy-who-had-been. He also felt an odd
pride that his son had not turned out to be as soft and
impractical as he had seemed five years before.

In that one sense Hale knew that his marriage had
been an unqualified success. The loss of Maya had
made Will into a man.

Hale walked up to the table where a desultory game
of draw poker was in progress. It was seven o'clock,
too early for Will to be there. Hale knew that. He had

counted on it. He wanted to be firmly entrenched in the game before Will arrived.

"Hello, stranger," said Leland Grant. "Haven't seen much of you since you moved into your castle."

"Hello, Lee," Hale said, nodding and taking the chair that Grant's boot nudged out from the table. "Gentlemen."

As the men murmured their greetings, Hale looked around the table and found no fault with it. Arthur Kroeber, the second-biggest lumberman on the redwood coast was there. He had long since dropped the pretense of organizing a redwood lumbermen's association and was now more or less openly scouting timberland for "several eastern clients," a polite reference that everyone knew to mean the Midwestern Lumber Company, the St. Paul firm which dominated the lumber trade east of the Rockies. Leland Grant was the second man at the table. Like Kroeber, Grant was a displaced Lake State lumberman. But unlike Kroeber, Grant was interested in actually logging, milling and shipping wood, whereas Kroeber was a pure speculator, specializing in the sale and resale of undeveloped timber grants. The third man at the table, Andrew Smythe, claimed to be the black sheep of an aristocratic English family. Whatever his putative bloodlines, Smythe had enough cash to regularly win and lose large sums at the Stock Exchange's tables.

In short, the three men could take the poker game to whatever limit Hale wished.

"Mind if I sit in?" Hale asked.

"Not at all," said Smythe. "Kroeber's feeling stingy tonight. Won't lose more than two hundred dollars on a hand."

Kroeber smiled lazily and tapped the ash of his cigar onto the sawdust-covered floor. "That's right. I don't have a cap on winning, though. Ask Lee."

"Ask me what? You're into me for a thousand and you know it. But don't worry. I've got my eye on those six hundred acres of yours on the south side of Warrior Creek. All you have to do is sign over that little piece of paper and—"

"Be laughed out of town," Kroeber interrupted. "That land is worth six thousand if it's worth a dime."

Smythe flipped a dime onto the table. The coin rang musically, spun and then settled into silence as the men laughed.

With a smile Hale sat down and settled into the familiar routine of masculine chaffing. Although he hadn't played much poker since his marriage, he had no doubt about his ability to hold his own with steady gamblers. Poker was one thing that had always come easily to him. If the reports he had received were correct, poker was something that came easily to his son as well.

By the time nine o'clock came around, Hale had lost eight hundred dollars and won twice that much. He had also steered the conversation to the topic of his son.

"Yes, Willy's a fine boy, but a bit impetuous still," Hale said, studying his cards.

Kroeber gave a bark of laughter. "Impetuous? You haven't seen much of him lately. Will Hawthorne is about as impetuous as a river bench redwood."

"What would you call it when a boy promises a wedding present too big for him to deliver?" Hale asked, blowing out a stream of cigar smoke as he picked up his two-card draw.

"What was the present?"

"One of those river bench redwoods you just mentioned. Twenty feet through at the butt if it's an inch. One of the biggest of the big trees. Three hundred and fifty feet tall, maybe more. Straight as a ruler and tough as granite. I don't really blame the boy for rethinking his gift."

"What in hell would you do with it?" Kroeber grunted.

"Panel the bedrooms of my new house."

"A tree that big could panel a thousand bedrooms," Grant pointed out.

"As I said. Impetuous. The boy not only promised the tree to me, he said he'd cut it down in a week. That was five weeks ago. The tree was still standing, last time I looked." Hale flipped three five dollar chips into the pot. "I'll see you, Kroeber, and raise ten more."

Grant looked at his hand and tossed in fifteen dollars. "Just as well he hasn't delivered. No one can mill a bastard like that."

Hale shrugged. "Impetuous."

"I'll see your fifteen," Smythe said, "and bump ten more."

Kroeber looked at his hand, pushed four chips into the pile and said, "Call. Tell you what, Hawthorne. If Will ever gets it felled, you just bring it to one of my mills and I'll saw it up for free. I've got a new head rig I want to test, but no one's cutting anything big enough for me. And I'll raise you fifty."

"I'll see you," Hale said, "and raise you fifty more."

The other men folded. Kroeber called and turned over his hand at the same time Hale did.

"Got him by a ten of spades," Grant said, shaking his head as Hale pulled in the pot. "Just as well your pretty wife keeps you at home most nights. We'd be begging for drinks on the waterfront if you came down here more often."

The rest of the men laughed, including Kroeber. As they anted up for the next hand, there was a stir at the entrance to the saloon, followed by the sound of high heels clicking as several of the Associate Members began escorting someone from the front door to the poker area.

"Must be Will," Smythe said without looking up from the deal. "Those girls just can't stay away from his handsome face."

Kroeber grinned. "Maybe that's why that tree's still standing—Will's been spending too much time lying down."

Smythe snickered.

"Those girls sure do take it out of a man, don't they?" Grant said, smiling and picking up his cards. "They'll squeeze you until you're dry as a summer forest. Isn't that right, Hale? Oh, I forgot. You've given up that sort of thing."

"I'm a married man. I have no need of soiled doves."

Will heard his father's smug statement and knew that he was meant to hear it. It took every ounce of Will's control not to show how his father's words affected him. Will had no doubt that Hale didn't need recourse to prostitutes. The memories of Maya's hot, generous sensuality had made other women uninteresting to Will by comparison. The thought of Hale riding Maya night after night in a storm of ecstasy was the one thing that threatened Will's icy self-discipline.

And when he looked into his father's triumphant eyes, Will knew that Hale was very much aware of the sole chink in his son's armor.

"Good evening, gentlemen, Father," Will said calmly. "is there room for one more?"

"Hey, here's the woodsman in the flesh," Grant said, smiling. "Sit down and tell us how you're going to do it."

"Do what?"

"Bring him a beer, Louise. He'll need it," Grant said. "Put it on my account."

One of the Associates left for the bar. The other girls looked at the men, realized that there would be no point in hustling anyone for a few hours and left. Louise returned with a glass of dark beer, leaned well over Will's shoulder to set the glass in front of him and pouted when he wouldn't kiss her in return. As Louise left with a sultry swirl of her silks, Will drank two swallows of the beer and turned back toward Grant.

"Now, what is it that I'm supposed to do?"

"More like what you were supposed to have done," Hale murmured as he cut the deck for Kroeber's deal. "Shall we deal you in, Willy?"

The despised nickname rankled, but Will showed nothing. Hale used the name precisely because it rankled, and Will knew it.

"By all means, deal me in." He tossed in a five dollar chip as an ante and turned toward Grant. "What's on your mind?"

"It's—"

"Just a silly matter of a wedding present," Hale interrupted, dismissing the subject with a wave of his hand. "It's all right, Willy. Youngsters often speak before they think. We men know that."

Grant nodded without looking up from the cards that were being dealt. "I don't blame you a bit for taking your time with that tree. There's no way that you can chop down a really big redwood in a week."

"Six days. And I'll have help. Henry Ising."

Kroeber grunted. "You'll need him and his whole heathen tribe to boot."

Grant stared hard at the cards he had fanned narrowly in his hand. "Six days? Have you gone daft? Don't answer. And don't distract me. This hand has possibilities. Let's just see how well the rest of you like your cards." With that, Grant flipped several chips into the pot. "Twenty-five or fold."

"Grant's just talking to hear himself talk, Willy," said Hale. "Words are easy. It's action that makes a man. Here's your twenty-five, plus twenty-five of my own."

With a sigh Kroeber drummed his fingers on the table. Finally he threw in chips worth fifty dollars. "I'm in."

The players weren't impressed by Kroeber's show of reluctance any more than they had been impressed by Grant's show of exuberance. Talk was indeed cheap. It was seeing someone else's cards that was expensive.

Will said only, "Fifty, plus fifty more."

Smythe folded.

"You shouldn't let being laughed at affect your judgment," Hale said, glancing up at Will. "I don't imagine there's a man over twenty-five who didn't learn the hard way not to say things that can't be backed up. Here's your fifty plus fifty more."

By the time it got back around to Will, everyone but Kroeber and Hale had folded.

Will smiled coolly at his father. "Don't call a load too heavy until somebody can't pick it up."

"Or chop it down?" suggested Hale. Then he dismissed the matter again. "Don't worry, Willy. I won't hold you to it."

"I'll see you," Will said, putting more chips into the pot. "And raise you three hundred."

Hale smiled. "Of course. Money is so much easier. Is the pot to be your wedding gift? I'll see you and raise you five hundred."

Kroeber tossed in his cards. Will put in five hundred dollars. "Call."

"Full house," Will said, turning his cards faceup. "Jacks over sevens."

"Straight flush, queen high." Hale turned over the queen and stroked the card almost lovingly. "My beautiful redheaded queen of hearts has been very good to me. Especially at night."

Will watched his father's blunt fingers trace the stylized woman's body on the face of the card and wondered why his father was deliberately baiting him. Did he expect to drive him away again?

"You'll have your wedding gift in six days, beginning at midnight tomorrow."

Hale just smiled and shook his head. "Don't worry yourself about it, boy. I understand. We both know that no two men alive can bring down the Guardian in six days. Take your time," he added, shuffling. "Although it would be nice to have the wood before next summer."

"That tree will be on the ground by midnight of September twentieth," Will said flatly, picking up his cards.

Smythe looked at his cards and then at Will. "I don't think so, Will. Now, you know I'm a friend of yours and I'm also a shameless gambler. I've made some incredibly stupid wagers—for instance, I'm seeing the five-dollar raise on this hand. And I'm bumping it another twenty. But even I would have to bet against you and Ising, and I haven't even seen the tree."

"Careful, sport," Grant said, and it wasn't clear whether the warning was for Smythe or for Will.

"There's no need for care," Will said. "The Guardian will fall, and it will fall on schedule."

"I don't think so, Willy," Hale said. "In fact, I'd be willing to wager a considerable amount on it. One thousand acres of mixed fir and redwood in Black Basin against your entire Black Basin timber holdings, which is somewhat less than one thousand acres if I remember correctly. I'll see you, Smythe, and raise you twelve hundred."

"Twelve hundred!"

Smythe's yelp fell into the spreading pool of silence that had descended around the table as gamblers and onlookers alike absorbed the nature of the parallel wager that was being made.

Everyone folded until the play reached Will.

"What about you, Willy? Are you in?"

"Oh, I'm in, father. But not at the stakes you outlined. Without my Black Basin acreage, yours is a dead loss. So we'll bet my thousand acres in Black Basin against all your felled logs in Weeber Basin."

Silence spread throughout the Stock Exchange.

"There are nearly two years' worth of logs on the ground," Hale said.

"Because of the drought. Yes, I know. That's why building the railroad is so important for Tres Santos Company. Drought or flood, the logs will come down to the mill. *But only if you can build a railroad that opens up Black Basin's ten thousand acres of timber.*"

Hale smiled. "Your one thousand acres in Black Basin plus your word never to interfere in my business again."

"Your felled logs in Weeber basin plus the deed to the redwood palace."

"Done." Hale's voice was calm, but his eyes glittered with triumph. "Beginning midnight tomorrow, you have until midnight of the twentieth to fell the Guardian with no other chopper but Henry Ising."

"Agreed." Will pushed back from the table and stood.

"Wait a minute," Smythe said. "What's in Hale's hand?"

"You had your chance to see it," Hale pointed out. "You folded." He reached for the pot.

Suddenly twelve hundred-dollar gold pieces rained down on the table.

"Call," Will said softly.

Hale hesitated, then shrugged and turned over the two, seven, nine and ten of hearts. The fifth card was the jack of clubs. Will revealed his own hand one card at a time. A two of diamonds, a six of clubs, an eight of spades, a nine of spades—and the queen of hearts.

"I have your queen," Will said. "Nothing else. But that's all that matters, isn't it?" Smiling, he swept the pot into his hat.

"Enjoy it until midnight of the twentieth," Hale said casually, lighting his cigar and blowing a fragrant stream of smoke across the table. "For on the twenty-first, you will have nothing but the memory of what a fool you were tonight."

Henry Ising had been grumbling steadily since four a.m., when Will had rousted him from a warm bed and told him to hitch up his bulls to the supply wagon that had been packed and waiting for three weeks.

"Did anyone ever tell you that you're a surly bastard in the morning?" Will asked cheerfully.

Ising looked up from checking the wagon load of axes, springboards, food, cooking equipment, tents and everything else that they would need in the next week. "I'm a bastard twenty-four hours a day. The surly part I throw in for special occasions."

Smiling, Will threw a handful of metal tent stakes into a tin bucket and shoved it into a space among the supplies. The metal rang and clattered loudly in the morning silence.

"Don't look so glum," Will said. "Before you got homesick and left Washington, we brought down firs together that were fifteen feet through at the butt and we did it in four days."

Ising grunted. "A twenty-footer is twice as big, and you only gave us six days. Redwood's trickier, too. I don't think it can be done by two men."

Will turned and looked at his friend with gray eyes that concealed nothing of the demon howling within.

"Not just two men, Henry. *Us.*"

For a moment old superstitions blew across Ising like a chill wind, rippling flesh on the back of his neck and arms. Then the moment passed, and Ising nodded as he shook out a tarp and flung it over the wagon with an easy, powerful motion of his arms.

"You're sure we can get this rig all the way into the Guardian's grove?" Will asked.

"We might have to swamp out a little brush in the last couple of miles, but a high-ballin' logger like you shouldn't worry about that."

With feline quickness Will grabbed the end of the rope that Ising snapped across the load to him. Will tied off a piece of the tarp and snaked the rope back over the load to Ising's side of the wagon.

"I thought you wanted to help me bring down just one big tree," Will said quietly.

"I didn't expect to do it in less time than God took to make the world."

"Win or lose, five thousand dollars is yours to keep."

Ising shot Will a black look. "Shove your god-damn money. I wouldn't commit this kind of foolishness for cash."

"If it wasn't for you I'd have died in that cold sea. Half of what I win is yours—and if Indians could hold claims legally, half of every timber claim I own would be in your name already."

"You staked me to my oxen," Ising said flatly. "We're even."

"Never. Half of what I own is yours."

"Dammit, Will, be serious. Even your white God only takes a tenth."

"And the Devil takes all." Suddenly Will laughed and grabbed the rope that came sailing back over the tarp. "Sure as hell will be interesting to find out which one we're working for, won't it?"

Chapter Twelve

"I'm the only one who's going to get rich this week," Johnny Ising said with true Yurok satisfaction. "I'm going to charge a dollar admission to every timber beast and woods monkey that wants to watch the Guardian fall. And that's only for white folks. I'll charge Yuroks the equivalent in dentalia. That's a fair price, isn't it, Will?"

Will, who was riding alongside the slow-moving wagon, looked over to where Johnny was sprawled comfortably on the canvas tarp that covered the load. Johnny smiled up with the easy charm of a seventeen-year-old youth to whom life has been largely kind.

"Rich? You've been in the sun too long," Will said. "Henry, did you know your brother was tetched? We're five miles out in the woods along a skid road that's been abandoned for four years. Only thing that's going to come and look at us is a thieving blue jay."

"There's going to be a hundred people out there," Johnny said. "Hell, some of the woods bosses are even thinking about giving their men a day off to go out and watch the Guardian fall. Most of those folks never get to see a tree like that, much less to watch one come down. Right, Henry?''

Ising's only reply was to curse the off ox that kept skirting its share of the light load.

Johnny sat up on one elbow. "What's the matter with you? You worried about the bet?''

Ising glanced over his shoulder. "You're being paid to fetch water, cook and keep the axes sharp, not to be some goddamn carnival huckster. Any people come, just keep 'em out of our way, hear?''

There was no conversation for the next mile. Will finally reined his horse close to the wagon again.

"Why don't you crawl in back and sleep while I drive?'' Will asked Ising.

"Because old Buck is in a worse mood than I am, that's why," Ising said, flicking the offending ox lightly with the whip. "Put Johnny's lazy ass on your horse, and you sleep instead. You need it more than I do, and for damn sure, more than he does.''

After a moment's hesitation Will took Ising's advice.

Will didn't awaken until the last hundred yards leading to the small meadow where they would camp. Low evergreen boughs and tall brush compressed by the wagon's passage groaned over the frame and then whipped free, threatening to sweep Will off the tarp. He rubbed his eyes, yawned and stretched. A look at the sky told him that they had made good time despite Ising's and Buck's foul mood. It was barely past noon.

The first thing Will saw was a Tres Santos woods boss and a timber beast lounging around a small campfire. Will's mouth flattened into a thin line as he understood his father's silent message: Will wasn't trusted to wait until midnight to start chopping down the Guardian.

"Afternoon, Will," said Curtis, the woods boss.

Will nodded.

Curtis looked uncomfortable. "This ain't my idear. A lot of men have bets out. They was worrying 'bout midnight. I drew the short straw."

"I understand. And you understand that if anyone gets in my way, I'll chop him off at the knees." Will jumped off the wagon. "Henry, peg out the oxen in the west corner of the meadow. Johnny, drag the camp stuff up to that little rise. Should be dry there."

"Hell," Johnny said. "It's dry everywhere. Haven't had a decent storm in twenty months."

"Don't complain to me about it. That's why there are so many Tres Santos logs still on the ground. No river to float them down to the mill."

Alone, Will walked from the meadow's edge into the surrounding forest. Overhead the sky was clear, cloudless, a blue so pure it made his eyes burn. Dead ferns crackled underfoot. The generous carpet of moss was stiff and tinted more brown than green. Life seemed to have almost withdrawn from the woods, shut down, waiting for the yearly renewal of winter rains.

For a long time Will stood at the foot of the Guardian and tried to ignore the memories surging and flashing like chain lightning against the darkness of his mind. Maya's eyes so clear, so deep, watching him with dawning wonder. Her fingertips trembling as she touched his eyelids, his cheek, his lips. The velvet contrast of ruby nipple and white breast. The gliding, searing perfection of being sheathed within her satin depths....

Why couldn't she have loved me just a little when I loved her so much?

"You all right?"

The sound of Ising's voice sliced through Will's turmoil of memories and regret. He closed his eyes. When they opened, they held nothing of love or loss—only icy violence and the calculations of revenge.

"Just thinking where to make the cut," Will said flatly.

Ising glanced sideways at his friend. Will's face held no expression. Neither did his voice. But for a moment Ising would have sworn Will had been in pain.

"It's a big bastard, isn't it?" Ising said, measuring the Guardian's height and massive trunk. "Slow to taper, too. If we were doing this for a sawmill, we'd start almost twenty feet up. Maybe less but not much."

"We're not doing this for a sawmill. We'll start twelve feet up."

Ising said something under his breath, then sighed. "You want to win this bet or not?"

"The last springboard goes in at twelve feet. I promised a log twenty feet in diameter. That's what I'll deliver."

Emotionless gray eyes measured the Guardian. In the absence of mist and moisture, the bark had dried out to a rich cinnamon-colored column that went up and up into the sky until finally the first dark swirl of branches appeared. As with all big evergreens, when the crown grew upward, the branches that were shaded beneath the crown died. Dry, brittle, weighing hundreds of pounds and polished by weather into lethal points, the widow-makers hung poised overhead, waiting to be released by wind or the simple passage of time.

"Where do you want to bring it down?" Ising asked.

"There."

Will pointed just to his right, where he and Maya had lain in a sensual tangle and created memories that still had the power to bring him awake in the middle of the night, his body hard and shuddering with a need that no woman since her had been able to assuage.

"We better lay it down damn straight, then, else it'll hang on that fir."

"You see a better way?"

Ising shook his head. "A tree that big, there's no clean track for a fall." He measured the Guardian from root to crown again. "Should go all the way across the meadow."

Will didn't answer. Motionless, he stared up at the Guardian's lofty green branches, remembering a woman who had grown dizzy looking at such magnificence, remembering a time in the past when he had held all of life within his arms and heard it call his name in ecstasy, remembering . . . too much.

And then in his mind he heard the future . . . the tearing, dying scream of the big tree as it fell. A shudder passed through him. When the Guardian no longer stood over the dead dreams of the past, perhaps then he would finally be free of Maya and of the demon gnawing at his soul.

At five minutes before midnight Will sat near the campfire, a double-bladed ax across his lap, eyes focused on darkness. Firelight ran and glittered over the razor edges of the ax. Other campfires flickered on the meadow, and the sound of voices shivered through the air. Horses stamped and nickered, disturbed by the people who milled around and laughed and laid bets.

Will came to his feet in a single motion. Ising and Johnny followed suit. They walked toward the column of darkness that was the Guardian rising into the moonlit sky. Each man carried two lanterns and two axes. The waxing moon was balanced in the Guardian's branches. People melted aside in front of Will, Ising and Johnny as they walked. No one spoke until Arthur Kroeber stepped forward.

"One minute," Kroeber said, looking at his watch. "It's not too late to back out. I'll even buy that Black Basin land from you at double the going price."

Will walked past Kroeber to the Guardian, pulled out his own watch and waited. Ising lit several of the kerosene lanterns with a single sulfur match. Soft circles of yellow light bloomed like huge, exotic flowers on the forest floor. When he was satisfied, Ising turned to Kroeber.

"It's not too late to raise the stakes, either."

Kroeber snorted. "What did you have in mind? Seashells?"

"My span of oxen against the ten acres you own at the edge of the old Yurok village."

"Five acres is all your span's worth."

"Ten or nothing. Going, going . . ."

"I'll take it." Kroeber looked at his watch. "Midnight. Good luck, boys. You're going to need it, because you sure as hell don't have brains."

Neither Will nor Ising moved for a long ten count while Will watched the hands of his own watch close with midnight. When they did, he snapped the watch shut. The sound was startlingly loud in the silence.

"Now it's midnight. Let's go, Henry." As they bent over the stack of springboards, Will said softly, "You didn't have to bet your oxen."

"Kroeber makes my butt tired. Besides, if we lose, I won't need the oxen."

"You won't?"

"Hell, no. We'll bring down this son of a bitch or die trying."

They worked two hours by lantern light. First they toenailed the three-foot-long springboards into the thick bark at intervals of five feet. Then they began the undercut that would determine the direction of the Guardian's fall. When the boards were in place, Will and Ising alternated testing the security of the boards and the sharpness of the heavy axes by ripping off chunks of foot-thick bark. Very quickly sapwood showed through, gleaming in the moonlight.

The transparent silvery light was deceptive, concealing as much as it illuminated. Even with lanterns it was too dangerous for the men to work in close to one another, alternating ax strokes in a rhythm familiar to loggers anywhere in the world. Finally Ising stepped back and gestured toward the few small trees that grew in the direction the Guardian would fall. Will nodded without looking away from the redwood's gleaming body. While Ising cleared the felling path, Will's axe flashed and sliced into wood with a solid, rhythmic *thunk . . . thunk . . . thunk* that rang through the damp night air.

After a few hours both men rolled into their blankets, having done all they could in the dark. Ising slept. Will lay awake, waiting for the sun's clear light to aid in his revenge.

The ringing blows of an ax woke Ising. He opened his eyes to the dark gray of early dawn. There was only enough light for him to see the face of his watch. Four-thirty. He propped himself on his elbow, letting the cold morning air awaken him.

"Johnny. Johnny! Get your lazy ass out and make breakfast."

Ising got up, walked into the woods for a few moments, then returned for two big axes. Balancing the heavy tools on his shoulder, he walked toward the towering redwood that had presided over seven hundred thousand dawns.

The first day was one of testing. Will and Ising tested themselves and each other, gauging their joined strength against the demands of their work. There was no easy way to fell the Guardian. It was so thick that they could not attack it with a crosscut saw. Even the longest woods saw—which was nothing more than two six-foot crosscut saws brazed together into a single band—was too short to make the undercut that would determine the line along which the redwood's massive bole would fall.

Instead of the faster, easier work of sawing, Will and Ising were faced with the task of chopping a deep wedge into the falling side of the trunk, carefully gauging the direction of the fall with an iron frame called a gunsight. When they were satisfied with the undercut, they would switch to the tree's opposite side and make another, larger wedge-shaped cut, chopping the cut deeper and deeper into the living bole until there wasn't enough structural integrity remaining to support the tree.

Will had estimated that the initial undercut would reach four feet into the trunk and would have to be four feet high. Most of the work could be done from the springboards that he and Ising had notched into the tree. But the off-side cut would have to be at least six feet from top to bottom, so that the two choppers would have room to swing their axes while reaching all the way into the heart of the Guardian, a distance of ten feet.

The volume of wood to be chipped away was enormous. To be done at all, the work required great skill, strength and concentration; but to be done in six days, it would require the kind of stamina from which legends were made.

After a time both men climbed down their springboard stairway and ate the mammoth breakfast that Johnny had cooked. The bole of the Guardian looked as though it had barely been nicked; despite the deep pile of chips that had begun to accumulate at the massive base of the tree.

A half hour later Will and Ising climbed back up the bole, took positions facing one another and began wielding the heavy double-bladed axes with an unvarying rhythm. After ten minutes they changed places so as to exercise the other side of their bodies. Despite the cool air they sweated profusely, darkening their flannel shirts until the plaid blurred into an undifferentiated black. Every thirty minutes they stopped for water. Sometimes they changed axes, taking up one that Johnny had just sharpened.

By ten o'clock that morning, most of the onlookers had drifted back to their own jobs in the woods. Curtis and the other man remained, watching and doing nothing until Will changed axes in rapid succession. Without a word Curtis picked up the discarded ax, thumbed the edge and took the sharpening steel from

Johnny's hands. Johnny started to object, decided better of it and went to get the spare steel.

Ten minutes later Curtis passed the ax blade over the back of his hand, frowned, and went back to work. Five minutes after that he tried again. He smiled as a fine patina of hair came off to coat the ax's edge.

"Yo! Will! Try this one!"

Will caught the ax handle, thumbed the edge of the blade and looked down at Curtis. "That's one I owe you."

"Like hell. A man gets right bored watching chips fall."

Johnny brought a big midmorning lunch, for Will and Ising were burning up an enormous amount of energy. He also brought two more axes that had been sharpened by Curtis's very skilled hands. Will and Ising worked until noon, then took a one-hour break for food and rest.

Ising lay on his blankets, listening to the sharp calling of Steller's jays in the branches overhead. The sunshine was a golden, weightless river of warmth. He closed his eyes, letting the sun warm his face as he rolled his stiff left shoulder, loosening cramped muscles.

Will lay on his own blankets, his head propped on his elbow. He knew he should try to nap, but he could not, any more than he had been able to sleep last night. Beneath his harsh self-control he hummed with raging energy that was a volatile mixture of hatred and desire. He had learned to channel that energy in the past; it had brought him a long, long way in just a few years, for while other men had slept and laughed and caroused, Will had planned and worked toward revenge with the singlemindedness that defined obses-

sion. Now he was within days of seeing his every plan
come to fruition. Now the demon was up and pacing
within the prison of his soul, testing his control,
snarling to be free, to dip its demon muzzle in the ruin
of Maya's life and howl victory to the black skies of
hell.

Abruptly Will sat up, impatient to be back at the
tree.

"It would be a lot quicker to chop off what hangs
between your legs," Ising said without opening his
eyes.

"Is that the Yurok solution?"

"Yuroks don't have the problem. We want something, we buy it. If a Yurok breaks tribal law, he pays
a fine. If he can't pay, he becomes a slave. If he wants
his father's woman, he knows just what the cost is in
advance. With dentalia everything is possible."

Will froze, wondering how Ising had known.

"But white men aren't the same," Ising continued.
"They have a thousand ways to drive themselves
crazy. A lot of them revolve around women. So chop
it off or find another woman."

"I've tried other women. It didn't work."

Ising sighed and opened his eyes. He didn't bother
to argue. He had seen Will's eyes when he had held
Maya's limp body in his arms after they had both been
pulled from the sea. Ising had tried to warn Will then
about getting crossways with fate. Will hadn't listened. He wouldn't listen now. It was too late. It had
been too late since the first moment he had looked at
Maya and marked her out as his.

The undercut was completed on the second morning despite an ax shaft that had split in Will's hands.

Just before lunch he replanted the springboards on the off-side of the Guardian. Ising watched with real satisfaction, not minding the ache of his body from balancing on the narrow springboard and swinging a heavy ax. As the last springboard was toenailed in, he smiled. They were doing well. Now all he had to do was to get Will to slow down before he burned out. At least he had slept most of last night. He should sleep well tonight, too, despite the *woge* that lived behind his gray eyes.

The men worked steadily through the afternoon, switching places with the same unvarying rhythm that they swung the whistling ax heads into the Guardian's trunk. There was no breeze, no cooling veil of mist or cloud, nothing to stir the hot silence of the forest but the metronome of steel ax blades chewing into living wood. Camp fire smoke hazed the little meadow. From time to time people would ride or walk through the woods, measure the amount of cut against the thickness of untouched trunk and shake their heads. Despite the heaped, fragrant mounds of chips, the men looked insignificant against the Guardian's massive bole.

As the last slanting rays of blood-red light filtered through the campfire smoke, Will broke the rhythm.

"Let's knock off for the day."

Ising smiled grimly and thanked his private gods for the return of common sense. Perhaps Will's devil wouldn't ride him into the ground with exhaustion before the Guardian fell. Or perhaps even demons needed rest.

As Ising swung down from the last springboard, he grunted at the impact of the ground. His feet and calves ached from the incessant balancing act on the narrow perch the springboard offered. Will groaned as well, then flexed his right hand repeatedly. When Ising looked over, Will turned away, concealing his palm. Ising's hand shot out and wrapped around Will's right wrist and held it in a ray of fading light.

A long, ragged cut bordered with bruises marked the place where the ax shaft had shattered in Will's grip. Ising looked at the other hand. No cut, but the shadows of bruises forming beneath the rime of callus were all too clear.

Ising said nothing. There was nothing to say. Will's hand had been hurt, and only time would heal it. He didn't have time.

"I'll wear gloves."

Ising shot him a look of disbelief. Any working man could see that it was too late for gloves. He let the matter pass, but that night, after they had eaten, he drew Johnny aside and gave him a careful set of instruction. Johnny listened, nodded and disappeared into the darkness.

If Will noticed Johnny's absence, he said nothing, not even the next morning when he awoke to find Ising preparing breakfast himself. The two men were back on the springboards by dawn. Will wore a pair of soft leather gloves. Ising watched from the corner of his eyes but could detect no awkwardness. Certainly there was no slowing of Will's pace nor of the depth of the ax blade's bite.

Three hours later Will and Ising were still on the boards, chopping, when Johnny returned. He was accompanied by a dozen Indians. There were eleven men plus a woman in her early twenties. She had a broad-featured, striking face and the strong, ample body of a well-bred member of the local aristocracy. She wore thirteen strings of dentalia around her neck, an extraordinary declaration of wealth and position.

Ising swung down from the springboard and shot a look of irritation at his brother.

"I said we needed a shaman, not an audience. And I asked for the Old-Woman-Who-Lives-Upstream."

Ising spoke in Yurok and used the nickname of the most powerful shaman in his village. To speak her given name in that language would have been the harshest personal insult possible in the Yurok culture.

The young woman's eyes narrowed as she met Ising's gaze. She gave him back a look that took in his white man's clothing and the oversized ax in his hands. She did not appear to be impressed with what she saw.

"She's Tolowa," Johnny said quickly. "None of the Yurok shamans would come to heal a white man. I met her and her brother on the river. The brother says she's the most famous shaman in her clan, even though she is young."

"Young? She's not old enough to have experienced pain, much less to know how to cure it."

"What do you know of pain, half-man?" she asked calmly.

"More than a whole man," Ising retorted. "What of you, woman?"

The shaman simply looked at him with unflinching black eyes. For an uneasy moment Ising felt as though he were seeing through a window into a place where ice was black and burned with cold crystal flames.

"I see you, shaman," Ising said, looking away.

The woman's eyelids flickered down for an instant, and then she smiled, showing him the face of a desirable young woman. "I see you, man."

In the twilight her heavy strings of shell money gleamed mysteriously with each breath she drew. Despite her youth she obviously had the confidence of her own kind. There was no other way a young woman could have garnered such wealth.

"Can you see the pain of a white man and heal him as well?" Ising asked. "It will be a simple thing. There is no evil spirit involved."

The shaman glanced aside at Will, who had said nothing since the Indians had come into camp.

"His spirit is . . . too powerful. To heal it will require that which I do not have."

"Balls," muttered Ising. "It's his hands I'm worried about. His soul is his own problem."

Will understood enough Yurok to catch the reference to white man and hands. When Ising gestured, Will turned away from the group.

"I'm fine," he said curtly.

The shaman's hands flashed out with surprising speed. She had the glove off Will's right hand before he could object. The battered skin oozed clear fluid mixed with blood. The bruises had darkened.

"Hell, you won't even be able to close that hand tomorrow," Ising said, "much less hold an ax handle."

"You're wrong."

Ising looked at Will and said no more. Will's eyes were the same window into a different, much darker reality that the shaman's eyes had been.

The woman touched the weeping cut firmly with her fingertips and prodded the bruises as well, watching Will's eyes as she did. He didn't flinch. After a few moments she nodded and pointed to his left hand. He peeled off that glove as well. The palm wasn't as bruised, but it still must have been painful. Even so, Will didn't move while the shaman's strong, narrow fingers tested the flesh and bone.

"I will give him a balm to keep the raw flesh sweet."

"Will he be able to keep chopping?" Ising demanded.

The shaman laughed. "Don't you know this man?" she asked softly. "He will chop if he must tie the ax to the bloody stump of his wrist."

The shaman and the Yuroks were not the only people drawn to the Guardian's grove. In the next twenty-four hours seven timber cruisers from the Stock Exchange wandered in with enough supplies to see them through the remainder of the bet. The men set up camp, then gathered around the Guardian and assessed the task still confronting the choppers. The cruisers were Will's colleagues, speculators all. They quickly split into two relatively good-natured camps—those few who thought Will and Ising might win and the overwhelming majority who backed Hale Hawthorne.

Then, about midafternoon of the third day, a mud-caked buggy rolled into the clearing. The driver was well dressed in the style of a steamboat gambler and very narrow between the eyes. The man with him was thickly built and sullen of face. The gambler got down from the buggy and eyed the clearing beneath the Guardian with anticipation. There were between twenty and thirty men lounging about with nothing better to do than drink and count chips falling. He wished he had thought to bring a few hurdy-gurdy girls and one or two outright prostitutes, as well. Even Chinese girls could be sold for good prices, if there were no other females around and if enough men were in a mood to celebrate.

The gambler glanced toward the small band of Yurok youths who idled around the fire and wondered if the boys knew of Indian women available for work. The Yuroks were still rumored to buy and sell slaves, and Indian women were better than no women at all. The gambler shot the cuffs of his brocaded shirt and headed for the crowd of Stock Exchange cruisers who were standing with heads thrown back, watching the two choppers on their springboards.

Within an hour several tables were set up, as well as a bar that consisted of a plank laid across two whiskey barrels. The impromptu bar was attended by the gambler's heavyset companion. Even at triple the usual price, there was no lack of customers for warm whiskey served in dirty shot glasses. It was the same for the gaming tables; triple the customary house percentage did nothing to discourage the spectators from trying their luck.

By late afternoon there were a half-dozen fires in the meadow sending smoke into the damp, still air. Loggers and sailors from Eureka continued to arrive to witness the progress of the impossible bet. Another small band of Yuroks showed up just before sunset and set up camp with their comrades, bringing the population of the Guardian's meadow to more than fifty.

Whoops of laughter and outrage drifted up from the gambling tables to fill the silences between ax strokes. Will found himself growing increasingly irritated at the audience the bet had attracted. In all the years that he had planned revenge, he hadn't foreseen that his private vendetta would end up as a public amusement for drunken louts. The anger Will felt didn't distract him; he used it to power his ax and to dull the pulse-beats of pain within his hands. Anger countered the weariness in his legs as he balanced on the narrow springboard. Anger dimmed the ache of a body that had known too little sleep.

At sunset Will and Ising climbed down wearily from their perches and made their way to their own camp, expecting to find Johnny preparing food. They were both startled to find the Tolowa shaman kneeling beside the fire, turning a whole haunch of venison on a spit.

"What are you doing here?" Ising demanded. "I thought you and your brother were headed for Trinidad. And what happened to Johnny?"

"Your brother is as lazy as a coyote," the woman said. "He went off to drink with some other lazy Yuroks this afternoon. Now he can't see the fire, much less cook food on it. You must eat, and so must your friend. So I cook for you."

With a quick, graceful strength the shaman stood up from the fire. She approached Will and held out her hands, indicating that she wished to see his palms again. With more gentleness than before, she stripped away the leather gloves that were now soaked dark with sweat and blood.

Ising drew a breath through clenched teeth at the sight of Will's hands. Both palms were dark and swollen with bruises. The right palm was crusted with blood and the clear serum that oozed through the broken skin and battered flesh.

"You're going to cripple yourself if you keep that up," Ising said.

Will said nothing.

The shaman said only, "You have been using the balm. Good."

By the end of the fourth day the meadow and the surrounding forest had become a carnival ground with several hundred spectators camped beneath the canopy of redwoods. The area around the base of the Guardian was littered with chips of wood. Beyond the tree, ferns and brush had been beaten flat for several hundred feet in all directions by the crowds that gathered to watch and to applaud or to disparage the efforts of Will and Ising. Some of the men from the Stock Exchange finally erected a rope barrier to keep the spectators at a reasonable distance from the work. Even so, Will and Ising were never alone; the sounds of carousing at the outlying campfires kept them awake long into the night. By day it was the same, male shouts and laughter drowning out even the beat of the ax heads into wood.

By noon of the fifth day gamblers stood at the base of the Guardian, timing the ax strokes and measuring the size of the resultant chips, comparing them with chips from the first day or two, looking for signs of weakness in Will and Ising. The arguments among the gamblers were like the buzzing of flies to Will—distant, small, meaningless. He was wholly consumed by the necessity of driving his own body beyond its human limits.

While the work so far had opened up a deep enough cut in the Guardian's bole that both men could stand on the stable platform of the living tree itself to chop, Will and Ising still had what appeared to be at least a third of the job in front of them. Canny handicappers and timber beasts were giving odds of five to one that the Guardian would still be standing on midnight of the sixth day.

The shaman remained in their camp. By day she cooked and nursed Will's wounded hands and massaged the knotted, aching muscles of both men. By night she lay with Ising, murmuring soft incantations to him and to Will as they slept. Will himself was so focused on shutting out pain that he barely noticed the world around him. When he walked to and from the Guardian, men learned to step out of his way for the simple reason that he would walk right over them if they didn't. When he closed his eyes he saw the flash of ax blade into wood, and when he woke it was the same.

Late on the fifth day Will's focus shifted. It began when he and Ising stopped to assess their progress. Will thought that he had allowed a shallow enough angle of entry to compensate for the difference between chopping down a fifteen-foot diameter fir and a twenty-foot diameter redwood. He had not. The cut was too steeply angled. It would not dive deeply enough into heartwood to fell the Guardian.

They had two choices: they could widen the cut, allowing themselves to force it past the heart of the tree, or they could push the triangular cut to its apex and then go to work with a crosscut "misery whip" and wedges, sawing through the final foot or two of trunk from one side.

The choice was difficult. Making a new angle on the cut would take longer, but it allowed them greater control over the path of the Guardian's fall. Sawing from beside the two cuts was faster, but it was dangerous, both to the sawyers and to the spectators. It raised the distinct possibility that the trunk wouldn't fall along the predicted path but to one side or the other. Under normal circumstances that risk was acceptable, but now there were hundreds of spectators, half of them drunk, crowding in around the Guardian.

Just as Will was about to call for the misery whip and let the unwanted, uninvited spectators take their chances, the sound of childish laughter penetrated his harsh focus on the Guardian. He looked down from his perch and saw children playing hide-and-seek around the base of the tree, saw other children burying each other in mounds of fresh chips, saw still more children fetching wood or water for their family's needs.

"Get them out of here!" Will said hoarsely.

Ising shook his head. "We've tried. It hasn't worked. No one believes the tree will come down in six days, so no one is worried about being in the way."

Will closed his eyes and tried to tell himself that it wasn't his problem. He had come here to bring down the Guardian—and with it, Maya and Hale Hawthorne. If spectators wanted to risk their lives and those of their children by treating the bet as though it were a carnival, that wasn't his concern.

Laughter drifted up to him. In the clear air it was impossible to tell how near or far the children were, whether they were boys or girls, whether it was now or fifteen years ago when Will and Beth had played the same games, laughing and chasing each other with no thought for the next instant or the one after that. He had inadvertently been the cause of Beth's panicked flight down the stairs and into blindness; suddenly he knew that he couldn't live with himself if he caused harm to another child.

He couldn't bring down a hundred tons of undirected tree into the midst of laughing children. Nor was there any way to keep the area around the Guardian clear for more than one hundred and fifteen yards in all directions, which was the absolute minimum safety would require.

Without a word Will went back to the springboard and began the agonizing job of widening the cut. When the gamblers realized what had happened, the posted odds against Will's success rose sharply. The children continued to race and laugh and play with unabated enthusiasm, aware only of themselves and the sun and the glistening mounds of chips freshly fallen from the axes whistling overhead.

Initially the decision not to saw seemed to give both Will and Ising new energy. Will swung his ax as though its weight had suddenly been halved. He knew that he had reduced his chance of success. He also knew that the only way of compensating for his choice was to redouble his efforts. After dinner he went back to work, swinging the ax by lantern light, pushing himself beyond any man's ability to endure, driven by the demon within.

On the morning of the next day Maya came to stand in the Guardian's fragrant shadow.

Chapter Thirteen

As Hale led her across the last bit of the meadow, Maya felt her panic ease. Nothing looked familiar. Nothing called up those memories from the past that had haunted her for years. Instead of being a soft, living green, the meadow was brown and littered with bottles. Instead of being infused with evergreens and sunshine, the breeze smelled of campfires, coffee and pots of beans simmering at the back of sooty grates. Instead of the elemental privacy and intimacy of Eden, there were people thronged ten deep, pushing and shoving to get closer to the roped-off area around the base of the Guardian.

This wasn't the place of her memories and dreams. There was no silence here, no serenity, no primal sensuality. She had been afraid that her memories would betray her if she came back to the grove, that somehow people would look at her and Will and know what had happened beneath the Guardian's fragrant silence five years before. That was why she had initially refused to accompany Hale to the meadow. He had been first surprised and finally angry at her stubbornness. In the end she had given in and gone to the meadow because Hale had left her no other choice except to tell him why she didn't want to go. That was the one thing Maya could not do.

She followed Hale while he pushed through the crowd, and she tried not to hear the fragments of conversation around her. It was impossible. Even if she hadn't overheard a single word, Hale's expression would have told her that Will wasn't doing well.

"... can tell you that Will is as game as they come, but he doesn't have a chance."

"Kroeber is giving eight to one against Will. That narrow-eyed gambler is giving nine."

"Seen his hands? It's a miracle he can pick up an ax, much less chop with it."

"Look at that big bastard. Why, a man could gnaw at it forever and not ..."

Maya wondered if Hale had heard the people, until he glanced over his shoulder to see if she was following him. His eyes were heavy-lidded, his expression calm and satisfied, as though he had just left her bed. Nausea twisted through Maya, shaking her. Suddenly, irrationally, she was quite certain that Hale knew what had taken place five years before in the Guardian's towering presence. Hale had never said a word to her, never chastised her, never so much as hinted that he knew she had lain with another man before she became Hale Hawthorne's wife.

He couldn't know. Will never told him and I bled in Hale's bed that first night as freely as any virgin ever did.

In the past Maya had told herself that the conflict between father and son had existed before Will had pulled her from the sea and proclaimed her to be his own. She might have intensified the conflict, yet she hadn't caused it; Will would have fought Hale even if

Maya had never been born. But would Hale have taken such pleasure in his son's destruction? Would Will have become hard and cruel, intent on ruining his father? In assuring her unborn children's future, had she unwittingly destroyed not only herself but another woman's son as well?

A shudder of rebellion went through Maya. She hated being near the Guardian again, hated seeing Will, hated seeing Hale's heavy-lidded triumph and knowing that she was the cause of it all, both the destruction and the cruel satisfaction.

The last of the crowd parted, giving a clear view of the Guardian and the two men who worked in such close harmony, swinging lethally sharp steel axes in an unvarying rhythm. Maya could not help the soft sound that escaped her lips at the sight of Will naked to the waist, shining with sweat, standing in the space he had chopped out of the redwood's living trunk. She had forgotten how strong he was, how his muscles slid and coiled so smoothly, so powerfully. Yet against the Guardian's massive elegance, even Will seemed but a toy man pecking at a tree too big to comprehend.

If the world were a ship, this would be its mast.

Will's words from the past returned, haunting Maya even as the sight of his grace and power swept through her, shaking her.

Standing beside Maya, Hale took in the tree, the two men and the newly angled cut with a single glance. "Looks as though you've got a problem, Willy. You hurried the cut. That's the trouble with youth. No foresight or patience."

The rhythmic sound of the axes stopped. Will spun around and looked down, leaning on his ax. When he saw Maya's upturned face he forgot the exhaustion draining his strength. The pity and pain she felt for him were so clear on her face that it enraged him.

"Hand her up, Father."

Hale looked startled. "I hardly think that—"

Impatiently Will interrupted. "Hand her up. Now!"

The command in Will's voice cracked like a bullwhip. Instinctively Hale knew that he could obey, or he could subject the Hawthorne family to a very public airing of very private injuries. Without a word Hale stepped onto one of the lower springboards and helped Maya mount the tree. The springboards had been placed for the convenience of unusually large men. In order for Maya to climb into the cut, Hale had to literally hand his wife up into his son's arms.

Will's nostrils flared as the remembered scent of Maya expanded through his senses. He saw her pupils dilate, darkening her green eyes. He felt the trembling of her body when he touched it. He heard the tiny, helpless sound she made when he tightened his strong hands and lifted her easily up to him.

"Frightened?" he asked coolly.

Maya couldn't answer. She had never thought to be this close to Will again. The reality of it made her dizzy. Without knowing it, she clung to the hard strength of his forearms. When he felt her nails digging into his flesh, passion scored through him. The smile he gave her was like a knife sliding free of its sheath—polished, brilliant, promising pain.

"I didn't want to come here," she whispered. "Will, please believe me. I didn't want to come!"

The darkness and wild glitter in his eyes didn't change. "I'm glad you came," he said softly, smiling. "My father brought you here to witness my defeat, but every time I look at you I feel hatred like raw lightning in my veins. I'm not tired any longer. I'm going to bring down this tree and my father with it. And you, Maya. You most of all."

She closed her eyes and swayed beneath the tangible waves of his hatred beating at her. Suddenly Will shifted his grip, lifting her from the fragrant cave he had chipped from the Guardian's living trunk. He said nothing in answer to her startled cry, simply dangled her over the lip of the cut until Hale reached up and took Maya by the waist.

"A sorry lumberman's wife," Will said, staring at his father. "She has no head for heights. Take her before she faints."

Without a backward look Will picked up his ax and attacked the Guardian as though it were the first day rather than the fifth.

The rude carnival that had sprung up around the meadow reached a fever pitch on the fifth night. The big grove was awash with the twisting light of campfires. The meadow had become a small town with its own residential neighborhoods and a small commercial district populated by drummers and merchants peddling food and whiskey from the back of wagons. There was even a rowdy red-light district where several gamblers had set up a dirt dance floor and a line of crib tents just beyond the firelight.

Hale found members of the Stock Exchange in residence at a campfire close to the drummers' wagons. His own tent was at the opposite side of the meadow, next to Will's camp. Maya, pleading exhaustion, had spent much of the day in the tent, eating little and saying less. After Maya heard Hale go off to a poker game to absorb the congratulations of his peers, she came out and sat and watched flames twist together in the heart of the campfire.

Long after darkness came, the sound of chopping echoed through the forest. Maya looked at her arms where Will had gripped her. His blood had crusted and dried on her skin. She touched the dark smudges with her fingertips, feeling a pain unlike any she had ever known spear through her.

Finally the sounds of axes biting into wood stopped, telling her that Will's self-imposed agony had ended for a time. With a soundless prayer of thanks she went back inside the tent. A few minutes later she heard him walking into his camp. She didn't question how she knew Will's footsteps from Ising's; she simply knew that Will sat with his back to her campsite and Ising did not. She heard the sound of dinner being scraped from tin plates, silence and then a stifled groan when Will rolled into his blankets and slept not ten feet from where Maya lay in her tent. Helplessly she touched the canvas separating them. When she realized what she had done, she wrenched herself over onto her opposite side and closed her eyes, praying for sleep with something close to despair.

She was still awake when Hale came back, smelling of whiskey and male desire. He fumbled the tent flap shut and felt his way to his own bedroll. Maya breathed carefully, evenly, as though she were deeply asleep.

"Lass?"

Maya said nothing, did nothing.

Her covers were dragged down. When his hand gripped her breast, she gasped.

"Dinna worry, lass. 'Tis only your husband."

When Hale began dragging up the hem of Maya's nightgown, a strange, icy anger blossomed in her.

"Not here," she said in a stranger's empty voice. "Not now."

There was no answer but that of his cold hands separating her thighs. The smell of whiskey washed over her.

"If you won't think of my physical health, at least respect me as your wife. Your *wife*, Mr. Hawthorne, not a whore to be taken on the dirt floor of a tent where everyone may hear your rutting noises. Or is that what you had in mind? Is it myself that you want, or is this just a way of proving to Will that you are still man enough to lie with a woman?"

For an instant Hale froze; then he rolled off Maya and went to his own bedroll without a word. Long after his hoarse, rhythmic breathing told her that he was asleep, Maya lay awake, shuddering, her eyes wide and painfully dry.

Will awakened before dawn, listening to the sounds of the forest. During the last hours of darkness a fog had come in. He could smell it, feel it, taste it, hear it dripping from evergreen boughs to the resilient forest floor. Cold and damp had stiffened him as he lay on the ground. He had slept fewer than five hours. It wasn't enough, but that no longer mattered, any more than his cramped muscles mattered. It was the same for his hands, which burned and bled even in his dreams. They didn't matter, either. All that mattered was the picture he kept in his mind, that of Hale coming out of Maya's room, slick with lust and satiation.

As Will kicked aside his covers and pulled on his boots, the shaman walked back into camp, carrying an armload of firewood. The sound of the wood being dropped to the ground roused Ising. They both ate a cold, silent breakfast before walking side by side to the Guardian. In the predawn gloaming the tree seemed untouched but for windrows of chips scattered like dark snow at the base. The springboards creaked as they took the weight of the men. Moments later, the rhythmic violence resumed, steel against living tree, two men against a towering redwood—and one man against the demon within, eating him alive.

The widening of the wedge-shaped cut went quickly, with foot-deep chunks of redwood leaping out from the trunk as though alive and fleeing the ax. Will and Ising worked steadily through the morning while the rest of the citizens of the tent city slept late, recovering from their bacchanalia the night before.

By noon spectators began to gather again. Murmurs of surprise went around as they realized that the wedge already had been widened and the men were now working again on deepening the cut itself. They were chopping directly beneath the butt of the redwood, working in the opening they had chipped out, standing well inside an overhanging ceiling of living tree. Every flying bit of redwood that leaped from their axes meant that much less fiber to balance and support the hundred tons of redwood that hung poised above their heads. Even using axes with handles four feet long, Will and Ising were forced to bend at an awkward angle to reach the remaining wood. Less than half of the heartwood remained.

From time to time Ising would stop, lean on his ax handle for a few moments, then resume the chopping rhythm. Will paused as well. Despite the cool air they had taken off their shirts. Suddenly a freshening wind set the tops of the trees to swaying.

"Wait!" Will said roughly.

Ising didn't need to be told twice. He leaned heavily on his ax and listened as intently as Will. Both men knew that giant evergreens usually gave some warning before they toppled, although that warning might be nothing more than an explosive popping noise as they pitched over and fell toward the ground. Sometimes evergreens remained upright and then shot straight down upon their stumps, rather than toppling sideways. If that happened without warning, Will and Ising would be crushed instantly. Even if the redwood fell properly, the butt might shatter on impact, sending a hail of spear-point "splinters" in all directions. Until the Guardian fell, no one could predict how the tree would act in its death throes.

"Anything?" Will asked.

Ising shook his head.

They both stepped out on springboards, laid their palms on the trunk above the cut and looked up and up and up to where wisps of fog still wreathed the Guardian's crown. There were no telltale vibrations in the trunk. Nor did the redwood's branches sway more to the breeze than those of neighboring trees.

As one, Will and Ising went back and crouched beneath the towering column of wood, chopping steadily, pausing from time to time to listen. They heard nothing as the long day wore on but the voices of spectators and sharpened steel singing through air to bury itself in wood.

Johnny brought their lunch, wearing a sheepish smile and a blinding hangover.

"The shaman told me to take care of you, or she would send a *woge* to gnaw on my liver."

"She's gone?" Will asked.

"Left an hour ago."

Will looked at Ising, who seemed undisturbed.

As though Will had asked a question, Ising said, "She is a shaman, now. When she is a woman as well, she will find me again."

After eating, Will and Ising climbed back up into their fragrant, man-made cavern. Steel sank into wood in a steady rhythm once more, and once more spectators pushed and crowded forward in order to better gauge the progress being made firsthand. Hale came to stand among the men. For a few minutes he looked up at the son who was bigger and stronger than he and then turned away.

Maya did not go to the tree. She lay in her bedroll with her eyes open, listening to each blow of the axes, knowing that with each stroke Will was trying to cut through the intangible cords that bound him to her. She listened, feeling each blow, holding the picture of her plump, healthy children in her mind as though her life depended on recalling just how sweet their smiles were.

She didn't know how long it was until the sound of the two axes faltered and died. One ax took up the rhythm again. Maya listened, breath achingly held, and then she sighed. Will's strength hadn't given out. It was his ax that still worked, a rhythmic steel chant continuing, ringing through the hours, singing death to the living tree.

As sunlight slanted into late afternoon, all chopping sounds stopped. Maya lay without moving, knowing that the two men would be coming toward camp to eat supper and take a half hour of rest. She heard footsteps, heard water being poured and the campfire pot being scraped, heard a hoarse groan as someone lay on the ground. A half hour later she heard the men go back to the tree once more. Soon steel rang again and again against redwood.

After a time Ising's ax no longer kept rhythm. There was a long interval, then Will's ax fell silent as well. Maya counted the minutes in the silence of her mind, and counted. And counted. The silence stretched beyond the time needed to drink water or to wrap the ax handle with new cloth so that Will's glove wouldn't slide despite the blood leaking through. Voices were raised in excitement. At first Maya held her breath, hoping to hear the crashing of a giant tree brought down. Instead she heard a stranger cry out.

"Ten to one against Will Hawthorne! Place your bets, gents! The odds won't get any better!"

Maya pulled herself to her feet, unconsciously smoothed down her dress and her unbraided hair and walked into the crimson sunset. Men were thronged around the rope barrier but they stepped aside for her. She went up to the barrier, slipped underneath and stood alone in the opening between rope and redwood.

Ising was nearby, stretched out on his back, asleep. Will was on his knees in the giant cut, slumped over his ax, every line of his body proclaiming utter exhaustion. Thin trails of blood showed on his face where it had been cut by a flying chip.

As though he sensed Maya's presence, Will's head lifted slowly. She said nothing, did nothing, simply looked at him with dark, fathomless eyes. The sight of her standing there, witnessing his weakness, his defeat, sent a surge of rage through Will. He came to his feet and attacked all that was available to him in his fury: the tree that had become the living symbol of Maya's hold over his unwilling soul.

At first the rhythm of Will's chopping was ragged, but with time it settled into an even pattern. As though called by the even strokes of the ax, Ising woke and climbed back up the trunk into the cut. Within minutes their chopping had settled into a pattern once more.

The last red light drained from the sky, and the wind came up to sweep the sky clean of any clouds. The evening star burned through a gap in the Guardian's boughs. After a time the full moon sent a transparent, ghostly silver illumination over the forest. Lanterns hung from poles and springboards and rested on the living floor where Will and Ising stood swinging their axes in unison, cleaving the night and the immense tree with steel blades.

Maya stood within the multiple circles of lantern light, motionless but for the breeze lifting her hair. She didn't notice Hale when he called to her from beyond the rope. She didn't speak to the men behind her or to the two men chopping above. Silent, unmoving, her face expressionless, she watched Will with eyes darker than the night.

After a time Ising stopped and leaned on his ax. Will kept on chopping. Sweat ran down his naked back in rivulets, making him gleam with the patina of a pagan idol cast in gold. Chips flew up and arced into the night like dark, frightened birds. Nearly every blow of Will's ax freed chunks of wood as big as a man's head, chips flying and falling and heaping up, chips thudding softly to the ground and rolling to Maya's feet.

Suddenly Will stopped. He reached directly above his head, touching the heartwood of the Guardian. After a moment he peeled off his glove and flattened his hand against the fresh cut. Ising's head lifted. He watched his friend with eerie intensity. Will stood with eyes closed, chest heaving and glistening, his whole attitude that of a man listening.

More than three hundred feet overhead, a soft wind swirled through the Guardian's crown. Will felt the breeze, but not on his sweat-soaked body. He felt the wind in the faint tremor that passed through the living tree to the heartwood and from there to his own hand. The tree trembled slightly again, and so did he. There was something vastly moving about the vibrations coming through his palm, as though a woman's body lay humming with promise beneath his touch.

Will cocked his head, listening intently. He heard only the whispering sigh of wind caressing the Guardian's invisible crown. There was no muffled snap, no popping of wood, no faint groaning caused by the ripping of thousands of tiny wood fibers. The tremors coincided with the gusts of wind passing overhead, ruffling the huge redwood's boughs, and focusing the full force of supporting and balancing the tree's immense weight within the few remaining feet of intact heartwood.

For an instant fury raced through Will, followed immediately by something very close to despair. The Guardian trembled in the wind, but it was still standing upright, still balanced against the wind, still strong. The massive redwood's death throes had not even begun.

From the crowd came an anonymous cry: "Nine-thirty!"

"Will?" Ising asked.

"I can feel the wind. Barely."

"That's all?"

"That's all."

Ising looked up. Encompassing the moon and half the stars, the lateral branches of the Guardian were a network of absolute black. The boughs were huge, the size of normal trees, and weighed thousands of pounds each. He looked to the crowd thronging the Guardian's entire girth. Children played hide-and-seek among the adults, and men who had known more whiskey than food in the last hours swayed like ferns in the wind.

"Somebody's going to get killed if they aren't careful," Ising said, his voice flattened by exhaustion.

Will looked out at the seething, changing ranks of people. He picked up a kerosene lantern and went to stand at the lip of the cut.

"This tree is over three hundred feet tall," he said, his voice carrying through the sudden hush. "I can feel the wind in the heartwood. Now, I don't care if a bunch of damned fools and drunks get killed, but I won't have children on my conscience." Will turned his head and looked directly at Hale. "Get those children cleared out or all bets are off."

"You've got a lot of chopping yet, Hawthorne," a man hollered. "That tree'll still be standing come sunup."

"Hell, yes!" another man yelled. "I seen big redwoods stand straight up for two days after they started groaning, and this here tree ain't even said a word yet!"

Will ignored the men. He watched Hale. After a long moment Hale nodded. He turned to the crowd.

"Take your children to a safe place or the bet is cancelled."

"You got no right—"

"This is my claim!" Will shouted hoarsely, cutting across the protest. "All of you are trespassing! Get those kids out of here!"

Maya turned and faced the crowd. It was the first time she had looked at anything except Will since she had come to stand by the Guardian at sunset. She stared at each of the women in the lantern light, picking them out one by one. What Hale's and Will's exhortations didn't accomplish, Maya's bleak eyes did. Women took their children and withdrew to the side of the Guardian opposite the felling path. They stood more than three hundred feet back in the darkness, faces turned toward the cluster of lanterns.

The sound of axes rang again in the night. The rhythm was ragged, stuttering. Each interruption for water or to switch sides sapped the men's concentration. It was obvious that they were working on nerve alone, forcing their bodies to lift, swing, retrieve the ax, lift, swing, retrieve the ax, lift, swing . . .

The self-appointed timekeeper called out, "Ten o'clock."

Five minutes later the Guardian made its first sound, a single sharp, dry, wooden snap so loud that it was painful. A nervous shiver swept through the crowd. Some of the spectators who weren't familiar with logging turned and hurried through darkness to the place where women and children watched. Logging men stayed near the tree. They knew that many, many square feet of heartwood stood between the Guardian and its moment of death.

The wind strengthened. Will and Ising froze in an attitude of intense concentration. A thin groan shivered through the tree as another strand of wood surrendered to the changing interplay of weight, wind and gravity. The two men stood motionless, waiting, waiting, praying for signs of the tree's weakness.

The Guardian made no other sound. Nor was there any outward sign of weakness. The tree stood as tall and as straight as ever.

As one, Will and Ising hefted their long-handled axes. Seconds later the *thunk . . . thunk . . . thunk* of blade biting into tree trunk resumed. It was punishing work. The tension in the remaining wood was extraordinary, repelling axes as though steel cables rather than wooden fibers supported the trunk.

"Ten-thirty!"

There was no sound from the tree, no continuous tremor, nothing to indicate that this night was different from any of the centuries of nights the Guardian had known in its long life. Ising's face was pale even in the lantern light, his expression grim. It was the same for Will, exhaustion carving deep lines in his face. The men chopped in a rhythm that was as ragged as their breathing. Chips flew up, flashed in the light and then were swallowed in darkness as they fell to the ground.

Suddenly Will went to his knees. He stayed there for a moment, head hanging, breathing hard. His arms trembled visibly. Ising went down as well, resting in the only way he trusted himself to. Both men knew if they lay down they wouldn't get up.

"Eleven o'clock!"

The announcement was greeted with cheers, groans and a new round of betting. Maya ignored the noise and movement. She had attention only for Will. Johnny ran forward, scrambled up the springboards and handed canteens of water to the men. Arms trembling visibly, Will held a canteen in both hands and drank, pouring the remainder over his head before returning the canteen.

"Eleven-fifteen!"

With an effort that was obvious, Will wiped his hands on his canvas pants, leaving dark smears of blood, sweat and water. Staggering slightly, he came to his feet and picked up the rhythm once more. Ising heaved himself to his feet and picked up his ax. Though neither man spoke, it became clear that they were driving themselves in a single, final effort to overcome the huge tree before midnight. In a frenzy of concentration they chopped at twenty strokes a minute, dragging huge chunks of wood fiber out of the Guardian's core. Five more minutes went by, and then another five, then five more.

"Eleven-thirty!"

Suddenly there was a sharp, ripping sound. Ising barked in pain. Simultaneously Will felt a slashing, stinging blow across his face, as though he had been cut with a buggy whip. He knew instantly what had happened. The tension building in the interior of the tree had made its way to the surface of the cut, where a bundle of wood fibers had snapped simultaneously, scattering splinters of redwood like shrapnel from an exploding cannon shell.

Will reached up and touched his cheek. His fingers came away bloody. Blood trickled from a scattering of places across his chest where the skin had been torn. Ising swore in English, a long, vicious bullwhacker's oath. Then he turned in the flickering lamplight. Will saw a six-inch splinter the thickness of a pencil sticking out from beneath the skin of Ising's massive forearm. Blood welled up around the wound. He grabbed the end of the splinter and pulled. His fingers slipped. The splinter remained imbedded in his clenched muscles.

"Pliers!" yelled Will.

Instants later Johnny lifted himself over the lip of the cut and ran over to Will. He took the pliers without looking away from Ising's wound.

"Ready?" Will asked.

Ising grunted then hissed in pain as Will clamped the pliers on the splinter and yanked. The wood came free, shining wetly in the light. Will examined the wound. It was bleeding freely. None of the muscles appeared to have been severed. Ising flexed his hand. It responded slowly, but it did respond. Without a word he picked up his ax and turned to face the Guardian's thick core once again.

"Chop at the edge," Will said flatly.

Ising hesitated, then walked unsteadily to the edge of the cut, where the tension on the fibers was not so deadly. It would not only be safer to chop there, it would be easier as well. Slowly both men began to work again, moving awkwardly, as though drunk or wading chest-deep against a heavy current. It was apparent to the spectators that the accident had destroyed the choppers' momentum, leaving them vulnerable to the exhaustion that was rapidly turning their muscles to sand.

"Eleven thirty-five!"

Two minutes later the Guardian began to groan. At first the sound was faint, thin, distant. Slowly it deepened into a throaty moan that was eerily reminiscent of a man in pain. Maya closed her eyes and swayed, shuddering. The sound passed, leaving a heavy silence in its wake.

The wind came up, making the forest tremble.

Will put his hand against the wood. The humming tension seemed greater, a vibration that went through his bones. It was no longer even remotely sensual; it was the forerunner of explosive violence.

"Eleven forty!"

Wind flexed again and the Guardian groaned. But the wind was coming from a different direction, swirling around the redwood's broad base, sending Maya's hair streaming away from her face, pushing the immense bulk of the tree away from the direction of the felling path. Wind swirled heavily, rushing around the bole, pushing against the tree, using the Guardian's vast crown as a lever against the redwood's stability. What man couldn't accomplish in hours, the wind might do in seconds.

"Get back!" Will shouted hoarsely. "The wind is shifting!"

"Let 'er rip, boy," shouted one logger drunkenly. "I'll ride that bastard down myself."

"Then you'll ride it straight to hell!"

The effort of shouting cost Will what little strength he had left. His legs gave way, sending him to his knees. Ising was no better off. He, too, was kneeling, using his ax as a brace to keep him upright. Blood covered his forearm.

The Guardian's groaning deepened until it seemed to make the air itself shiver. Most of the people backed off, clearing a semicircle with the felling path in the center. Hale slipped under the rope for the first time and went to stand by Maya.

"It's not safe for you here. The tree won't fall for hours, but there could be another explosion of splinters at any instant."

Maya ignored him.

"Come with me," Hale said, stepping in front of her.

"Get out of my way. I can't see Will."

It was the same voice she had used in the tent when she had refused Hale for the first time in their marriage. It was a stranger's voice, lacking warmth, lacking emotion, lacking everything but a bleakness that chilled Hale to his soul. His hand dropped. He looked at Maya's eyes and saw nothing but darkness. Silently he took one step aside, no longer blocking her view.

"Eleven forty-five!"

The timekeeper's voice was all but buried beneath a gust of wind. There was a flurry of new wagers as the lumbermen in the crowd bet heavily against Will and the townspeople changed sides to become his ally. The timber beasts smiled and took the bets confidently. They knew what the city men did not: eating away at the heartwood of a tree the Guardian's size was a delicate, time-consuming process made even more dangerous by the gusting wind. The cut had to be worked on from the edge of the tree inward, unless the choppers took the insane risk of crawling under the narrow, deepest edge of the cut where fibers exploded and the massive trunk itself hung over the axman's head. It would take a kneeling man at least fifteen seconds to come to his feet, run the width of the deep cut and from there to the relative safety of the ground. A man at the outer edge of the cut would have five seconds head start, which was about the time it took for a tree to fall.

It took only a second for a man to die.

"Eleven forty-eight!"

The timekeeper's voice was nearly lost in the trembling groan of the Guardian. Will couldn't tell whether it was the tree or himself moaning as he tilted his head back and looked up the trunk. It was leaning perceptibly against the blazing white circle of the moon. As he watched, a gust of wind straightened the bole, then sent it leaning slightly away from the felling path. The experienced loggers saw the motion as well. They withdrew well into the darkness, taking their drunken friends along.

"Eleven fifty!" The timekeeper's voice came from a distance, but there was no mistaking the words.

Maya watched Will try to come to his feet—and fail. He tried again and failed again. He knelt over the handle of his ax, his body running with sweat. The wind gusted wildly, sending lantern flames leaping and making her hair whip like dark flames around her face. The Guardian keened in a long, rising note, then fell silent for a moment. Again Will tried to lever himself to his feet, using the ax. His hands slipped and he went to his knees. He stayed there, head hanging, his body shaking with each ragged breath that he drew.

"*Will.*"

At first Will thought that he was dreaming the sound of his name being called by Maya's gentle, beautiful voice. His eyes opened. Wearily he brushed away sweat until he could see. She stood at the base of the tree in a shaft of lantern light, her hair loose, incandescent with light. He reached toward her with a hand that was black with blood, and then he realized that she was real, not a dream. She was real, and she was standing there as she had always been, just beyond his reach, tormenting him, watching him fail once more, boy not man. And there beside her was his father—her husband, her lover, the father of her children.

With an inchoate cry, Will staggered to his feet once more, only to have his legs give way. Because he couldn't stand, he crawled back into the cut, all the way in, stopping only when he was within reach of the Guardian's deepest heartwood. His ax came back over his shoulder, glittered briefly in the lantern light, then sank into the straining, groaning heartwood. A shower of splinters ensued. He didn't notice. He was beyond normal human responses, driven wholly by the demon that had ridden him for five years. He felt as though he were a meteor arcing across the sky, burning out of control, burning to ash and memory long before meeting the earth.

There would be solace in that. There would at least be release.

Ising watched his friend for the space of a long breath, then closed his eyes and prayed to all the gods he knew and to the ones he didn't know as well. Above the sound of the wind and the keening, moaning tree came the clear laughter of Johnny as he stood three hundred feet away, just aside of the felling path, taunting the tree in Yurok. Ising wanted to shout at Johnny but he lacked the strength. Instead, Ising dragged himself over next to Will, lifted his ax and sank the blade into the Guardian's straining trunk.

As though called by the primitive rhythms of rage, the wind leaped, sweeping across the sky, bending the forest roof in deep waves.

"Eleven fifty-six!"

The words were lost to Will and Ising in the rifle-shot sounds of snapping wood. Bunches of fiber popped in the uncut heart, showering them with splinters that stuck to their clothes and speared through their skin. They kept chopping, eyes closed, faces turned away, chopping by memory alone, memory and a demon that had lived too long within a human soul. Slowly, ponderously, the Guardian began to sway. At the base the movement was imperceptible, but at the crown, the tree's motions swept across the face of the moon. The Guardian's moaning became a sustained, unearthly keening that consumed the wind, the silence, the night itself.

As one, Will and Ising threw themselves out of the cut and over the edge, running against the wind, sweeping Maya and Hale before them as they fled the death throes of the immense redwood. Behind them the twisting, shuddering, screaming tree sank slowly through the darkness toward the forest floor.

The crown was a hundred feet wide, heavy, and left behind a swath of destruction as the Guardian brought down other trees with its own fall. Limbs and whole tree trunks snapped off with the sound of cannons firing. The explosion of noise reached a crescendo as the butt of the log thundered to the ground, sending a shockwave through the earth.

Will stopped running and spun around. Where the Guardian had once stood he saw nothing but a fantastically splintered stump reaching toward the moon. A feeling of wild elation swept through him. Over the popping and snapping of settling boughs he heard someone cry out.

"Twelve o'clock!"

There was silence, then a ragged cheer. The wind swept the sounds away, making room for a high, thin cry as someone called out Ising's name in agony. The cry wavered then sank beneath the wind once more.

"Johnny!" yelled Ising. *"Johnny!"*

There was no answer.

Will and Ising sprinted toward the sound, their exhaustion forgotten in a wave of adrenaline. When Will passed the stump of the Guardian, he snatched up a flickering lantern. For the first hundred and fifty feet of the way, the path along the redwood's trunk was smooth and uncluttered by limbs. Then the men were slowed by the wreckage of broken boughs and chunks of bark that had been stripped off neighboring trees by the falling monarch. Abruptly the men's progress was blocked by a segment of a three-foot-thick Douglas fir that had been cleanly snapped off and thrown to the ground by the falling redwood.

"Johnny?"

Ising's call was answered by a wail of pain. They fought through the fir's dense boughs, drawn by Johnny's wounded cries. Despite the unpredictable wind the Guardian had fallen less than eight degrees off the line Will had chosen. The tree lay partially cushioned on the falling bed and partially tangled in the wreckage of smaller trees that its fall had destroyed. Ising and Will were forced to their hands and knees by the tangle of evergreens. They were more than two hundred feet along the redwood's massive trunk when suddenly Will stopped.

"Listen," he hissed.

Ising heard the thin, faint moan. "He's up ahead."

"No. There's something else."

Both men were quiet again for a moment. Then Ising heard it, too, another kind of groaning, the kind the dying Guardian had made. Somewhere up ahead another tree trunk was under enormous stress. The massive redwood hadn't fallen cleanly. Part of its huge weight was held above the ground by another tree. The entire tangle of wreckage was alive with tension, a trap set and baited, waiting for something to release its lethal energy.

"I hear you, Tree," Ising said in Yurok. "Johnny is but a foolish boy. He didn't mean his taunts. You who have lived so long and so magnificently wouldn't take the life of such an insignificant creature as my brother."

With that, Ising crawled forward once more. Will followed. They found Johnny in the boneyard of limbs that had been the crown of the Guardian. They also found the springy young cedar that was bearing the load of the collapsed redwood. The cedar was bent almost double by the enormous weight, shivering and groaning beneath its impossible burden. Ising and Will pushed carefully through the tangled boughs, knowing that any movement could upset the delicate balance of the trap that was waiting to be sprung. Over their heads, the cedar held the massive redwood at bay, but it was a doomed effort. Both men knew it. At any second the smaller tree could give way, letting the Guardian finish its last, crashing descent to earth.

Lantern light picked out the form of Johnny amid the green wreckage. He had almost escaped the redwood's dying embrace, but the same whiskey that had made him fling taunts at the big tree had betrayed him when he had turned to flee the falling monarch. His left arm was pinned between a huge redwood limb and the trunk of the cedar. He was slumped against the smaller tree, dazed with pain but held upright by his trapped arm.

Ising seized Johnny, removing the boy's weight from his injured arm. Will held the lantern close, saying nothing, for there was nothing that words could change. Johnny's arm was a mangled, bloody ruin, its bones smashed beyond any hope of mending; yet muscles and tendons remained intact, chaining Johnny to the useless limb. His face was the color of the bone that gleamed through skin and blood. He moaned with each breath, writhing as he instinctively tried to free himself from the wooden trap whose jaws were holding him in place for the Guardian's death blow.

"Get an ax," Ising said.

"It won't work. You cut that bough and the whole thing will come crashing down."

The cedar groaned and shuddered as the redwood's massive trunk settled inevitably toward the ground. Johnny screamed.

"Not the tree," Ising said. "His arm."

For an instant Will looked at the sweat standing on Ising's face and at the boy lying slackly in his half brother's arms. Then Will looked at the ax that he had held onto even as he fled the Guardian's violent end. Without a word he set down the lantern, whipped off his belt and cinched it tightly around Johnny's maimed arm, cutting off the flow of blood. Johnny screamed. Will clenched his teeth against the nausea rising in his throat as he tightened the belt even more.

The smell of blood and cedar hung thickly in the silence. Will raised the ax above his head and brought it down with every bit of strength he had left. The sound of the ax blow and Johnny Ising's scream were

lost in the wailing of wood stressed beyond its ability
to endure.

Ising swung Johnny into his arms and blindly followed Will as he broke through the tangled boughs to
the night beyond. They had gone no more than fifteen feet when the cedar exploded behind them, dying
in the instant of its release. The Guardian thudded
heavily to earth, covering the place where Johnny's
blood soaked into the forest floor.

Chapter Fourteen

Hands folded in outward calm, Maya stared out into the empty blue sky instead of at the graceful, intricate curves and whorls that curled across the redwood panels lining her sitting room. The same bird's-eye grain was present in her bedroom, which adjoined the sitting room. The elegant redwood panels were the Guardian's legacy. They appeared throughout the Hawthorne house. There was nowhere Maya could go in her own home that didn't whisper to her of Will's hot, sensual embrace almost six years ago, and of his icy hatred now.

Most people who saw the paneling admired its unique beauty. Maya did her best not to see the wood at all. Each time she looked at the Guardian's red bones, she felt a little more of her life drain away. She had asked Hale not to put the panels in her rooms. Hale had ignored her. Although he said nothing to her on the subject, Maya knew that Will had somehow induced Hale to install the wood in her private rooms as well as in the rest of the house. Will wanted her to look at the panels, to remember, to live with the memory of her betrayal always before her eyes. Betrayal—and Johnny's screams. Even after six months she heard him cry out in her nightmares. She would hear those terrible, thin screams until the day she died.

So much unhappiness. So much pain. So much hatred. All of it stemming from the bittersweet abandonment of the afternoon when she had given in to the sensuality that she had stifled for a lifetime.

Dry-eyed, Maya stared at the empty sky, trying to conjure up the faces of her children, reminding herself that not all of life was futility and pain. There was Emily, with her curly cinnamon hair and quick mind, her clever, long-fingered hands reaching out to life, grabbing it, holding onto it with laughter and mischief dancing in her gray-green eyes. And Justine, soft, gray-eyed Justine, whose chubby cheeks and bubbling laughter never failed to delight the people around her.

Even Will. More than once Maya had come across Will sitting on the floor in grave conversation with Emily while Justine sat in his lap, drooling her adoration of the man who would smile at her while she teethed on his thumb. The sight of Will's gentle smile had turned Maya's heart inside out. But that smile was only for babes and for Beth, who was blind. To the rest of the world Will gave the hard gleam of teeth that reflected the demon within.

Winning the bet with Hale hadn't made Will kinder, more merciful, more at peace with himself and the world. If anything he was worse, a man poised at the thin edge of his self-control.

Maya understood how Will felt, what private whirlwind of destruction he rode. Seeing him every day, passing him in the hallway of the Hawthorne house, sitting across from him at dinner—her own self-control was stretched like a wire, stretched until it hummed a high note of distress, and each day pulled that wire tighter than the day before, straining her beyond her ability to endure. There were moments when she was afraid that she would go mad.

And there were moments when she was afraid that she would not.

Maya closed her eyes, trying to alleviate the burn of unshed tears. The ache was so much a part of her that she didn't even notice it anymore. She hadn't cried in a long, long time, no matter how great her pain. It was too late to begin now. It was too late for too many things.

Laughter drifted down from the tower room overhead. The sound subtly eased Maya. At least something good had come from that terrible day when the Guardian had fallen. Johnny Ising had survived to bring laughter and a belated childhood to Beth. It had been a near thing, though. For the first few weeks after he had been brought to the Hawthorne house, Johnny had hovered at the point of death. Maya had refused to let him die. She had nearly ruined her own health nursing him around the clock, until Beth started coming into the room, learning how to care for Johnny, learning to calm him when he awakened in the middle of the night frightened by pain and fever dreams or by his unfamiliar surroundings.

Beth had understood Johnny's fears better than anyone else. She, too, had awakened once from unexpected injury into a strange, painful, lightless world. She had learned how to cope with darkness and the agonizing headaches that sometimes struck her without warning. She taught Johnny what she had learned—how to get beyond the pain of what was missing to the pleasure of what still remained. By the time Johnny had recovered enough to limp down to meals in the kitchen, he and Beth had become such a common sight that no one really noticed them, except to smile at the blind girl leading the one-armed, stiff-kneed Indian boy through each ornate nook and cranny of the Hawthorne house.

Maya waited, breath unconsciously held, hoping to hear Beth's laughter again. Nothing came but the distant calling of a bird. Maya's eyes opened slowly. She looked around her sitting room. There was nothing there to hold her emotions, nothing to soothe the raw ache of nerves stretched too tightly for too many years. The stained-glass window in the northern wall was pretty, but essentially empty. It was the same for the Mexican onyx fireplace and the Oriental carpet and the French furniture and the Spanish lace curtains. Only the Guardian's legacy was alive; the extraordinary bird's-eye pattern seemed like a thousand eyes watching her, seeing into her, sliding past her careful outward serenity to the inner darkness of her soul.

I did what you said, Mother. I didn't marry for my heart, for my soul. And you were right. My babies thrive. Now tell me just one thing, Mother. Tell me how to live without a heart and soul.

Abruptly Maya came to her feet, unable to bear her elegant redwood prison any longer. Usually when these moments of wildness came to her, she calmed herself by playing with Emily or Justine, but they were asleep now. Or they were with Will. It seemed that everywhere she turned lately, Will was already there, watching her, driving her away from even her own children, her only succor in a world where each choice had such terrible consequences.

In the hallway Maya hesitated between heading up-stairs for the tower room and going outside into the gazebo. She started for the third story, then changed her mind. Beth would be too caught up in playing make-believe with Johnny to have time for talking with her restless stepmother. Nor was it fair of Maya to intrude upon the laughter Beth had finally found.

Outside the sun shone with painful brilliance in a sky devoid of any clouds. Maya walked from the backyard to the long, winding path leading up to the gazebo. At the edge of the forest, salmonberry was in full bloom. The first rhododendrons and delicate Douglas iris were already making their appearances, even though it was only April. It was much too warm for spring. In normal years eighty inches of rain fell on the redwood coast between October and the end of April. But that year less than thirty inches of rain had fallen in the past eight months; now the rainy season was already giving way to an early summer.

Maya couldn't remember such a dry winter and spring. The past two winters had been unusually dry. The rivers were already running shallow, their pools warming in the unfiltered sunlight of a cloudless spring. Despite the fact that lumbermen from all over were heading into the woods a month early, Hale hadn't mentioned the dry weather. It was as though rain or the lack of it had no effect on him; yet Maya knew that Tres Santos logs lay behind a dam in Wee-ber Basin, waiting for enough water to float them to the timber-hungry mill on Humboldt Bay. Before the Guardian's fall Hale had spent a lot of time staring at the sky, looking for signs of rain. After the Guardian Hale seemed not to care. Even the railroad that had consumed so much of his attention no longer seemed to interest him. He spent more time in his mill and less at home. And he drank every night in his room.

At first Hale's drinking had made Maya tense with fear, for in the past he had always come to her after he had been drinking. That, too, had changed. Since she had refused him in the Guardian's meadow, he had not opened her bedroom door. Maya was profoundly grateful for Hale's restraint. She knew her duty as a Christian wife, but the thought of Hale rooting and grunting between her legs was unbearable. To compensate, she had redoubled her other attentions to Hale, pampering him in overt ways.

It was more than guilt for not wanting Hale that moved Maya; there was a lost, almost childlike quality about Hale lately that tugged at her compassion. So she cared for him as she would a beloved child, seeing that he had clean clothes and favorite foods, trimming his nails and his hair, tending the small cuts and splinters he picked up at the mill, offering him encouraging smiles and gentle touches when he was silent too long.

And every time she did, Hale would watch her with sad understanding in his sunken eyes, but Will would watch her with naked hatred.

Maya walked quickly from the path into the filtered sunlight of the gazebo. There she sat on the padded bench, head resting on her drawn-up knees, her unbound hair rippling with subtle fire at each shift of the breeze. If she had looked up, she would have seen the flash of sunlight off the house's third-story windows, where the girls' nursery was, and where Beth and Johnny laughed at jokes only they understood.

They were still laughing now, but quietly, not wanting to disturb the rest of the household.

"Is she in the gazebo?" Beth asked, standing in a warm square of sunlight.

"Yeah. She spends a lot of time there, doesn't she?"

"It helps her to be outdoors when she's unhappy."

Johnny turned and looked at the young blond goddess who stood in the sunlight that was darker than her hair. Since he had awakened in the Hawthorne house, he had known warmth, security and luxury for the first time in his life. For that he cheerfully put up with weekly baths, reading lessons, counting lessons and a future that didn't bear close examination. A penniless Indian was one thing; a penniless crippled Indian was a far worse thing. But Johnny didn't think much about that. All that worrying about tomorrow had ever accomplished for him was to make today unhappy. Tomorrow would come soon enough. Until then, today was here to be enjoyed.

"How could anyone living in this big house be sad?"

Beth's expression took on a melancholy that was years too old for the angelic innocence of her face. "Perhaps she mourns the babies she lost."

"Can't she have more?"

Mentally Beth counted the months since Justine had been born. "Yes. It would be safe now, I suppose. But Maya gets thinner each time I hug her and she hardly laughs at all. I don't think she's well."

With a frown, Johnny turned away from the window. Ising had told him that Maya was a woman set apart from all others since the wreck of the *Brother Samuel*. Ising had said the same about Beth, but she was neither melancholy nor distant. Smiling, Johnny limped over to stand next to Beth in the sunlight.

There was only a little time before he had to report for work at the mill. Before then he wanted to hold Beth once more.

"I see you, woman," he whispered, stroking Beth's hair and shoulder with his hand.

"I see you, man," Beth whispered back.

Beth ran her hands over Johnny's hair and lips and chest, seeing him in the only way that she could, the way that had first led to the piercing sweetness of being caressed in return. She couldn't get enough of that kind of "seeing." Touching and being touched by Johnny was a secret glory that made Beth feel as though she had swallowed the sun. With one hand she touched his mouth, for that way she could tell when he smiled. With her other hand she stroked him. She felt him smile at her caresses, then felt his smile tighten when her hand slid down his torso. He hardened beneath her hand with a speed that made her breath quicken. Slowly, sensually she kneaded his rapidly changing flesh.

"Do you think that they're all asleep?" he asked thickly, moving rhythmically against her small hand.

"I'll be very quiet."

"No, you won't. You'll whimper and moan while you ride me. You always do."

Johnny's laugh became a groan when Beth's hand opened his pants and moved between his legs, teasing him with the instinctive skill of one to whom touch was the whole world. He sank to the floor, bringing her down after him, sliding his hand up beneath her skirt. She opened to him instantly, moving against his probing fingers, her face incandescent with the pleasure of being caressed. Within moments she was slick and as hot as he.

"Lift up your skirts," he said urgently, lying back on the floor.

Smiling, Beth lifted her skirts. "Remember how awkward it was the first time?" she whispered.

Johnny's laugh was short, breathless. He remembered. He had come at the first intimate brush of her flesh over him, but it hadn't mattered. Her innocent pleasure in his touch had hardened him again instantly. Laughing, fumbling, too hot to care, they had finally discovered that if he lay on his back, neither his stiff knee nor his absent arm mattered.

"Where are you?" she whispered.

"Right here," he said hoarsely, his black eyes riveted on the vee where white legs joined in a nest of pale gold hair.

Beth patted the air for a moment until he took her hand and guided it to his erect, straining flesh. Smiling, she lifted herself over him, letting her skirts settle onto him in a scented cloud. As he took her, she threw back her head and tried not to cry out with joy. It was so wonderful not to be alone in her darkness. Long before she had known Johnny, she had discovered the sensual secrets of her own body, but it was so much hotter and sweeter when it was shared. She had taught him what she knew about pleasuring her, and he had learned very well. Each time it was better, so much better that she thought she must cry out or die.

"Soon," she whispered, bending blindly over Johnny. "Soon we'll have our own house, our own rooms, our own—oh!"

Johnny felt Beth tighten around his thrusting flesh and moved against her again harder, harder, driving small, hoarse cries from her lips as she tried to finish telling him about the future she envisioned for the two of them. He heard her words, but they meant no more to him than the oddly rhyming story of knights and ladies that she read to him from pages that were no more than papers with pinpricks throughout—shaman words in writing, alien rhythms, shaman tales of men with removable iron skins, words and tales told by a shaman with eyes in her fingertips and golden paradise between her legs.

Flickering candlelight played on the redwood panels of the dining room. Maya sat at one end of the table, Hale at the other, and Beth and Will on opposite sides. There was little conversation except for Beth's chatter about how clever Johnny had become at counting.

"You should see him," she said eagerly. "Why, he would be a wonderful clerk for your business. Remember, Daddy? You were saying that you needed someone you could trust not to sell your accounts to a competitor? Johnny would be a perfect—"

"He's an Indian," Hale said, interrupting Beth. "I had a hard enough time finding him work as a sweeper in my mill at night. What do you think my men would do if they knew a Yurok was adding up their pay each week? I'd have a riot on my hands. Besides, Johnny's just a boy. He has no more sense of responsibility than a sparrow. I don't mind him staying in the gardener's house, and I don't mind him taking his meals in the kitchen. We owe him that much, I guess. But I won't turn my mill upside down for him. If he hadn't been drinking that night, the damned tree never would have caught him in the first place."

Beth's rosy lips settled into a mutinous line. Maya saw and stifled a sigh. Since Beth had nursed Johnny back to health, she had become quite self-confident. That was good, most of the time. And some of the time it made for unpleasant friction.

"Just give him a chance," Beth began.

"The subject is closed."

There was a tight silence followed by Will's lazy voice. "Don't worry, Mouse. If he's half as good as you say, he can keep books for my business. I have a lot more need of him. My business has more than doubled since the Guardian fell. Father's hasn't. Has it, Father?"

Two pairs of gray eyes met for an instant, then Hale looked away.

Maya looked at her plate, but not before she saw defeat settle across Hale's face. It had been that way ever since he had lost his bet with Will, as though the more the son grew the smaller the father became. Will didn't help any by undercutting Hale's authority at every turn. From the redwood paneling on the walls to the type of meat served at the table, Will's wish was the deciding one. If Hale objected, he never said so. Nor had he objected when Will had moved his belongings into a suite of rooms on the second floor, just down the hall from her own rooms. Perhaps that was why Hale no longer came to her bedroom. Perhaps he didn't want to walk past his son's rooms on the way to his wife's bed.

"Pass the salt, please, Mrs. Hawthorne," Will said.

Maya set the salt on the table near Will's hand, taking no chance that she would touch him by accident. She was careful not to look at him, either. She wanted to do nothing that might attract the icy edge of his anger. Usually she was safe in Beth's presence. Usually, but not always. Will was predictable in only one thing: his contempt for her.

Tell me, how is my father's whore today?

The greeting was spoken aloud only when he found her alone. The rest of the time the words burned behind his gray eyes.

"Will you really hire him?" Beth asked, turning her face toward her brother with uncanny accuracy.

Will looked at the smooth innocence of Beth's cheeks and the heartbreaking clarity of her blind blue eyes. She looked more like an angel than a mouse; the purity of her blond beauty made him want to protect her from the world's careless corruption and injury.

"I'll give him a chance," Will promised.

Beth's face was transformed by her smile. She groped across the table for her brother's hand. When Will gave it to her, she raised the callused fingers to her lips and then cradled his palm against her tear-streaked cheek.

"Oh, thank you, Will. Thank you, thank you, thank you!"

He looked surprised, then almost embarrassed. "Hey, it's nothing to get upset about. I'm giving Johnny the same chance I'd give any other boy, that's all."

"That's everything. It's just everything! I've been so afraid...."

Uneasily Maya looked at the relief that shone so clearly on Beth's transparent young face.

"What were you afraid of?" Maya asked softly.

"I didn't want Johnny to go away. I couldn't live without him. Now he'll stay with me forever."

Will smiled with the gentle indulgence he reserved for Beth and the other two children. "Forever is a long time, Mouse."

Beth just grinned and attacked her dinner with more appetite than she had shown for food in the past few months. Maya watched, smiling as Will was smiling. It was good to see Beth eat. She was too thin and her color hadn't been good. Maya had been worried that Beth was ill. The cook had mentioned that Beth hadn't eaten breakfast very often lately.

Suddenly Maya's smile froze, and all pleasure drained from her in a cold rush of fear. Automatically she arranged and rearranged the food on her plate, appearing to eat without actually putting more than a few bites into her mouth. She thought quickly, frantically, denying the possibility of her fears being true even as she thought about ways to deflect the disaster that she feared was coming.

"You're not eating, Mrs. Hawthorne," Will said. "Is the beef too tough?"

Maya started, recalled from her grim speculations. "No. It's fine."

"Then there must be another cause for your flagging appetite. Let me be the first to congratulate you on the happy occasion."

Her head snapped up as she turned to face him. "What?"

"The baby."

Maya was speechless, wondering frantically how Will had known. Or was it simply a lucky guess? She swallowed. "What baby?"

Will's mouth thinned into a sardonic curl. "There's no need to be shy. We're a family. You needn't hide your condition as though it were something shameful. You're a married woman, after all."

"I'm not pregnant," Maya said baldly, too relieved to be tactful.

"Really? Or is it just too early to be certain?" Will asked, his tone pleasant and his eyes like ice.

"There is no possibility of pregnancy."

For a moment Will met Maya's bleak green glance. Then he nodded and turned to talk to Hale. The older man shoved back his chair and left the table without a word, heading for the office where he kept his books. And his brandy.

"I'll join you as soon as I'm finished," Will said. "We have some business to discuss."

Hale said nothing. The door shut firmly behind him.

Will finished his meal, teasing Beth between bites, ignoring Maya as though she didn't exist. Then he put his napkin on the table, pushed back his chair and excused himself to Beth. He went right to the office, wanting to get there before his father eluded him by the simple expediency of getting drunk.

With the easy coordination that marked all his movements, Will opened the office door, closed it behind him and stood for a moment looking down at the man who had once dominated his world. Hale appeared older than his years, his skin worn and loose, his eyes dull. With a faint shock Will realized that his father's hair was completely white. Hale's hands trembled slightly as he lifted a heavy crystal decanter and poured brandy into a snifter.

Will looked away, wanting to deny the reality of what his father had become. Old. Shrunken. Indefinably less of a man, as though some vital spirit had died when the Guardian had died.

The exultation that Will had known after the Guardian fell had faded too quickly. Revenge on his father and Maya had been the very reason for Will's continued existence when he had awakened lost, injured, ill and betrayed on a ship bound for foreign lands. At first he had burned with fierce triumph when he saw defeat in his father's eyes. Now Will felt something close to discomfort when he looked at the ruin of what had once been a formidable foe. Sometimes when he saw his father, Will felt an emotion uncomfortably close to pity. It was inside him right now, a mixture of sadness and anger and the whispered questioning of all that he had done in the name of revenge.

Suddenly Will cursed beneath his breath, furious to realize that all softness hadn't been burned out of him. The man in front of him had manipulated, abused, humiliated and ultimately betrayed his son. He deserved nothing but the same in return.

"That won't get your empire back," Will said coolly as Hale lifted the brandy snifter to his lips. "Nor will it get Maya pregnant."

Hale ignored him. He emptied the contents of the snifter in three long, fiery draughts, coughed, wiped his eyes and poured more brandy.

"Damn you!" Will snarled, striding to the desk and leaning forward over his clenched fists. "Don't just give up! Fight me!"

Hale smiled as he swirled brandy around in the snifter. The hard curve of his lips made him look for an instant like his son. Then the curve dissolved, leaving nothing but an old man who had fought too many battles to give a damn about one more.

"You could go to Yesler, to a Lake State bank—hell, even to Kroeber for a loan," Will said tightly. "You could use it for operating expenses at the mill, to buy timber rights, to build another mill, another railroad, anything. Everything! You could do any damn thing you want!"

Hale waved the snifter in Will's direction in a careless salute. "Except win. Each thing I did to cut my losses or increase my profit would initiate a more powerful countermove on your part. I'm an old poker player, Willy. I know when to raise and when to call... and when to get the hell out of the game."

With barely leashed violence, Will grabbed a big leather ledger and slapped it onto the desk.

"Last summer you invested more than three hundred thousand dollars in timber rights and logging operations in the Weeber Basin. The investment covered not only the redwoods and the cost of their harvest but nearly a hundred thousand dollars for the splash dam and river streambed dredging so that the logs would float all the way to Humboldt Bay and the Tres Santos mill."

Hale shrugged. "A bad bet. A dead loss."

"No," Will countered. "A brilliant bet! No other mill owner had the guts to do anything but whine about rivers that only ran deep a few months of the year. You were the only man who thought of making a river deeper artificially, just long enough to get a year's harvest of logs to the mill. With that splash dam you could deliver logs at a time when other mills had cut up their stockpiles and were shutting down their operations. And there you would be with the sawlogs everyone would pay a premium price for. It was a brilliant plan. There was no way you could have known that there would be two drought years in a row."

"But there were," Hale said. "Even worse, there was you. I made a man out of you. You made a eunuch out of me." Hale swallowed brandy, coughed and settled back in his chair, waiting for the world to blur comfortably around the edges. "But I still have *her*, Willy. I have her and you don't. Think of that when I walk down the hall to her room tonight. I'll have a son of her yet." He laughed softly.

Will said a single, vicious word before he controlled his temper. "Do what you like with your whore. All that matters to me is how much water is behind the dam in Weeber Basin."

Hale tipped his head, studying the brandy as though the future swirled within, trapped as he was trapped. "How would I know? I haven't been in the woods for months."

"You had a man out in Weeber Basin two days ago asking questions. How much water is there behind the dam?"

For a moment there was silence. Then Hale laughed again. "Two feet, maybe three of water in a few places. But there's mud showing in other places." Hale's mouth curled down. "Not enough water, Willy. Not nearly enough. The engineers told me that I'd need forty to fifty acre-feet of water to move those logs all the way to Humboldt Bay. At most the pond has fifteen feet backed up, and the river is already shrinking. It will probably be down to pools and trickles by Independence Day. Those logs are going to stay on the ground for at least another season. So you see, Willy, you shot a crippled duck. Drought would have bankrupted me even if you hadn't. You didn't beat me. Life did. In the long run it makes losers of us all. Your turn will come, Willy. Your turn will come."

Hale looked at his furious son and laughed and laughed until tears came.

Maya waited for dessert to be cleared away before she spoke to Beth. "Come up to my rooms with me. We need to talk."

Beth hesitated, sensing the command beneath the soft voice, but she made no overt objection. Maya said nothing until they were in her sitting room and the door had swung shut noiselessly on its well-oiled hinges.

"It occurs to me that I've been lax in one part of your education," Maya said calmly, not even waiting for Beth to feel her way to the settee. "Do you know how babies are made?"

There was an instant of astonished silence, followed by a sweeping flush up Beth's cheeks. For a moment Maya wavered, but the memory of Beth's mature body rising from the bath made it imperative that the question be answered.

"Beth?"

"Yes," she whispered.

"Yes, what?"

"Yes, I know how babies are made."

There was a long silence while Maya turned words over and over in her mind, but there was no delicate way to ask the question that was clawing at her mind.

"Have you and Johnny... ?"

Beth looked stricken. She began to tremble.

"I'm sorry," Maya said evenly, "but I must know. I look at you and see a child. It's the same for me when I look at Johnny. But you see things with your fingertips, not your eyes."

"It's not what you think!" Beth burst out. "It's not wicked or evil! It's so beautiful when we're together. It's like being able to see again, and everywhere I look the sun is shining!"

Maya swayed and closed her eyes. "Oh, my God," she whispered. "You're lovers."

"It's all right," Beth said quickly. "Everything will be all right. I've thought about it a lot. Will promised Johnny a job. After we're married, we'll—"

"Married?" Maya's voice sliced across Beth's tumbling words like a razor made of ice. When Maya heard the fear and fury in her own voice she closed her eyes and fought for self-possession. "Beth," she said carefully, "there will be no marriage. Your father simply will not permit it."

"I know he won't want to. He still thinks I'm a baby. You all do. But I'm not. I'm a woman."

"It's not your age. It's Johnny."

"I know he lost an arm, and he walks with a limp but that doesn't matter to me. He's good with numbers. He can earn a living that way."

"Beth," Maya whispered. "Beth . . . even if Johnny were as straight and whole as Will, and as rich, your father would never permit the marriage. No clergyman would join you. You're white. Johnny is Indian. No matter what you say or do or how you pout, that fact won't change. Your father will never allow you to marry Johnny Ising."

"He will. He'll have to. I've made sure of it."

The cold that washed over Maya settled into the marrow of her bones. "How?"

"I'm pregnant."

Maya looked at the radiant triumph in Beth's face and wished that she were as blind as the girl. "You're pregnant?"

Beth's small, white hands smoothed over her abdomen. "Oh, yes. I'm pregnant. I'll have my own baby to make greedy noises at my breast. I'll have my own baby to tickle and hug and hold against my heart. Oh, Maya, I can't wait!"

There was a harsh sound as Maya tried to control her anger and despair. "How many periods have you missed?"

"Three."

The pride in that single word snapped Maya's control. She seized Beth's shoulders in an aching grip. "Didn't you think? Don't you understand? This is the one thing in a woman's life that changes everything. Sex as such is nothing. But to be pregnant . . . ! You have a baby growing inside you. It can't be wished away. It can't be washed away. It exists, changing everything. Now and forever, it exists and everything is changed!"

As the truth of her own words hit her, Maya let go of Beth and stepped away. Maya felt helpless, adrift, as though the floor were the deck of the *Brother Samuel*, and the river bar loomed ahead out of the mist and storm.

"Sometimes," Maya said in a hollow voice, "sometimes I think that God must have hated women who have foresight, for He cursed them with living only for their future children, while men . . . men cast their seed and walk away. Away. Dear God, that I could go away too...but then who would take care of the babes?''

A shudder wracked Maya.

Beth reached out blindly for the other woman, frightened by the quality of Maya's voice. "Maya? Maya, where are you? Don't go away! Don't go into your own darkness! I need you! Who will teach me how to care for my baby?''

Maya spun around toward Beth even as the bedroom door crashed open to reveal Hale standing in the doorway, his face flushed with brandy and outrage.

"Baby? What wicked talk is this to soil the tongue of a young lass?'' he demanded.

"I'm not young and it's not wicked,'' Beth said, distraught beyond any thought of caution. "I'm going to have Johnny's baby and I'm glad. Do you hear me? I'm glad!''

Hale went white. For a moment he stood absolutely motionless. Then with a strangled cry of fury he reached for Beth. Maya threw herself forward, deflecting his attack. Brandy and her unexpected weight staggered him. He sprawled off-balance onto the settee, sending it crashing against the wall.

"Go to your room and lock your door, Beth,'' Maya said urgently. "If you love your baby, go!''

With a stricken look, Beth hurried from the room. Hale struggled upright, panting with exertion and fury. Maya tried to talk to him, to reason with him, but it was impossible. The indignities and losses of the last months had eroded Hale's self-control. He was beyond rationality. He lashed out, sending Maya staggering across the room with a broken cry. Before she could come to her feet, he was out of the door and down the hall. She picked up her skirts and ran after him, racing down the stairs with no thought of her own safety, terrified for Beth.

Maya reached the bottom of the stairs, turned down the hall and heard the front door slam shut with shattering impact.

"Beth?" she called. "Beth!"

A frightened voice came from the back of the house, where Beth's rooms were. "Maya?"

Maya sagged against the banister in relief. Beth was safe. "Yes, it's me. It's all right now, Beth. It's all right."

Only then did Maya realize that in the extremity of her terror she had been calling Will's name.

Chapter Fifteen

Chanting softly in Yurok, Johnny made the rounds of the Tres Santos mill with a lantern in one hand and a broom clamped beneath the stump of his left arm. There was a flask in his hip pocket as well. From time to time he set the lantern down, took a long pull on the flask and then went back to sweeping up mounds of fragrant sawdust and piling them to one side for later collection. As he was only one-third through his shift as sweeper, he was only one-third drunk.

Johnny wielded the broom indifferently. His job was the most menial sort, but he didn't resent that fact. He knew that his injuries had left him too stiff and awkward to be a sugler or a logger or a fisherman. While sweeping up in the mill didn't pay much, it was more than he would have made emptying out spittoons along the waterfront. It was easier work, too. He reached for his hip pocket again, paused then shrugged. Sweeping up sawdust was a thirsty business. He uncapped the flask, tipped back his head and took a long drink, shuddering at the familiar, fiery bite of whiskey in his throat.

The mill echoed with darkness and a cavernous silence as Johnny went back to sweeping. Head saws held in suspension for tomorrow gleamed dimly, reflecting back pale, cold shadows of the lantern's warm yellow light. At one time the mill had worked around the clock to process logs. Now there were barely enough logs to keep a single shift going. The other mills were similarly quiet. Too many logs were scattered across the timberlands of the redwood coast, logs waiting for rains that never came to fill rivers that wound like limp silver strings through their rocky beds.

The sound of a wagon rushing up to the mill made Johnny pause, resting the broom against a red-gold pile of sawdust higher than his knees. The continuous crackling of a buggy whip underlined the urgency of the driver, as did the rattle and skid of wheels. A horse whinnied wildly, overriding the bass cursing of the driver. Johnny picked up the lantern and broom and went toward the darkened mill entrance, wondering what was going on. He had walked only a short way toward the door when a voice inside the mill called from the darkness beyond the circle of lantern light.

"Is this how you repay me, you crawling redskin bastard? Come here and face me like a man!"

The voice echoed around the empty mill, confusing Johnny. He turned in a slow circle. Whiskey and the swinging lantern made him dizzy.

"Who's tha'?" Johnny asked, slurring the words.

"Hale Hawthorne, you son of a bitch!"

"Oh. You come to check on my work?"

Laughter came back, the kind of laughter that made Johnny think of *woges* and the black heart of the deepest redwood forest. Lantern light picked out the flash of Hale's eyes as he slowly walked across the saw room floor toward the now-silent steam carriage where

Johnny waited. Hale's footfalls were muffled by the sawdust that coated the room wherever Johnny hadn't been—and often where he had been as well.

Johnny raised the lantern, holding it beside his head, peering out at Hale. "I can't see you too good."

With complete disregard for the highly flammable sawdust heaped around, Johnny set down the lantern. A few fumbling adjustments brought the flame up to a high leap.

"Tha's better," he said, looking around with satisfaction. The shadows were farther away, now, but they still waited just beyond the ring of light.

Hale crossed the saw room. His eyes never left Johnny, silhouetted by the single wild flame of the lantern.

"Mr. Hawthorne?" Johnny asked, unease penetrating the warm layer that whiskey put between himself and the world. In the flickering leap of the kerosene lamp, the older man's face looked more demonic than human. "You sure?"

"It's me. Take a good look, heathen. I'm the last thing you'll see this side of hell."

Johnny grabbed the lantern and began backing up, moving awkwardly with his stiff knee. "Somethin' wrong?"

"Just you, and I'm going to fix that. You've raped your last white girl."

Hale closed the distance between himself and Johnny with a lunge. Reflexively Johnny swung the lantern in self-protection. Hale threw himself aside just in time, going down into a huge drift of sawdust. Tiny, resinous particles of pine sprayed outward, mixing with the less volatile but still quite flammable redwood sawdust.

"I didn't rape no one," Johnny said, forgetting under stress all the grammar that Beth had so patiently taught him. "Any girl I give it to wanted it, and that's a fact."

"Liar! My little Beth would never want such a disgusting thing done to her! The only way you'd be able to take her is to rape her!"

Covered in sawdust, Hale erupted toward Johnny, who swung the lantern wildly again, aiming for the other man's head. Off-balance from whiskey and the loss of his arm, Johnny missed Hale's head. Instead, the lantern crashed into his shoulder. Glass shattered, and kerosene splashed out past the wick, saturating a small spot on Hale's black wool coat. A small flame blossomed.

"Sweet Jesus!" Hale gasped, as the possibility of personal danger penetrated his fog of rage and brandy. He swatted at the flame, then smothered it with his bare hand.

Johnny turned and tried to run. Hale caught the motion and leaped. Johnny lashed out with the lantern again. The metal base slashed Hale across the forehead just as Johnny tripped and went sprawling into the same drift of sawdust that had cushioned Hale's earlier fall. The older man jumped forward, clawing for the lantern, unable to see for the veil of blood across his eyes.

"You're making a mistake," Johnny said, scrambling backward frantically. "Beth wanted it same as I did! Hell, she wanted it more. She taught me things that I—"

Johnny's words became a scream as Hale flung himself forward, his fingers digging like talons into Johnny's throat. The boy struggled frantically, but he was overmatched. The smell of whiskey rose from the sawdust as the flask in his pocket broke. Kerosene spattered randomly as he flailed with the lantern. Finally he grabbed the lantern by its guard wires and began smashing it against Hale's head again and again. Hale bucked abruptly, knocking the lantern free of Johnny's hand. The light spun end over end to land upside down in the mound of sawdust.

Instants later a sudden, brilliant ball of flame flared up and swallowed the struggling men.

Will was a block away, riding his horse through the gentle rain at a full gallop when he saw a flash of light. Seconds later there was a muffled *whump* as the shock wave of an explosion raced through the night. Above the Tres Santos mill smoke billowed up, blackening the moon. By the time Will lashed his horse through the front gate of Tres Santos, flames were reaching hungrily from the windows. Fed by sawdust and resinous scraps of pine, the fire burned with such explosive violence that the very air turned to flame.

The heat was so great that Will's clothes smoked even before he reached the main door. The thin rain outside was no deterrent to the fire storm. Will raced to the horse trough, threw himself in the water and emerged soaked. Suit coat over his head, he tried again to get past the leading edge of the inferno. It was hopeless. He ran to the side of the building, kicked in a locked door and tried again.

The interior of the mill was a foretaste of hell. Will could go no more than a few steps before he was driven to his knees by the searing heat and lack of oxygen. Coughing, choking, calling out to Hale and Johnny and hearing nothing but the ravenous voice of the inferno in return, Will finally was forced to retreat. As soon as he emerged, men appeared through the thin drizzle and dragged him into the chill of night, beating out flames from his clothes.

"I'm all—right," Will gasped. "My father—Johnny—in there!"

Men exchanged glances. Finally the floor boss shifted on his feet and met Will's eyes.

"Ain't no one coming out of that there fire alive, Mr. Hawthorne, an' that's God's own truth."

More men came scrambling out of the darkness, dragging the mill's small hand pumper into position to fight the fire. From the distance came the clanging of the municipal fire bell in the barn near the top end of First Street. More help was on the way, but Will could see that it would arrive too late. Nothing short of an act of God could reverse a mill fire once it took hold.

Grimly Will went to work with the men who were using the mill's pumper on the raging fire. The thin stream of water turned to steam long before it touched a single licking flame. Around Will, stitching through the whisper of rain, came the high screams of panicked lumberyard mules from the nearby stable. Men cursed and dragged the beasts out into the darkness beyond the reach of flames. Other men ran to the wharf beside the mill, where deck hands were scrambling to get a pair of three-masted brigantines beyond the reach of the ravenous fire. The swirling, leaping flames had already spread to the structure that housed the lumber grading room. From there the fire spread through the old section of the mill like water thundering out from behind a burst dam.

The municipal fire pumper came boiling into the yard, the four-horse team scattering the crowd as though they were no more than quail. The fire in the pumper's boiler was already burning, building steam pressure to drive the pump. Dozens of hands dragged hose off the cart, peeling it away until the brass reel spun and shimmered with reflected flames. Seconds later a heavy rush of water was joining the tiny, wavering stream that issued from the hand-powered mill machine.

Will left the smaller pump and went to organize the mill workers into a bucket brigade to bring water from the wharf to the burning building. It was a futile effort. Within minutes Will was forced to admit that the Tres Santos mill was a dead loss.

He grabbed men, shouted at them, pointed them toward different targets. Under his directions the volunteers began soaking the roofs of nearby, woodframe buildings, hoping to prevent the spread of the fire. Although the mill had been lost, they still hoped to save the waterfront and the town itself.

As night wore on the rain strengthened, finally allowing the men to defeat the flames. By dawn the Tres Santos mill was a pile of smoldering wreckage, with fugitive flames still burning in some of the heavier timbers. More than half the yarded lumber was lost, as was the wharf itself and one of the two brigantines that had been anchored just off it. The roofs of nearby buildings had been set afire, and one of the structures had been burned so badly it would have to be razed. But the advance of the flames had been stopped short of the commercial district with its tightly spaced stores and ornate, heavily occupied hotels.

Will leaned wearily against the municipal pumper's brightly painted wheel as dawn spread a different, cooler fire across the rain-glistening face of the land.

He was as sweaty and sooty and exhausted as any of the men milling around him. The only thing that was keeping him upright was the knowledge that someone had to search the hot remains of the building.

In all the hours that the fire had been fought, no one had seen Hale Hawthorne or Johnny Ising.

The shrill hooting of a steam whistle turned all eyes toward the water, where a tugboat was approaching the dock with unusual speed. The deck was crowded with Tres Santos loggers. The first man to leap onto the wharf and make his way through the crowd to the pumper was Henry Ising.

"We came as quick as we could," Ising said. "Anybody hurt?"

Will looked at the broad, dark face of his only friend and wondered how to tell Ising that life had played one last, cruel joke on the boy who had never believed that tomorrow would come.

"I'm afraid that two men died. My father was one. Johnny was the other."

Ising's face showed pain, then nothing at all. "Where is Johnny's body?"

"In there."

Ising looked toward the skeletal black ruins of the mill. "Your father?"

"With Johnny," Will said roughly. "Come. We'll search together."

Hale Hawthorne's funeral was the biggest that Eureka had ever seen. Every flag within the city limits flew at half-staff. Competitors' mills closed at noon so that their men could attend. Four hundred of the region's most important citizens filled the sanctuary of Reverend Cleary's church, a church that had been built with Tres Santos redwood donated by Hale Hawthorne. More than two thousand people gathered in the street outside, waiting for a glimpse of the redwood coast's most powerful citizens as they came to pay their respects to one of their own.

Maya noticed nothing of her surroundings, nor did she hear the hushed murmurs of the crowd as she stepped down from the handsome black carriage with its polished brass fittings and matched pair of ebony horses. No one but Maya, Beth, Will and Henry Ising knew what had happened the night that the Tres Santos Mill had burned to the ground. When questions were asked, Maya had simply said that Hale often inspected his mill at night. As that was known to be true, all further speculation centered upon how the accident had occurred. Will's suggestion that his father had had a seizure and Johnny had been trying to help him and somehow a lantern had been knocked over was generally accepted.

With Justine on one arm and Emily clinging to her hand, Maya preceded Will and Beth into the packed church. Maya looked straight ahead as she walked slowly up the aisle, her face heavily veiled, her eyes nearly as dark as her mourning clothes. The strain of the months since Will's return had cost her every bit of inner strength she had. She had none left with which to face the crisis of widowhood. She hadn't loved Hale, but she had respected him as her husband. He had been an important part of her life and of her thoughts, the father of her children, the source of her children's security.

All of that had burned to ash with the mill. Though Maya knew nothing of Hale's finances, she was aware that the logging industry of the redwood coast had been depressed by the drought. To lose the mill on top of that boded ill; worst of all, to lose the driving force behind Hale Hawthorne's redwood empire presaged disaster.

Maya settled into the front pew, which was so familiar to her from Sundays past. Justine fretted softly for a moment then calmed when Maya held out a small, favorite toy. Emily sat unnaturally still, her eyes huge, her little face solemn. Beth sat beside her, pale as salt, secure within the strong circle of Will's arm. A helpless longing flared in Maya, a yearning to be held just once like that, trust and affection transmitted by touch, a shoulder on which to dry her tears.

But then, she had no tears to dry. Her emotions were in a state of terrible stillness, balanced on the thin edge of breaking. When people complimented her on her strength and courage in the face of Hale's death, she spoke softly in response, hoping that only she could hear the madness skirling at the edges of her quietness. She faced an unending battery of decisions, each choice loaded with hidden, possibly dangerous, ramifications for her children. She could bear no more; yet there was so much more to bear before her children would be secure once again.

And Beth—child herself, soon to be a mother. Beth's babe would need Maya, for Beth herself was as locked in grief as she was in darkness. Maya had no more of herself to give, yet she could not turn her back on Beth any more than she could sell her own babies into slavery. She would have to find the strength somewhere, somehow, to bring the family intact through this crisis.

"Mama, is Father up there in that long box?"

Emily's question speared through Maya's control. She forced words past the constriction in her throat that came whenever she thought of the awful night when Hale had turned on his pregnant daughter and then rushed out into the darkness to find her lover. Hale had found Johnny, and he had found death as well. What was left of the two men had been discovered locked together. With the exception of the shortened bone of Johnny's severed arm, it was impossible to label the remains as Hale Hawthorne or Johnny Ising, white or Indian, murderer or murdered. Half of the bones had been brought to a local undertaker. The rest had been turned over to Henry Ising for burial according to Yurok customs.

"Yes, part of your father is up there. The rest of him, the most important part, is with God."

"I can't see him when he's with God, can I?"

"No, sweetheart. You can't."

"Will I ever see him again?"

"No."

The word was as soft as it was final.

Although Emily had heard the explanation of Hale's absence many times by now, she began weeping with a thin-lipped silence that tore at Maya's heart. She pulled Emily close, holding both her children against her body. Motionless but for small gestures to calm them, Maya endured the sermon and the eulogies, her mind as empty as her heart.

A cold wind blew in off the Pacific, pushing a spring storm before it, rattling the windows of the Hawthorne house with a thousand clawing fingers of rain. The clock had just struck midnight, but Maya was still awake. Wide-eyed, motionless, candle flames reflected in her dark eyes, she sat by Beth's bedside. Beth's small, slender hand lay lax and cool within Maya's. The sedative that the doctor had given Beth had finally brought relief to the girl.

The fire in the hearth burned brightly. As Maya watched it she remembered that she would have to order more wood for the house; they were down to the last half cord of the oak that had been cut by a Tres Santos work crew and hauled down the coast last summer to dry in the mill's kiln. As the thought came, Maya flinched. The mill was utterly gone. Even the heavy saws and metal rails of the steam carriage had been bent and warped by the fire. The massive office safes had fared little better. Except for the funeral itself, Will had spent almost all his time going through the scorched papers in the mill safes and talking with Jeffrey Lockhart, Hale's lawyer.

That was where Will was now, late at night when most people slept. He was going over the requirements of Hale's will and estate. Soon Will would come back to the house. Soon Maya would have to face him once more, would have to see again the contempt and accusation in his eyes. Soon.

She didn't know where she would find the strength to bear up much longer. She knew as well as he did that none of it would have happened had she not put the lives of her future children above the lives of everyone else—Will, Hale, herself. Even Beth had inadvertently paid the price of Emily's and Justine's security. Were it not for the deadly rivalry between Hale and Will, the Guardian never would have fallen on Johnny Ising, bringing him to the Hawthorne house, to Beth's lonely life.

And to an early death.

For a long time there was no movement in the room, no noise but that from erratic gusts of wind and scattered rain and Beth's slow breaths. Finally the sound of a horse's hooves on the driveway brought Maya out of her reverie. With great care she disentangled Beth's fingers, stood and walked soundlessly from the room. With trembling fingers Maya parted the heavy brocade curtains an inch. She noticed the tremor in her hand with a distant sense of surprise. She had hoped to be stronger than this when it came time to face Will. If only for the sake of her children's future, she must be strong.

Rain had given way to a heavy mist that the gaslight at the front gate transformed into a shimmering halo of pale gold. A man on horseback passed through the outer edge of the light beyond the wrought iron fence. He wore a dark coat with the collar turned up and a straight-brimmed hat pulled down low over his eyes. His shoulders were wide and straight, and his powerful body moved easily as he adjusted to the horse's gait.

Yet Will felt anything but easy as he rode the tired horse to the stable at the side of the house. He was still reeling with the shock of what he had discovered among his father's papers. The envelope had been new, its wax seal hard but unbroken. Across the paper's creamy face had been written: "For William Hale Hawthorne. To be opened by him, and only by him, in the event of my death."

It had been dated the week after the Guardian fell and was in his father's handwriting. There was no chance of a mistake. Will wished that there were. What the letter had told him was corroding his soul.

He tried to put it out of his mind. It was impossible. Each word burned in him with a separate violence.

There is a reason that the Lord God reserved vengeance for Himself. He is so much better at it than mere man.

By now you have ruined my Redwood Empire beyond hope of anyone saving it. Even you. You have mortgaged too much of your own property to begin to salvage mine. I leave a bankrupt estate, a penniless widow and two children with no future.

Yes. Two children, not three. Look at Emily's right ear as I did four years ago. She is your child, not mine. She'll be the same as her mother was, rootless in the land until she becomes a drudge or a prostitute or some older man marries her for her youth and beauty and fertile womb.

I salute the vengeance God has visited upon the child of your wanton lust.

Will finished rubbing down his mount and left the cold stable behind him with long strides. He didn't notice that the mist had turned to wind-driven rain once more, a hard, chilling rain that ran from the eaves of the big house onto the grass below. He wrenched open the front door.

Maya stood just inside, a small oil lamp in her hand. She watched him with eyes that reflected flame but nothing more, no inner life, nothing but darkness beneath. Taking the lamp from her hand, Will brushed past her and went to the room where Emily and Justine slept. Despite his turmoil he was careful not to wake either child. He stared at Emily's sleeping face, trying to see himself rather than the father he had hated. She had the same slightly dimpled chin that Will had; but Hale, too, had owned such a chin. It was the same for the color of her eyes, a gray-green that could have come from a combination of Maya plus father or son.

With a hand that trembled slightly, Will eased aside the cinnamon locks that spilled in such profusion onto Emily's pillow. Her right ear was tiny, perfectly shaped—and tucked just beneath the upper rim was a hole so tiny that no one who hadn't been looking for it would have seen it. Barely big enough to hold a pierced earring, the hole bore silent testimony to Will's paternity.

He turned and looked at Maya with eyes half-mad. In that instant he hated her more than he ever had before. She had taken from him not only her love, but also the child their love had conceived.

Will's fingers wrapped around Maya's arms so harshly that nerves rubbed against bone. Other than a stifled gasp of pain, she said nothing as she was dragged from the children's room to Hale's office downstairs. Once the door was shut, Will let go of Maya as though she were a burning brand. Afraid to trust himself to speech at that instant, he worked on the fire that had been laid in the hearth. Within minutes flames were dancing over aged oak logs.

"Did the doctor come?" he demanded, his back still to Maya.

"Yes."

"Well?"

"Beth is distraught, but otherwise healthy. The baby will be born in October."

Maya's voice reminded Will of the wood he was feeding into the fire—slightly rough, dry, utterly dead. He turned and looked at her. In the semidarkness of the office her green velvet robe was the same color as her eyes, black with vague intimations of green where firelight touched. Her skin was pale, perfect, and her breasts curved softly in the opening of the robe.

He yanked off his hat and dripping suit coat and flung them into a nearby chair. With the same savagely controlled motions he poured himself two fingers of brandy, took a swallow and felt a different kind of heat than that of rage spread through his belly. For a moment he cupped the snifter in his hand, warming the amber fluid, making its vapors rise. He drew a breath from the crystal mouth of the snifter. The fragrance was like vengeance ... sweet and wild at first whiff, brutally harsh when taken in too great a quantity.

"Lockhart was unhappy to discover that he wasn't Father's executor," Will said.

"Was he?"

The words were soft, distant, more polite than interested. Will went on speaking anyway, holding onto the brandy because it was all that kept him from grabbing Maya; and if he touched her again, he didn't know whether he would kill her or make savage love to her. He didn't want to know. So he spoke about Hale's business.

"Lockhart had cut a deal with Kroeber on selling off the estate." Will stared over the rim of the snifter to Maya. If she understood what he was saying, it didn't show on the flawless skin of her face. "Lockhart, for twenty percent of the take, was going to gut the estate and give it to Kroeber."

"Lockhart was a dinner guest in this house last week."

There was no emotion in Maya's voice. She offered the statement not in outrage or denial, but as a simple fact.

"I doubt that there was anything personal in it," Will said dryly, "either the dinner or the deal with Kroeber. Kroeber had Lockhart over a barrel. Lockhart is half owner of a bank that issued a new block of capital stock last month. Rumor has it that some Chicago holding company bought up every share of that bank's stock. Rumor is right, for once. The holding company was a front for Kroeber's backers, Shirmer and Stout Lumber. Right now they have a lot of leverage with Lockhart. If they want something, he'll do what he can to deliver it. And they wanted Tres Santos lumber out of business for good."

Maya waited, watching blankly, wondering if what Will was saying had any immediate bearing on the future of her children.

"My father thought that Shirmer and Stout would never get out of the Lake States," Will said absently as he swirled brandy. "He was wrong. They're finally running out of timber in the Middle West. Either they come to the redwood coast or they die. Shirmer and Stout had been trying to get leverage on Father through Kroeber for years. When Father lost three bets in a row, they had him."

"I don't understand."

Will smiled thinly. "It's quite simple. First he bet on a splash dam to get his logs down the hill. Then he bet on a normal rainfall to make the dam work. When he came up dry, he floated rumors of building a railroad. Kroeber's backers took the bait. They loaned

Father money. He made feints in the direction of laying track, but what he wanted the money for was operating expenses for his logging operations. That's
what he used the loan for, betting that a normal rainfall would come last winter and the dam would fill and
the logs would rush down to the bay. Then he could
sell the logs, pay off the loan and have enough left
over to build two railroads if he wanted to.

"But the rain didn't fall. He still might have pulled
it out if he could have taken a loan against the logs and
this house. After the Guardian fell, no loans were
possible. He lost, but give the Devil his due. My father was one hell of a gutsy gambler."

The firelight gleamed on Will's teeth as he grinned.
For an instant Maya saw in that grin the youth she had
begun falling in love with nearly six years before, when
he had put himself at risk to save his sister from the
swinging captain's chair. Then Will's grin hardened
into a cold smile, and Maya closed her eyes, not
wanting to hear what was coming next, knowing that
there was no choice but to hear.

There was a long pause. The big house was filled
with silence, save for the drumming rain and the soft
popping sounds of dry oak being consumed by flames.

"You still don't understand, do you?" Will asked,
watching Maya narrowly.

Her eyes opened. There was no color but darkness
in them.

"You chose the wrong man to be your husband,"
Will said, savoring each word as though it were perfectly aged brandy. "My father left you bankrupt, utterly without recourse, not a penny to your name.
Kroeber holds paper on the mill and any timber rights
worth having. I own every log in Weeber Basin.

"And the house, Maya. I own this house as well.
There's nothing between your children and starvation
but whatever Christian charity I might have left in my
soul."

Chapter Sixteen

Maya's face lost all color. After all that she had sacrificed, all that she had endured to assure her babies' future—it couldn't be for nothing. She couldn't be back where her mother had been years before, adrift in an indifferent world with no more to support herself and her children than whatever work was left in her worn body.

"Oh, dear God, no," she whispered in unconscious plea.

The smile on Will's face did nothing to reassure her.

"Oh, yes, Maya. I've waited years for this moment. Now, finally, you know how I felt when all that I cherished in life was taken from me by the betrayal of someone I had trusted. Now you know what it is to lose everything in a single instant."

The terrible stillness that had been growing for years within Maya's soul, consuming her darkly, exploded in a torrent of words.

"What would you have had me do?" she demanded, her voice rising. "Marry a boy who knew nothing of misery and want? Marry a handsome, passionate child who believed that failure was impossible for him?"

"Yes!" Will retorted harshly. He leaned toward Maya, his eyes narrowed in an anger as passionate as hers. "I could have taken care of you. I could have moved Heaven and Hell for you, Maya. *I did move them.* You should have believed in me. But you didn't. You didn't even give me a chance!"

Maya laughed, and the chilling sounds made Will's skin ripple in primal response.

"Is that what I should tell Emily?" Maya asked, her mouth twisted in an amusement that was as unnatural as her laughter had been. "Should I tell her to believe in the first boy who sets her body afire? Beth did. Do the results please you?"

Will's eyelids flickered, but he said nothing.

"Answer me, Will. What should I tell Emily?" Maya demanded, her voice high and tight with the strain of not screaming. "My mother married a handsome, charming boy. He meant well, he had dreams bigger than the world, and he failed at everything but getting children. He succeeded very well at that, to his family's everlasting despair. I was the first. I watched my mother grow old and worn before her time. I listened to dreams and promises that meant less than the air they were spun from. I watched and I listened. And I learned, Will. I learned! Life taught me never to marry a man my own age, because he wouldn't be able to support the babies he got upon my body one after the other, without regard for the future or the hungry cries of the children already born."

Will started to speak but Maya's words rushed on, sweeping his protests aside.

"I buried two sisters and three brothers with my own hands," she said in a high, thin voice. "But the winter winds didn't care. When the mule died we ate it and that spring mother and I hitched ourselves to the plow because father was gone, and little Arthur guided the plow until mother fainted in the traces, and then I pulled the plow alone, and it wasn't enough. The rains came late, and the corn died, and we went hungry, and baby Jessica died."

"Maya—"

"No! Let me—" Her voice broke. She twisted her fingers together, shuddered and went on in a hoarse voice. "Jessie died in the winter. Mama was ill, Father was dying, there was no one but me to wrap that sad little body and read from the Bible.... The ground was frozen. I had to chop out her grave with the hatchet. And with every stroke, every frozen bit of dirt, I vowed to God and the Devil that I would never do what my mother had done. I would never make my babes pay for my mistakes. I would never let my heart and my body lead my future babies into an endless hell of misery and want. I would never have to go into the fields and see my children eat grass until they vomit. I would never watch my babe dwindle and die and then have to bury a tiny corpse that weighed no more than a handful of leaves."

For a moment Will closed his eyes, unable to bear any longer the sight of Maya's face as she remembered her past. He tried to envision his own sister in a muddy spring field, strapped like an animal to a plow, pulling her young heart out because it was that or watch her family starve...and then to watch her baby sister starve anyway. He had seen children like that in ports all over the world, bones like match sticks, eyes dulled by hunger, death a cold shadow seeping into their bodies, draining them, claiming them.

The thought of Maya struggling to feed her brothers and sisters in the face of such overwhelming poverty went like a knife into Will's soul, turning, slicing, tearing, making him bleed in ways that he hadn't thought himself capable of any longer. His eyes opened, dark with a new kind of pain.

"Maya...my God...don't..."

She didn't even hear Will's hoarse words. She was the captive of her own memories and the breaking of the terrible silence that had claimed her soul for too many years.

"I kept my vow," Maya said, her voice stretched to the point of shattering as she focused on Will for the first time. "I married a man who was no longer young. I married a man who could give my babies a life without hunger and want. I sold myself for my children's future.

"And I lived with my heart a raw wound and you the salt in it! I hungered for you until I couldn't eat, couldn't sleep, couldn't think, until I dreamed of madness as I had once dreamed of warmth and food. But Emily and Justine slept snug and warm, and they ate food every day. Every day, Will! Do you know how much of a miracle that is? My babies ate as much as they wanted, whenever they wanted. That was the bargain I had made with God and the Devil. That was the bargain I kept."

As suddenly as it had come, the strength and the fire rushed out of Maya. Her voice broke, only to return as a raw whisper of sound.

"And now...and now I have two children whom I love and can't feed. I have a child pregnant with another babe, and a house owned by a man who would laugh to see my soul writhing in Hell. I learned from my mother's mistake, but what will my daughters learn from mine? What shall I tell Emily when she looks at a young man and her heart turns inside out? If she lives that long. If she lives...."

Will tried to speak, but couldn't force words past the tension in his throat.

Maya shuddered and then became very still as a thought slowly condensed from the black, swirling pain of her mind—a possibility so perfect, so alluring, that it glittered like faceted, polished jet as she turned it over and over in her mind. Images suffused her, memories of Will talking to Emily while Justine teethed and drooled in his lap, Will smiling at her babies and Beth with gentleness that did not exist in him for the rest of the world. But it existed for them, for the innocents born into a tangled web of mistakes that they had never made.

Yes.

The eyes that watched Will with new awareness made a chill gather in his soul. The shadows that had always been a part of Maya had deepened, become more intense. Consuming.

"Tell me," she said in a stranger's voice. "If you came across my children in the street, starving, would you turn aside from them?"

"My God, of course not!"

Maya smiled gently, and it was by far the most painful thing that Will had yet endured.

"As I hoped...your hatred is for me, not for my children. So I give them to you," she said simply. "I will leave now, tonight. You will take care of Emily and Justine, Beth and her unborn babe. You will see that they are neither cold nor hungry, that when a storm rushes in from the ocean, they are wearing warm clothes beneath a sound roof. You will do that because they are innocent children who had nothing to do with my mistake, my betrayal. In return, I will vow never to come back again.

"And," she added softly, "I keep my vows."

Will stared at Maya, remembering the morning when he had watched her from the woods while Justine nursed at her breast and Emily played with butterflies and Beth lay with her head in her beloved stepmother's lap to enjoy the slow caresses of Maya's hand. Maya's love for the three girls had been so clear, so overwhelmingly deep, that Will could not imagine her abandoning them for any reason short of death.

"You'll never again talk to them, never again write to them, never again so much as watch them from a distance?" he probed, watching Maya through narrowed eyes that glittered in the firelight.

"Never."

"Then you must mean to die," he said flatly.

Maya met his glance with dark, unflinching eyes. "I have lived for my children. I sold my life for them before they were even born. My death will be a small thing . . . to me most of all."

The calm words were more agonizing to Will than a scream would have been. He had lived solely in hope of drinking the wine of revenge, and he had achieved that, only to discover that it was turning to vinegar even as he swallowed it. Maya had lived for her children's security, and she had achieved it, only to discover that security was as fragile as the bittersweet taste of victory.

"'I have lived with my heart a raw wound and you the salt in it,'" Will whispered, reaching toward Maya with hands that trembled from the force of the emotions twisting within him. "Has it really been that way for you?"

Hearing her own painful words returning on Will's lips was so unexpected that Maya couldn't speak. Slowly she nodded. When his fingertips lightly touched her cheek, she began to tremble. His thumb touched her lower lip, then rested on a small scar just below.

"This is new," Will said, tracing the scar. "You didn't have it when we lay beneath the Guardian. I would have remembered it. I remember everything about that day, those hours, you." As though memorizing the change in Maya's skin, his thumb skimmed lightly, repeatedly over the tiny, nearly invisible white line. "What happened?"

Her lip quivered beneath his touch. "The n-night you came back from the woods and f-found that I had married...I heard you cry out when you left. I wanted to scream, too, but your father would have heard, so I b-bit my lip against the cry."

Will closed his eyes as memories flooded him. "I hated you," he said, his tone low, intense. He released Maya from his touch. "I hated the knowledge that you had found pleasure with any other man, much less my father."

"Pleasure?" Maya made an odd sound as she remembered the pain and humiliation she had felt with Hale. "Hate me because I betrayed you, but don't hate me for the forced intimacies of the marriage bed. There was no pleasure for me."

His eyes opened. He searched her drawn face intently. "You are a sensual woman. The most sensual I've ever known."

It was a statement rather than a question, but Maya answered anyway, understanding the question that lay beneath his words. "Long ago, yes, perhaps. With you. Once. But never since. The marriage bed killed that in me. The thought of sex repels me. Hate me for my other sins, but not for lust. I have none left in me."

"But it wasn't lust between us," Will said. "If it had been just that, other women could have eased me. I would have outgrown you as I outgrew so much else. But I didn't. You consumed me. That's not lust. Lust doesn't care who slakes it, which whore is beneath it while it ruts."

How is my father's whore this morning?

The contemptuous, oft-repeated greeting echoed in Maya's mind, breaking her fragile hold on herself. Tears burned behind her eyelids but would not form to soothe and fall, giving her ease. There was no release for her any longer, save one.

"Will," she whispered, trembling beneath the weight of choices made, losses counted. "Please, don't hate me after I'm...gone. I can bear anything but not that. I have known beauty three times in my life. Twice when I looked at the face of my newborn babies and knew that they wouldn't starve; and once with you beneath the Guardian. I never meant to hurt you. If it had been just my own life you asked for, I would have given it to you and never known a single moment of regret. But it wasn't just my life. It was the lives of all the babes I would have as well. I couldn't make them pay for my loving the wrong man."

"Loving?"

Will's hand went out to Maya once more. His fingers tightened on her chin as he turned her face up to his intense scrutiny.

"Did you love me?"

"Yes," she whispered.

"No. You turned your back on me."

"I loved you," she said, trembling. "Then. Now. Always. But loving you didn't change the fact that my duty was to the helpless unborn. You weren't a man in your own right. Without your father's generosity, you hadn't enough money to clothe and feed and shelter yourself, yet you believed that the world would always bow to your own desires simply because you were Hale Hawthorne's son and had never known hunger. Had I not come between you and your father, you would have grown up forever tied to his purse strings."

Maya searched Will's eyes, wondering if he were truly listening to her, if her words were penetrating the rage that she sensed was still seething in him. He said nothing to give her a clue to his thoughts. He simply watched her with unblinking eyes whose dark centers had expanded to swallow all but a thinly glittering rim of gray.

"I knew your immaturity," Maya said in a low tone, "but still I was drawn to you. Beneath all my practical thoughts was the secret hope that there would be time for us, time for you to grow, time for me to have both a man my heart wanted and the man my mind knew that my babes would need. Then you touched me, held me, taught me that my fine thoughts and foresight were no protection against my reckless, unthinking passion.

"And then there was no more time, only the chance of a helpless, hapless babe growing in my womb. You hadn't thought of that. You hadn't thought beyond the moment you would have your pleasure of me. You were no more ready for the responsibilities of marriage than a sea hawk soaring above the waves.''

Will wanted to turn away, to deny what Maya was saying about the boy who had lived years ago in the shadow of his powerful father; Will wanted to deny, but he could not. There was truth in what Maya was saying. He could have left home at any time since he turned fourteen and made his own way in the woods as other boys had been doing, as his father had done. Yet Will had stayed at home, held by his love for Beth and by the more insidious bonds of physical comfort and future inheritance.

Even as Will told himself that he would have broken with his overweening father whether or not Maya had ever been born, Will wondered if he would have left the empire that Hale had wanted his son to inherit—at the price of the son's own manhood and independence.

"You hated me because I had betrayed you," Maya continued raggedly. "Yet how would you feel toward a woman who betrayed her own helpless children *and knew what she was doing while she betrayed them*?" She searched Will's eyes, saw the pain-darkened centers rimmed with crystalline gray. "Do you finally understand? If I had it to do all over again I would have to betray you again."

Suddenly, unexpectedly, tears spilled from Maya's eyes as she heard her own words.

"Oh, God," she cried. "I couldn't do it—yet how could I not? I would try to turn away from you instead of betraying my own helpless babies. Even knowing what was to come, I would try, but it would be easier by far to die than to betray you again! I have lived these years knowing that your name will be the last word on my lips when I die and that I will go to God wondering if it wouldn't have been better never to have been born at all!''

"But I'm the one who brought you to ruin," Will said, his voice rough with suppressed emotion. "I made you pregnant and then I dedicated my life to bringing down the man you married for the security he could give your children. My father went bankrupt because I knew him, knew his mind, knew how he worked, how he planned. I destroyed him and you without a single thought to your children's future. They weren't real to me, not in way revenge was. Even Beth wasn't real. I saw how much she loved you, saw how much your innocent children needed you, yet nothing truly mattered to me but my own needs, my own revenge. Don't you realize that yet?''

Slowly Maya nodded. She knew what Will was saying. He had knowingly destroyed the very thing for which she had sacrificed so much: the security of her children.

"Yes, I understand. It doesn't change anything." She smiled sadly. "If people had to be perfect in order to love and be loved, life would be terrible beyond bearing." She took a trembling breath and continued. "I understand what you were. I also understand what you are now. My children are real to you now. They will be as safe with you as any baby ever born into this uncertain life. We've come full circle," she whispered. "I am you and you are me once more. When you talk about me to my children, remember that. Please don't hate me, Will. I can't bear to go to God with your hatred on my soul.''

Will felt Maya's tears burning over his hand as he held her face, felt the searing hot tears in his own eyes, tears more scalding than any hatred he had ever known. He tried to speak but found no words to comfort either her or himself. His arms closed around her as he pulled her close, rocking her slowly against his chest, whispering her name again and again because it was the only word that he could say.

Maya heard the litany Will made of her name, tasted his tears on her own lips, and the last of her fragile hold on her own emotions dissolved. A lifetime of unwept tears welled up and swept over her, tearing her apart. Crying uncontrollably, she clung to Will as she had once before, when he had come to her out of a cold ocean mist holding salvation in his hands. He held on to her in the same way, letting her wild grief shake both of their bodies.

Only after a long time did Maya become aware of herself and her surroundings once again. She was surprised to discover that she was lying on her bed, a soft comforter pulled up beneath her chin. She had no memory of being carried to her room. Will was gently bathing her face and hands with a cool cloth. She touched his cheek with fingers that trembled.

"I know that I'm dreaming," she whispered, "but don't awaken me."

Maya's voice was almost too husky to be audible, but Will understood her. He smiled at Maya as though she were Beth before he turned and wrung out the cloth in a basin of cool, lavender-scented water. When the soft cloth moved lightly over Maya's face, soothing her tear-inflamed skin, she made an incoherent sound that could have been Will's name.

After that there was nothing but silence and the occasional ripple of water when the cloth was refreshed. From time to time he supported her head with one hand and tilted a crystal glass against her lips with the other. Then she would drink, easing the rawness of her throat.

"Better?" Will finally asked, his voice soft as he set the glass aside once again.

She nodded, touching his cheek again, enjoying the rasp of his growing beard because it told her that she was not dreaming. Will was real. She was real. The moment was real.

As though Will understood Maya's thoughts, he gently trapped her hand with his own and turned his head, kissing her palm. What began with a light pressure turned into an almost painful caress as he gripped her hand with work-hardened fingers and a strength that was unused to measuring itself against a woman's softness.

"There will be no more talk of dying," Will said, watching Maya's haunted green eyes. "Promise me."

"Will—"

"Promise me that you'll live," he interrupted fiercely, wanting only to hear that from Maya. "I swear I'll demand nothing else of you, but I must have that!"

Her lips trembled. "I promise."

With a visible effort Will forced himself to release his grip on Maya's hand. When she didn't remove it from his cheek, he closed his eyes and savored the sweetness of her touch, moving his head slowly, slowly, rubbing his cheek against her palm, then against her wrist, then against the soft, slender arm that was revealed by her robe's loose sleeve. Every few breaths he turned his lips reverently against her skin, brushing her taut flesh, breathing in her fragrance.

Finally he became aware of the fact that she was shivering.

"You're cold," he said, tucking the comforter more closely around her.

"No."

Will heard the strain in Maya's voice. "You're frightened," he said sadly. "Of me? Is my presence so hateful to you?"

Maya caught Will's hand between her own and drew it to her lips. She kissed him with the same haunting gentleness that he had used in caressing her.

Will's breath stopped and then his heart leaped with each brush of Maya's lips against his palm. In a few moments he, too, was shivering. He leaned forward, breathing in the scent of tears and womanly warmth and the subtly spicy fragrance that was Maya's alone. He whispered her name against the curve of her ear, her cheek, the corner of her mouth. And then she turned to him, giving him the sweetness of lips he had thought never again to kiss. He savored the moment, lengthened it, creating a new world where the two of them could live with time suspended, nothing real but the warmth of their lips learning once more the beauty of a shared kiss.

At first the chaste, gentle, sliding touch of Will's lips was enough for Maya, more than she had ever hoped to have. Yet as the soft kisses continued, she remembered a time when his tongue had caressed her mouth intimately and his taste had spread through her with a sweet, living fire that no wine had ever equalled.

"Will," she breathed. "Do you . . . ?"

He waited, but no more words came, just the soft pressure of her lips against his.

"What?" he whispered.

She hesitated, but in the end the words could not be held back. "Do you still taste like life itself?"

A groan ripped through Will. The pressure of his mouth on Maya's changed as he parted her lips with a single twisting motion of his head. As his tongue entered her mouth, he felt her nails dig suddenly into his arms. Sanity returned to him. His tongue retreated from her mouth, only to have her follow. When the tip of her tongue caressed him, the sensuous taste of her made a violent tremor run through his body. Suddenly he was kissing her without restraint, flattening her into the bed, his body moving over her, covering her while their mouths mated.

Without warning he wrenched his mouth free of hers.

"You are a fire in my body, in my mind, in my soul," Will said, breathing harshly, hating the loss of self-control that he had vowed to himself would never threaten him again. "A single kiss and I'm a boy again, out of control. What have you done to me?"

Maya opened dazed eyes. "It's all right. This is just a dream. I'm naked beneath the Guardian, and you're kneeling between my legs, touching me, touching me and I'm wild with your touch and I see you bending down to me, filling me...and then I wake. Empty. Just a dream."

With an anguished sound, Will threw himself aside and onto his back. The violent movement sent him to the edge of the mattress. His broad shoulder hit the bedside table, sending a crystal flagon skidding off. Reflexively he caught the delicate bottle, but not in time to save the stopper. It crashed to the floor even as some of the bottle's contents splashed over his hand. Will expected the smell of perfume to fill the air, but there was no scent at all to the liquid. It was clear, thick, oily.

Maya saw Will's puzzlement and almost laughed. The memories associated with the bottle were too bitter for laughter, however.

"You hold in your hand the secret to the sensual pleasures of the marriage bed for which you hated me all these years," she said, her tone both sad and bleakly amused. "Without that oil I would have bled like a virgin each time."

Will's hand tightened around the bottle with crushing force when he realized what Maya was saying. He remembered the heat of her overflowing at his intimate caresses, remembered the gliding ease of his entry despite her virginal tightness. The knowledge that Maya had spent her married years in a state of dry endurance should have pleased him; instead, he was enraged at the thought of her lying beneath a man while she was forced time and again, month after month, year after year.

With a choked cry Will threw the bottle away from him. It hit the far wall and exploded into a thousand razor shards.

"I should have killed him the night I came back from Black Basin," Will said savagely. "God knows I wanted to!"

Maya rolled onto her side and looked at Will's enraged face. "It wasn't Hale's fault," she said quietly. "It would have been the same with any man but you. I gave my husband thin-lipped duty and he asked for no more. He was as gentle as he could be and still get children. I bear him no hatred. How could I? He is Justine's father, Beth's father, yours.... How could I hate the man who gave life to those I love?"

"And Emily? Don't you love her?"

"Oh, yes," Maya said softly. "But she is not Hale's."

Will thought of the tiny hole in Emily's ear, legacy of a grandmother she had never known. "When did he tell you?"

"He? Do you mean Hale?"

"Yes."

"Tell me what?"

"That Emily was my daughter, not his."

Maya's shock was plain. "He didn't know! There was nothing on her, no birthmark, no color of eye or hair, nothing to suggest that she was your daughter."

"Oh, but there was. He knew. Not at first, but later."

Maya's breath filled her throat until she could barely whisper, "What are you talking about?"

"The tiny hole just beneath the rim of Emily's right ear. My mother had one. So, I'm told, did her father. My brother who died at three weeks had one as well. Nothing like that existed in my father's family."

Maya went as pale as the sheets upon which she lay.

"You didn't know?" Will said, reading the answer on her face.

Slowly she shook her head.

"Then why were you so certain that Emily was mine?"

Maya tried to speak, failed, licked her lips and tried again. When she finally spoke her voice was dry, hurting. "Believing that I had something of you to love . . . it was the only thing that kept me sane."

Will closed his eyes, unable to bear the truth in hers. He had misjudged Maya as badly as she had once misjudged him. Even after he had seen her in the garden, seen the radiance her love cast over those around her, he had refused to believe that Maya was anything but a whore. The thought of what he had done to her and her children chilled him to his soul.

He had believed that he had caged the demon within himself. He had not. He had become it.

"Hold me," Will whispered. "I don't deserve it, but I must have it to live. . . ."

When he felt the warmth of Maya coming into his arms, the relief was so great that it was nearly pain. He pulled her closer, lifting her onto his chest, needing to feel the weight of her as she held him. He was racked with an agony of regret, silently screaming to turn back time, to have today's knowledge somehow change the sad mistakes of the past, but that wasn't possible. All he could do was hold Maya, letting her warmth seep into his soul, driving out the icy demon that had ruled him far too long.

This time when Maya's mouth met and mingled with his, Will didn't pull away. He no longer feared the deep, overwhelming passion that Maya alone was able to arouse in him. He finally understood that he would not lose his soul within her. He would discover it.

Slowly Will rolled onto his side, carrying Maya with him as he moved, never breaking the warmth of the kiss. She opened her eyes as the world gently spun around her. She saw the thick darkness of his eyelashes, the intense concentration revealed in his expression and the unfocused, unreal room beyond his wide shoulders. Her fingers kneaded through his hair, traced the corded tendons of his neck and probed the hard muscle beneath his fine cloth shirt, reassuring herself with each pressure against his resilient flesh.

"You're real," Maya whispered, kissing Will with each word, amazement and discovery in her voice. "You're real and I'm not dreaming. Tell me that I'm not dreaming."

He looked at her and told her what he had always known and had just discovered. "I love you, Maya."

Though she moved not at all, the room spun again, and her heart turned over within her body. "Now I know that I'm dreaming," she said, her voice shaking. "Oh, God, may I never wake again."

Then she could say no more, for he had claimed her mouth once more, filling her with the sensual caress of tongue against tongue. Without knowing it she moaned and pulled him closer, needing to feel his weight pressing against her, pinning her within a sensual dream that she wanted never to end.

Will swept the comforter from between their bodies with a single motion, sending the soft folds tumbling to the floor. Maya no longer had need of its warmth. Wherever his lips touched her, heat followed, a growing flush of passion claiming her white skin. The green velvet of her robe slid from one shoulder, then the next, then followed the quilt to the floor. Maya knew nothing of her growing dishabille as she twisted slowly within Will's arms, caressing him with her body as much as she caressed him with her hands, trying to feel all of him at once because it had been so long since she had felt anything at all.

When Will's hands found Maya's breasts and cherished the velvety peaks that rose beneath the cloth, she couldn't stifle the cries that rippled from her with each changing pressure of his skilled fingers. The bows holding together the front of her nightgown gave way one by one, revealing breasts that had the smooth lus-

ter of satin. Her nipples were as pink as her lips, as
tempting as her tongue. He bent over her breasts,
kissing first one and then the other, teasing her with
the tip of his tongue until her back arched in silent
plea. He took what she offered, drawing her breast
deeply into his mouth, tugging on her with a slow, elemental rhythm that sent pleasure spearing through
her body, leaving echoes of her soft cries in its wake.
When the last echo faded, she was naked, and he was
kneeling between her legs.

"You are so perfect," Will said, his voice raw, his
eyes burning as he looked at Maya, touching every
part of her while he cherished her with words. "No
mouth ever kissed more sweetly. No shoulders ever
curved more gracefully. No breasts ever fed child and
lover alike so generously."

His fingertips slid down her body, touched the almost invisibly fine marks that were the legacy of the
children she had borne. He bent low again, kissing the
soft skin over her womb, tracing each faint silver line
with the tip of his tongue.

"No body ever held both babe and lover half so
well," he whispered.

His fingers rubbed through the warm hair between
her legs, seeking the hot core of her, finding it. He
made a thick sound of satisfaction when her body answered his sliding caress with tiny, secret meltings. He
looked at her, all of her, and he smiled to see Maya
opening to him, watching him even as he watched her.

"And no woman ever inflamed me half so much,"
he said huskily, bending down to her once more. "I
have no words, only this...."

The first intimate touch of Will's tongue shocked a
sound of surprise from Maya. She tried to say his

name, but speech was impossible to her. His mouth had found and sweetly imprisoned her most sensitive flesh. Pleasure speared through her, arching her back in primal response, tearing a ragged cry from her throat. She meant to push him away but when her fingers tangled in his hair it was to hold him close, closer, her body twisting while ecstasy grew inside her, pressing against her even as he did, ecstasy expanding with each rapid heartbeat until she could bear no more and it burst within her, drenching her with pulsing, shimmering fire.

When Maya could lift her head again Will was sitting beside her, watching her as he had all along, smiling. His hand stroked her body slowly, and his eyes glittered with the reflection of her passion.

"That is just one of the things a man can do to pleasure the woman he loves," Will said almost roughly. "There is no fear of pregnancy in that for you. Or in this."

She shivered when he caressed her with his fingertips, sending aftershocks of ecstasy radiating through her. She caught his hand, stilling it, for when he touched her she couldn't think. And she wanted to think, to learn, to bathe him in the same ecstatic fire she had just known.

"Is there . . . is there a way for a woman to pleasure the man she loves?"

Will couldn't conceal the shudder of need that went through him. "Yes."

"Teach me," she whispered.

"I don't trust myself not to take you."

Maya's eyes widened at the blunt statement. She remembered the steel discipline that Will had. The thought that she could affect him to that extent was as exciting to her as the wildest of his caresses. She sat up slowly, smiling when she saw his eyes lingering on the newly taut peaks of her breasts.

"Please," she murmured. "Teach me."

Maya brushed her open mouth over Will's shoulder, his chest, his bare neck above his shirt, and all the while she twisted slowly, rubbing her hard-tipped breasts against him. The hot, moist, repeated touch of her tongue made him groan. The nuzzling of her breasts made him clench with the painful need to know their sensuous peaks hard against his tongue. When he felt her fingers fumbling with the buttons on his shirt he didn't know whether to laugh or swear. He caught her hands. She kissed his fingers, bit them gently, took one into her mouth and suckled as though she were a babe, tasting him, tugging on him, caressing him always with the soft rasp of her tongue.

And watching his response with curious, passionate eyes.

"God," Will said roughly, more groan than word.

Buttons popped and rolled unnoticed across the bed as Will yanked off his shirt and threw it aside.

"Touch me," he said, lying down, pulling Maya after him. "Touch me the way I touched you."

She rubbed her hands across the hot skin of his chest, liking the slight roughness of his thick hair. Her mouth followed her fingers, tasting him, drawing taut groans from him. When her palm brushed the smooth, flat circle of his nipple, he jerked in response. She remembered how it had felt to have his mouth caressing her. Her hair slid forward in another kind of caress, bathing him in silk as her tongue found his nipple. When she teased the nipple until it tightened into a nub, he made a thick sound of pleasure. She tugged on him gently with her lips and teeth while she stroked the warm mat of hair that grew down his torso, feeling his powerful muscles tighten in passionate reflex. Soon her mouth followed her caressing fingers. His hips moved slowly, as though seeking her touch.

The belt buckle was cold against Maya's cheek, an alien intrusion into the shared heat of their bodies. Slowly she lifted her head. She saw Will's passionate hunger in every tight line on his face, in his narrowed eyes and in his lips thinned against a groan. His muscular torso glistened with a fine mist of heat. Each muscle stood in high relief, clenched in need and anticipation. She could see the hard ridge of flesh rising beneath his buckle. Suddenly she wanted to touch him, to hold him.

"Will?" Maya asked huskily, her hands on the buckle.

"Anything," he groaned. "Though I may die of your sweet teasing."

Metal buckle and leather belt gave way before Maya's gentle, insistent fingers. She unfastened his pants slowly, inadvertently brushing against his rigid flesh with each motion of her hands. As the pants fell open, her touches became intentional, exploratory, consuming; and Will's hips moved in helpless response. Her fingers lingered, shaping him, discovering and exploring the tightly drawn flesh just below, nestling the twin weight of him in one hand while she explored the visible pulsing of his blood with the other.

Will's breathing became hoarse, rapid and he looked like a man being drawn on the rack as he lay caught between her caressing hands until she reluctantly withdrew to finish the task of undressing him. When the last of his clothes slid to the floor, she knelt between his legs and looked at her handiwork with open pleasure. He made a stifled sound and clenched his fists against the need to reach for Maya. Having her look admiringly at his naked body was like being brushed by fire. Being touched by her exploring fingertips traveling the length of his legs from ankle to thigh was a sweet agony. The warmth of her mouth on the long muscles of his abdomen was a passionate brand whose like he had never known.

Her long hair fell across his skin, concealing his nakedness in a curtain of silken flame. Beneath the curtain her lips brushed him, hesitated, brushed again. At the first tentative touch of her tongue his whole body went rigid. Her tongue went over him with sensual curiosity, as though memorizing every unexpected change in texture. When she finally drew him into the moist heat of her mouth, he cried out.

The hoarse sound made Maya tremble. She looked up, afraid that she had shocked him.

"Isn't it allowed?" she asked.

"Allowed?" Will gave a harsh crack of laughter. "Whatever you want is *allowed*."

"But you cried out."

"So did you, when you lay in my place. Was it pain or a pleasure so great you felt as though you were dying of it?"

"Pleasure . . . dying of pleasure."

"Bring that sweet death to me, Maya," he said huskily.

His eyes blazed into hers, and his hips moved in slow rhythms against her hand. Smiling, she bent over him again, learning him as he had once learned her, drawing him deeply into her heat, tugging on him, drowning him in fire. Finally he could hold no longer against the incandescent, exploding pleasure. He forced her head up until she had to stop caressing him.

"Hold me in your hands," he said through clenched teeth. "Yes. Like that. Oh, God. Don't stop. Don't. Stop."

He moved within the hands that held him lovingly, and when she answered his need with increasing pressure, closing her fingers around him, he gave himself over to her with a harsh cry, his head thrown back, his whole body shuddering with the wild pulses of ecstasy that poured from him.

When Will was quiet once more, Maya flowed up his body to lie beside him, holding him close, loving him with every beat of her heart. His arms came around her immediately, molding her to the length of his body. When his still rigid flesh snuggled against her belly, he shuddered and moved almost helplessly, increasing the sweet contact. Her arms tightened and her body returned the caress. He turned his head and nuzzled at her swollen lips. Smiling, she nibbled and nuzzled in turn. For a long time they lay intertwined, kissing slowly, learning the beauty of simply holding and being held in return.

Gradually the kisses changed, became more intense, and their breathing quickened with the race of sensation through their aroused bodies. Hands smoothed and caressed, encircled and teased until neither he nor she knew who sought and who found, who moaned and who cried out, who shivered and who pleaded, who demanded and who gave. Hard, aching flesh slid between soft thighs, then pressed hungrily against even greater softness. Melting warmth overflowed, begging for a slow, intimate penetration.

"Maya, we've got to stop," Will said, turning his head aside from her clinging lips, breathing harshly.

"Why?"

"I'm an inch from taking you, that's why!"

"An inch?"

Her hips moved, pressing against him until he parted her just enough to drive them both wild.

"Enough," he said, trying to withdraw but unable to because the hot, moist caress of her body felt too good.

She moved again, pushing him slightly deeper into her softness.

"For God's sake, I'm not made of stone," he said harshly. "Help me to stop!"

Maya opened her eyes. Her pupils were fully dilated, leaving only a rim of green color that was as deep as the redwood forest, as mysterious, serene and wild at the same time.

"I want to have your baby," she said softly. "I want to carry the baby knowing that it is yours. I want to hear the baby's first cry and know that it is an echo of your voice. I want to watch the baby nurse at my breast and know that once, just once, I lived with every part of me swept clean of fear. I love you, Will. I love you."

Her words became a soft cry as he took her slowly, totally, and felt himself taken just as completely in return. He watched her face, her eyes, while he retreated and returned, taking and giving, probing and caressing deeply, loving her with every bit of his powerful body. She watched him while they loved, lifting herself to meet him, sighing at the gliding retreat, rising to meet his gentle penetration again and then again in a sensual dance of creation that knew no time, no

place, nothing but cries of ecstasy endlessly repeated
until flesh could bear no more.

They slept still joined, lips brushing, breath mingling, hearts beating in a single slow rhythm of peace.

Chapter Seventeen

Though it was early in the morning, the gentle tapping on the kitchen door wasn't unexpected; Will had
sent word that he wanted to speak with Henry Ising.
When Will opened the door, Ising was standing patiently on the porch, his big slicker damp with the mild
rain that had been falling on and off for several days.

"Come in," Will said in a hushed voice. "Beth and
Maya are still asleep."

Ising looked sharply at Will's face, trying to guess
the cause of the unexpected summons. There was no
sign of new trouble in Will's expression. If anything,
his friend looked more at peace than he had in years.

"What's happened? Beth's all right, isn't she?"

"She's no longer hysterical," Will said, leading Ising in and closing the door. "I don't know what that
Tolowa shaman you sent over said or did, but Beth
was much more calm afterward. Maybe the chants put
her to sleep. The shaman told Maya that Beth and the
baby would both be fine. Our doctor said the same
thing." Will rubbed his hand wearily over his hair. "I
just wish that she would talk about it with me, but she
won't. She hasn't even admitted to me that she's
pregnant." He caught Ising's compassionate look and

grimaced. "But that's not why I asked you to come here. I need someone to go to Weeber Basin for me."

Ising nodded as though he had been expecting the request. "The logs. I was wondering when you would get around to them." Something in Will's face stopped Ising. "That's what this is all about, isn't it? There were a dozen witnesses to that bet. Your father's estate can be made to pay even if he'd dead, no matter how that lawyer screams."

"If I collected from the estate, Maya would be destitute."

"Congratulations. That's exactly what you've been trying to do for the last six years, isn't it?" Ising retorted. "Make her and your father poorer than a one-legged Indian?"

"I've changed my mind. It may be too late, but I've changed my mind."

"May be too late? Hell, Will. It's years too late! Kroeber and his backers smell blood. It's the talk of the timber beasts. No bank is going to walk away from foreclosure out of sympathy for widows or children. They'll pick Maya's bones as clean as you did your father's. And if you're in with her, they'll skin you alive on the way by."

"They'll have to catch me first. The logs are the key. Once they're in the bay, Tres Santos will have more money than it needs to pay off its outstanding loans. Every mill within fifty miles is screaming for logs. That's what I'm going to give them—at a price that will make them scream even louder."

"When? The talk I hear says the railroad loan comes due in three days."

Will nodded curtly.

"How the hell do you expect to get those logs down here before then? On your back?"

"Haven't you heard? It's raining."

Ising gave his friend an incredulous look. "You don't have to be a shaman to know that this piss-ant rain isn't going to fill any rivers."

"I've signed over my land in Black Basin to Maya," Will said calmly. "No matter what happens, Maya won't be left a complete pauper."

"What about you? What about all the rest of your land that's mortgaged to the tops of the trees? Black Basin was the only thing you really owned. Without it, all you have left is a strong back and a thick head!"

"That's all I had before, too." When Ising opened his mouth to object, Will said, "No. It's done. I won't have Maya hurt anymore."

The look on Will's face and the gentleness in his voice when he spoke of Maya told Ising all that he needed to know. The demon of revenge no longer rode his friend's soul. Silently, Ising thanked whatever gods might be listening for the healing of Will's spirit. Even if Black Basin had been cast in solid gold, it was well worth the trade.

Ising gripped Will's shoulder in his big hand. "What do you want me to do in Weeber Basin?"

"Check the lake behind the splash dam. Check the logs. See if they're together against the dam or bogged down in the shallows. Check the river itself. I would go, but—"

"Your women need you," Ising interrupted.

Will smiled thinly. "I also have a few final details to clarify with my father's creditors."

The hard curve of Will's mouth told Ising that his friend might have softened on the subject of Maya, but the rest of the world was still in for a rough ride. Ising wasn't disturbed that Will's transformation hadn't been complete; in fact, Ising was pleased. The world deserved a rough ride from time to time.

"I doubt that there's been enough rain in the last few days to float a stack of shingles down to the bay, much less two years' worth of logs," Ising said bluntly. "But you know that, don't you?"

Will said only, "The tugboat captain is expecting you. There will be a horse waiting on the other side."

"I'll be back by supper," Ising said, turning away even as he spoke.

"Henry..."

Ising looked back.

"Thank you."

With a flash of white teeth and a careless wave, Ising stepped off the porch into the rain. He pulled up the collar of his wool shirt, tugged his knit cap more tightly into place and set off for the wharf. It would be a long, damp trip to Weeber Basin.

Beneath a thin veil of rain, Weeber Basin looked like a war zone. On the lower hillsides, cut two years ago, the dripping fireweed and alder had grown back, covering the scars of logging. But on the higher, more recently logged slopes, shattered stumps loomed from the gouged and channeled earth. Their hunched, rumpled outlines reminded Ising of hunting dogs chained out in the weather, stoically awaiting the call of their master.

Amid the hacked remains of forest a few huge trees survived. Their size had protected them from man's ax, yet they seemed oddly naked as they thrust straight through the rain into an invisible sky. From those lone, gigantic survivors would come the seeds of eventual rebirth far below on the forest floor; but on this gray day, the Weeber Basin looked more like a charnel house than a nursery.

Ising looked around with an ambivalence that was new to him. The weeping fireweed and the destroyed forest seemed a proper match for the events of the past days. Like the fallen trees, Hale Hawthorne and Johnny would never again know the sunshine of this life. And, eventually, neither would Ising himself. He had always known that and accepted it, but riding through the ruined basin in a futile rain made man's uncertain life span seem a melancholy solution to the gods' original problem of what to do with the handful of mud that had been left over after the world was created.

The logging camp was at the edge of the river, next to the log landing. The river was surprisingly muddy for such a minor rainfall. Usually it took a hard, long rain to dirty the water. There had been no such flood of rain. Nor was there one in sight.

Above the Narrows, the shallow river looked as slack and dispirited as the thin rain. The camp itself was no better. No one appeared as Ising rode in and dismounted. Most of the timber beasts had drifted away, seeking other work, anticipating that the death of Tres Santos would surely follow that of Hale Hawthorne. The rest of the loggers were either at the Indian camp or drinking rotgut in their sodden tents.

A gust of wind made the long tents billow and roughed up the brown puddles that had gathered in ruts and depressions throughout the camp. A thin ribbon of smoke rose from the cookhouse chimney, telling Ising that there was a least one timber beast

who hadn't deserted the company—one of the old-
timers most likely, a logger who had been there too
long to start over in a new forest, competing for work
with boys half his age and twice his strength.

Ising tied his horse in the now-empty ox stable,
wondering if the oxen had been sold off or simply
moved in closer to help with the job of cleaning up the
burned mill site. Suddenly he was very glad that his
gentle, patient oxen weren't in danger of being sold to
strangers who might be careless or cruel. Not only did
Ising care for his oxen more than a man should care
for dumb beasts, he also had a feeling that their big,
warm bodies and hay-scented breath would bring a
smile to Beth's wan face. That would be worth trying. A woman carrying a baby should be at peace with
the world.

"Yo! That you Ising?"

He turned and recognized the woods boss, Joe
Larson, calling out from the porch of the cookhouse.

"Hello, Joe."

"Didn't recognize you without your oxen. Come
out to inspect the wreckage, have you?"

"Hell, no," Ising replied as he crossed the yard in
long strides. The raw lumber steps of the camp kitchen
were slippery with rainwater. "I just love riding in the
rain."

"You call this rain?" Joe turned and spat a stream
of tobacco juice into the runoff from the porch roof.
"I could piss a bigger rain than this."

The wind gusted again, swirling smoke and rain-
drops alike.

"If you plan to beat this storm in a pissing con-
test," Ising said, looking up at the thickening clouds,
"you better start drinking the river. Looks like we

might finally get something worth putting on a slicker for.''

Larson squinted up at the sky, shrugged, and said, "Come on in. They ain't sold off the coffeepot yet."

Ising stopped under the shelter of the kitchen porch, peeled off his slicker and shook it to get rid of the water that had beaded up on it. He looked at Larson, who had made no move to go into the kitchen. Curiosity was plain on the old Swede's face.

"How long has it been raining out here?" asked Ising.

"Three days, more or less."

"Lot of runoff for just a few days."

Larson nodded as he surveyed the denuded and debris-strewn hillsides of the basin. "That's Gospel truth," he agreed. "She's a comin' off them hills like it was a good winter rain."

Ising glanced quickly at the woods boss. "How's the level in the lake?"

"Up some, I guess."

"When did you last check it?"

"Yesterday."

"Then the level could be rising."

"I guess." Larson pulled out a plug of tobacco, bit off a hunk and talked around it. "It don't matter. River's no ways near full enough to do any good."

Ising thought of Will and Maya, and Beth, pregnant with his half brother's child. Wearily Ising pulled his slicker back on. "I'll have coffee later. Let's take a look at the pond."

"Can't hurt," Larson said laconically, "but it can't do no good, neither. Winter's long gone. Them logs ain't going nowheres this year."

Larson leaned into the cookhouse, grabbed his own slicker off a hook beside the door and stepped out into the thickening rain with Ising. Together the two men trudged across the soggy camp yard and down a slippery trail to the edge of the shallow lake that had formed behind the splash dam that had been built at the bottom of a ravine. It was hard to tell where the logs ended and the muddy water began. The depression was entirely covered with a mat of logs, the product of Hale Hawthorne's two years of gambling.

Ising looked at the logs, mentally added up their worth and whistled soundlessly. No wonder Hale had gone crazy. It must have been killing him to know that millions of board feet of lumber—his financial salvation—lay up in Weeber Basin, just beyond reach, held hostage by two dry winters. The most important bet Hale had lost had not been with Will but with Mother Nature.

Larson squinted off to the left, gave a grunt of surprise and said, "Damn pond's come up 'bout four inches since yesterday. Used to take three, maybe four days to come up like that."

"You sure it's up?"

"See that willow thicket yonder?" he asked, pointing. "The roots was dry yesterday."

Ising's black eyes surveyed not only the willow thicket but the surrounding basin. Most of the rivers on the redwood coast took between one and three days before even a hard rainfall raised their level. The Weeber River had always been slow to respond, because its watershed was thickly forested, soaking up rainwater like a vast green sponge.

Yet Larson was saying that the lake had come up at least four inches after a few days of mild rain.

"There's one of the reasons." Ising gestured to his right, toward a thick, swift brown stream rolling through a shallow ravine and dumping into the lake. "The ground isn't holding water worth a damn."

Larson spat. "Weren't like this last year."

"Last year only half the forest was lying on its back down in the basin. Come on. Let's check the splash dam."

As they walked the trail toward the head of the small lake, the wind gusted again. Ising stopped, realizing what had been nagging at him for the past hour. The temperature was warmer than it should have been on a rainy spring day. For a few minutes he studied the clouds that came scudding in overhead, pushed by the rising wind.

"That's Weeber Peak, isn't it?" Ising asked at last, pointing toward the east where all but the lowest slope of a mountain lay hidden by clouds.

Larson looked at him in disbelief. "Course it is. You gone crazy?"

Ising turned his back on the peak and said nothing, having attention only for the wind blowing in over the low peak. A western wind. A summer wind. And it was carrying a summer storm on its back. The clouds were lowering even as he watched, their thick, soft bodies trapped by the bowl that was Weeber Basin. Warm wind, heavy clouds, rain pouring down over the Weeber River's changed watershed. Maybe, just maybe...

Against all common sense Ising began to hope that the son would win another bet that the father had lost.

When they reached the dam, Larson climbed up on the heavy log structure. "She's up, all right," he said as Ising clambered up beside him and studied the in-

tricate mechanism of gates and splashboards at the
heart of the dam. "More like six inches than four,"
Larson added, glancing at a scale gauge that extended down into the water on the lake side of the
dam.

"That's higher than the water got all last winter,
isn't it?" Ising asked.

Larson grunted. He studied the Yurok carefully for
a full ten seconds. "You thinkin' what I think you're
thinkin'?"

"I'm thinking those logs are worth a hell of a lot
more down in the bay than up here in this mud puddle."

A stream of tobacco juice joined the brown water.
"That's just the point," Larson said. "This here
puddle is purely choked on logs. Now, floating them
logs right here ain't enough. What with the way the
river is low and all, we gotta be able to open the gates
for near eight hours before she'd come up enough to
carry these here logs down past the Narrows. Ain't no
eight hours of water in here yet, and that's Gospel."

"But in another day? Two days?"

Larson chewed thoughtfully, checked the wind and
the clouds, spat and sighed. "If that was a northern
wind jamming them clouds, maybe. But it ain't.
Southern storms is like southern women—mighty
juicy for a few hours, and then dry as a chewed bone.
Like my Daddy said—you want staying power, you
need a northern wind and a Swede woman every
time."

Thunder rolled lightly through the basin. As though
summoned, the rain began to fall in earnest. Against
the gloom, lightning skipped. Each bolt seemed to release more of the clouds' thick burden. Rain came

down hard and fast, reducing visibility to less than a full span of oxen.

"Like I said," Larson muttered. "Real juicy. You need me, I'll be in the cookhouse."

"Wait. How many men are left?"

"Ten. Mebbe fifteen. They drift in about supper-time. Smell of ham and beans brings 'em in like skunks."

"Tell them to start pushing logs out of the shallows and up closer to the dam."

"Waste of time. Ain't enough water now. Ain't gonna be enough water tomorrow. Loan's due the day after."

"Tell them."

Larson shrugged. "I'll tell 'em."

Rain was still pouring down in near-tropical tor-rents five hours later when Ising finished rousting timber beasts out of their lairs and putting them to work rounding up logs. He rode past the dam once more and noted that the level had risen an astonish-ing inch an hour. The denuded slopes of the basin were shedding water faster with each moment.

As he rode down the rutted wagon trail that ran be-side the river, Ising studied the pools and rills. Before the last rain the river had all but dried up, reduced to little more than a three-inch-deep trickle that joined the deeper pools. The water was dirty now, its depth impossible to judge. But as the horse waded across, Ising swore that the river was at least an inch or two deeper. If it was rising so swiftly in the basin, might it not be even deeper downstream, where the east and south fork of the Weeber River came in?

Just before dark Ising strode into the small office Will had rented in the building across the street from the Tres Santos mill site. Will glanced quickly at the Yurok's face, then back at the document he had been studying.

"How high is the water?" Will asked.

"Not enough."

"How high?"

Ising had heard that tone of voice too many times since they had awakened chained together in the stinking crew quarters of a southbound ship. Whatever peace Will and Maya had achieved together hadn't removed Will's ability to be ruthless when the stakes were high enough.

"The pond was a foot below the waste gates when I left," Ising said. "We aren't putting water down the spillway yet, which means the river below the dam to the Narrows isn't getting any help from its headwaters."

"Go on."

"That's it. Not enough damned water until you get past the Narrows. Then the south fork comes in and a quarter mile later the east fork comes in as well. Won't do you a damned bit of good, though. There's not enough depth in the river to get the logs to the Narrows, and not enough water in the pond to make the difference." Ising still hesitated. Then he shrugged. "Hell, I could get some of the logs down past the Narrows to the bay for you, but not all of them. A quarter of them, maybe a few more, and I'd leave three logs jammed up behind boulders for every one I got down."

Will looked at his hands for a long moment. He had expected as much, but he had hoped. . . .

"A quarter of the logs won't pay off the loan," Will said absently, thinking of many things, but most of all of the fact that he had had so little time with the woman he loved.

Unease moved in Ising at the bleak acceptance he saw on Will's face. "Will—"

"What are the roads like?" Will asked, cutting off whatever Ising had been going to say.

"Muddy in the logged areas, good in the rest."

"Could your ox team pull a small wagon to Weeber Basin by dawn?"

"Hell, Segup could do that by himself before moonrise."

Will smiled slightly. The effect was to heighten rather than to soften the underlying harshness of his expression.

"The wagon has dynamite and blasting caps aboard. If you don't want to take it, I'll understand."

"I've hauled worse. What are you going to do, clear out snags below the dam?"

"The wagon is waiting for you on the other side of the bay. Everything is loaded, lashed tight, ready to go. I'll meet you in the camp sometime before dawn."

"What are you going to do?"

Pray for a miracle. But the bitter thought went no farther than Will's mind. Aloud he said simply, "I won't know until I see the lake."

It was not quite the truth. Will was all but certain of what would come with the dawn. Talking about it would change nothing, however, and would quickly lead to the kind of public interest that had turned the felling of the Guardian into a circus. Will didn't want that. What he was going to do would be far more dangerous to spectators than the Guardian's death had been.

Even more to the point, Will didn't want Maya to have the least suspicion of what he was going to do.

Long after Ising had left, Will looked out the window, watching the rainstorm that held his future in its elusive gray grasp. Off across the roofs of downtown Eureka, rank after rank of clouds boiled in from the Pacific, laden with sweet, warm rain. For a moment Will felt a twinge of the same emotion that Ising had been struggling to suppress all day—hope.

Bet everything on the turn of one card, he thought, remembering what he had found among his father's papers. *Is that what you were going to do, Father? And then I came along, offering you what looked like a much better, safer bet. No wonder you took it so quickly. I wish to Christ that someone would come along and offer the same bet to me.*

The room was silent, save for the sound of rain against the glass of the window. No voice came from the night to whisper of another, better gamble. There would be no alternative to what awaited him at dawn. Will turned back to the desk covered with papers. There was less than an hour before dinner would be waiting for him at the Hawthorne house. Tonight, of all nights, he wanted to eat with the people he loved, to see his just-discovered daughter laughing up at him, to have Justine's tiny weight in his arms, to tease Beth gently and to hold Maya until he could not tell the difference between her body and his own.

Maya heard the sound of Will's footsteps coming up the path from the stable. Instantly her heartbeat quickened. She smoothed her hands down the exquisitely fitted dress that she wore, touching the silk-covered buttons as though they were talismans. Widow's black became her, giving her skin the sensuous sheen of Oriental pearls. The intense green of her eyes was in vivid contrast to her creamy skin and to the dark, almost secret fire in her mahogany hair. She had been told many times in her life that she was beautiful, but she had never understood what that meant until she saw the pleasure in Will's eyes now as he watched her.

It was difficult not to rush into his arms after the kitchen door opened and he stood there watching her. He looked worn and yet so handsome that she had to close her eyes or lose her self-control entirely. The housekeeper and nanny had gone home, but Mrs. Chou remained. Maya had no wish to give Eureka's gossips another Hawthorne scandal to talk about. It was bad enough that the talk of Tres Santos's imminent bankruptcy had reached the point where the servants bluntly asked to be paid on a daily basis.

"Good evening, Will," Maya said softly. "You look tired. Let me take your coat."

When he smiled at her, the lines of his face changed dramatically. The bleak, forbidding look vanished, and in its place was a love so clear that Maya felt her throat tighten with emotion. Unknowingly she smiled at him in the same way, her radiance so vivid that Will wanted to go to her and hold her, just hold her, and let the cares and compromises of the day fade into insignificance.

Though it wasn't necessary, Maya helped Will out of his coat, cherishing the small intimacy of having cloth still warm from his body folded over her arm. As she had with Hale, Maya pampered Will, but in Will's case she acted from love rather than from guilt at her inability to love. She had taken great pleasure in arranging the household for Will's comfort; his favorite chair had been moved close to the hearth, his slippers awaited his feet, his preferred soap lay next to the downstairs wash basin alongside a fine linen hand towel on which Maya had recently embroidered his initials. She enjoyed making life more pleasant for Will in even the smallest way.

"Thank you," Will said, as Maya took his coat, but his eyes said far more. "Is Beth well enough to eat with us?"

"I think so."

"I'd like that. What of the children? Are they asleep already?"

"Yes."

"Would it . . . could I see them for just a moment? I won't wake them."

Maya searched Will's brilliant gray eyes, sensing something she couldn't name. "Of course."

Will followed her up the stairs to the third story, which had been given over to the children. The girls were asleep in a large, airy room whose walls had been painted by Maya with characters from their favorite fairy tales. The images were life-size and lifelike, and Maya took almost as much pleasure in them as her daughters did. A small oil lamp burned in a secure niche on the wall, casting just enough light to reassure the little girls if they woke up in the night.

Emily slept as she lived, with the complete abandonment of a confident child. She lay on her back, her small hand curled next to her face and her other hand next to her waist. The lace coverlet was rumpled and askew, and her unruly cinnamon hair reflected lamp flame in waves of shimmering gold each time her head moved. Will ran his fingertips over the long, tumbled locks, feeling as though he could sense the little girl's shimmering life even in her cool hair. With tender care Will drew up the coverlet and tucked it around her small face. She stirred. Her eyes opened. More asleep than awake, she focused on Will.

"'Lo," she murmured, smiling. Her fingers closed around his hard thumb. "Kiss?"

"Hello," he whispered, bending down and giving Emily the kiss she had requested. "Now go back to sleep, little love."

Long eyelashes fluttered down as Emily fell asleep between one breath and the next. After a few more slow breaths her grip on Will's thumb loosened. Only then did he straighten. He stood for a long time without moving; then he reached down and smoothed his fingertips once more over her vibrant hair.

Justine was asleep in her white crib, her tiny face suffused with color and health. Very gently Will ran the back of his index finger over her soft little cheek. The texture of her skin was unbelievably fine. It was the same for her hair, which was as black as Hale's had once been. The thickly lashed eyelids were closed, but if they had been open, they would have revealed eyes of extraordinary clarity, quicksilver eyes that watched the world with consuming interest.

Softly Will caressed Justine's cheek once more, feeling love turn inside him almost painfully. He no longer cared that Justine was Hale's child; like Maya, Will had come to realize that he couldn't hate the man who had given life to Beth, to Justine, to himself. Justine's life was doubly precious to Will, for he knew that her birth had kept Maya from sliding so far into melancholy that a descent into madness would soon have followed. Then Will would never have known the peace he knew now, for he would never have purged the bitterness of the past in Maya's loving arms.

"Will?" Maya whispered, watching expressions come and go from his face in the soft glow of reflected lamplight. "What is it?"

"I was just thinking how beautiful she is when she sits on my lap and looks at me with those big gray eyes."

"And drools while she chews on your thumb."

"Yes, that too. That most of all." Will's smile was heartbreaking to see. "I would hold her, but I don't want to disturb her sleep."

Without a word Maya bent over the crib and lifted the sleeping baby into Will's arms. She didn't know why, but she sensed that it was important to Will that he hold Justine. The look on his face when Justine was put into his arms was indescribable. Maya fought tears for a moment, then lost and did not care. Knowing that Will loved Justine as much as he did Emily moved Maya deeply.

When Will looked up from Justine's sleeping face he saw the tears caught in Maya's smile. He bent slowly, brushed his lips over the clear drops and whispered his love for Maya across the body of her sleeping child. The words came back to him, spoken just as softly, the returned kiss equally sweet. Justine murmured sleepily. Will turned and lowered her into the crib, his calloused hands careful as he lay her back in her warm nest and covered her with her favorite blanket.

For a long time Will watched Justine sleep. Then he turned and brought Maya into his arms, holding her as gently as though she were a child, kissing her in the same way. He tasted Maya's tears again and knew that she sensed the emotions that he barely held in check. He could not lie to her, so he gave her what he could of the truth.

"Sometimes knowing that death is always near makes life unbearably precious," he whispered. "You bring life to me, my love."

Before Maya could answer, Will kissed her again, cherishing her with such gentleness that she could only cling to him and whisper her love for him over and over again.

From the hallway below came Beth's soft voice calling out to her brother. Will and Maya clung together for a moment more then left the nursery and walked down the hall hand in hand before reluctantly separating at the stairway.

"There you are," Beth said, turning as she heard their familiar footsteps descending the stairs. Her voice was as pale and strained as her face, and her blind eyes were red from crying. "Mrs. Chou said she thought you were checking on the girls. Are they all right?"

"They're fine," Maya said.

"They're perfect," Will said.

Unconsciously Beth put her hands on her own womb.

"Your baby will be perfect, too," Will said, putting his large hands over hers.

Beth's transparent face showed first shock, then a mixture of love and hope so desperate that it was all but tangible.

"Do you really mean that?" Beth asked. "You don't hate it and me because of what happened to Father?"

Will's arms closed around Beth in an enveloping hug. "I could never hate you or anything that's a part of you," he said, his voice rough with the effort of controlling his emotions. "You know that, don't you?"

"Father hated m-me," Beth blurted out, twisting her hands together and trying not to sob. "Maya had to s-stop him from hitting m-me. He d-didn't understand. I was s-so afraid!"

It was the first time that Beth had spoken of what had happened that night. Will didn't want to hear the painful details, yet he knew that Beth had to talk before she would begin to heal. So he held her and stroked her hair and listened, sensing Beth's feelings of guilt and hurt in the shuddering of her body as she talked about her dreams of marriage and a family of her own, of having someone who would always be within reach, as much a part of her as her own heartbeat. It had been like that with Johnny, sometimes. She knew now that she had been wrong to expect other people to understand. She had been wrong to seduce Johnny, but it had been so beautiful....

When Beth finally fell silent once more, Will kissed her cheek and tilted her face up until he could see her expression. "Father didn't hate you, Mouse. He didn't run out of the house because he couldn't stand seeing you any longer. He ran out because he wasn't in control of himself. What happened at the mill wasn't your fault, either. Too many things had gone wrong for Father in the last year. He couldn't deal with it any longer. That's not your fault. It's his...and mine."

Abruptly Beth burst into tears. "Father had been drinking. Johnny had been drinking, too," she admitted. "I asked him not to but he did anyway, almost all the time. Why did he do that?"

Will closed his eyes. "It's called innocence. He was too young to believe that tomorrow really comes, and with it the consequences for today's choices."

"I'm not like that anymore, but it's too late, isn't it? I'm sorry, so sorry, but that doesn't change anything. No matter how I cry or pray or scream, they're still dead. It's too late! It will always be too late!"

Gently Will rocked Beth against his chest, murmuring soothing words. Over her bright blond hair, his eyes met Maya's. Although neither spoke, they both knew what the other was thinking. They, too, had once been innocent. They, too, had once made choices with reckless disregard for the well-being of the people around them. And they, too, had paid and would go on paying for the rest of their lives. Nothing could retrieve the mistakes of the past, not even love.

But love could forgive.

When Beth was calm once more, Will led both women into the dining room. Beth ate slowly, but with a growing appetite, clearly reassured by Will's gentle words and his acceptance of the baby that was growing within her. As Maya watched, she felt some of her own tension slowly subside. Though she had said nothing, part of Maya had been afraid that after losing Johnny, Beth would slide into the despair that had nearly claimed Maya's own sanity before Justine's birth.

By the time dessert was served, Beth was yawning delicately behind her napkin. Will pushed back his chair, plucked Beth out of hers and carried her down the hallway as though she were eleven and he were sixteen once more. Then he sat by her bed, holding her hand until she fell into a deep sleep. Only then did he give in to his own weariness. He went slowly up the stairs and opened the door to his bedroom.

Maya was waiting for him, wearing the forest-green robe of soft velvet that he loved to touch. There was a low fire in the bedroom hearth. Beside it a hip bath steamed in silent welcome. Without a word Maya kissed him gently, led him to the bath and undressed him as though he were her child rather than her lover. When Will sank down into the heated water, he closed his eyes and sighed with the sheer luxury of setting aside his worries and fears for a time. Maya rubbed his scalp, his neck, his powerful shoulders, loosening the tension she sensed deep within his silence.

While Will's head lay relaxed against the towel which she had made into a pillow, Maya sharpened the straightedge razor and shaved him with gentle skill. When she was finished she put aside her robe, revealing the soft folds of her nightgown and the even softer flesh beneath. She soaped up a cloth and bathed Will, leaning over him, brushing his skin with lips that demanded nothing in return, loving him with her silky touch and smiles. He watched her through half-closed eyes, enjoying the pleasure she took from touching him. Heartbeat by heartbeat, he felt his weariness being replaced by growing strength.

When Will stood so that Maya could rinse him, his arousal was as evident as the naked strength of his body. With a small smile playing about her lips, Maya poured warm water over Will, smoothing his skin with her hand. There was a sensuous, unhurried thoroughness in her movements as she rinsed every last bit of soap clinging to his dark, springy body hair. Where she had leaned against the tub, her gown clung to her

skin, held by transparent bands of water. The deep
pink of her nipples stood out clearly against the thin
cloth.

After Will stepped out of the tub, Maya dried him
with a huge towel that she had warmed by the hearth.
The cloth was soft, almost velvety. She made certain
that not one drop of water was left on his muscular
torso before she knelt gracefully in front of him to dry
his legs. The towel rubbed the length of his right leg
from ankle to thigh, then his left. With teasing delicacy she blew on his most sensitive flesh before she
lifted the towel to dry him as thoroughly as she had
rinsed him.

Heavy-lidded, smiling, face darkened by the sensual heat that was sweeping through him with each
touch of Maya's elegant hands, Will watched the
woman he loved. When the towel slid away and was
replaced by her mouth, he made a hoarse sound. His
body tightened as though he had stepped into live
flame, and he felt as though he had, heat twisting and
turning in him with each velvet stroke of her tongue.
The sultry caresses were so lovingly given to him, so
obviously enjoyed by Maya as well, that he could
scarcely believe he wasn't dreaming.

"Enough," he finally said, his voice husky as he
watched her with eyes so dilated that they held only a
thin crystalline band of gray.

"I can never love you enough," Maya whispered,
turning her flushed face from side to side against his
hard thigh, glorying in the scent and masculine textures of his body. "I want to give you everything that
I am, that I can be, that I ever will be. I want to look
into your eyes and see only the future, not the past.
Let me love you, Will."

He pulled Maya to her feet in a single motion that ended only when his mouth was joined with hers. The taste of himself on her lips made Will tremble with both passion and the more complex emotion of a love for her that grew greater with each breath he drew. He had wanted to take all night loving Maya, to tell her with his body all the things for which he had no words, but that was impossible now. His need was too great, tearing him apart in agonizing waves that took from him even the ability to speak. He lifted her and didn't let go until they were on the bed and he had sheathed himself in her so deeply that she gasped. Instantly he tried to retreat, only to feel her fingernails bite into his buttocks as her hips moved, demanding all of him once more.

"Maya," Will said, fighting for self-control. "Maya..."

She tried to say his name but wild, shuddering bursts of sensation had claimed her body. When Will felt the hot, melting pulses wash through her, he realized that she had gasped not because he had taken her too soon, but because the first hard thrust of his body filling her had sent her over the edge into fulfillment. He tried to control himself, wanting to freeze time so that he could always watch Maya's face drawn taut by the exquisite pleasure of their joining.

Caught in the fiery transformations of ecstasy, Maya gave herself to Will with a fierce, sensuous abandon that made a mockery of his attempts at self-control. Crying out hoarsely, he thrust into her with a power that would have shocked him had he not been instantly hurled into the same ecstasy that already had claimed Maya. He gave of himself as she had, no thought of holding back, knowing only the wild, sweet violence of their shared climax.

Will didn't know how much time had passed until he became aware of the bed and the room around him once more, but most of all he was aware of Maya's hands stroking his head and back. He lay with his face between her breasts as she murmured loving words against his hair. The lace cloth of her nightgown was pushed up into a knot beneath his cheek, silent testimony to the overwhelming urgency with which he had taken her. He stirred, only to feel her arms tighten around him.

"Sleep," Maya whispered. "I want to hold you while you fall asleep. Then I'll go."

"Stay with me. I'll see that you get to your room before dawn."

Maya looked into Will's eyes and felt her heart turn over. She loved him as she had never thought to love anything in her life, even her own children. He kissed her and then he pulled up the blankets to cover their flushed bodies, settled her deeply in his arms. He fell asleep whispering his love into her rose-scented hair.

Just after midnight Will stirred. The first thing he sensed was the sweet weight of Maya against his body. The second thing he sensed was the silence. He wondered why that should have awakened him. Then he understood. The rain had stopped falling. A line from the Bible came to him, taunting and haunting at the same instant. "The Lord giveth and the Lord taketh away. Blessed be the name of the Lord."

For a moment Will wanted to shout against the unfairness of a life that gave him everything his soul had longed for, only to take it away almost as soon as it had been given. But there was no point in railing against what was. If he had learned nothing else in the past six years, he had learned that.

With a gentleness that was at odds with his grim thoughts, he eased from the warm entanglement of sheets and limbs. The moonlight was so bright that he had no trouble finding his robe. He pulled it on, tossed hers over his arm and went to the bed. When he picked Maya up, she stirred sleepily, murmured something and snuggled against his chest. He carried her to her room, enjoying the feel of her breath against his skin with every step.

As Will lowered Maya into her bed, she stirred again, drawing back from the cold sheets. He hushed her gently before he turned and brought the hearth fire into crackling life. Then he lay beside her and pulled up the covers, knowing that his big body would quickly warm the bed for her.

He planned to stay for only a few minutes, but the sight of moonlight playing across Maya's face was so beautiful that he forgot the passage of time. Beneath the covers his hand smoothed tenderly over her. Though soft, her nightgown was no match for her skin. His fingers slid beneath the hem until there was only her body and his hand and the secret rustle of cloth sliding up her legs. The texture of the skin between her thighs made even the finest silk seem coarse by comparison.

Will eased the covers away from Maya, wanting to see her but not wanting to wake her. He shifted until he could straddle her thighs. Slowly, gently he untied each bow until the nightgown fell open from neck to hem. She was so beautiful that his breath caught. For long moments he looked at her without touching her, until finally he could bear it no more. He brushed feather kisses over her eyelids, the hollow of her cheeks, the full curve of her mouth. The elegant line of her throat tempted him and he followed it until the luxuriant softness of her breasts could no longer be denied. As Will nuzzled and kissed and suckled, Maya gave a soft whimper and moved to ease his way. He thought that he had awakened her, but when he looked up he saw that she was still asleep; and even in sleep she gave herself to him. The realization of how deeply they were joined both humbled and exalted him. Reverently he bent over her once more.

Slowly Maya's breathing changed. She moved languidly, sinuously, caught in the sensual vise of a familiar dream. She was lying beneath the Guardian, sunlight flowing like warm honey over her nude body. But it was more than sunlight. It was Will touching her, Will's hands smoothing apart her legs until there were no more secrets between them, only sweet flesh for him to cherish. His mouth was hot, knowing, sending ecstatic shivers through her with each movement of his tongue. She moaned and opened for him even more, and he smiled, caressing her.

In the instant of awakening Maya thought that she had dreamed the old dream again, that she would awaken cold and alone, reaching for Will only to remember that she had driven him away years before, but still she reached for him with an agony of yearning that knew no end.

Then Maya saw the moonlight pouring over Will's naked body, dream and lover united, his hair black against her skin as he caressed her with a delicacy that sent wave after rhythmic wave of pleasure expanding through her. She tried to speak, but all that came out were soft moans as he put his warm hands behind her knees, slowly drawing her legs up until she was curled against her own body in a sensual abandon that she hadn't imagined possible. Shivering, too caught in pleasure to move except at her lover's touch, she felt ecstasy steal through her in an expanding flush of heat. She cried out, unable to bear the beauty he was bringing to her.

And still he ravished her, biting her softly, teasing her with the heat and intimacy of his mouth, taking her body away from her, making it his. Softly she cried out again and again, twisting in slow motion, held in the loving vise he had created, rippling with the ebb and flow of ecstasy through her body. And still he caressed her, riding the incandescent waves with her, drawing yet more response from her with each changing pressure of his mouth. She wept softly, moving against him, with him, turning sinuously, helplessly, lost to everything but him, feeling something both terrifying and beautiful growing deep within her body, consuming her even as he did until she moaned, "Will...ah, Will, I'm dying...."

Only then did he come to her, drawing her legs up even farther as he filled her satin depths completely with his own body. He moved slowly, deeply, advance and retreat, and she sobbed with each motion. Slow, sensual convulsions swept through her at every new penetration. She cried out with each stroke, her voice shattered by ecstasy, until he withdrew and came to her once more, and she arched in languid violence like a drawn bow.

Only his mouth mating with hers kept her scream of ecstasy and his triumphant shout within the bedroom walls. His body arched as fiercely as hers, and his last coherent thought as he poured his soul into her was that he had cheated the death that waited for him tomorrow by dying in Maya's arms tonight.

Chapter Eighteen

The last of the rain stopped falling in Weeber Basin
with the first glimmering of false dawn. Will rode in
shortly afterward to find Ising waiting on the cookhouse porch, a cup of coffee in each hand. Joe Larson was standing beside him. Without a word Ising
handed the coffee to Will. As Will drank, the sun
emerged over an eastern ridge, sending thick yellow
light through the dissipating clouds.

Will looked at the clearing sky. "It's going to be a
beautiful day."

"Rain floats logs better than sunshine," Ising muttered.

"We've got to make do with what we have." Will
snapped his wrist, sending the dregs of his coffee into
the mud. "I'm going to have a look at the pond."

The other men followed Will, slipping and sliding
and skidding down the muddy bank as they made their
way to the dam. The freshets and runoff streams were
still pouring their contributions into a lake that was
now the color of café au lait. Will waded through a
knee-deep stream, knowing that within hours the

chocolate runoff streams would vanish as though they had never existed.

Will climbed up the dam structure and made his way across the catwalk to the depth gauge. He knelt beside it, peering at the level. It was still five inches below the waste gates. If he opened the splashboards for a controlled release of water, there might be enough in the pond to fill the river between there and the Narrows, but there wouldn't be enough water to keep the river level up long enough to float all the logs past the Narrows and into the larger river beyond.

Without a word Will studied the dam, staring at the twenty-foot-tall stack of neatly matched and rounded logs, and at the cable-operated splashboards on the downstream side of the dam. On the pond side, a large, roomlike box stuck out. One side of the big box was the dam itself and the splashboards. The other three sides of the box held back water from the pond. The interior of the box was dry. On the side of the box opposite the dam were the big gates. When they opened, water flowed into the huge box. The weight of the incoming water triggered the mechanism that would hoist the splashboards, thus releasing water from behind the dam at a predictable rate that was controlled by the width of the main gates.

While sturdy, the splashboards were of wood that was only two inches thick. They were meant to be used during a very brief transition phase between the holding back of water and the releasing of it. The dam and the walls of the attached box were far thicker; they had been designed to hold back the weight of millions of pounds of water and logs. The splashboards had not.

Will was hoping that they would give way as soon as the full weight of the pond pressed against them.

And if he were unlucky and the splashboards held, he was going to bet his life that they would continue holding long enough for him to set the charge that ultimately would blow them wide open.

"Henry," Will said, "I want you to take off downstream and warn anyone who might be between here and the Narrows that the middle fork of the Weeber is going to rise hard and fast. I'll give you two hours' start. After that, hunt a piece of high ground and stay there."

"What are you going to do?"

Will pulled out his watch, looked at its face and then looked directly at Ising. "Better get going."

Ising stared at Will's bleak gray eyes and knew that arguing against whatever Will had planned would be futile. Ising turned on his heel and strode off downstream. Will watched until his friend was out of sight. Only then did he turn toward Larson.

"I'll need your help with the gates."

"What fer? Ain't enough water in the pond for more than two hours. Take at least three hours to float all them logs past the Narrows."

"The way I'll do it, there will be plenty of water."

"Hell's fire," Larson said in disgust, spitting out a stream of tobacco juice over the dry side of the dam. "Only way them logs will get to saltwater this year is if'n the dam gives way all at once, and that ain't likely. She was built to last. I know. I helped pick them logs myself."

"That's why my father bought a wagonload of dynamite six months ago."

Larson blinked. "You ain't gonna..."

"I sure as hell am," Will said, measuring the dam with unflinching eyes.

Maya awoke an hour after dawn with a feeling of uneasiness pervading her. She reached out for Will before she remembered that he had left hours ago. Suddenly memories of the previous night washed over her and with them a sensual shivering that shortened her breath. She didn't know what the future held for Will and herself; she only knew that there had to be a future for them together. The alternative was as unthinkable as the darkness that had nearly claimed her before Justine's birth.

Hurriedly Maya dressed and peeked into the nursery. Justine was awake but content for the moment with chewing on her coverlet. Emily slept deeply, undisturbed by the filtered sunlight coming into the room. Without making a sound, Maya turned from the doorway and went down the stairs to the kitchen. Mrs. Chou was already at work, up to her elbows in flour dust as she kneaded bread dough.

"Good morning, Mrs. Chou," Maya said.

The old Chinese woman grunted. "No good. Dam' fool get kill."

Maya stared at her. Mrs. Chou had been with the Hawthornes since Will's birth and, in addition to being the absolute ruler of the kitchen, she was considered almost a member of the family. As such, she spoke freely, though her English tended to be opaque, particularly when she was upset. The vigor with which she kneaded the bread dough indicated that the cook was very upset indeed.

"I beg your pardon?" Maya said.

"Get self kill!"

"Who?"

"Willy. Dam' same kind dam' fool father!"

With a force that made the crockery bowl dance, Mrs. Chou slammed the dough in and set it aside to rise. Maya clasped her hands together and tried to control the cold fear that was creeping through her.

"How is Will going to get himself killed?" Maya asked with desperate calm.

"Dam' logs dam' kill."

"Logs... at the mill?"

Mrs. Chou jerked her head toward the mountains. "Up way Weeba Liva."

"Weeber River? Logs? But there hasn't been enough rain to move the logs. I don't understand."

"Logs stay dam, yes?"

"The logs are behind the dam, yes."

"Dam go, logs go. Shoom! All once go, quick-quick. Dam' fool die quick-quick same time!"

Maya closed her eyes and prayed that she wasn't understanding the old woman. "Are you saying that Will is going to blow up the Weeber Basin dam?"

Mrs. Chou nodded curtly.

"Are you sure?"

"Sure same die quick-quick," she grunted.

"How do you know?" Maya demanded.

"Second son's bossman sell Willy fire caps. Take Weeba Liva. Go shoom all once, quick-quick."

"Fire caps? What are...oh, God. Blasting caps? Is that what Will bought? Blasting caps for dynamite?"

The woman's head bobbed in vigorous agreement. "Yes-yes. Caps. Shoom!" Her arms swept up and out violently, describing an explosion. "Go quick-quick. Die same time. Dam' fool!"

Maya turned and ran to her room, her skirts held high. Moments later she emerged in a riding outfit. She ran down the stairs and through the kitchen to the stables beyond. In a matter of minutes she appeared again, bent low over the back of her favorite mount as the horse gained speed with every frantic stride, urged on by the unaccustomed lash of a riding crop.

Mrs. Chou watched until Maya had vanished, then turned back to the kitchen again. "Quick-quick lady. Dam' fool die same way."

Will threw up his hands in disgust, frustrated by Larson's endless arguments. "First you tell me that if the whole dam goes at once the logs will be scattered from hell to breakfast, and then you tell me that there's not enough water behind the dam for a controlled release. I've listened to you for two hours, and the level in the pond hasn't gone up an inch. There's as much water in there now as there ever will be. So tell me, old man, which is the better gamble—take out the splashboards alone or blow the whole works to hell and gone!"

For a long, long minute Larson stood on the catwalk chewing tobacco and cracking his knuckles one after the other. Finally he spat, hitched up his pants and turned toward Will.

"Take out the main gates by hand. If'n you get lucky, the splashboards will break an' you won't have to tiptoe 'round the downstream side setting charges an' hoping that dynamite don't blow it all to hell an' you with it." Larson paused then looked right into

Will's bleak gray eyes. "But I'm telling you, boy. Them splashboards will hold, leastways for a time. Maybe half a week. Maybe half a minute. No way of knowing. Good wood in them boards, but they're like women. Each piece is different."

"I don't have half a week. I don't even have half a day. The runoff's slowing down while we talk. Look at it."

Larson didn't have to. He knew as well as anyone that the pond wasn't going to rise any farther. But that wasn't the point, at least not to Larson. "Can you set a charge in half a minute?"

"No."

Larson spat over the side and said nothing at all. He knew that if Will set the charge in advance, there would be no way to time the fuse to give him the moments needed to get out of the way before the wall of water released through the main gates hit and either broke the splashboards or doused the fuse. If the splashboards were blown first, the big gates couldn't be opened quickly enough to assure that the mass of logs wouldn't jam up against the partially opened gates themselves, preventing the gates from opening wide and allowing all the logs through before the water escaped.

"Even if'n you blow them splashboards without getting killed, herding logs through the opening ain't gonna be no picnic, neither. If'n you ain't fast and tricky as a pig, them logs will chew you up sure as God made little green apples. I'm too old to do you any good on the water. You shoulda kept Henry. That big Injun can make them logs dance."

"I know." That was precisely why Will had made sure Ising wouldn't be around.

Will pulled out his watch and looked at it. Two hours had gone by. Ising would be far away by now, where he wouldn't be able to grab a pike pole and risk his life herding logs into the voracious gap where gates had once been.

"Let's get those gates open and see if this is my lucky day," Will said.

Without a word Larson turned and went to work disabling the mechanism that would have lifted the splashboards at the first impact of water rushing in. While he worked, Will went down to the base of the dam with a handful of nails and a hammer. A few minutes later he was back on the catwalk, helping Larson with the big gates. Muddy water swirled slowly, sucked into the box as the gates gradually opened. The box filled, and still the gates opened, wider and wider, until there was nothing at all holding the weight of the pond and its burden of logs back from the river bed except the splashboards, the weakest link in the chain of the dam stretched across the ravine.

The splashboards held.

Logs bumped and banged against the boards as a new dynamic balance was achieved between water and dam. Water dribbled and squirted through imperfections where the splashboards had been joined to each other and to the dam itself. Thirty seconds went by. A minute. Two minutes.

The boards held.

Three minutes. Eight. Twelve. The flow of water squeezed between the splashboards didn't increase. Seventeen minutes. Twenty. Thirty.

Will's watchcase clicked distinctly as he closed it and returned it to his pocket. Without a word he headed for the wagon that held the dynamite. When he returned, he walked very carefully, disturbing the blasting caps as little as possible. Although the caps were very well packed in cotton, their unpredictability was legend. He eased down the slippery ravine to the base of the dam.

Water the color of earth trickled and spilled and sprayed through the rough-sawn splashboards. Will stood directly in front of the lumber barrier that contained the lake. He rested his hand against the two-inch-thick boards and sensed their convex tension as they were stressed by the weight of logs and lake. The pent energy could be released at any instant, and if it went now, he would be dead before he could scream.

With a silent prayer Will reached up to one of the nails he had driven home before the main gates had been opened. In that much, at least, he had been lucky. There were no leaks nearby to douse the fuse. He hung the leather satchel that contained the capped and primed dynamite in place. Working quickly, carefully, he wedged a log against the charge to further channel the force of the blast into the taut boards. Only when he was satisfied that the charge was correctly secured did he retreat to the structure of the dam itself. He climbed up it rapidly, paying out thin, coiled fuse behind him as he went. His body still tingled with the vibrations he had sensed in the splashboards, the quivering of wood stressed beyond endurance. He had felt a similar vibration before, when the Guardian had trembled beneath the slashing onslaught of his ax.

Will knelt on top of the dam, steadied the tarred fuse in one hand and struck a match on the seat of his pants with the other. The thin fuse seemed to shimmer in the flame for a few instants before a whiff of acrid smoke puffed out. Gently he laid the spitting fuse on the catwalk, turned and scrambled down from the dam to join Larson on the bank of the pond. Will wasn't surprised to see that there were other men around, timber beasts who had either met Ising on the downstream side or had otherwise heard that something was going on at the Weeber Basin dam. Fire was the second-fastest thing in the forest; gossip was the first.

The men milled nervously behind the shelter of a rock face, torn between seeking shelter from the blast and wanting to see the monster of water and logs unleashed. A hush fell over the group as the seconds ran out. The only sounds to be heard were from three crows cawing to one another as they passed overhead. One of the Yurok timber beasts muttered a low chant. It could have been a prayer or a curse.

The sound of the blast was muffled by the dam to no more than a soft *whump* that was subsumed almost instantly by the roar of the giant cataract. Water burst through the sudden breach left by the shattered two-inch splashboards. The timber walls of the dam contained the sudden, enormous torrent for perhaps a minute before a sound like a cannon shot sliced through the roar of escaping water; a second later the dam was torn apart by forces it hadn't been designed to withstand. Splintered timbers leaped into the air only to fall back into the violence of released water. The stone-sheathed earthen banks of the dam held, shaping the flow, keeping it from overwhelming the natural contours of the river bed.

The logs first in line behind the new, wider gap were sucked through in an instant. They emerged on the other side as splinters, smashed against the rocks of the streambed by thousands of tons of pouring water. For a few seconds clouds of mist billowed up, obscuring the narrow opening in the ravine that once had been closed by the wooden part of the dam. Slowly the mist cleared to reveal a steady, regular flow of logs sliding through the broken dam and racing down the rejuvenated middle fork of the Weeber River.

The timber beasts cheered, but Will knew that the drive had only begun. He turned toward the men.

"Grab your poles and keep logs from getting stuck in the shallows. When the rest of the dam gives way, this pond will empty in ten minutes flat. And stay the hell away from the gap itself."

Timber beasts picked up their iron-tipped poles and leaped lightly onto the bobbing backs of ten-foot sawlogs, some of which were more than ten feet in diameter. The men danced out across the lake on bridges of submerged logs, jabbing and shoving and herding with their pike poles, trying to impose order like policemen in the middle of a riot. The men didn't need a second warning to stay away from the gap in the dam. No one wanted to face the maelstrom of forces that was sucking huge logs down as though they were no more than matchsticks.

Will grabbed a pole and leaped onto a log that was slowly being drawn toward the vortex of the whirlpool that had formed at the head of the lake. That was where the trouble would come, where logs could stick or jam and pile up in a turmoil that would slow the passage of other logs while precious water raced away. He leaped and skipped across logs headed toward the gap, coming closer to the churning, roaring opening with each step. He went from log to bobbing log with the ease of years of practice, sensing when a log would kick and when it would turn under his feet. Soon he was at the edge of the whirlpool, leaping and dancing like a madman from log to log, just one slip away from the grinding death of the maelstrom. Poking, pushing, bumping, jumping, cursing, Will kept the logs from getting hopelessly tangled as they were sucked into the current and shot through the gap.

To Will's private amazement, the earthen banks inside their sheath of rocks held against the swirling, churning water. The pond emptied at a pace far too fast to be called controlled, but not so fast as to be a single standing wave of water grinding down the deep ravine. For nearly an hour Will leaped and skidded as he herded logs, landing and balancing on the teeth of a gnashing monster made of logs, his life dependent on luck, skill and the needle-pointed calks on his boots. He worked with the massive momentum of water and logs, his pike pole a magic wand and he the magician who sent log after recalcitrant log spinning through the gap.

Then the rush of logs thinned, and he had time to look up. The level of the pond had dropped by several feet, and the flow over the brink of the remaining dam was gradually slowing. Soon it would be as safe to work at the gap as it would be along any turbulent stretch of river water. The timber beasts had already realized it. They were working closer and closer to Will with each passing minute. Soon they were working alongside him.

Will knew that he wasn't needed at the pond any longer. He walked logs to the muddy shallows and waded to dry land. Once ashore he turned and surveyed what had been a large, placid pond filled to the brim with logs. A two-foot wide border of chocolate brown mud marked the high-water line of the former lake. A hundred yards away a score of mud-slicked logs lay like beached whales. The rest of the shoreline was clear, no logs left behind to wait until next year or the year after. A two-year stockpile of sawlogs was bumping and sliding and grinding down the Weeber to Humboldt Bay.

Dimly Will felt that he should shout or laugh or jump into the air, but he had just discovered that he was too exhausted to do more than stand upright and breathe. He leaned against his pike pole as relief poured through him like water through the broken dam. The emptying pond had swept with it two million board feet of lumber, enough to build a small city, more than enough to put Tres Santos back on its feet. He had risked death too many times in the last hour, but it was all worth it. He had won.

Now he had only one last gamble to face, one final bet to make, and it had to be done at the Hawthorne house rather than in Weeber Basin.

"Hawthorne! Hawthorne, come a running!" Larson yelled. "The drive is snagged at the Narrows!"

For a moment Will didn't seem to hear. Then he straightened, balanced his pike pole over his shoulder and went over to where Larson stood. Will didn't need to hear the details to know what had happened. In his mind's eye he could all too easily envision the kind of jam-up that could take place in the Narrows—a gorge with walls thirty feet high and a boulder-strewn riverbed that was scarcely wider. Once caught, the logs would stay. The water released from the dam wouldn't. It would spurt through the logjam until nothing was left behind but a heap of drying logs.

"How many logs got through before it jammed?" Will demanded.

"Couple hundred, maybe."

Not enough. Not nearly enough.

"What about the river?" Will asked.

"Henry gives you an hour, maybe, before she drops. Half an hour for sure. I took the oxen off the wagon an' put in horses."

"Thanks."

Will turned and began running for the dynamite wagon. Larson followed, scrambling over the muddy ground and up onto the wagon seat with an agility that belied his grumbling about his age. When Will picked up the reins, Larson was no more than a few seconds behind. He reached over the back of the seat and pulled the brightly painted box of blasting caps into his lap.

"Let 'er rip," Larson said.

"It's my problem, not yours."

Larson looked at Will. "Your daddy was a hard man, but fair. Tres Santos come as close to a home as I ever got."

For an instant Will hesitated. Then he nodded, picked up the whip and shouted at the horses.

It was two miles to the Narrows. The whistling lash of the leather whip never let up as the team plunged down the rough lumbering road, cases of dynamite bouncing harmlessly around the wagon box and the volatile caps held in Larson's hands as the wagon slewed around curves at runaway speed. By the time Will pulled to a stop beside the gang of timber beasts gathered by the road at the Narrows, the horses were wild-eyed and lathered. With Larson holding the caps, Will had saved ten minutes on the run down the road.

From the other direction came another horse, galloping hard, its shoulders and flanks white with lather. Will was pulling a case of dynamite out of the wagon when he heard the drumroll of hooves and looked up to see Maya's long, mahogany hair whipping in the wind. She brought her horse to a plunging halt beside the wagon, relief clear on her white face when she saw Will standing there unharmed. She had just enough self-control left to prevent herself from sliding off the horse and into his arms in front of the curious timber beasts.

"I was worried," she said, her voice harsh with barely controlled emotions. "I heard an explosion, and later the water got muddy but only a few logs came through."

"They're jammed down there," Will said, looking at Maya for an instant, wishing that she weren't there and fiercely glad that she was because in the darkest part of his mind he hadn't expected to see her again.

"I'm going to blast it loose while there's still water in the river."

The relief that Maya had felt vanished as she watched him stuff dynamite and a coil of fuse into a knapsack.

"No," she said. "It's too dangerous. Surely those logs don't mean so much to you that you'd risk your life for the money they would bring!"

"Those logs are your future. Without them Tres Santos is bankrupt."

"I've been poor before. I survived."

"But the babies didn't, did they? Larson! Over here with those caps!"

"Will, I—" Maya began, her voice as anguished as her dark green eyes, but a sudden outcry from the timber beasts cut off whatever she had been going to say.

"It shifted!"

"He's trapped!"

"Is he dead?"

The shouts overlapped each other, but Will realized instantly what must have happened. He ran to the edge of the bank that overlooked the river thirty feet below. At first all he saw was the tangled mass of redwood sawlogs jammed like an imperfect cork in the gap between two granite walls. Muddy water gushed through openings in the log pile, spurting out in brown fountains, falling thirty feet downstream in fierce torrents. The massive log tangle was dangerously haphazard, a devil's jackstraw pile that could come apart entirely or collapse in upon itself even more tightly at any moment. Logs were still sliding downstream from the dam, colliding heavily, adding their weight to the precarious pile. The narrow canyon seemed to vibrate with pent-up energy.

And then Will leaned closer, staring at the logjam in sudden horror. Henry Ising lay motionless on one of the big logs at the leading edge of the jam.

"Men say the big one with the bole on it is the key-log," Larson said, pointing to the massive log where Ising lay. "It hung up on that rock finger yonder. Move that log and all the rest move. Guess Ising gave it a try."

Maya's hand gripped Will's forearm. "Henry isn't moving."

"Get me an ax and a pike," Will said to Larson.

Maya said nothing, but her fingers dug into Will's hard flesh with enough force to bruise.

"Too many deaths," she said softly. "Too much dying..."

"If the logs get through, your children will never die of hunger or cold."

Maya flinched as though a whip had been laid across her shoulders. "No."

"I have to go to him," Will said. "Could you live with me, with yourself, if I did less than I could for Henry?"

She made a low, anguished sound. Slowly her fingers unclenched from his arm as she looked up at him. For an instant they were the only human beings in creation.

Will turned away quickly, shrugged into the straps of the knapsack, picked up the ax and the pole that had been brought to him and went to the very edge of the bank. A rope had already been thrown over the side of the canyon down the steep slope. In moments

Will had scrambled down and dropped onto the rocks at the river's edge. He put aside the knapsack he was wearing; dynamite would do Ising no good at all.

As Will stepped onto the tangle of logs, it trembled as though it were a living beast crouched in ambush. The sound of the water thundering through the haphazardly piled logs was deafening. Will was drenched to the skin instantly, buffeted by sound and fiercely frothing water. He had felt nothing like it since the wave had broken over the *Brother Samuel*, sweeping everyone aboard into the icy sea, killing all but three of the passengers. And had it not been for Henry Ising, no one would have escaped; the destruction would have been complete.

Will leaped and scrambled over logs that were shoved together at every imaginable angle. Many of the logs were loose, held back only by the key-log ahead, the single log that had begun the jam. If he were quick enough, and lucky enough, he could get Ising out and remove the key-log before other, more difficult tangles were created by new logs being forced against the old. As he worked his way across the jam, he kept stealing glances at Ising. He hadn't moved.

The last part of the crossing was the easiest. A ridge of water-smoothed granite thrust out from the canyon wall into the river. It was the granite which had caused the jam. Logs groaned against stone and water hissed. Ising lay chest down on the key-log. Will could clearly see a livid bruise where something had struck Ising on the side of the face. Will touched Ising's neck, probing for a pulse. It was there, weak but steady. He probed the bruises gently. The skull beneath felt solid, intact. He started to lift Ising, only to discover that his left arm was pinned by something beneath the water.

The pain of being moved roused Ising. His eyes opened for a moment, stared at Will without comprehension, then flickered closed. His groan was all but lost in the churning of water and logs. Will knelt and groped beneath the surface of the water, exploring the puzzle of wood and flesh. He quickly discovered that his friend's arm was wedged between two logs. Gentle, steady pulling accomplished nothing. Nor did more forceful attempts help. When he brought his hand away again, blood was mixed with the muddy water.

At the edge of his vision Will saw a sudden shifting of logs as the jam moved in accordance with the unknown, constantly changing dynamics of water and new logs arriving with every instant that passed. The big log he and Ising were on jerked. Ising groaned harshly.

Will swiped the back of his hand across his eyes, trying to clear his vision of the sweat that was stinging his eyes. But even cleared, his eyes could find no escape from the thing that his soul shrank from doing.

"No," he said, even as his hand reached for the ax whose gleaming blade he had buried in the log. The tangle of logs shifted very slightly. Ising groaned again.

Will came to his feet in a single gesture. Two quick motions set the calks of his boots deeply into the wet log. As he raised his ax over his head, the vision of Johnny Ising flashed through his mind.

"*No!*"

The ax whistled down in a lethal curve. A splash of color flared as the blade dug a chunk of blood-red bark from the log beside Henry's arm. Instantly Will swung again and then again, shifting his balance with each stirring of the log, sending the blade deeply into bark that lay not one inch from flesh, meeting and matching the massive shift and shivering of the log-jam. Each blow of the ax took a new bite from the sawlog. Each blow came closer to flesh and then closer, until the final blow parted the fabric of Ising's shirt.

As soon as the bark on the closer log had been scaled away, Will sank the ax blade into the log and went to work with the pike pole, levering its steel point into the space between the bark and the heartwood. Once the pike found its mark, Will began to apply pressure. He levered down with his powerful arms, and down, muscles bunching and straining all across his big body until the shirt he wore split across the shoulders and the pike pole's tough wood creaked on the edge of breaking. Ising groaned from the sudden, biting increase in pressure as the massive equation of logs and water shifted slightly once again.

Suddenly the pike slid beneath the strip of bark that remained beneath Ising's arm. Will withdrew the pike, knelt and flailed beneath the water, ripping away the loosened bark with his bare fingers rather than take the chance of sending the pike's steel point through Ising's flesh. When no more bark came away, he pulled gently, firmly, on Ising's arm.

It was still wedged.

His arm knocked against the ax as he bent over again, but he ignored the instant solution that lay so close by. He could slice through Ising's arm with a single stroke, freeing him, and that way there would still be time to blow the logjam before all the water leaked away.

Johnny all over again, crippled for life because he had come too close to the bitter quarrel between Hawthorne father and Hawthorne son. Drunken, one-armed Johnny dying because there was no way to live. Only this time it would be Henry, whose biggest mistake had been to pull Hawthorne children from the uncaring sea. And Maya, beautiful Maya.

Shaman woman, living for a future only she could see.

Will clawed beneath the water again but could detect no release. He switched back to Ising's arm, ignoring his friend's unconscious protests. Steadily increasing the pressure, Will pulled on Ising's arm, putting more and more of his enormous strength into the work, shaking his head to clear sweat and tears from his eyes. Suddenly the arm jerked forward into the notch that had been carved to receive it.

Ising was free.

The arm hung bloody and useless, but the savage pain had aroused Ising. He stared uncomprehendingly at Will for a moment, then tried to say something. Will leaned closer.

"Should have used . . . the ax," Ising rasped.

"Never. Can you sit up?" Will demanded.

Ising answered by struggling upright, then nearly falling back again. He panted with exertion. There was no way that he was going to walk off that logjam, and Will knew it.

Will grabbed Ising beneath the armpits and dragged his big friend the length of the log to the granite spur that had caused all the trouble in the first place. The timber beasts at the top of the wall had anticipated him. A rope dangled within easy reach.

"Stand up," Will said, dragging Ising into an upright position. The Yurok was only two inches shorter than Will and weighed at least as much. "Lean on me, but stand up!"

Ising struggled to get his feet under him as Will lifted. Finally Ising half rose, half clawed his way up with the help of the rock wall. Will whipped the heavy rope around Ising's chest and shoulders, making a harness and securing it with an immovable knot.

"Haul!"

At Will's yell the rope tightened around Ising's body. Soon he was bumping up the rock face, turning slowly, rising more swiftly with each second.

Will watched long enough to be certain that nothing would go wrong. Then he ran upstream and seized the knapsack. Working as quickly as he could, he wrapped up twelve sticks of dynamite in a length of fuse cord. He stuck one end of the remaining length of fuse cord into the cap, crimped it closed with his teeth and then jammed the cap into the center stick of the bundle. Only then did he study the tangled mass of logs.

Ising had been right. The key-log, the pivot point of the tangle, seemed to be the redwood log eight feet in diameter with a heavy bole growing like a tumor from one side. In the beginning it might have been moved by a man with a pike pole. Ising had tried and been unlucky. It was too late for poles now. Each new log coming downstream had wedged the tangle more tightly.

With the bundled charge in one hand and a coil of fuse in the other, Will made his way into the tense heart of the jam, ignoring the tortured groans of logs being twisted to the point of an explosion such as the one which had caught Ising. Refusing to hurry despite the hammering of his own heart, Will circled the key-log until he found what he had hoped for. There was a little cavern that extended back into the heart of the tangle. He crept into the space and nestled the dynamite into place where a flag of thick bark had been gouged out. He started to pay out the fuse, only to discover that just four feet remained. There would be thirty seconds, at most, before the fuse burned down to the explosive cap—and then there would be no more time at all.

Thirty seconds.

Will looked from the key-log to the rope dangling down the granite wall of the Narrows. Then he looked at the watermark along the river. A dark band showed on both sides, telling him that the water had already begun to drop, leaving the Tres Santos's logs behind.

There was no dry surface on which to strike a match. Will flicked the head with his thumbnail once, twice, three times, and on the fourth the head sputtered to life. A fragment of burning sulfur caught beneath his nail. He ignored the pain, concentrating only on making sure that the fuse was lit. It sizzled and burned with a white point of light. He set the fuse down carefully and then turned and ran from the cavern, skipping and jumping over logs with reckless speed. He gained the granite ledge with a single tremendous leap, skidding and falling on his calks until he found his balance again and raced for the rope that dangled so invitingly.

Ten seconds gone.

Will didn't even hear the cheers and shouts of encouragement from the watching timber beasts. He twisted the rope around his fist, set his feet against the wall and began hauling himself up hand over hand, kicking and gouging with his feet for purchase as he climbed.

Fifteen seconds gone.

He was a third of the way up the wall when the steel calks on his boots betrayed him. Metal screeched over stone, then his feet shot out and he smashed face-first into the rock wall. For an instant he was stunned. Rope burned through his hands before he tightened his grip, catching himself. He shook his head hard, trying to clear it, and all he heard was the pounding of his own blood keeping time with the fleeing seconds.

Twenty seconds gone.

Grimly Will flexed his arms, taking his whole weight on his hands as he jackknifed, bringing his feet into contact with the wall once more. At the edge of his vision he saw arms reaching down, hands gripping the rope, hauling him up even as he climbed toward safety. But there would be no safety when that charge went, blowing jagged hunks of logs hundreds of feet in all directions.

And Maya stood at the brink, her mahogany hair whipping in the wind, her hands reaching toward him.

"Get back!" Will shouted while he clawed his way hand over hand up the rope. "Back!"

The hands remained, pulling him up the wall far more quickly than he could have climbed unaided.

And Maya remained, pulling as hard as any timber beast.

Will reached the brink with four seconds to spare. The momentum of his ascent flung him over the lip of the canyon. As he lunged to his feet, men scattered, knowing the danger as well as he did. Will grabbed Maya and sprinted for the far side of the road. When the clock in his head ran out, he flung Maya to the ground and covered her body with his own; at the same instant an explosion blew out the heart of the logjam.

For the space of several heartbeats there was silence. Then debris began to hail down around them, great chunks of wood and ragged banners of bark, with splinters and chaff and water all mixed together. The bombardment continued for what seemed like a lifetime. When it was finally over, Will rolled aside, freeing Maya.

"Are you all right?" he asked hoarsely.

She nodded, her eyes huge in her pale face. She was still shaking from the moment she had seen Will smash against the rock face and begin to drop, sliding down the rope, sliding away from her forever.

Will dragged himself to his feet, pulling Maya up as well. Together they stood on the lip of the canyon and looked down. The tangled mass of redwood logs looked as solid as ever. Wearily Will turned away, heading for the dynamite wagon once more, knowing that he was at the end of his strength.

"No," Maya said, her voice low, vibrant. "Look!"

The raft of logs was seething, shifting, dissolving away before their eyes. First one log, then another, then another and another bobbed and slid past the Narrows, log after log moving past until there were too many to count, logs floating downstream faster and faster, weaving and reweaving loose patterns as they floated smoothly down toward the sea.

Together Will and Maya watched until the last log had vanished into the distance. Only then did he turn toward her, his eyes dark with the knowledge that he had lived to place the final bet, the one that mattered more to him than any that had gone before.

Without a word Will helped Maya up into the wagon and drove down the mountain.

Maya sat in Hale's office, listening to the silence in the big house. In the three days since the log drive, Will had not been to the house for more than hurried meals and to check on Ising's progress, which had been startling. His shaman had come for him that day at sunset. They had left shortly afterward. Maya had objected, but to no avail. Ising's arm was stiff, bruised, slightly swollen; his injury not at all the kind that would keep him tied down when the shaman's black eyes smiled his way.

There was no sound in the house save the soft hiss of flames in the hearth. Maya knew that she should go to bed. She also knew that she would not. She needed to discover what lay behind Will's silences during the past few days. She needed to know why he had not come to her despite the longing he couldn't conceal.

The sound of a horse's hoofbeats brought Maya to her feet in a rush. She smoothed her velvet robe nervously. When she heard the kitchen door open, she walked into the hall.

"Will?"

He turned toward her soft voice instantly. His hands were full of papers. "I was going to wait until morning, but since you're up..."

Maya heard the undercurrent of darkness in Will's voice, saw it in his face, sensed it in the reluctance of his body as he walked toward her. Without a word she turned and went back to the office, trying to fight back the cold panic gnawing at her soul.

"What is it?" she asked as she heard Will shut the door behind himself. "What's wrong?"

"Nothing," Will said, walking around the desk until he could face Maya. He threw down the papers he had been holding. They fanned out across the polished wood. "Read these."

"Will?" she asked, looking at his eyes. They were empty of all but the kind of dark waiting she had thought never to see again in him.

"Read them."

One by one Maya picked up the papers and glanced through them. A deed to the house—in her name. Loans taken out by Hale Hawthorne and paid off by Will Hawthorne's logs—and the collateral signed over to Maya Hawthorne. Black Basin's valuable timber holdings—signed over to her.

Paper after paper was picked up in Maya's trembling fingers, only to slip away as soon as she saw her own name in place of Will's. Finally she looked up at him with troubled green eyes.

"I don't understand," she said softly. "All of this should be yours. You have given me more than Hale lost to you, more than Hale ever owned, everything you've worked for. There is nothing left for you.'' Her voice died as fear claimed her. Was he leaving? Was that why he had given everything to her. "Why?'' she whispered, her voice breaking.

"Henry once told me that you were a woman set apart, a shaman, and that your choices wouldn't necessarily be the ones I wanted you to make. You would do as you pleased. He was right...and he was wrong. You've never been able to choose freely. Always you've chosen for your children's future, whether they were born or lived only in your mind.'' Will gestured toward the papers heaped on the desk. "If you sold that all off tomorrow, you would have more money than Beth and your children could spend in their lifetimes. If you want to sell, Kroeber will buy.''

"I don't understand.''

"You're free,'' Will said simply. "You need never fear for your children's future again. You can choose to marry...or you can choose to live as a shaman, knowing no man unless it pleases you for the moment. Your choice, Maya. Your own choice, freely made. You are free of all men if you wish. Even me.''

Maya trembled as she looked at Will. "And if I give it all back to you?'' she asked in a raw voice, grabbing a pen from its holder and slashing wildly across papers as she cried. "Then will you love me again? That's what I want. You! Just you!''

Hard fingers closed around Maya's wrist, and the pen went springing away. Will caught her chin with his other hand and held her very still, looking at her as though she were newly discovered, wholly unknown, a prize beyond measure or comprehension. His eyes were no longer empty. They blazed with emotion.

"Are you sure, Maya?" he asked. "This is your only chance, because if you come to me again I'll never let you go."

"Yes, never let me go, and I'll never let you go because if you go... if you go..." Her voice broke and she wept.

Will lifted Maya into his arms, holding her close, kissing away the quicksilver tears on her cheeks, hearing her words of love given freely to him, giving them back with each breath, each caress. As he turned to carry her from the room, the hem of her robe swirled out, sweeping the desk clean. Neither he nor she noticed the rustling slide of documents falling to the floor, the bittersweet past whispering from each thick paper, legacy of loss and betrayal, vengeance and ecstasy and a love they had only begun to measure.

Epilogue

The Guardian was the last giant redwood ever cut by the Hawthorne family. Will and Maya loved the vast, fragrant silences and the massive elegance of the big trees too much to shatter them with the inventions that later made possible the economic logging of even the biggest trees and the most remote forests. Tres Santos Redwood Enterprises logged with a shaman's eye, a vision of the future that no one else could see.

Will and Maya taught all the Hawthorne children to see in the same way. Ising's offspring and Beth's son played hide-and-seek with their cousins beneath Black Basin's massive redwoods. As the children grew and had children of their own, each succeeding generation came to walk amid Black Basin's redwood groves, absorbing silent lessons about life and man and time.

On the one hundredth anniversary of Tres Santos Redwood Enterprises, the Hawthornes gave Black Basin to the nation that they had helped to build. Along with other people from all over the world, Hawthornes still walk the basin's pathways and watch mist dance gracefully along shafts of pale gold sunlight. Hawthornes still go to the basin when they are soul-weary, and they still receive the gift of perspective and peace from the redwood forest.

Hawthornes will still be there when you, too, are drawn to Black Basin's ancient trees. Somewhere on the mysterious pathways a child with quicksilver eyes will be staring in awed silence at the primeval forest that lived long before western civilization was born and would live on undisturbed long after that civilization was no more than a rumor whispered from bough to bough.

*   *   *   *   *

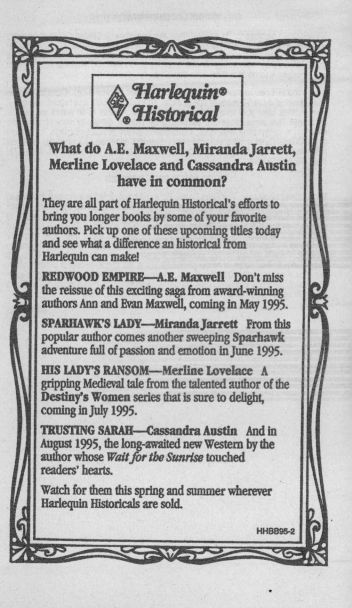

MILLION DOLLAR SWEEPSTAKES (III)

No purchase necessary. To enter, follow the directions published. Method of entry may vary. For eligibility, entries must be received no later than March 31, 1996. No liability is assumed for printing errors, lost, late or misdirected entries. Odds of winning are determined by the number of eligible entries distributed and received. Prizewinners will be determined no later than June 30, 1996.

Sweepstakes open to residents of the U.S. (except Puerto Rico), Canada, Europe and Taiwan who are 18 years of age or older. All applicable laws and regulations apply. Sweepstakes offer void wherever prohibited by law. Values of all prizes are in U.S. currency. This sweepstakes is presented by Torstar Corp., its subsidiaries and affiliates, in conjunction with book, merchandise and/or product offerings. For a copy of the Official Rules send a self-addressed, stamped envelope (WA residents need not affix return postage) to: MILLION DOLLAR SWEEPSTAKES (III) Rules, P.O. Box 4573, Blair, NE 68009, USA.

EXTRA BONUS PRIZE DRAWING

No purchase necessary. The Extra Bonus Prize will be awarded in a random drawing to be conducted no later than 5/30/96 from among all entries received. To qualify, entries must be received by 3/31/96 and comply with published directions. Drawing open to residents of the U.S. (except Puerto Rico), Canada, Europe and Taiwan who are 18 years of age or older. All applicable laws and regulations apply; offer void wherever prohibited by law. Odds of winning are dependent upon number of eligible entries received. Prize is valued in U.S. currency. The offer is presented by Torstar Corp., its subsidiaries and affiliates in conjunction with book, merchandise and/or product offering. For a copy of the Official Rules governing this sweepstakes, send a self-addressed, stamped envelope (WA residents need not affix return postage) to: Extra Bonus Prize Drawing Rules, P.O. Box 4590, Blair, NE 68009, USA.

SWP-H595

In June, get ready for thrilling romances
and FREE BOOKS—Western-style—
with...

WESTERN *Lovers*

You can receive the first 2 Western Lovers titles FREE!

June 1995 brings Harlequin and Silhouette's
WESTERN LOVERS series, which combines larger-than-life love stories set in the American West! And WESTERN
LOVERS brings you stories with your favorite themes...
"Ranch Rogues," "Hitched In Haste," "Ranchin' Dads,"
"Reunited Hearts" the packaging on each book
highlights the popular theme found in each WESTERN
LOVERS story!

And in June, when you buy either of the Men Made In
America titles, you will receive a WESTERN LOVERS title
absolutely FREE! Look for these fabulous combinations:

◆ Buy ALL IN THE FAMILY
  by Heather Graham Pozzessere (Men Made In
  America) and receive a FREE copy of
  BETRAYED BY LOVE by Diana Palmer
  (Western Lovers)

◆ Buy THE WAITING GAME
  by Jayne Ann Krentz (Men Made In America)
  and receive a FREE copy of
  IN A CLASS BY HIMSELF by JoAnn Ross
  (Western Lovers)

Look for the special, extra-value shrink-wrapped
packages at your favorite retail outlet!

HARLEQUIN® *Silhouette*®

WL-T

WOMEN OF THE WEST

Exciting stories of the old West and the women whose dreams
and passions shaped a new land!

Join Harlequin Historicals every month as we bring you
these unforgettable tales.

May 1995 #270—**JUSTIN'S BRIDE**
Susan Macias w/a Susan Mallery

June 1995 #273—**SADDLE THE WIND**
Pat Tracy

July 1995 #277—**ADDIE'S LAMENT**
DeLoras Scott

August 1995 #279—**TRUSTING SARAH**
Cassandra Austin

September 1995 #286—**CECILIA AND THE STRANGER**
Liz Ireland

October 1995 #288—**SAINT OR SINNER**
Cheryl St.John

November 1995 #294—**LYDIA**
Elizabeth Lane

Don't miss any of our **Women of the West!**

Relive the romance... This June, Harlequin and
Silhouette are proud to bring you

by Request®

THERE'S SOMETHING ABOUT A Cowboy

Hard livin', hard lovin', hard to resist...

Three complete novels by your favorite authors—
in one special collection!

WILDCAT by Candace Schuler
THE BLACK SHEEP by Susan Fox
DIAMOND VALLEY by Margaret Way

Long on pride, short on patience, these sexy cowboys
will ride right into your dreams!

Available wherever
Harlequin and Silhouette books are sold.

HARLEQUIN® ♥ Silhouette®

HREQ695

Announcing
the New **Pages & Privileges**™ Program
from Harlequin® and Silhouette®

Get All This FREE
With Just One Proof-of-Purchase!

- **FREE Travel Service** with the guaranteed lowest available airfares plus 5% cash back on every ticket

- **FREE Hotel Discounts** of up to 60% off at leading hotels in the U.S., Canada and Europe

- **FREE Petite Parfumerie** collection (a $50 Retail value)

- **FREE $25 Travel Voucher** to use on any ticket on any airline booked through our Travel Service

- **FREE Insider Tips Letter** full of fascinating information and hot sneak previews of upcoming books

- **FREE Mystery Gift** (if you enroll before May 31/95)

And there are more great gifts and benefits to come!
Enroll today and become Privileged!

(see insert for details)